PORTRAIT

A face began to take shape on the blank page—a lean bearded face, with deep eyes and a patrician nose above a stern, passionate mouth. The face was surmounted by a conical helmet of steel over a chain mail coif, in the style of the late thirteenth century. Adam's own eyes widened as he realized that Peregrine was seeing him not as he was now, but as the Knight Templar he had been nearly seven hundred years ago. . . .

THE ADEPT SERIES
by Katherine Kurtz and Deborah Turner Harris

THE ADEPT
THE LODGE OF THE LYNX
THE TEMPLAR TREASURE
DAGGER MAGIC
DEATH OF AN ADEPT

Also available from Ace Books by
Deborah Turner Harris

CALEDON OF THE MISTS
THE QUEEN OF ASHES

THE ADEPT

KATHERINE KURTZ and
DEBORAH TURNER HARRIS

ACE BOOKS, NEW YORK

This book is an Ace original edition,
and has never been previously published.

THE ADEPT

An Ace Book / published by arrangement with
Bill Fawcett and Associates

PRINTING HISTORY
Ace edition / March 1991

Cover art by Tom Kidd.

For information address: The Berkley Publishing Group,
a member of Penguin Putnam Inc.,
200 Madison Avenue, New York, New York 10016.

The Penguin Putnam Inc. World Wide Web site address is
http://www.penguinputnam.com

ISBN: 0-441-00343-5

ACE®
Ace Books are published by The Berkley Publishing Group,
a member of Penguin Putnam Inc.,
200 Madison Avenue, New York, New York 10016.
ACE and the "A" design
are trademarks belonging to Charter Communications, Inc.

PRINTED IN THE UNITED STATES OF AMERICA

20 19 18 17 16 15 14 13 12 11 10

For

Betty Ballantine,

who has a special knack

for finding and encouraging new authors.

She bought a first trilogy from each of us,

across a fifteen-year stretch,

and then had the uncommon good sense

to introduce us.

Thanks, Betty!

ACKNOWLEDGEMENTS

Sincere thanks are due to the following people who contributed materially to the realization of this book:

Dr. Richard Oram, for his authoritative advice concerning matters of medieval Scottish history and archaeology, especially with respect to early Scottish cartography;

Mr. Kenneth Fraser of the St. Andrews University Research Library, for his valuable assistance in locating difficult-to-find research materials;

Dr. William Such, for his help in rendering the Greek terminology used in this book;

Robert Harris, for his help in reviewing the Latin;

Mr. G.H. Forsyth, caretaker at Melrose Abbey, for his useful information on the whereabouts of Michael Scot's grave;

And finally, the staff of the St. Andrews Tourist Information Bureau, especially Mrs. Maggie Pitkethly and Mr. Andrew Purvis, for providing a wealth of miscellaneous information not to be found in history books.

THE ADEPT

Prologue

THE autumn night was clear and sharp, with a bite to the still air that promised frost before morning. No moon eased the darkness, but the starlight cast its own faint luminescence over the Scottish countryside.

Partway up the slope of a wooded hill, a black-clad man waited in the shadow of ancient beech trees, hugging himself against the cold, now and again flexing black-gloved hands to keep his fingers supple for the work ahead. Several times in the last half hour, he had peeled back the cuff of his left glove to peer at the face of a military wristwatch. Now he did so again. The luminous dial read half past two.

The rear windows of Mossiecairn House were blind and dark. Upstairs, the last light had gone out some time ago. The old caretaker had long ago completed his last rounds, and could be expected not to budge again from his gate lodge until after daylight. The time would never be better.

Smiling slightly, the man in black zipped his leather jacket closer and pushed a black knitted watch cap up off his ears for better hearing, flexing his fingers again as he started working his way down the slope. He covered the distance swiftly, moving with the quiet assurance of a man well-schooled in night maneuvers, keeping to the shadows. A shallow burn was crossed by leaping lightly across a string of exposed stones. He paused for a final precautionary survey of the area before darting off across the open lawn, finally gaining shelter in the shadow of a porch over the kitchen entrance.

Disarming the house's security alarms presented little challenge to the man in black. By American standards, Mossiecairn's alarm system was woefully unsophisticated. Besides, the man in black had been in the house earlier in the day as a tourist, making note of everything that was likely to present problems when he returned.

Now he eased his way carefully across the darkened kitchen, lighting his way with a tiny pocket torch that cast a pencil-thin beam. He spared not a glance for the shelved candelabra and punch bowls and ice buckets, or the drawers full of silver flatware, as he passed through the butler's pantry and into the dining room. Likewise disregarding a valuable tea service displayed on the dining room table, he made his way swiftly along the inside wall to the double doors at the other end. There a deft twist of a lock pick let him into the adjoining library, avoiding the outer corridor and the electric eyes guarding the doors into it.

Again he paid little attention to the many valuable items on display as he swept his light around, avoiding the windows. The portraits were particularly fine, ranging from the Jacobean builder of the house down to the present owner. The one above the ornate fireplace he had admired earlier in the day: a Cavalier gentleman in velvets and silks the color of fine port wine, with a froth of lace at his throat and the curls of a long, dark wig showing under his plumed hat.

Antique weapons and other military accoutrements studded the walls between the paintings, and smaller items were displayed under glass in a series of shallow table cases set along the walls. Rare books occupied a heavy library table in the center of the room.

The intruder passed them by without a second glance, heading for the cases flanking the fireplace. Most of the items in the cases were medals and decorations won by previous occupants of the house, or oddments of domesticity such as watch fobs and ladies' fans and miniatures painted on ivory. A few, however, were bits of memorabilia associated with notables of Scotland's heroic past: Bonnie Dundee or Mary Queen of Scots or Bonnie Prince Charlie. Noting one silk-tied lock of hair in passing, cased in a golden locket of breathtaking workmanship, the man in black wondered how the Stuart pretender had managed to have any hair left at all, by the time he escaped over the sea of Skye and then took up his sad exile in France. It reminded him of all the splinters of the true Cross he had seen over the years—which, if put together, would have made enough crosses to crucify a dozen Kings of the Jews.

So he supposed the Scots could have their relics too. It mattered not to him. And the Scottish relic of tonight's interest would bring a pretty sum.

He smiled as he approached its case and shone his light through the glass, heedless of the Cavalier watching from above the mantel. The swept-hilt rapier and its scabbard lay on a bed of dark blue velvet, elegant tributes to the ornate style favored by Italian armorers of the late sixteenth century. The gold of the hilt and guard was deeply chased, and gold-washed etching glittered on the blued blade.

The scabbard was a more modest item, executed in Moroccan leather, but several semiprecious gems flashed discreetly along its length and at the throat. Between blade and scabbard, creamy white against the dark blue velvet, a small card carried a terse three-line inscription in an elegant copperplate hand:

The Hepburn Sword
once owned by Sir Francis Hepburn
the "Wizard Earl" of Bothwell, d. 1624

The man in black breathed a small grunt of satisfaction. Taking the tiny flashlight in his teeth, he extracted a delicate lock pick from an inner pocket and probed briefly at the case's lock. When it yielded, he raised the lid and engaged its stops. The hilt of the sword fit his gloved hand as if made for it, and he felt a thrill of imagination as he drew the weapon from the case and tried its balance, sighting along its blade where the etching caught the torchlight. Why, oh, why had he not been born a Cavalier?

Only briefly savoring the rush of excitement he felt as he picked up the sword, the man in black flourished the sword in ironic salute to the portrait above the marble mantelpiece, then pulled the scabbard out of the case and sheathed the weapon with brisk efficiency.

The sword of the Wizard Earl, indeed! Games were well and good, but he had *not* been born a Cavalier; and if he lingered long, he might begin to regret he had ever been born at all. His employer was said to be a most exacting man, if eccentric in his tastes.

All business again now, the man in black reached inside his jacket and pulled out a much-folded black nylon duffel bag, long and narrow to suit his needs. Into its open end he slipped the sheathed sword, pausing to tie it firmly closed before slinging it over his back.

Then, before closing the case and locking it again, he produced from yet another pocket a small card similar to the one already there. This one read: *Display Removed for Conservation.*

After that, it was simply a matter of retracing his steps. On his way out, he showed no more interest in any of the other contents of the museum than he had shown on the way in. Once outside the kitchen door, he paused briefly to re-arm the security system, but then he faded back into the shadows up the hill, silent as a whisper, heading for the shelter of the woods and a service lane behind the house.

His transport was waiting—not the charger that would have been a Cavalier's steed, but a powerful Japanese-built motorcycle that had seen him through many an escapade since being assigned to overseas duty. His imagination transformed the black crash helmet into a tilting helm as he donned it and wheeled the machine out of the underbrush, giving a strong push with his weight behind it. As the motorcycle rolled forward, gathering momentum on the downhill slope, he mounted on the run, letting the machine coast down the zigzag trail. Only at the foot of the hill, well out of earshot of the house, did he kick in the engine—and within minutes was roaring westward up a two-lane country road, into the frosty Scottish night.

An hour later, after an exhilarating run along the M8 Motorway, the rider was threading a more sedate course through the sleeping streets of Glasgow. Following precise instructions, he headed away from the city-center on a route that eventually brought him into a wilderness of abandoned buildings in the heart of the docklands of Clydebank. The low rumble of the engine echoed dully off the cobbles as he drew up outside the gates of a disused shipyard, going suddenly silent as he cut the ignition.

The man in black removed his helmet. Five minutes passed. The man glanced at his watch, got off his machine, and began slowly pacing back and forth, keeping to the shadows. His breath plumed on the frosty, salt-tinged air, and he stifled a sneeze.

Finally, as he turned in his tracks for the fourth time, his straining ears picked up the quiet murmur of a powerful car approaching. He returned to his machine. A moment later, a sleek, dark-colored Mercedes emerged from a side-alley and came to a smooth halt on the opposite side of the street.

As the headlamps were extinguished, the dark-tinted windows on the right side of the car glided down in automated unison. Pale face-blurs of a driver and a rear passenger showed in the darkness.

Relieved, the motorcyclist set his helmet on the saddle of his bike and sauntered over to the side of the car. Bending from the waist, he favored the passenger in the backseat with an ironic salute and drawled, "Morning, Mr. Raeburn."

The backseat's occupant acknowledged the greeting with a cool nod. "Good morning, Sergeant. I believe you have something for me?"

The sergeant pulled a cocky smile, exposing strong white teeth in a face weathered by years under Texas suns.

"Christmas gets earlier every year," he replied. "Just call me Santa Claus."

With an exaggerated flourish he unslung the duffel bag he still carried over his shoulder. The Mercedes' passenger elevated an eyebrow.

"Did you encounter any difficulties?"

The American gave a derisive snort. "Are you kiddin' me? I'd have had more trouble taking candy from a baby. What folks your side of the Atlantic don't know about security must cost your insurance people a mint."

As he began methodically unlacing the neck of the duffel

bag, the man in the backseat of the Mercedes watched his every move.

"I trust," said the man, "that you were not tempted to exploit the situation beyond the terms of our contract?"

His tone was conversational, but there was more than a hint of steel beneath the silken inquiry. It elicited a sharp glance from the sergeant, and an almost petulant disclaimer.

"Hey, I got a reputation to maintain!"

The man in the car smiled in chilly satisfaction. "You reassure me. Reliable help is not always easy to find nowadays."

The American did not bother to acknowledge the comment. As he jerked open the mouth of the duffel bag and drew forth the sword by its hilt, a map light came on inside the car. The light glinted off the gold and cut-steel as he passed it through the open window, point first.

"It's a pretty enough toy, I'll grant you," he remarked, "but I guess you know you could've had half a dozen fancy swords made for half what you're paying me to steal this one."

His employer took the Hepburn Sword in both gloved hands, briefly drawing the blade partway from the scabbard, then sheathed it with a sigh and laid it carefully across his knees.

"An object's worth is not always to be measured in terms of money," the man murmured.

The sergeant shrugged. "Whatever you say, Mr. Raeburn. You're a collector, and you know what you want. Me, I'm a—an acquisitions agent." He savored the sound of the title on his tongue. "And us agents do what we do for the money."

"Of course," said his employer coolly. "You've fulfilled your part of the agreement. I am now prepared to fulfill mine."

He nodded to his driver in the rearview mirror. The man in the front of the Mercedes wordlessly reached into the breast of his coat and drew out a fat leather wallet, handing it through the open window without comment. The recipient opened it casually and riffled through the thick sheaf of

American currency inside, one eyebrow raising in pleased surprise.

"As you see, I have included a small bonus," the man in the backseat said.

"Yes, sir, Mr. Raeburn," the American said with a broad grin. "It's been a pleasure doing business with you."

"I think I may safely say the same."

The man in the backseat drew the glove from his right hand. A signet ring set with a blood-red carnelian seal glittered richly on the third finger as he extended his hand through the open window.

The American accepted the proffered handshake. His employer's clasp was surprisingly hard. The man in the car gave a savage downward jerk, and the thief found himself staring into the muzzle of a silencer—one of the sleek West German ones.

This alone the American had time to grasp, even as the man in the car pulled the trigger at point-blank range. He never heard the quiet cough of the first shot, much less the second or third.

His body crumpled to the pavement with a loose-limbed thud as his hand was released. When he did not move, his killer slipped the silenced automatic carefully under the seat and signalled his driver to go on. The sound of the Mercedes' engine turning over was far louder than the shots had been, but neither raised any ripple of curiosity as the car crept almost soundlessly out of the Glasgow docklands.

CHAPTER ONE

IT was not until the following Monday, while waiting for his breakfast, that Sir Adam Sinclair became aware of the incident in Glasgow. He was still in riding clothes, having just come in from a brisk, early morning canter over the grounds of his country estate, not far from Edinburgh. Sunlight was pouring into the little parlor always called the "honey-bee room," because of the pale gold pattern of bees and flowers on the wallpaper, so he shrugged out of his hacking jacket and tossed it over the back of a nearby settee before pulling out the chair set before the little table in the wide window bay.

On the table, centered on a snowy tablecloth of fine Irish linen, a crystal vase of cut chrysanthemums reigned over a single place setting of antique silver and fine delft breakfast china. On top of his leather-bound appointment book, the morning edition of *The Scotsman* lay neatly folded in its customary place to the right of the china and cutlery. Adam unfolded it with a sharp flick of the wrist and scanned the main headlines as he sat down, absently loosening the knot of his tie.

Nothing of major interest had happened over the weekend. The European Parliament was poised to ratify a new set of air pollution control standards; a Japanese electronics firm had announced its intention to open up a manufacturing plant in Dundee; members of the Scottish Nationalist Party had staged another protest against the poll tax. He almost missed the item tucked away in the paper's lower lefthand corner: *Body of Alleged Drug Dealer to Be Returned to U.S.*

Raising an eyebrow, Adam folded down the top half of the paper and continued reading. As a physician and sometime police consultant, he tried to keep up with progress—or lack thereof—in the ongoing war against illegal drugs, but this seemed to be a follow-up to a story he somehow had missed, toward the end of last week. According to the article, the body of an American serviceman had been found in a derelict area of Glasgow's docklands—probably the victim of a drug deal gone wrong, judging by the execution-style shooting and the amount of money found on the body.

Given only what was in the article, Adam allowed that the police theory probably was correct, for drug trafficking, unfortunately, was becoming more and more a fixture in Scotland's largest city. Still, the thought crossed his mind, for no rational reason he could fathom, that the case might not be as open-and-shut as the Glasgow police seemed to think it was.

Further speculation was diverted by the arrival of Humphrey, his butler and valet of some twenty years' service, bearing a laden silver breakfast tray.

"Good morning, Humphrey," Adam said easily, lowering the paper as the butler set down a rack of buttered toast and a steaming porcelain teapot beside the immaculate breakfast service.

"Good morning, sir. I trust you had a pleasant ride."

"Yes, Humphrey, I did. I rode up by the castle ruins. I was appalled to discover that there are several small trees growing out of the debris on top of the first floor vaulting. And the ivy doesn't bear thinking about."

Humphrey gave a subdued chuckle as he poured his master a cup of tea.

"I understand that even the Queen Mother wages a constant war against ivy, sir," he murmured. "Absolutely hates the stuff. It's said that weekend guests are apt to be drafted to help pull it down. Perhaps we might consider the same tactic, here at Strathmourne."

"Hmmm, yes," Adam replied, with a twitch of his newspaper. "Well, I didn't realize ours had gotten so bad over the summer. I left a message for MacDonald to get a crew up there today, if possible, and start clearing it away. If he should call, you can confirm that for me. We can't have the thing collapsing any more, just when I'm intending to start restoring it next spring."

"Indeed not, sir," Humphrey agreed. "I'll see to it."

As the butler retreated to the kitchen, Adam helped himself to toast and opened the paper to pages two and three. He skimmed over the first few headlines on the left-hand page, not paying particularly close attention, until his gaze was arrested by another item, tucked away in the lower right-hand column: *Antique Sword Goes Missing*.

The dark brows raised slightly as Adam bent for a closer look. As a connoisseur and sometime collector of edged weaponry himself, such an article never failed to pique his interest. He scanned it once through, quickly, then turned the paper inside-out and folded it in half to read the article again, while he sipped his tea, trying to supply what the article did *not* say.

> Lothian and Borders Police are investigating the disappearance of a historic sword from the museum in Mossiecairn House, outside Edinburgh. The sixteenth-century Italian rapier, known as the "Hepburn Sword," has long been associated with Sir Francis Hepburn, the fifth Earl of Bothwell, who died in 1624. The sword is presumed stolen, but the actual date of the theft is uncertain. Its disappearance was not noticed for several days, owing to confusion on the part of museum staff, who were under the impression that the weapon had been removed from its case for cleaning. The sword is valued at approximately £2000. A reward is offered for information leading to its recovery. . . .

Adam sat back in his chair, lips pursed, dark brows drawn together in a deep frown. Though he told himself that his interest came of the subject matter in general, some sixth sense insisted that this story almost certainly reflected more than met the eye. Taking a pen from beside his appointment book, he drew a circle around the entire article. Then he reached around behind him and leaned back in his chair to snare the telephone off a side-table next to the settee.

The number of the Lothian and Borders Police in Edinburgh was a familiar one. He dialled swiftly, identified himself, and asked to speak with Detective Chief Inspector Noel McLeod. There was a short delay while the police operator transferred the call to Press Liaison. Then a familiar, bass voice rumbled in his ear.

"Is that you, Sir Adam? Good morning. What can I do for you?"

"Good morning, Noel. I've just been casting my eye over the morning paper. If you've got a moment, I'd like a word with you concerning one of the items on page two of *The Scotsman*."

"Oh, aye?" The voice on the other end of the line sounded anything but surprised. "I suppose that'll be the piece about the Hepburn Sword."

"You seem quite certain it wasn't the report on the latest sighting of the Loch Ness Monster," Adam said, smiling.

"Monster sightings," said McLeod, "are five pence a dozen. And you wouldn't be phoning me, you'd be phoning the constabulary up at Inverness. On the other hand, the theft of a sword that once belonged to Sir Francis Hepburn might well be of interest to you—given the good earl's reputation."

"As a wizard?" Adam replied, careful to phrase his next words with suitable ambiguity, just in case anyone should chance to listen in. "I know of no reason," he said ingenuously, "to dispute with tradition on that account."

There was just the slightest of hesitations on the other end of the line, before McLeod replied, "I see."

"As a collector of edged weaponry myself," Adam went on, "I was disappointed that the newspaper account was so thin on detail. It's a beautiful sword. Can you supply any additional information?"

McLeod made a noise between a growl and a snort, back now on more neutral ground.

"I wish I could," he said. "We've got two good men assigned to the case, but they've not got much to show for their pains. One thing's for certain: it wasn't a conventional theft. Nothing else in the place was lifted—not so much as a silver spoon."

"Which means," Adam replied, "that the thief was after the sword, and that alone. Was it an amateur job?"

"Most definitely not," McLeod said emphatically. "Quite the reverse. Our jolly thief disarmed the security alarms at the back of the house and then avoided the hall sensors by going through the dining room and picking the lock on the connecting doors. We figure he must have visited the house at least once to case it, so we're following that lead, to see if any of the staff remembers anyone suspicious."

His sigh conveyed a world of exasperation.

"Unfortunately, I doubt any of this will come to anything. We're not even certain when the theft occurred, because our boy left a sign in the case: *Display Removed for Conservation*. Oh, he was clever, this one. Needless to say, we didn't find any prints."

"In other words," said Adam, "you haven't any leads."

"Not one worth a wooden ha'penny," came the tart reply. "We'll just have to keep our eyes open, and hope for a break. It's possible the sword will turn up eventually in one of the auction rooms or arms fairs—though I doubt it. The case has all the earmarks of a contract acquisition for some collector who fancies items with odd provenances."

"Hmmm, as a collector with similar proclivities, I would tend to agree," Adam said, "—though you can rest easy, Noel," he hastened to add, smiling. "*I* haven't got your sword!"

McLeod's easy chuckle left no doubt that the inspector had never even considered such a notion.

"It *would* help if we had some idea what kind of person might go after an item like the Hepburn Sword," McLeod said. "As a psychiatrist as well as a collector, would you care to speculate?"

It was an unofficial way of inviting Adam to tender an opinion—and to articulate an idea that probably had already occurred to the canny McLeod, though he would never dare to admit it in any official capacity.

"Well," Adam said, again choosing his words carefully, "I believe we can rule out a simple profit motive. A £2000 sword simply isn't worth the effort and expertise it took to evade the security system and steal it. The fact that nothing else is missing would tend to support that theory. This means that the thief was after this specific sword."

"Aye," McLeod agreed.

"So we must ask ourselves, what sort of a person would want this particular sword?" Adam went on. "It isn't especially unique for its kind; I have several similar blades in my collection, some of them previously owned by men far more historically important than the Earl of Bothwell.

"So it has to be something else about the sword's past. What else do we know? It belonged to the *Wizard* Earl of Bothwell. I shouldn't want this to be taken wrong, Noel, but it is not inconçeivable that the thief—or someone for whom he is acting—is someone who believes that the sword is imbued with some measure of the powers ascribed to its former owner."

"Now there's an interesting thought," McLeod said. The tone of this noncommittal reply made it quite clear to Adam that the other man was well aware of the Wizard Earl's legendary fame as a necromancer.

"Assuming less esoteric motives, however," McLeod continued blandly, "I think I'll still have my chaps keep an eye on the auction rooms and arms fairs."

"That's what *I* would do," Adam agreed.

McLeod snorted. "Somehow I figured you would! Meanwhile, if some poor sod turns up impaled on Francis Hepburn's blade, in culmination of some satanic rite, I'll be sure to let you know before the press get wind of it."

"Thank you," Adam said drily. "I'd appreciate that." He pushed the newspaper aside thoughtfully. "Oh, there was one other item I wanted to ask you about, since I've got you on the line. I don't suppose you've formulated any personal theories concerning that American serviceman who turned up dead in Glasgow?"

"No. I was just relieved that he didn't turn up dead in my jurisdiction," McLeod said baldly. "The Glasgow police have been getting a hell of a row from the people at the Home Office, who have been getting a hell of a row from the American embassy—" He broke off abruptly. "Do you think there might be some connection between the two cases?"

"I don't know," said Adam. "I was merely wondering."

"That," said McLeod, "is anything but reassuring. Whenever you start wondering, I know it's only a matter of time before something happens that I'm going to have trouble explaining to the satisfaction of the media."

Adam allowed himself a companionable chuckle. "I *am* sorry, Noel. If this case produces any unusual complications, you know you can count on my help."

"Oh, aye," came the gruff reply. "But as they say somewhere or other: I knew the job was dangerous. Anyway, I've got another bloody phone ringing. Call me if anything else occurs to you, all right?"

"You know I will."

With this assurance, Adam rang off and resumed his breakfast, thinking about the Hepburn Sword. He was just finishing his second cup of tea, and thumbing through his day's appointments, when Humphrey reappeared with the morning's post on a silver tray.

Adam accepted the stack of mail with a murmur of thanks and gave it a cursory riffle, then set it aside and handed Humphrey the front section of *The Scotsman*.

"I've circled an article on page two. I'd be obliged if you'd file it for me. We may have occasion to refer to it again."

"I understand, sir." Humphrey folded the paper and tucked it neatly under his arm before casting an eye over the table. "Are you quite finished here, sir?"

Adam nodded, rising as he gave a glance to his watch. "Yes, I am. Good Lord, where does the time go? I want to call in at Kintoul House before I head into Edinburgh."

Humphrey paused in the act of clearing the table, his expression all at once one of concern. "Nothing wrong with Lady Laura, I hope, sir?"

Adam grimaced. "I don't know yet, Humphrey. I won't know until I see her. Incidentally, did you remember that I'm dining with the Bishop of Saint Andrew's tonight?"

"Of course, sir. I've laid out your dark grey suit, and there's a fresh shirt in your briefcase."

"Perfect!" Adam said with a grin, pulling off his tie as he headed for the stairs. "If anyone wants me, then, you know where I'll be. Oh, and if Inspector McLeod should happen to ring after I've left the hospital, tell him where I'm dining, and that I'll get back with him directly."

"Very good, sir," said Humphrey. "I'll attend to everything."

Chapter Two

A SCANT twenty minutes later, freshly showered and shaved, Adam emerged from his private apartments, riding clothes replaced by the crisp white shirt and formal three-piece suit that are the uniform of the medical profession.

The images that kept pace with him in the mirrors that lined the entry hall of Strathmourne House were those of a tall, dark-haired man in his vigorous forties, who moved with the purposeful air of one to whom time is always precious and in all too short supply. He had been a fencer and a promising dressage rider in his younger days, before the allure of medicine and other pursuits turned his energies to different priorities. The grace and suppleness required to excel at either sport persisted in an elegance of carriage that could not be taught, only inborn. The silver at his temples softened a patrician profile that, in other men, might have been regarded as severe.

Yet any severity of temperament was that of a man who expects more of himself than of anyone else around him. And it was compassion that tempered the air of brilliant intensity that Adam Sinclair wore as naturally as he wore his clothes. Even in unguarded moments of relaxation, the dark eyes promised the smouldering potential of a banked peat fire—a glow that could kindle spontaneously into comforting warmth or, more rarely, flare into sudden, formidable anger. The latter instances were rare, indeed, and usually balanced by a dry wit that could defuse nearly any taut situation.

His sense of humor came through now, as he passed from the hall into the vestibule. Outside, Humphrey had brought up the sedate and conservative blue Range Rover that Adam usually took into the city when he drove himself, and was waiting to hand him trenchcoat, hat, and briefcase; but as the day was promising to be fine, Adam shook his head as he emerged, heading for the garage instead.

"I've changed my mind, Humphrey," he said, bidding him toss case, coat, and hat under the tonneau cover of a dark blue XJ-S convertible, a recent and prized acquisition. "It's a perfect day for the Jag. If I get out of Jordanburn on time, it should still be light when I drive up to Perth. I don't believe the bishop's seen this beauty yet. If he's very respectful, I may even let him drive her before dinner."

Humphrey chuckled as he helped Adam zip back the tonneau cover on the driver's side and tuck it behind the leather seat.

"The bishop should enjoy that, sir."

"Yes, he should. She's a very fine motorcar." He grinned as he slid behind the wheel and began pulling on driving gloves.

"Then, after I have eaten his food and drunk his very fine port—and so that he shan't feel totally deprived—I shall hand him a rather substantial cheque for the cathedral fabric fund. I believe Saint Ninian's could do with some roof work."

"Can you name me a cathedral that couldn't, sir?" Humphrey replied with an answering smile, as Adam turned the key in the ignition and the powerful engine roared to life.

Soon he was easing the big car out the stableyard gate and down the tree-lined avenue, bare-headed under the sun, enjoying the breeze in his hair. The copper beeches were at their very best on this mid-October day, and as he turned the first curve, the gothic front of Strathmourne vanished from his rearview mirror in a sea of flame-colored leaves.

He kept his speed down as he threaded past a row of cottages belonging to the estate. Beyond the houses, the fields were patchworked brown and gold, dotted with circular bales of new-mown hay. Up on the high ground, one of Adam's three tenant farmers was ploughing up the soil in preparation for sowing a winter crop of barley. A cloud of white birds circled in the wake of the plough, screeching and diving for grubs and worms in the newly turned earth.

Nearly a mile from the house, the drive passed through a second set of gates, usually left open, and gave onto a good but narrow secondary road. Adam turned left rather than going right toward Edinburgh, winding along a series of "B" roads until at last he approached the main entrance to the Kintoul estate, marked by the distinctive blue-and-white sign bearing the stylized symbol of a castle.

Gravel hissed under the tires as he nosed the Jag under the arch of the stone-built gate house and on down the long avenue. The autumn color at Kintoul—the fiery shades that were Lady Laura's favorites—was as spectacular as that at Strathmourne, and as Adam continued toward the house, he found himself wondering again why he had been summoned.

Since he had known Lady Laura since boyhood, there were any number of possibilities, of course, both professional and personal. He had received her brief note just before the weekend, enjoining him to come up to Kintoul on Monday. The tone had been casual and witty, as was Laura's usual wont, but Adam had been left with the lingering impression that the invitation was issued to some unstated purpose besides the mere pleasure of his company. He had phoned Kintoul House the same morning, but Lady Laura firmly declined his offer to come sooner. This strengthened Adam's suspicion that she had chosen this particular day for a reason.

Beyond the gatehouse, the dense plantation shortly gave way to rolling pastures, finally affording Adam a glimpse of the great, sprawling pile that was Kintoul House. Seen from a distance, it presented a fairy-tale silhouette of towers, turrets, and battlements, the rugged roughness of its ancient stone work overlaid with silver-white harling. The corbels supporting the parapets, like the timbers framing the windows, were painted a smoky shade of grey that matched the slates covering the rooftops. The bright blue and white of

Scotland's national standard—the Saint Andrew's flag or, more familiarly, the "blue blanket"—fluttered from a staff atop one of the highest turrets, but the Kintoul banner was not in evidence, indicating that the Earl of Kintoul, Lady Laura's oldest son, was not at home.

This did not surprise Adam, for Kintoul, like many historic houses in Scotland, had become as much a museum and showplace as it was a residence. In the summertime, the earl opened the grounds and twelve of its twenty-eight rooms to public view. It was a matter of economics. Everything was still well maintained; but picnic tables, a visitor center, and a children's playground now occupied a stretch of lawn that formerly had been reserved for croquet and badminton. It saddened Adam, in a way, but it was better than having historic properties like Kintoul turned into hotels, or broken up for conversion into flats. He hoped he could spare Strathmourne that fate.

Remembering shuttlecocks and croquet hoops and the summer days of a childhood now long past, Adam carried on past the visitors' car park, all but deserted now that the tourist season was nearly over. A paved extension to the public drive took him through a gateway and around the eastern end of the house into a smaller parking area adjoining the family's private entrance.

He parked the Jaguar next to a car he did not remember having seen at Kintoul House before: a Morris Minor Traveller, with dark green paintwork and recently refinished timber on the sides. The backseat had been folded down to accommodate several large canvases, all of them blank so far as Adam could see. As he took off his gloves and briefly ran a comb through his hair, he wondered briefly who the owner might be, but he put the curiosity aside as he mounted the steps to the Kintoul side door.

The bell was answered by a liveried manservant Adam had never seen before. As he conducted Adam into the vestibule, they were joined by Anna Irvine, Lady Laura's personal maid and sometime secretary.

"Sir Adam, it's good to see you," she said, welcoming him with a strong handshake and a smile that was tinged with worry. "Her ladyship is in the long gallery. I'll take you to her, if you'll just follow me."

The gallery ran the full length of the north wing—a narrow, chilly chamber, more like a hallway than a room. A handsome Persian carpet stretched along its length, boldly patterned in rose and peacock blue, but because it was little used as a living area, the furniture consisted mainly of a row of delicate, spindle-legged chairs arranged along the interior wall, interrupted by the occasional sideboard or hall table. In its heyday, the gallery had been intended to provide the occupants of the house with space for indoor exercise during times of inclement weather. Nowadays, it served mainly as a corridor connecting the other reception rooms on the ground floor, except when summer visitors came to view the Kintoul collection of family portraits.

Today, however, the far end of the gallery had been transformed into something resembling a stage set. As they approached it, Adam recognized several pieces of furniture from other parts of the house—a settee, a wing-backed chair, an ornamental screen—brought together to create the illusion of a much smaller room. Set in profile in the midst of this artificial setting, regal as a porcelain costume doll, stood a pert, elderly woman in a floor-length white ball-gown. A length of tartan sash was brooched to one shoulder and across her breast, its silken fringes bright against the gown's brocade, and a diamond tiara glittered like a crown of ice crystals on her soft, upswept white hair.

As the maid led Adam nearer, he saw that a large canvas had been mounted on a tall standing easel positioned a few yards back from the composed little scene. He caught the piney smell of turpentine, and then just a glimpse of someone moving behind the easel. Before he could gain any clear impression of the artist, the woman in the tiara turned her head and saw him, her face lighting in a delighted smile.

"Adam! My dear!" she called. "Stay where you are, and I'll be right with you."

With an apologetic wave in the direction of the artist, she abandoned her pose in front of the screen and came eagerly down the gallery to meet him. Watching her with the critical eye of a physician, Adam was reassured to see no signs of weakness or hesitation in her bearing. She held out two thin, blue-veined hands to him as the distance between them closed. Adam bent down as he took them, and received a swift, motherly kiss on one cheek.

"Adam, I can't tell you how delighted I am to see you," Lady Laura said, as he, in turn, kissed both her hands. "It was so good of you to come."

"Did you really think I could ignore an invitation from my favorite lady?" he said with a smile. Then his expression sobered. "How are you, my dear?"

Lady Laura dismissed the question with a small shrug, also waving dismissal to the maid.

"I'm as well as can possibly be expected, given the conditions of my age," she said easily. "Never mind me. How are *you* getting on, with your latest covey of student-doctors?"

"Not too badly—though life would be much simpler if I could persuade them not to go haring off after every new theory that comes along, with nary a second thought for common sense." He gave her a rueful grin. "There are days when I feel strongly akin to a sheepdog."

"Ah, and you know you love it!" she scoffed, with a knowing twinkle in her eyes.

"Yes, I suppose I do, or I wouldn't keep at it." Adam stood back and surveyed his hostess appraisingly. "But *you*—Laura, you look positively *splendid* in all your regalia! You really ought to have your portrait painted more often."

"Perish the thought!" The Dowager Countess of Kintoul rolled her china blue eyes in mild dismay. "This is only my second sitting—or *standing*, as I suppose I should say—and I assure you that the novelty of the whole experience is already beginning to wear quite thin. I can only hope that Peregrine won't insist on too many refinements."

"Peregrine?" Adam cocked his head in new interest. "That wouldn't be Peregrine Lovat, would it?"

"Why, yes," Lady Laura replied, looking quite pleased with herself. "May I take it that you've seen his work?"

"Indeed, I have," Adam said. "Some of his portraits were hanging at the Royal Scottish Academy, the last time

I went. I was quite impressed. There was a luminance to his style, an artistic insight—one almost had the impression that he was painting more about his subject than would be visible to the naked eye. I should very much like to meet the man himself."

"I'm very pleased to hear you say that," she said, "because I should very much like him to meet you, too."

This candid disclosure earned her a penetrating look from her visitor.

"I don't suppose that would be the reason you asked me here today?"

Biting at her lower lip, Lady Laura breathed a long sigh and averted her eyes.

"I think he needs your help, Adam," she said quietly, linking her arm in his and leading him farther out of possible earshot of their subject. "Perhaps I've no business meddling, but—Peregrine is more than a casual acquaintance. You probably don't remember, but he was a friend of Alasdair's. They met at Cambridge. Alasdair used to bring him up to the lodge at Ballater for the salmon fishing—before the accident."

Encouraged by Adam's attentive silence, Lady Laura continued. Alasdair had been her youngest and favorite son.

"Peregrine was away painting in Vienna when it happened," she went on a bit more strongly, "but he came home for the funeral. That was the last I saw of him for quite some time, though he wrote regularly to let me know where he was and how he was doing. At times, I almost felt I had a replacement son.

"So you can imagine my delight when I learned he'd rented a studio in Edinburgh," she went on brightly. "I immediately invited him to come up and paint the children. He drove up the following week to do the preliminary sketches. If I—hadn't arranged the meeting in the first place, I hardly would have recognized him."

She made a show of studying one of the tassels on the front edge of her plaid. "He was always rather a quiet boy," she went on more slowly, "with more reserve, perhaps, than was strictly good for him. But he had quite a charming smile when he forgot to be serious. And now—now he hardly seems to have any life in him at all. It's almost as if he—wants to cut himself off from the rest of the world. And if someone doesn't come to his rescue soon," she finished bleakly, "I'm afraid he might very well succeed."

As she raised her eyes to meet Adam's at last, her expression was one of mute appeal. Adam gave her frail hand a comforting squeeze.

"Whatever else may be said about this young man of yours," he said with a gentle smile, "he is fortunate in his friends. Why don't you come and help us make one another's acquaintance?"

Peregrine Lovat was standing behind the easel as they approached, nervously dabbing at a palette with a brush whose end was well chewed. Every line of his body suggested tension. Seen at close range, he was a classically attractive young man of middling height, apparently in his late twenties or early thirties, with fine bones and shapely, strong-fingered hands. Fair-skinned and fair-haired, he was meticulously attired in light-weight wool trousers and a vee-neck cashmere sweater, both in muted shades of grey. The sleeves of the sweater had been pushed up, the cuffs of the ivory shirt turned back neatly. The silk tie knotted precisely at his throat proclaimed his Oxford connection, and permitted no allowance for relaxation, even when he was working. His oval face and symmetrical features might have provided a study for da Vinci, except for the gold wire-framed spectacles riding on the bridge of his nose. The large lenses made it difficult to read the color of his eyes.

As Lady Laura embarked on the necessary introductions, Adam set himself to refining his initial impression, going beyond mere physical appearance. What he saw at a second, more searching glance lent substance to the fears the countess had expressed on Lovat's behalf.

Everything about the younger man suggested a state of acute emotional repression. The thick, bronze-pale hair had been barbered to the point of ruthlessness at sides and back, and the chilly monochrome of his attire only served to leach any remaining color from a face already pale and drawn, thinner than it should have been. The line of the tight-lipped mouth was strained and unsmiling.

Lady Laura's voice recalled Adam from his impromptu assessment. She was speaking, he realized, to the artist.

"Adam's a psychiatrist, Peregrine, but don't let that put you off," she was saying. "He's also an old and dear friend—and an admirer of your work."

"I am, indeed, Mr. Lovat," Adam said, smoothly picking up his cue. "I'm very pleased to meet you."

He smiled and offered a handshake, but he was not surprised when Peregrine found a way to avoid it.

"Forgive me, Sir Adam," the younger man murmured, nervously displaying a set of paint-smudged fingers. "I'm afraid I'm in no fit state to return your courtesy."

With this tight-lipped apology, he retreated to the work-table next to the easel and began wiping his hands on a linen paint-rag. His fingers were not entirely steady. When Adam moved a step closer, as though to view the work in progress on the easel, Peregrine reached out and hastily flicked a flap of cream-colored hessian over the partly-finished canvas.

"No matter, Mr. Lovat," Adam said, affecting not to notice. "I apologize if I've interrupted your work. Judging by what I've been privileged to see in the past, you have a rare talent for portraiture. I was particularly taken by your study of Lady Douglas-McKay and her two children. In my opinion, it was one of the finest pieces in this year's RSA exhibition."

Peregrine shot Adam a fleeting, almost furtive glance from under lowered lids, then pointedly returned his attention to the brush he had started cleaning.

"I'm obliged to you for the compliment, sir," he mumbled stiffly.

"Your handling of children as subjects is particularly masterful," Adam continued calmly. "I was visiting the Gordon-Scotts only last week, and couldn't help but notice your recent portrait of their son and daughter. I knew it for your work even without seeing the signature. Your gift for capturing the spirit behind each face you paint is really quite distinctive."

The younger man murmured an incoherent phrase that might have been self-deprecation and put aside his paint rag. He glanced at Adam again, then abruptly took off his glasses and scowled at them as though dissatisfied. Out from behind the glasses, his eyes were a dull shade of hazel, with dark hollows underscoring them.

"Now, Adam," Lady Laura said abruptly, from behind them, "if you and Peregrine are going to debate the relative merits of artistic technique, I'm sure we can do it far more comfortably somewhere other than this draughty hall. If the pair of you will excuse me, I'll go tell Anna to have coffee sent up to the morning room."

She was gone before Peregrine could raise an objection—and Adam was not about to lose the opportunity she had created. The artist hastily put his glasses back on and followed the countess' departure with eyes that held an expression akin to numb desperation. Adam wondered why.

"Well, as ever, Lady Laura is a very perceptive and practical woman," Adam said amiably, affecting to rub his hands together against the chill. "Coffee would be most welcome, just about now. I'm surprised your fingers aren't too stiff to paint. May I?"

Before Peregrine could prevent him, Adam crossed to the easel in two easy strides and was reaching for the hessian drop-curtain. The smoothness of the sudden movement caught Peregrine completely off guard, and he instinctively reached out a hand as if to grasp at Adam's sleeve, only recollecting himself at the last moment.

"No—please!" he protested, his hand fluttering helplessly to his side as Adam started to lift an edge of the cloth. "I'd—really rather that you didn't—I mean, I don't like anyone to see my work before it's properly finished—"

Adam gave the younger man a sudden, piercing look. It stopped Peregrine in his tracks, his voice subsiding abruptly into silence. Adam returned his gaze to the canvas. With studied deliberation, he lifted aside the hessian drop so that the painting beneath was exposed to full view.

The canvas was an almost surreal fusion of scenes that might have been taken from two totally different pictures. Adam knew the three Kintoul grandchildren. In the foreground, Walter, Marjory, and Peter Michael gazed happily out at the world with bright, laughing eyes. Their portion of the canvas was vividly aglow with warmth, life, and color.

The expression of mischievous innocence in young Peter's round face elicited an involuntary smile from Adam. The smile died as his eyes travelled upward to take in the other half of the portrait.

The graceful figure presiding in the background was that of Lady Laura. The likeness was faultless, but where the children's forms were bright and solid, Lady Laura's was pale and insubstantial, like an image printed on water. The expression in the eyes was sweet and sad, the mouth wistful as a word of farewell. The scene glimpsed through the window behind her was of a white winter garden sleeping under a blanket of fallen snow.

Adam stared at the painting for a long moment in unbroken silence. Then he released the curtain so that it settled gently back over the canvas.

"Now I understand," he said softly, still facing the painting. "You see it. Don't you?"

Behind him, Peregrine gave a small strangled gasp. Surprised, Adam turned to look him squarely in the face. Behind the wired lenses, the younger man's eyes were full of pain and bewilderment. Quite clearly, Peregrine Lovat had no idea what had prompted him to paint what he had painted.

"I *am* sorry," Adam said softly, his own dark eyes softening with compassion. "I see now that you didn't actually know. But yes, she *is* dying, Mr. Lovat. I doubt if half a dozen people in this world know—and she doesn't want them to—but you can see it. Or rather," he finished quietly, "you can't help but see it."

Peregrine's gaze widened. He took two steps backward, then halted, visibly shivering. His mouth worked, but no sound came out.

"My dear boy, it's all right," Adam murmured. "There are many ways of seeing; some of them are tantamount to knowing. This faculty of yours is a gift, not a curse, You *can* learn to use it, rather than letting it use you."

Peregrine made a small, defensive gesture with trembling hands and swallowed hard. "I don't know what you're talking about," he said hoarsely.

"No, it's clear that you don't—at least not now," Adam

agreed. "But for your own sake, I hope you'll at least consider what I've just said."

A small stir at the eastern end of the gallery prevented either of them from saying more. Lady Laura's maid soon joined them to announce that coffee was now ready, up in the morning room, where the countess was waiting to receive them. Peregrine excused himself from accompanying Adam, claiming that he would follow as soon as he had a chance to wash his hands. Adam made no demur, but went on to the morning room alone, leaving the younger man to regain at least some semblance of composure.

The morning room, in contrast with the more formal gallery, was cheerfully done up in sunny shades of gold and leafy green. Adam arrived to find Lady Laura comfortably ensconced on a chintz-covered sofa before the fireplace, where a log fire crackled cheerily. A matching chair faced the sofa across a small table holding the coffee service.

"A most interesting young man," he said in response to her inquiring look, as he sat down beside her. "You were right to bring him to my attention."

"Will he be all right?" she asked, clearly still worried. "Adam, what's wrong with him? Do you know?"

Adam patted her hand and smiled reassuringly. "On such a short contact, I can only make an educated guess, but I believe I've given him something to think about. Let's just wait and see, shall we?"

Peregrine seemed uneasy and rigidly self-contained when he joined them a few minutes later, though the monochromatic grey now was broken by a smart navy blazer with shiny gold buttons. He accepted a cup of coffee from Lady Laura and sat down across from her, but he declined anything to eat. Reassured by a look from Adam, Lady Laura smoothly took command of further conversation, embarking on a series of comic anecdotes revolving around some of the more eccentric characters represented in the family portrait gallery. Presently Adam set aside his cup and saucer and consulted a handsome silver pocket watch.

"Ah, do forgive me, Laura, but I'm afraid I'm going to have to run," he said, slipping the watch back into a vest pocket. "I'm expected on rounds in half an hour, and goodness knows what new flights of speculation will lure our fine student-doctors off in all directions, if I'm not there to supervise. Sometimes I wish that psychiatry was a more exact science."

"You're forgiven, my dear," Laura said, smiling. "Far be it from me to monopolize your time at the expense of your duty."

Adam stood up smoothly. "The temptation to linger," he said with a laugh, "is by no means inconsiderable. Thank you very much for the coffee. If I may, I'll try to call round again on Wednesday."

"You know you're welcome any time," she replied, turning her cheek for his kiss. "Thank you for coming, Adam."

"The pleasure was all mine, dear lady."

He turned to Peregrine, sitting withdrawn and silent on the other side of the little table.

"And Mr. Lovat," he continued, "I'm very happy to have made your acquaintance." Then he reached into the inside breast pocket of his coat for a monogrammed card case.

"Here's my card," he told Peregrine, handing one across. "Please feel free to call upon me in the near future. After what I've seen today, I should like very much to discuss the possibility of your painting my portrait."

Chapter Three

THE next two days passed without hearing anything from Peregrine Lovat. On Wednesday afternoon, Adam returned to Kintoul House for his promised visit. To his surprise, Peregrine Lovat was not there. After satisfying himself that Lady Laura was in good spirits and reasonably comfortable, Adam inquired after the young man.

"I can't really say, Adam," she said, sipping tea with him in the morning room. "He didn't show up yesterday; and then he rang me this morning to say that something had come up with an agent from some gallery in London. If I didn't know better, I would accuse you of having frightened him away."

"Well, he's certainly frightened," Adam agreed soberly. "Unfortunately, there isn't a great deal I can do to help him until he becomes more afraid of himself than he is of me."

He turned the conversation to other subjects after that, for he did not want to reveal the reasons for his interest in Peregrine Lovat—not to Lady Laura Kintoul, whose impending death Peregrine had seen. After chatting for nearly an hour, and exacting her promise to call if she should feel the need of him either as a physician or a friend, he took affectionate leave of her.

In the normal course of things, Adam would have called in to Lady Laura again on Friday, but on Thursday a bleak autumnal tempest swept in off the North Sea, bringing blustery gales, torrential rains, and a spectacular thunderstorm. Within the space of twenty-four hours, the trees on the northeast flanks of the hills had been stripped bare of their leaves, the furrows in the fields turned into long ribbons of standing water. The storm left the air charged, sending several of Adam's patients at Jordanburn into suicidal depressions. He was kept busy far beyond his usual clinic hours, helping the staff cope, and consequently Peregrine Lovat was even farther from his thoughts than Laura Kintoul.

Professional crises were under control by Saturday morning, however, in time to embark upon his weekend social obligations as planned. The weather was still unsettled, but by ten, as Humphrey drove him out of the car park at Jordanburn and headed west, the sky to the north hinted of a possible clearing later on. The elegant old Bentley that was Adam's favorite vehicle, even above the Jaguar, lived up to its reputation as the "silent sportscar" as they bowled along the M8 toward Glasgow and Ferniegair, to the south.

His lunchtime engagement was at Chatelherault, a magnificent hunting lodge built in the early eighteenth century for the Duke of Hamilton, where Adam had promised to deliver a birthday tribute in honor of the present duke. As the old man had been a close personal friend of Adam's father, Adam regarded his own contribution to the festivities as a pleasure rather than a duty. Bringing the Bentley today was another way of demonstrating his affection, for his father and the duke had been old car buffs together.

He would have preferred to take the wheel himself, but delegating that task to Humphrey allowed time to read over the text of the speech he had prepared. During the drive he also reviewed his notes for a second address he was to make later that evening in Edinburgh, at a charity performance of *Die Zauberflöte*—which was another good reason to have Humphrey drive. Adam hated having to park in the city. In addition, since the day's tight scheduling precluded any return to Strathmourne between engagements, he had had Humphrey bring along a complete set of dinner clothes, so he could change before setting out for the concert hall. It was a fairly typical Saturday for Sir Adam Sinclair, Baronet.

The Hamilton affair went off without a hitch, despite the persistence of poor weather. During a lull in the rain, Adam took the old duke out to the car park to kick the Bentley's tires and reminisce about the old days, when he and Adam's father used to drive far older cars far faster than Adam or Humphrey drove the stately Mark VI. Afterward, Adam was persuaded to stay for drinks after most of the other guests had left, so that he had just enough time to change before leaving Chatelherault to pick up his companion for the evening.

She was ready on schedule, and they arrived at the concert hall in good time. Janet, Lady Fraser, was the wife of one of Adam's medical colleagues who had been called away on a consultation in Paris. The Frasers lived just north of Edinburgh, on the other side of the Firth, and like Adam, were generous patrons of the opera. Both Frasers had been friends since Adam's childhood.

Janet Fraser also was an incurable romantic, who teased Adam unmercifully about his bachelor eligibility and was forever trying to arrange matches with young ladies of suitable lineage. Once Adam had made his speech and returned to their box, she confined her good-natured badgering to the intervals, letting him lose himself in the magic of the music, but she could not resist further sly digs once they were safely ensconced in the privacy of the Bentley and on their way home.

"You really are impossible, Adam," Janet was saying, as Humphrey drove them north across the Forth Road Bridge. "I'm always delighted to have you as an escort when Matthew has to be away on one of his trips, but you need a lady of your own. You could have had any of a number of bright young things on your arm tonight."

Adam sighed and sat back in the Bentley's deeply cushioned leather, beginning to tire of the game. He had not yet abandoned the hope of eventually sharing his life with a wife and family, but the lady of his admittedly exacting dreams seemed to be maddeningly elusive.

That was not Janet's fault, of course. Still, he was glad she could not see how her persistent harping on the subject was beginning to annoy him. Though the white of his scarf and wing-collared shirt would be starkly visible above the black of his dinner jacket, he knew that his face was only a vague blur. She was wearing ubiquitous black as well, and blended almost invisibly into the darkness of the backseat, except where a choker of diamonds glittered against a vee of white throat opening upward toward the whiter patch that was her face.

"Must I keep reminding you that I'm saving myself for the right woman?" he quipped, giving her the light-hearted rejoinder that he knew she expected. "You're already married, after all."

"Oh, Adam! You are *so* incorrigible. It isn't that you don't have normal appetites—I know that from long ago. Lately, though, you seem to *enjoy* living like a monk!"

Adam considered the accusation. In that part of his life that he shared with only a few close intimates, some aspects of their common work did recall the discipline and dedication required of monks; but that was hardly anything he was prepared to discuss with Janet, dear a friend as she might be.

"Will you think me less monkish if we stop at Strathmourne for a drink, before I take you home?" he asked lightly. "I hasten to remind you that this is *only* an invitation for a drink. Lovely married ladies are always welcome at Strathmourne Abbey's refectory table, but my monkish cell remains sacrosanct."

"Oh, Adam," she giggled. "I don't know why I put up with you. I don't know why I ever did."

But she allowed him to change the subject, once he had told Humphrey to make the necessary diversion, settling into drowsy companionship with her head against his shoulder by the time Humphrey turned up the avenue to Strathmourne.

The Bentley prowled up the winding track toward the gate-arch in a hiss of wet gravel. As they rounded the last bend below the house, Humphrey reached for the remote control box to unlock the gate. Then he uttered a startled exclamation and applied the brakes.

The Bentley skidded to a halt in a back-sheet of rainwater. Adam sat up sharply and peered ahead through the forward windscreen, Janet stirring sleepily beside him. Drawn up at the closed wrought-iron gate and blocking it was a dark green Morris Minor with timber sides. To the left of the car, a slight, rain-drenched figure spun around in the full glare of the Bentley's headlamps.

"Good God, is that Peregrine Lovat?" Adam exclaimed, already reaching for the door handle.

The artist was wearing neither hat nor scarf. The rain had soaked through his trenchcoat, and his fair hair was plastered flat to his skull. He evidently had been pacing beside his car for some time, for his feet had worn a path through the wet carpet of fallen leaves. For an instant he stood arrested, as though mesmerized by the headlights; then he lurched forward, staggering toward the Bentley like a sleepwalker. He was not wearing his glasses.

"Is he drunk?" Janet asked.

"I don't think so."

Throwing his topcoat around his shoulders, Adam stepped out of the car just in time to catch the younger man before he fell to his knees. Seen at close range, in the merciless revelation of the headlights, Peregrine looked even worse than Adam had imagined. His eyes were bloodshot and deeply hollowed from lack of sleep, and an ugly bruise stained his right temple.

"Peregrine, what on earth has happened to you?" Adam demanded. "You look dreadful!"

Peregrine made a sound between a sob and a moan and clutched at Adam's sleeve with rain-chilled fingers.

"Help me," he mumbled brokenly. "Please—you have to help me."

"Of course I'll help," Adam assured him. "But let's get you in out of the weather first."

Humphrey had left the driver's seat of the Bentley, and was coming around the front of the bonnet to join them. Janet's face was a pale blur in the opening of the left rear door. With sudden decision, Adam headed Peregrine toward the Morris Minor, putting his own coat around the younger man's shoulders before bundling him into the passenger seat with Humphrey's help.

"I'll deal with this," he told the butler, as he closed the door on Peregrine and headed around to the driver's door.

"You drive Lady Fraser home. Tell her I'll ring her tomorrow and explain."

As Humphrey retreated to the Bentley, bending to speak to Janet as he closed the door, Adam glanced at Peregrine. Huddled deep in Adam's coat, the artist was shakily pulling his spectacles from an inner pocket, sliding them onto his face with trembling hands. Adam reached for the ignition, for he wanted to get Peregrine back to the house, but the keys were not there.

"I'll need the car keys, Peregrine," he said quietly, holding out his hand.

Peregrine dragged them clumsily from his coat pocket. When he unclenched his fingers to drop the keys into Adam's waiting hand, Adam caught sight of a row of raw, half-moon gouges across his palm where he evidently had driven his own fingernails deep into the skin. Adam said nothing for a moment, merely locating the correct key by the light of the Bentley's headlamps and then starting the car.

Humphrey activated the gate from inside the Bentley, and Adam put the Morris into gear and eased it through, glancing sidelong at his silent passenger as he negotiated the few dozen yards to the garage. Floodlights came on as he pulled into the stableyard, triggered by an electric eye, and Adam parked the Morris under one of them.

"I'm—sorry to be such a bother," Peregrine murmured huskily, when Adam had pulled on the hand brake and switched off the ignition. "I wouldn't have come here, but I had nowhere else to turn. I—think I must be going mad."

Adam's dark gaze was steady. "Why do you say that?"

Peregrine made a small gesture of miserable helplessness, not daring to meet Adam's eyes.

"I wanted to kill myself earlier," he muttered. "If I'd had a gun in the studio, I probably would have done it. Then I thought of gouging out my eyes with a palette knife. I only just managed to stop myself, by clenching my fists as hard as I could and slamming my head against a wall." He gave a bitter, half-hysterical laugh. "If that's not mad, I don't know what is."

"Why don't you let *me* be the judge of that?" Adam said

quietly. "Can you tell me what made you suddenly decide on this course of self-destruction?"

A long shudder wracked the younger man from head to foot. "Lady Laura," he said hoarsely. "She's dead. She died this afternoon."

This bald announcement kindled a gleam of enlightenment as well as grief in Adam's steady gaze.

"You were right to come to me tonight," he said, after a heartbeat's silence. "I'm only sorry, for your sake, that you didn't come sooner."

"Then you think you can help me?" Peregrine asked disbelievingly.

"I think you can be helped," Adam corrected carefully, still taking it all in. "For my part, I shall do whatever lies within my power. Meanwhile, we should get you out of those wet things."

With Humphrey otherwise engaged, it fell to Adam to manage the domestic details. After showing Peregrine the location of the library, he shepherded the younger man upstairs to one of the auxiliary bedrooms and laid out dry clothing from his own wardrobe, returning downstairs then to make a phone call. The tear-choked voice that answered at Kintoul House belonged to Anna, Lady Laura's maid, and confirmed, without having to ask, that Peregrine had told the bare truth about Lady Laura.

Adam identified himself and apologized for the lateness of the call, then gently related what he had been told. The maid supplied sparse details in a voice close to breaking—how Lady Laura had died shortly before four o'clock that afternoon, slipping away peacefully in the middle of an afternoon nap. Her eldest son and other members of the immediate family were now all gathered at the house. Funeral arrangements had not yet been decided.

It was the expected scenario for a death in a noble family. Nor did the death itself come as any surprise to Adam, whose long-time friendship had widened to include professional attendance when Laura Kintoul first learned of her terminal illness. He requested a brief word with the earl in order to convey his condolences, along with his willingness to render any personal service the family might require.

Then he rang off with the promise to call by Kintoul in the morning.

As he laid the receiver gently back in its cradle, he found it increasingly difficult to hold at bay his own feeling of sudden loss, coupled with a fleeting twinge of doubt, that perhaps he had not done all he could.

I knew this was only a matter of time, he thought. *Perhaps I should have been there*. To which another part of himself responded, *All had been done that needed to be done. Laura was ready to make this journey. You yourself opened her eyes to the way. . . .*

A sound in the hall outside the library recalled him to more practical considerations, and things needing doing for one still living. Seconds later, Peregrine appeared hesitantly at the library door, shuffling in outsized velvet slippers bearing Adam's heraldic crest and wrapped up in a quilted blue dressing-gown at least two sizes too large for him. He said nothing as he allowed himself to be steered numbly to a chair beside the library hearth.

He was still deathly pale from cold and the trauma of the afternoon and evening. He was also terrified. Feigning unconcern, Adam went to the drinks cabinet in the corner and poured two stiff measures of whiskey into cut crystal tumblers. He gave Peregrine a reassuring smile as he pressed one into his chilled hands.

"Here—drink this," Adam advised. "I've just rung Kintoul House. Let me get a fire going, and we'll talk about it."

He put his own drink on the mantel and bent wearily to the hearth, slipping a fire-starter briquette under the kindling already laid and lighting it with a long match. When he had nursed it to a healthy blaze, he took back his drink and sat opposite Peregrine.

"I spoke to Anna, Lady Laura's maid," he said quietly, in answer to the artist's look of shrinking inquiry. "Of course she confirmed what you told me earlier. But you mustn't mourn for *her*. She travels now in bright company."

Peregrine's eyes flew wide at this calm statement of assurance.

"What do you mean?" he demanded shakily. "You speak as if you *know*."

"I do."

"But—how can you know that? Who—what are you, anyway?"

Adam schooled his expression to one of bland neutrality, wondering just how much Peregrine was seeing.

"You know my name. You see my face," he ventured.

Confusion and fear flared again in Peregrine's taut face.

"Yes," he whispered. "That's part of what frightens me. Oh, God, if only I could stop seeing!" he moaned, shaking his head. "If you have some kind of power—if—if you're some sort of—of wizard or something—for God's sake, lift this curse!"

His eyes were feverish bright, his hands clenched so tightly around the tumbler that Adam feared he might crush it.

"I told you, it isn't a curse!" he said sharply. "And I haven't the power to *make* you stop seeing, even if I had the authority. Before we carry this conversation much further, though, you're going to have to try to relax." He jerked his own glass pointedly at the one in Peregrine's hand. "I wouldn't want to have to pick glass out of your very talented hands, if that shatters. If the whiskey isn't to your liking," he added more gently, "I can give you a sedative."

Peregrine blanched and shook his head, alarmed, but he did loosen his death-grip on the glass.

"N-no, please. No sedative. That only makes matters worse. If I take pills, I lose what little control I have left over this vision of mine."

"Then you *do* have *some* control."

Peregrine gave an unsteady, mirthless laugh.

"You're humoring me, aren't you? You think I really have gone mad."

"No, I am genuinely interested to hear what you have to say," Adam said truthfully. "But if I'm to help you, you must make up your mind, here and now, to be absolutely candid with me—however outrageous you may think you sound! I promise not to judge—but I have to know. It's a leap of faith, I realize—you hardly know me—but I can't help you unless you do your part."

Adam waited. Peregrine stared at him for a long, taut moment, totally motionless, then breathed out a long sigh, running a hand over his face and through his drying hair, dislodging his glasses.

"I'm sorry. I—there's really never been anyone I could talk to, about this. Where shall I start?"

"The beginning is usually best," Adam replied. "When do you first remember—*seeing*?"

Peregrine swallowed painfully, removing his glasses for a moment to rub the back of his hand across his eyes. Then he put the glasses back on, to stare down at the whiskey in his tumbler.

"I—can hardly remember a time when I *couldn't*," he murmured. "When I was a child, I used to see all kinds of things—things that weren't really there. I used to see pictures on walls that afterward turned out to be blank. I used to see other faces in mirrors, besides my own. Sometimes I would see things happening around me that seemed to belong to other times. . . ." His voice trailed off.

"Were you frightened by what you were seeing?" Adam asked.

The question seemed to take Peregrine off guard. He frowned, remembering.

"No, now that you mention it, I wasn't," he said. "But it scared the hell out of my father, when he found out about it. He thought there was something seriously wrong with me."

He took a breath before continuing. "When I was really small, I had a whole host of friends who used to come and talk to me all the time—tell me stories, play games with me. I know that lots of kids have imaginary friends, but eventually they outgrow them. Mine seemed very real. When I first went away to school, some of them used to help me with my studies. Sometimes they even gave me clues during exams—though they would never actually tell me the answer."

He shot an oblique glance at Adam, encouraged when Adam remained attentively silent.

"It—seemed so natural that I never thought much about it," he went on, "—until I started talking to some of the other boys. That was when I realized that—no one else was aware of my friends' existence. Eventually I made the mistake of asking my father about it."

"Why was that a mistake?"

Peregrine hunched his shoulders and grimaced. "If you had known my father, you wouldn't have to ask. He was very much the hard-nosed realist. He was appalled to think that any son of his should be so fanciful."

"Then, you discussed the matter in some detail?"

"I wouldn't say that we *discussed* it," Peregrine said, with a bitter curl of his lip. "Let's say that we had words. It was made quite clear to me that my overactive imagination was not to be indulged. Unfortunately, that wasn't much help. In fact, it only made the problem worse. It seemed like the more confused and upset I got, the more prone I became to seeing things. . . ." He glared down into the liquor in his glass.

"How old were you?" Adam asked.

"About eleven," Peregrine replied tonelessly.

"And do you know if your father ever considered submitting you for psychiatric evaluation?"

Peregrine shook his head, not daring to look Adam in the eyes.

"He thought it would reflect badly on the family, if word ever got out. Eventually he abandoned trying to reason with me, and simply made it clear that if I—wanted to continue being his son, I had better learn to control my delusions."

Adam only nodded. He had seen the pattern too many times before.

"Go on."

Peregrine closed his eyes briefly and then continued.

"As you can imagine, the threat was a good one. I made every mortal effort to shut my eyes to the other world. I suppose his methods were vindicated, because by the time I turned thirteen, I'd finally succeeded in blotting it all out."

The tone in his voice was dreary, rather than triumphant. After a pause, Adam said casually, "Let's leave that for a moment. When did you first start drawing and painting?"

Peregrine looked relieved.

"That's easy enough," he said. "It was at the beginning of my third year of prep—about the time everything else had shut down. I took an art class as an honors elective." He smiled wanly. "It was incredible. I'd never known I had it in me to draw. After that, it was as if a whole new world had opened up for me, to replace the one I'd lost."

"What did you draw?" Adam asked, trying to steer him away from the emotional mine field of his sight.

"Oh, nice, safe landscapes and buildings, for the first year, with a strong emphasis on perspective." Peregrine's voice had a more confident ring to it, as he talked about his art. "Most of my classmates hated the technical assignments, but for me, the exercises in perspective were like a kind of—oh, I don't know—a form of magic, I suppose. There were rules you had to follow, but the possibilities were almost infinite. The art mistress was very supportive, and I started picking up the pieces of my self-confidence."

He took a tentative sip of the whiskey before continuing thoughtfully.

"It got even better, once we started in on life studies. Portraiture was my forte from the start. In my final year, I did a portrait of the headmaster as Robert the Bruce that was good enough to win me an important prize. My father was dubious about all this artistic effort—he would have preferred excellence in sports, I think—but you can't argue with a picture on the cover of *Scottish Field*. Fortunately, my exams were good enough that even he couldn't complain about *that*.

"I wanted to go to art school next—he wanted me to read law—so we compromised on art history at Oxford, and then art school." He grimaced. "I wish now that I'd done as he wanted and read law—or even become a banker or an economist."

"Do you?" Adam carefully kept his tone uninflected.

"Yes!" Peregrine declared vehemently. "Oh, I started out well enough, during those first few years after I finished art school. I got a lot of lucky breaks, thanks to Lady Laura and others. I was even on the way to gaining a reputation, when things took a turn for the worse."

"In what way?"

"My vision—changed," Peregrine said. He took another swallow of whiskey. "I started seeing things again. I tried to control it, but I couldn't always. More and more often, when I started on a new portrait, I began to see things I had no business seeing. Sometimes when I looked at a subject's face, I would catch myself looking into his future—"

"Seeing his death, you mean." Adam made it a statement.

Peregrine's mouth tightened grimly. "It didn't happen every time. But it happened often enough to convince me that painting anyone over the age of legal majority was courting insanity."

"Which is why you've mainly painted children, in the last few years," Adam finished, nodding. "What persuaded you to paint Lady Laura?"

"Did *you* ever try saying no to Lady Laura?" Peregrine replied, giving Adam an almost incredulous glance. "Besides, the original commission was to paint her grandchildren. It was only after I'd started that she asked to be included in the picture. I couldn't very well refuse her; she was the kindest and most generous of patrons—almost like a mother, if you really want to know. That's why, when I realized what I was painting—"

He drew a deep, unsteady breath and tried to go on.

"I tried to tell myself that it couldn't be true," he whispered. "It was all I could do to continue working. I tried to blot out the knowledge, but I couldn't. Then *you* showed up—and continuing to deny it became out of the question. Now she's dead, as I foresaw. And I—haven't got any tears left for her."

He buried his face in his hands, a single dry sob wracking his frame. Sharing his grief, Adam reached across to lay a comforting hand on one taut shoulder.

"Peregrine," he said quietly, "Lady Laura Kintoul was diagnosed with terminal cancer nearly six months ago. That was long before you made a start on her portrait. Foreseeing someone's death is not the same thing as causing it."

When Peregrine offered no response, Adam tried another tack.

"Is death the only thing that you see?"

Peregrine gave a quick shake of his head.

"What else do you see?" Adam prompted.

Peregrine lifted his head, making a gallant attempt to get his emotions under control again.

"Well, it's—hard to describe," he said hesitantly. "I see—the sorts of things I seem to remember seeing when I was very young. Sometimes it's only the background that changes—and then it's as if I'm looking into some other time or some other place. Sometimes the face itself changes when I look at it from another angle, or in another light. It's still the same person—but different somehow."

Adam nodded. "Can you give me an example?"

Peregrine bit his lip. "Well, take you, for instance. Even as I sit here, I can't be entirely sure what you look like. Something about your aspect keeps changing. I see you differently now than I did only a minute ago."

Adam was listening intently. "Is it my death that you see?"

Peregrine flinched at the question, then recovered himself. "No. Not your death . . ." He narrowed his eyes and cocked his head at several different angles, as though trying to stabilize his vision.

"It's no use," he said after a labored pause. "I can't tell you what it is I see."

Adam sat silent for a moment, weighing his next words very carefully.

"I think we ought to see if there isn't some way to remedy that," he said at last, setting aside his untouched glass. "There are ways to separate and clarify one's perceptions. If you're willing, I propose carrying out a simple experiment."

"An experiment?" A wild, almost cornered look flitted briefly behind Peregrine's eyes, but then he took an impulsive gulp of whiskey.

"Why not?" he said, suddenly reckless. "I certainly can't go on the way I have been. If this experiment of yours offers any hope at all, I'm willing to give it a try."

Chapter Four

"GOOD lad," said Adam approvingly. "Now all we need are a few simple props."

He left his seat and shifted a small rosewood side table away from the end of the adjoining settee and into the space directly in front of Peregrine's chair. Then he returned to the drinks cabinet to rummage in a bottom drawer. When he rejoined Peregrine a moment later, he was carrying a fisherman's float made of transparent, pale green glass. He handed it to Peregrine, who set aside his tumbler to take it.

"A crystal ball?" the artist said, with more than a trace of skepticism in his tone.

"If you wish," Adam replied, smiling. "I'll explain everything in a moment. You can decide then if you want to carry this any further."

From the mantelpiece he took one of the pair of silver candlesticks flanking an oil of a hunting scene, bending to light the stub of a long fireplace match from the fire and then using that to light the candle in the silver candlestick. This he brought to Peregrine's table, setting it carefully in the center. Peregrine watched all these preparations with mingled fascination and uncertainty. By the flickering candlelight, the intricate inlay pattern in the top of the rosewood table seemed almost to glow.

"Now," Adam said, as he resumed his seat opposite Peregrine. "As you probably already know, the keys to most upheavals of the psyche generally lie buried in the individual's unconscious mind. Before we can get at those keys, we need to set the conscious mind at rest. There are chemical ways of doing this, of course, but they all have their side effects. Besides, you've already told me that drugs just make your problem worse.

"What I propose, then—and what I prefer anyway—is that we use one of several meditational techniques I've found useful in the past. One of the ways the unconscious guards its secrets is by projecting fear into the conscious. So I'd like to direct you in a simple relaxation exercise, to see if we can't bypass that fear and get down to what's really troubling you."

"I *know* what's troubling me," Peregrine muttered. "I keep *seeing* things I *shouldn't*!"

"Why don't you humor me by pretending that I do know what I'm doing?" Adam said mildly. "I know you're a bundle of nerves—and I understand why—but it isn't going to get any better if you won't let me help you."

Brought up short by this gentle rebuke, Peregrine blinked owlishly at Adam from behind his spectacles, then drew a determined breath.

"I'm sorry," he said, subdued. "What do you want me to do?"

"First of all," Adam said easily, "I want you to take the float between your two hands and hold it so that you can see the flame of the candle through the glass."

"All right." Peregrine turned the glass globe around experimentally, peering through it from several different angles. "Should I take off my glasses first?" he asked.

"You may, if it will make you feel more comfortable. How well do you see without them?"

"Oh, well enough, this close," Peregrine replied. "They're really for distance. Will it make any difference with the experiment?"

"Not really."

"In that case, I'll leave them on." He glanced doubtfully at Adam. "Are you going to hypnotize me?"

"So, you know my tricks already," Adam said, leaning back in his chair with a look of faint amusement. "You needn't worry. It won't be like Svengali or Count Dracula, robbing his victim of all power of will. I promise you, you'll remain in control of the situation at all times."

The assurance produced the desired smile, if still a bit strained. Subsiding, Peregrine bent his gaze to the float and the light of the candle. Seen through the slight distortion of the hand-blown glass, the flame seemed to take on a life of its own, expanding and contracting in a succession of bright dancing forms.

By degrees, as Adam's low voice began urging relaxation and a centering on the image of the flame, Peregrine felt himself drawn closer to the warm, lively glow, bathing in its brightness as it filled his field of vision. A growing lightness seemed to permeate his limbs, as though his body were shedding its weight. Far from being strange, the sensation was oddly familiar, even comforting.

Peregrine closed his eyes, trying to recall when and where he might have felt this way before. At the same time, he heard Adam Sinclair's deep, resonant voice speaking to him in words that were clear but remote, as though carried over a great distance.

"That's right. . . . Go ahead and close your eyes. Relax and float. There's nothing to fear now. You're perfectly safe. Just relax. Relax. . . ."

Gradually the remaining tension drained away from the young artist's face. As he began to relax, his breathing came more easily, with the shallow regularity of someone just on the verge of sleep. Adam fell silent for a few seconds, to see if he would rouse himself, but Peregrine only gave a little sigh and seemed to settle even more.

"That's very good," Adam said softly. "Can you hear me clearly?"

"Yes." The answer was almost inaudible.

"Excellent." Adam kept his tone quiet and reassuring. "At the moment, you're perfectly aware of what's going on around you; it's simply too much bother to pay attention to other things. You're relaxed and safe and perfectly at peace. Now, I'm going to fetch something from across the room. When I return, I shall ask you to perform a simple task for me—one that is perfectly within your ability. Will that be all right?"

"Yes."

Satisfied, Adam went to the desk at the far end of the

room, returning with a pencil and a blank pad of paper. Peregrine was sitting as he had left him—relaxed and motionless, eyes closed.

"You're doing just fine," Adam reassured him, in the same quiet tone he had used throughout. "We're finished with the float for now, so I'm going to take it out of your hands," he said, suiting action to words. "I'm giving you a pencil and some paper instead. I want you to take a few more deep breaths, to let go of any remaining tension or anxiety that might still be with you. Then, when you're ready, I want you to open your eyes and look at me, with all your inner intuition as well as your physical eyes, and draw what you see. Do you understand?"

Peregrine nodded his assent, his closed eyelids fluttering as he drew a slow, deep breath. Quietly Adam retreated to his chair, sitting back casually to watch, legs crossed. When the artist looked up, a few seconds later, the dull, hazel eyes had taken on an inner luminance, like lamps newly kindled.

Adam neither moved nor spoke, only watching his subject's minute nuances of expression, feeling Peregrine's eyes on his face. After a moment's searching scrutiny, the artist brought pencil and paper together and began to sketch rapidly, his gaze rarely leaving his subject. After a moment he frowned and scribbled vigorously over what he had drawn. and began on another. When he scribbled out the second sketch and started again, looking more and more confused, Adam quietly rose and came to set one hand on his shoulder in gentle restraint, the other pressing lightly to his forehead.

"Close your eyes and relax, Peregrine," he murmured. "Relax and let yourself drift. It seems I've set you a more difficult task than I realized. Just relax and rest easy for a few minutes, while I see what you've drawn."

Peregrine surrendered the pad and pencil without resistance, eyes closing and hands fluttering to his lap with a relieved sigh. Adam watched him for a few seconds, absently sticking the pencil through the spiral binding at the top of the pad, then turned his attention to what Peregrine had drawn.

Fortunately, the scribbling had not entirely obliterated the work. The sketch at the top showed a lean, bearded face with deep eyes and a patrician nose set above a stern, passionate mouth. A chain mail coif surrounded the face, surmounted by a conical helmet in the style of the late thirteenth century. The device delicately shaded on the left shoulder of the mantle was the distinctive, eight-pointed Maltese cross of, among others, the Knights Templar.

Adam pursed his lips, nodding as he realized what Peregrine had glimpsed—echoes of a past life whose details were only accessible to Adam himself when in a deeply altered trance state, and mostly elusive during ordinary consciousness. As a psychiatrist, he preferred to believe that his "far memories" were psychological constructs—tricks that the mind played, in order to deal with material more acceptably couched in the fantasy of a past existence than in the cold, stark terms of reality. The mystical part of him preferred to believe that it all was literally true, in some way he could not begin to explain.

As a compromise, he permitted himself to function *as if* it were true, simply accepting and using the insights he sometimes received from his "previous selves," because they usually worked—even if the methods he employed often did not square with his medical training or blunt logic, much less his affiliation with the religious establishment to which he gave generous support.

Meanwhile, more tangible proofs confirmed that Sir Adam Sinclair, Baronet, did have ancestral ties, at least, to the Knights of the Temple of Jerusalem. The tower house awaiting restoration in the north field had been in the Sinclair family for at least five hundred years—a former Templar site, as, indeed, were most places in Scotland with "temple" in the name. It was Templemor, not Strathmourne, from which the Sinclair family took their baronial title. And it was said that Templar blood ran in the Sinclair line as well, from the dark times after the Order had been suppressed nearly everywhere except Scotland.

At this remove, some of the historical "proofs" were hazy, of course—not that it really mattered. Some truths simply *were*. And the ultimate truth about the Templars, which even history books tended to substantiate—and which Adam's heart had never doubted—was that the Knights of the Temple of Jerusalem had pursued a course of single-minded devotion to the defense of hallowed ground and the guardianship of secret truths, many suffering burning martyrdom rather than betray what the Order held sacred. And though a fourteenth-century King of France had set out to destroy the Order, hoping to gain possession of their legendary wealth, he was never to know that the greatest treasure of the Templars lay not in gold, but in knowledge. . . .

Knowledge. Peregrine Lovat seemed to have it—though it was clear that he did not know what he had. Thoughtful, Adam returned his attention to the young man's work. Behind the scribbling, the second sketch showed the same strength of determination as the first, but the face was clean-shaved and hawk-visaged, framed in lappets of boldly striped linen. The tall headpiece Peregrine had sketched above the linen was the double crown of Upper and Lower Egypt, incorporating a solar disk set between tall ostrich plumes—the adornment of an Egyptian high priest.

No longer really seeing the sketch, Adam turned slightly to gaze into the fire. The second drawing was far more startling than the Templar Knight had been, for it depicted the most vivid of Adam's far memories. He wondered, briefly, what other faces Peregrine might have sketched, had Adam not stopped him.

The boy had the gift, though. There was no doubting that. The question was, who was Peregrine Lovat, that he should possess the ability to penetrate beyond the mask of matter and *see* another's soul, especially that of one trained as Adam had been trained? The answer to that question might well have far-reaching consequences, not only for Peregrine, but for Adam and his associates as well.

He turned to regard the young artist for a long moment, reaching deep inside himself for guidance on how to proceed. Peregrine was sitting quietly, hands lying gently cupped in his lap, the eyes closed behind the wire-rimmed spectacles, but Adam had some doubt that the level of trance was deep enough for what he had in mind to do next.

Setting the pad on the mantel, he decided to find out how good a hypnotic subject Peregrine was.

"Peregrine," he said quietly, "I'd like to take this a step further, if I may. Will you trust that what I ask is only for your well being?"

At the younger man's drowsy affirmative, Adam reached down and gently removed the glasses, so he could monitor better by watching the eyelids.

"Just keep your eyes closed now," Adam directed. "I've taken off your glasses so you can be more comfortable. You don't need to see for a while anyway. I want you to take a deep breath and concentrate on your heartbeat. I'm going to count your pulse, and I want you to count with me." He pressed his fingertips against Peregrine's wrist and felt the pulse, strong and steady.

"Take a deep breath and concentrate on your heartbeat," he continued. "Feel the pulse and rhythm of your life gently taking you even deeper and more relaxed as we count down from ten—nine—eight—seven—"

He could see Peregrine's lips moving, continuing the counting, and he could feel him slipping deeper, hardly even whispering the final, "One."

"Good," Adam replied, half-breathing the word himself. "Very relaxed . . . very deeply relaxed. And now, as my hand touches your forehead, I want you to sink into an even deeper—sleep."

At the word "sleep," he shifted upward to touch his subject lightly between the eyes. A quiver of eye movement registered briefly beneath the lowered lids, but then Peregrine drew a long, even breath and exhaled on a shallow sigh, his head lolling forward slightly, nodding.

The response was precisely what Adam was looking for. Leaning down to take one of the slack hands, he lifted his subject's arm to shoulder level and stretched it out straight, running his free hand down it several times from shoulder to wrist.

"Now imagine that your arm is becoming as stiff and rigid as an iron bar," Adam said, testing at the lock of the elbow for emphasis. "It's becoming so rigid that neither you nor I can bend it, and you cannot lower it. Try if you wish, but you cannot bend your arm."

Peregrine did seem to try. Adam could see the consternation on the younger man's face, but the arm did not budge. Quickly, before Peregrine alarmed himself or did move the arm, Adam stroked along its length again.

"That's fine, Peregrine. Your arm is going back to normal now. It's no longer stiff. You can stop trying to move it, and relax. Let your arm return to your side. It's perfectly normal now, and you will have no aftereffects. Sleep now. Deep sleep."

Silently Adam considered what to do next. He *could* simply try to regress Peregrine to a past life, hoping to find some clue to his problems in the present; but there was a quicker way, and one far more certain. It was hardly a usual psychiatric procedure—most of his medical colleagues would be scandalized—but then, there did not seem to be much that was usual about Peregrine Lovat.

"Now, Peregrine," he finally said, "you're doing very well indeed. You've achieved a very useful level of deep trance, and in a moment I'm going to ask you to go deeper still.

"For now, however, I have further instructions for you. For reasons I'll eventually explain, you're to remember nothing of what is about to happen, when you wake up later on. But if and when I ask you to recall it at some later date, it will come back to you in full detail. I have my reasons for asking this, but it isn't appropriate for you to know them just now. So you will retain no conscious memory of anything you might hear or experience in the next little while, for your own well being. Nod if you understand and accept this."

When Peregrine nodded, Adam drew his own chair closer to the rosewood table, reducing the distance between himself and his subject.

"Thank you. I will not betray the trust you've given me. Now, I want you to go very, very deep—twice as deep as you are now. Go so deep that nothing you may hear with your ears will register on any conscious level until I touch your wrist like this and tell you to come back." He briefly pressed Peregrine's wrist between the first two fingers of both hands.

"Only if real physical danger should threaten, such as a fire, will you counter this instruction and come out of trance. Now lean your head back and sleep. Sleep deeply, hear nothing, and remember nothing. Deep asleep."

When he was satisfied that Peregrine was, indeed, oblivious to his surroundings, Adam moved behind the chair, reaching into his coat pocket to take out a heavy gold signet ring set with a handsome sapphire. Slipping it onto the third finger of his right hand, he touched the stone briefly to his lips, then laid the backs of his hands along the tops of the chair wings to either side of Peregrine's head, open palms turned upward. Taking as a centering point the candle still burning on the table before Peregrine, he drew a deep, centering breath and slowly exhaled, at the same time breathing the opening words of an almost silent invocation, couched in the Hellenic Greek and Latin of third-century Alexandria:

"*Ego prosphero epainon to photi . . .*"

He offered the rest in the silence of his mind, lifting his heart and his hands in selfless oblation.

I offer praise to the Light in the person of Ra: Pantocrator, Deus de deo. . . . of Horus: Logos, Veritas veritatis. . . . of Isis: Hagia Sophia, Regina Caeli. . . . and of Osiris: Nous, Lumen de lumine. . . . Thou, O Lord, art Light Eternal, Alpha and Omega, Source and Ending. Preserve us unto everlasting day. Amen.

Briefly he brought his hands together, palm to palm, touching the fingertips to his lips reverently, in salute to That which he served. Then, drawing a deep breath, he set his hands on the chair wings again, to either side of Peregrine Lovat's bowed head, closing his eyes to the physical flame before him.

"As Above, so Below," he murmured. "As Without, so Within. . . ."

The brightness of the flame's after-image shimmered behind his eyelids, establishing a glowing point of reference. He focused on that point to the exclusion of all other internal images. As it receded, twin threads of brilliant silver unreeled in parallel against the expanding ground of his internal vision, fine as spider-silk. One was the silver cord of his own life; the other, he knew, was Peregrine Lovat's. The threads began to spiral as he plunged after them, not falling but flying.

In the still, pristine silence of his own mind, Adam made himself a part of that cosmic spiral. It gathered momentum, whirling faster and faster through gauzy fields of lights like scattered stars. The star-points elongated into other silver threads, all wheeling and spinning. The myriad filaments all converged toward a single distant point, like the heart of a coalescing nebula.

Never relenting, Adam fixed on the unbroken spiral of Peregrine's silver cord and followed it into the shimmering midst of the dance. Anticipated, but never quite expected—as usual—came an icy thrill of disorientation that left him momentarily breathless and slightly dizzy. When the universe righted itself again, he found himself standing in spirit before two immense doors of immeasurable height, robed in white, his feet bared to tread on holy ground. It was familiar ground—the eye of the cyclone, the calm at the center of the storm, the hub of the wheel—but the awe was always new.

Adam had the Word of an Adeptus Major. As he spoke it, the doors opened with ponderous majesty. Beyond lay timeless vaults of silence: the unmapped and unmappable halls of the Akashic Records, the imperishable archives of all lives for all time. Into the vaults of the future, he might not go; but guided by the silver cord that was Peregrine's connection into the Sephiroth, Adam passed into the vaults of the past, threading a circular, inward-tending course along corridors iridescent as mother-of-pearl. At the heart of the labyrinth lay a convoluted chamber, whorled and curved like the walls of a nautilus shell. And at its center, on a canopied altar, lay a great book. As Adam approached the altar, the book opened of its own accord.

Hands pressed palm to palm in respect, Adam bent his head over the book, framing his intent in wordless query. As if conjured by some mystic wind, the pages began to turn and images to be presented for his gaze—the strands of the thread that linked the many lives of the one now known as Peregrine Lovat.

He skimmed over the early material, searching for the key—that initial moment of awakening, the point at which the soul first encountered its own spiritual likeness mirrored in the greater soul of the Divine Light. For Peregrine Lovat, that epiphany had taken place at Delphi in the age of Pericles. The oracular gift bestowed at that instant of enlightenment was what made itself known now, as the gift of seeing. Not to many was such vision given; and to endure the gift, its use—and disuse—must be mastered. Such would be the task of Peregrine Lovat—and of Adam, to teach him.

So. The soul that now was Adam Sinclair bore witness to the mandate: to make of a potential curse a gift, a tool for his own further spiritual advancement and in the service of the Light—for Peregrine had made that unreserved dedication to service before. It remained but to reawaken him in this life—a task which Adam, as a healer of souls as well as of minds, had performed before.

But as he closed the book, preparing to go, light darted from roof to floor to roof again in quicksilver flashes too swift for the eye to follow, lively as summer lightning. The signature was unique, portending the imminent arrival of one of those to whom Adam answered on the Inner Planes.

Stilling his curiosity, for he had not asked for audience, Adam acknowledged the authority of One who had long ago progressed beyond the need to manifest in physical form, bowing his head and opening his hands at his sides in a posture of receptivity. The other manifested in a beam of pure white light that pooled momentarily on the floor of the dais beneath Adam's feet and then surged up and around to envelope him in a shimmering pillar of opalescent fire.

Restive forces brood at the edge of the Abyss, Master of the Hunt, came the unexpected warning. *Do you seek our help?*

The question startled Adam, for he had perceived no threat requiring his attention. He had been functioning in his capacity as a physician of souls tonight, not as a cosmic keeper of the peace.

No, Master. I have come on an errand of mercy, as a healer of souls.

Explain.

It is written that all pilgrim souls must enter the world as children, and that so long as the personality is immature, the intellect untrained, even an Adept may be kept from achieving his full potential. There is such a one come to me—an Adept, I find, of rare gifts—who has been crippled, half-broken in childhood, before mind and intellect had sufficiently matured to protect the indwelling spirit. I believe his destiny may lie within the mandate of my mission, but the fledgling hawk must be re-pinioned, before he is ready to rejoin the Hunt. I would help him learn to fly again, that the potential of his gifts may be regained.

The desire is worthy, came the response, *but you should know that opposition threatens, and a risk is involved.*

What opposition, and what risk?

The Veil obscures details, even from us, but a threat exists. You will be a focus, though even the opposition will not know it for some time.

I am not afraid to face this threat, Adam replied. *But, is the fledgling to become an ally, then? How, if I can neutralize the self-doubt that cripples him, so that his potential is released? May he take his rightful place before the Light?*

He may. If the fledgling proves steadfast, you have authority to receive him; but this is by no means fore-ordained. Do you accept the commission to rehabilitate this soul?

The question bore of no answer but one.

My office as physician in the Outer was not lightly undertaken, Master. Nor do I take lightly my vows on the Inner, as a sentinel of the Light. I see the spark in Peregrine Lovat—a spark too bright to be wasted in aimless wandering, when it could be directed to Service. I accept the commission.

So be it, then, Master of the Hunt. But tread softly, lest he and you should plummet into the Abyss.

It shall be so, Adam replied, with a deep bow.

Between one heartbeat and the next, the enfolding

presence simply was not there any longer. The Chamber of Records wavered around Adam and then disappeared, and he arrowed back toward the material world. The slight disorientation of soul-flight ended with the faint psychic jolt that signalled the spirit's reunion with matter. When Adam opened his eyes, swaying a little on his feet, he was standing once again in the familiar library at Strathmourne, hands resting on the back of the chair where Peregrine Lovat slept. Details of what had just transpired grew more hazy by the second, but a clear plan of action lay before him now.

Almost perfunctorily, he brought his palms together in salute to the Light, the touch of his fingertips to his lips closing and sealing the rite he had just performed. Then he came around in front of Peregrine's chair, settling fully back into his role as physician and teacher.

The younger man was as Adam had left him, head tilted back in the angle of the wing-backed chair, eyes closed. After blowing out the candle, Adam bent to touch Peregrine's wrist lightly in pre-arranged signal.

"Peregrine, listen to my voice," he said firmly, no longer uncertain of his way. "Can you hear what I am saying?"

The younger man's lips parted slightly, in a scarcely breathed, "Yes."

"Excellent," Adam said. "In a moment, I am going to ask you to return to waking consciousness. Before I do that, however, there is something you should know, even though it may be some time before you arrive at a full understanding of what I am about to tell you."

He settled carefully back into his chair, watching the other man closely.

"It is a fact, though I cannot prove it to you in any rational, scientific manner, that an individual's personal history often goes back beyond the boundaries of his present lifetime. I have reason to believe that the vision which you have been at pains to suppress since childhood is actually a valuable legacy from earlier stages of your development. And there is no doubt that you can control it—provided that you acknowledge the gift for what it is."

Vague hope stirred the trembling eyelids as Peregrine's lips moved soundlessly to frame a single word.

"How?"

"First," Adam said, "you must learn to sort out the different kinds of information that, up until now, have been coming in uncontrolled. In a word, you must learn to focus your talent, and to turn it on and off when *you* decide—not just when it happens. The techniques for doing this already exist in your own subconscious mind, but they are buried. They can be retrieved through dreams. I should like to leave you with a posthypnotic suggestion to strengthen your ability to remember those dreams. Do you agree?"

Peregrine nodded his acceptance.

"Very good. Then, you will accept that suggestion, and know that you *will* dream the knowledge that will set you free. You will dream it as you are ready to receive it, and you will remember what you dream."

"Yes," Peregrine whispered, his head nodding slightly.

After a slight pause, Adam also nodded.

"Now, in a very few minutes, you are going to wake up of your own accord. At that time you will have no conscious memory of the conversation that has just passed between us. However, the ideas themselves will filter through to you in the course of the next few nights, couched in dreams that you will remember very clearly. I want you to record any dream that should happen to come to you—write it down, or make a sketch, if that suits you better—and then we'll talk about it at the first opportunity. Will you do that for me?"

"Yes," came the whispered response.

"Very good. Now in addition, because looking at people with your artist's eye seems to be what triggers your vision, I'm going to suggest that you not set out to draw anything for several days, other than in connection with your dreams. Give yourself a bit of a rest, while your unconscious begins sorting things out. Lady Laura's death has been a shock, I know, but it's also the catalyst that seems to have brought everything to a head. Then, after a few days, I *will* ask you to draw quite a lot. If you can link your ability to see with an intention to draw or paint the results, that can be the first step toward gaining conscious control.

"Now, in your own good time, awaken feeling refreshed and relaxed and remembering my instructions."

He sat back in his chair and waited, making a steeple of his forefingers and tapping them lightly against his chin. A few moments later, as instructed, Peregrine stirred and sighed, then opened his eyes. Seeing Adam in watchful attendance, he drew himself upright and stretched a little sheepishly.

"I was half-expecting to find myself sprawled out on the sofa in my studio," he said. "How long have I been under?"

"Hmmm, the best part of an hour," Adam said, glancing at an ornate carriage clock on a side table, "but never mind. For what it's worth, I think we've made a very good beginning. How do you feel?"

Peregrine summoned a crooked attempt at a smile. "Not too bad. More tired than anything else—which is a distinct improvement." He flexed stiff shoulders, then glanced down at his wristwatch. "Good Lord, if that really is the time, I ought to retrieve my own clothes and go home while there's still time for you to get a few hours' sleep."

"Sleep is a luxury I can do well enough without, now and then," Adam said. "Besides, you're not really in any fit state to drive. The room where you changed can be yours. I expect Humphrey can supply anything you need."

"Well, I don't want to impose," Peregrine began.

"It's no imposition—simply common sense. As a matter of fact," he continued casually, at the artist's look of continued uncertainty, "it would probably be no bad thing if you were to move in here at Strathmourne for a few days. It's clear from what you've told me tonight that you have a lot of soul-searching to do. And in my experience, it's generally a good idea not to embark on that kind of inner journey without the benefit of someone standing by, ready to step in, if you feel the need of a mediator."

Peregrine flushed slightly. "That's uncommonly generous of you, Sir Adam, and I'm very grateful—but as you know, I didn't exactly come prepared for an extended visit."

"That needn't worry you in the least," said Adam with a deep chuckle. "It's one of the many good reasons for having a faithful manservant. I'll give your keys to Humphrey, and he can drive down to Edinburgh first thing in the morning and collect whatever you need from your flat."

A relieved smile eased the younger man's weariness. "You think of everything, don't you? In that case, I'll take you up on your invitation—at least for a few days. I can't seem to summon up the energy to argue with you."

"You'll find it rarely does any good, when I set my mind on something," Adam said lightly, getting to his feet. "And we'll discuss the length of your stay when you're more rested. In the meantime, I highly recommend a late-night snack before we turn in. I heard Humphrey come in a little while ago. He makes exceptionally good hot ham sandwiches, and his recipe for cocoa, I'm convinced, has more than a touch of brandy in it."

CHAPTER FIVE

HALF an hour later, feeling relaxed and comfortably full-fed for what seemed like the first time in days, Peregrine bade his host a drowsy good-night and made his way upstairs to the room he had used earlier. Though he had been in no condition to appreciate it before, the room was spacious and elegant, like most of what he had seen, thus far, at Strathmourne. The walls were a cool shade of Wedgewood blue, with the woodwork and cornices picked out in white. The center section of the coffered ceiling had been painted to resemble the sky by night. When he had shed his slippers and robe and climbed wearily under the chintz-covered comforter, he lay back on the feather pillows and gazed up dreamily at the tempera fresco of clouds and constellations for several minutes before switching off the bedside lamp. It was the serene image of a starry firmament that he carried with him as he settled unresisting into deep, untroubled sleep.

Overwhelmed by sheer fatigue, he had no dreams that he could clearly remember. When at long last he roused again to full awareness, the room was suffused with a subdued submarine glow, and from far, far away, he could hear the sound of church bells. Shrugging himself out from under the bedclothes, he padded barefoot over to the curtained window-bay and parted the blue damask drapes. Sunlight poured into the room, and outside, the sky was clear and bright.

But the continued ringing of the church bells told him that it must be far later than he first had thought. Blinking, he retired to the bedside table and snatched up his wrist watch. To his amazement, it was nearly half past eleven. Could he really have slept so late?

He found his clothes of the night before, clean and neatly pressed, laid out over the back of a chair to the right of the bathroom door—Humphrey's work, no doubt. On the counter beside the bathroom sink were his shaving kit and other small, assorted personal effects, obviously retrieved, according to plan, from his flat in Edinburgh. A quick foray back into the bedroom to inspect chests of drawers and wardrobes revealed that a thorough selection of the rest of his clothing had been brought as well. Marveling at the efficiency of Adam Sinclair's soft-spoken manservant, Peregrine made shrift to bathe and dress as quickly as possible, wondering what he had gotten himself into.

There was no sign of Humphrey, when Peregrine made his way downstairs. Nor, at first, could he find evidence of anyone's presence. As he paused on the bottom-most step to get his bearings, however, he noticed that the door to the library was standing slightly ajar. Taking his courage firmly in hand, he went up to the threshold and rapped lightly on the paneled oak.

"Come in," said Adam Sinclair's deep voice from inside.

Peregrine pushed the door open and stepped timorously into the room. Adam was sitting at his desk with his back to the window, the sleeves of an immaculate white shirt aglow in the morning sun against a dark waistcoat and cravat. The jacket of the morning suit was hanging over the back of another chair. Peregrine was surprised to see his host so formally attired until he remembered, with a pang, that Adam had promised to pay a sympathy call on the Kintoul family that morning, and apparently had done so.

"You've already been up to Kintoul House, haven't you?" Peregrine said, flinching from the direct gaze as Adam looked up. "I—I meant to go with you. You shouldn't have let me sleep."

Smiling, Adam set aside a newspaper cutting he had been reading, laying it on a stack of similar items in an open manila file folder.

"I felt that you needed the sleep more than the family

needed yet another caller this morning," he said easily. "There will be ample time for a more meaningful visit in the week to come. Besides," he added, not unkindly, "I think you may be sure that Lady Laura would not have begrudged you the benefit of a good night's sleep."

Peregrine opened his mouth as if to protest, then shut it again when he realized that Adam had spoken no more than the truth. While he was still searching for a suitably chastened rejoinder, Adam said, "Humphrey's set up a table for brunch in the room across the hall from this one. If you're sufficiently wide awake to feel peckish, I'll ring down to let him know we're ready for something to eat."

When Peregrine made no demur, Adam reached across the bay to tug at an embroidered bellpull, then returned his attention to tidying up the stack of cuttings in his file. The motion drew Peregrine's gaze like a magnet, and the words, "Antique Sword," jumped out at him from the headline on the top cutting, just as Adam closed the folder.

"You'll find I have a variety of interests," Adam said casually, taking no apparent note of the slightly guilty look of surprise on Peregrine's face as the artist quickly looked up. "Every once in a while, I get asked to assist the police with cases that have aspects of the—shall we say, *unusual* about them. For quite some time now, I've made a habit of saving anything in the papers that happens to catch my eye. More than once, this eccentricity has given me advance warning that my services may be called for."

Peregrine blinked and nodded, but he had the sudden, inexplicable feeling that something had just gone totally over his head. Adam's manner seemed as relaxed as ever, but Peregrine abruptly was certain of one thing: his host's apparently simple and open explanation was camouflage for something far from simple. Whatever the nature of the case involving this mysterious sword, Sir Adam Sinclair had some personal stake in the affair.

"I'm sorry, Sir Adam," Peregrine said stiffly. "I didn't mean to pry."

Adam cocked his head at Peregrine in some amusement. "*Sir* Adam?" he said archly. "If we're going to work together, Peregrine, I think you *might* be entitled to drop the

Sir, at least in private. And you're not prying. If you'd not been meant to see this, do you think I would have been reading it when I knew you might come in at any time? Besides, it's all been in the newspapers at one time or other. Have a look, if you're interested."

He held out the file folder, still smiling, but Peregrine shook his head, aware of feeling a little silly to have made such a fuss, yet quite certain that Adam was not laughing *at* him.

"That isn't necessary," he murmured. "I—just didn't want you to think I'd take advantage of your kindness. And frankly, even if I did read that," he jutted his chin toward the folder with a sheepish grin, "I doubt I'd be any the wiser."

"Perhaps not," Adam agreed with a chuckle. He opened a drawer on the right-hand side of the desk and deposited the folder inside before reaching for his jacket. "Shall we go? I seem to recall that Humphrey mentioned something about fresh salmon. . . ."

Later, after they had disposed of the salmon, not to mention eggs Benedict and fresh asparagus, Adam took Peregrine on a long guided tour of the house. The present Strathmourne House was not of any great antiquity, having been rebuilt on the site of an earlier house ravaged by fire in the mid-nineteenth century—which, in turn, had been built on an old monastic site. In its present form, it was a Victorian rendering of Scottish vernacular architecture, designed and built, at the instigation of Adam's grandfather, by a talented local architect named Forbes. Pundits south of the Solway and River Tweed tended to label Forbes' distinctive style as neo-Gothic; Adam, when feeling particularly irreverent, was reminded of a favorite childhood picture book of *Wind in the Willows*, with its illustrations of Toad Hall.

"Toad Hall" notwithstanding, Forbes had gained a sufficient reputation to eventually be awarded a knighthood, in recognition of the excellence of his architectural achievements; and it was widely accepted that Strathmourne exemplified some of his best technical work. Peregrine's artistic sensibilities were impressed, not only by the layout of the rooms and galleries, but by the close attention Forbes had paid to small details of embellishment. The vine-leaf friezes adorning the walls throughout the rooms on the ground floor were reminiscent of the best designs of the High Gothic period. Similarly, the stained glass window in the private chapel depicted the dream of Jacob with a medieval richness of jewel-like color.

Peregrine was particularly struck by a heraldic crest carved and painted on the central boss of the ceiling in the great hall—a phoenix taking flight out of a nest of fire, within a traditional Scottish buckle and strap.

"That's a striking crest," he said, shading his eyes with both hands to peer up at it. "Is it a Sinclair device?"

"Aye, one of several." Adam smiled. "According to the Alexandrian Physiologus, the phoenix betokens life eternal. When it reaches extreme old age, it builds itself a pyre of Arabian spices and is consumed, to rise up again out of the flames as a new creature, reborn to ongoing life."

"Reincarnation," Peregrine murmured. "Do you think such a thing is possible?"

Adam flashed him a penetrating look from under raised brows. "Is it possible that we are born again and again in the course of fulfilling our individual spiritual destinies? Don't ask me. Ask yourself."

Glancing startledly at the chiseled face of his companion, Peregrine found himself without a word to say.

They left the great hall and moved upstairs. Peregrine's discomfiture gradually subsided as they wandered in and out of the apartments in the north wing. The pair of adjoining rooms at the end of the corridor boasted an intriguing collection of Edwardian toys.

"This was the nursery, when my father and his brother were boys," Adam said, watching indulgently as Peregrine bent to inspect a child-sized mechanical pony and cart. "My sister tells me that when she was a child, she used to regard it as a special treat to be allowed to come and play up here. That was one of her favorites."

The mechanical pony had a removable leather harness, and a mane and tail of real horsehair. Peregrine fingered the brass rail behind the seat on the cart, cocking his head to admire the designs stenciled on the side.

"I didn't know you had a sister," he said. Somehow, in spite of all his social grace and obvious charm, Adam Sinclair seemed strangely solitary—as though somehow set apart even from his friends.

"Theodora's quite a bit older than I am," Adam replied. "Actually, she's my half-sister—not that it matters. Her mother was my father's first wife. There's quite a good portrait of her in the room next to yours. Come along and I'll show it to you."

The portrait was full-length, and showed a slender, dark-haired girl with laughing eyes, hugging a shawl of tartan silk over an elegant white ballgown.

"That was painted shortly before Theo's twenty-first birthday," Adam said. "The following year she married Sir Thomas MacAllan. He was in the diplomatic service. They've spent most of their married life in the Far East, though they're home now. All three of the children were born abroad. I'd love to see what you'd do for a family portrait of all of them."

"Where is home now?" Peregrine asked.

"Over in Argyllshire, not far from Inveraray," Adam replied. "It's a pretty place, if a trifle tame after the Orient. But Theo, I think, was more than ready to settle down in one spot, after so many years spent in foreign climes. Thomas retired a few years ago. Theo tells me he rather enjoys being his own man for a change."

The rest of the tour was taken up with travel anecdotes, ending up in the library once more. While they were waiting for Humphrey to bring up the tea tray, and Adam was making a phone call, Peregrine prowled idly up and down the array of bookcases that lined the walls adjoining the desk. A handsome volume bound in Moroccan leather caught his eye.

On an impulse, he drew it off the shelf and turned it over in his hands, appreciating the workmanship of the fine binding. Riffling through the pages, he discovered that it was a first edition of *Psychologie und Alchemie* by Carl Jung, dated 1944. On the flyleaf, a handwritten note read:

"To Philippa Sinclair," followed by an inscription in German. The signature was that of Jung himself.

A shadow fell across Peregrine's right shoulder. "My mother was a student of Jung's," Adam said from behind him. "She's also a psychiatrist. He sent her that book shortly after she and my father were married."

Peregrine turned to glance at his host, the book still open in his hands. "Is she Swiss, then?"

"No, she's an American," Adam said, "but she was in Switzerland, studying with Jung, when the Second World War broke out. When the United States entered the war in 1942, she joined the U.S. Army Medical Corps. She and my father met up in a field hospital behind the lines—and the rest, as they say, is history."

Peregrine closed the book and carefully returned it to its place on the shelf. "I gather she's still alive?"

"Oh, quite," Adam returned with a laugh. "At the moment she's in America, supervising the running of her clinic in New Hampshire. That was a bone of contention while my father was alive, since he thought she should be here all the time, attending to her duties as lady of the manor. Since his death, however, that's where she spends most of her time. She maintains that the work keeps her young."

He might have said more, but at that moment Humphrey's discreet knock heralded the arrival of tea and scones. As Peregrine followed Adam back to the fireside, he reflected that a capacity for remarkable achievements seemed to run in the Sinclair family.

They passed the evening quietly at Strathmourne. A simple but excellent dinner was followed by brandy in the now-familiar environs of the library.

"I suggest we make an early evening of it," Adam said. "I think you'll agree that last night was—ah—something less than restful, and tomorrow, after I make my rounds down at Jordanburn, I've got to drive up to Gleneagles for the afternoon. It's the quarterly meeting of the Royal Scottish Preservation Trust, and I'm speaking. Perhaps you'd like to come along."

"Well, I—"

"It's no intrusion, if that's what you're thinking," Adam said with a smile. "I think you'd enjoy it—and it would give me the chance to present you to some good friends of mine who are members of the Trust—friends who might be the source of future commissions," he added, raising his glass in smiling salute, "if the prospect of my company for the day and a bunch of probably boring lectures aren't sufficient enticements."

Warmed through by the brandy and the glow of their growing camaraderie, Peregrine found himself agreeing. Only much later, after he had retired to his room for the night and was drifting off to sleep, did it occur to him that this was the first social engagement in months that he had allowed himself to accept. Nor had he thought even once about the despair that had driven him here to Strathmourne not twenty-four hours before.

The next day, Monday, dawned fair and fine. After an early breakfast, Adam left Peregrine on his own for a few hours while he zipped into Edinburgh to see patients, returning just after eleven to pick him up.

"Traffic was lighter than I expected," Adam said, as he leaned across to open the passenger door of the Jaguar for Peregrine. "We may even have time for a proper lunch. I told some friends we'd try to join them, if we got there before one."

They arrived at the Gleneagles Hotel with plenty of time to spare. Adam's friends turned out to be the Duke of Glendearn, who was president and principal patron of the Trust, and several other titled notables, several of whom were acquainted with Peregrine's work. The warmth of their reception did much to dispel Peregrine's initial shyness, and by the time lunch was finished, he was well on the way to finding himself at home.

Peregrine glanced at the program leaflet Adam handed him as they went into the lecture room. The morning's program, he found, had included the society's business meeting and several addresses on various aspects of Scottish history. The events scheduled for the afternoon included several more speeches and a series of panel discussions—

none of which turned out to be at all boring, so far as Peregrine was concerned.

Adam's own contribution, last on the agenda, was a lecture on the subject he termed "Intuitive Archaeology." Interestingly enough, to Peregrine's way of thinking, no one seemed inclined to leave early. In fact, people who had been wandering in and out during the afternoon made a point to come back in as the duke was introducing Adam. Evidently Sir Adam Sinclair was one of their more popular speakers.

"This is intended to be an exercise in creative speculation," Adam warned his listeners, with a smile that compelled their instant attention. "What I am proposing is that, for the next fifty minutes, we waive all consideration of empirical methodology, in order to examine the intuition as a prime tool for archaeological investigation."

"Intuition," he repeated, looking around the room. "It's something that many people think women have more of than men do." That comment brought a chuckle. "People working in the so-called 'hard sciences' tend to mistrust it, because it can't be 'proven' by scientific logic. People working in the 'soft' sciences—and psychiatry is one of them—know that intuition can be a very valuable tool, especially when confirmed by results. Perhaps, then, the line between logic and intuition is not as hard and fast as the hard scientists would have us believe."

As Adam turned to the next page in his notes, Peregrine settled down contentedly to take it all in. This was turning out to be every bit as interesting as he had hoped it might be.

"Actually, many hard scientists do use intuition," Adam went on, "though most of them would squirm, if forced to admit it. After all, it isn't 'logical.' However, it is no secret that some researchers are infinitely more adept than others at arriving at correct hypotheses on the basis of slender or confusing physical evidence. Putting this into an historical perspective, I would like to suggest that intuition may, in fact, play a very large role in reconstructing history on the basis of artifacts. . . ."

There followed a series of factual anecdotes involving a number of eminent archaeologists and their discoveries. As

Peregrine listened, it began to dawn on him that the faculty Adam was describing was, by any other name, a kind of extrasensory perception. He glanced around him, wondering if any of the other members of the audience had caught the masked drift of the discourse. Before he could form any distinct impressions, the presentation took an even more radical turn.

"If we accept that intuition does, in fact, play a vital expository role in archaeological investigation," Adam said coolly, "we may well find ourselves obliged to modify our definition of physical reality. To that end, I am going to suspend, for a moment, all consideration of Newtonian physics in order to broaden the concept of nature to include that elusive field in which the intuition operates."

This announcement generated an interested stir amongst those present. Without pausing to refer to his notes, Adam continued, leaning forward conspiratorially on the podium.

"All physical reality is traditionally quantifiable in terms of three dimensions: height, width, and depth. But such an assessment fails to take account of the fact that objects—and people, for that matter—also exist in the dimension of time. This temporal factor is something that, for lack of a better term, I should like to call Resonance."

Peregrine sat forward in his chair. He felt suddenly as if he were on the brink of hearing something of vital personal importance.

"To draw an analogy," Adam went on calmly, "resonance can be interpreted as a kind of existential echo: a subtle shadow of how things used to be. As a theoretical psychologist, I would submit that the ability to perceive resonance is a rare function of the human psyche. In antique times, that faculty was the trademark of priests, seers, and mystics. In these latter days, it is still a factor among those whose livelihood depends on their developing that faculty of vision: archaeologists, psychiatrists, artists. . . ."

Artists? Startled, Peregrine was suddenly swamped by a host of half-realized implications. Was this why Adam had wanted him to come along? He was still struggling to untangle his own thoughts when he was roused from his reverie by an outburst of hand-clapping. He looked up to see Adam descending from the podium into a crowd of would-be questioners.

It was some time before Adam was free again to join him. By then Peregrine was sufficiently master of his own whirling speculations to follow along gracefully while friends and acquaintances offered their congratulations and goodbyes. The shadows were lengthening by the time they pulled out of the car park. Peregrine held his tongue until they were back on the main road toward Strathmourne, then abruptly voiced the question that he had been at pains to suppress for more than an hour.

"This business of resonance that you spoke of—is that another way of saying that objects can somehow generate images from their temporal past?"

Wry amusement plucked at the corner of Adam's long mouth. "You were listening closely, weren't you? Yes, that's the basic idea. The same principle applies to people as well. Those resonances are sometimes described, in psychic circles, as 'auras.' And they can resonate forward in time, as well as backwards."

"Oh," said Peregrine. For a moment he stared hard at the road ahead. Then in a rush he said, "This problem of mine—this problem with seeing things that other people can't see—could it be somehow related to this notion of resonance?"

"It's at least a theory," said Adam. "But I can't give you any hard answers. I suggest you sleep on it."

That proved to be his last word on the subject. Balked in several further attempts to draw out his host in greater detail, Peregrine at last gave up and allowed the conversation to drift into other channels, equally fascinating, but of far less personal import, so far as Peregrine could tell. Later that night, none the wiser, he went to bed with no expectation of falling asleep readily, let alone dreaming.

But as he lay in bed, staring up at the starry patterns on the ceiling, his thoughts drifted so subtly from conscious into subconscious awareness that he was not aware of having fallen asleep until the onset of the Dream.

Chapter Six

THE dream began as though he were waking up from a light doze. He was still in bed in the Blue Room at Strathmourne, but the door was standing half-open, emitting a wedge of unearthly light. Peregrine rose from the bed and crossed to the doorway. When he looked beyond the confines of the room, he realized that he was standing on the threshold of some other reality.

He should have been facing another door, in a corridor papered in a willow-herb pattern designed by William Morris. Instead, he was confronting a square chamber, empty and bare, whose blank walls had the silvery sheen of mirrors. The wall to his right was broken by a high archway, affording him a view of a succession of other rooms beyond. The light that suffused all the rooms seemed to be emanating from somewhere off in the distance, in that direction.

Peregrine was seized by a sudden desire to locate the source of the light. His dream-self stepped out into the middle of the square chamber, and his own reflection sprang out at him from three sides. He fetched up short, for the reflection did not match up with his appearance.

His dream-persona was wearing the modern clothes he had worn when he had fled to Adam Sinclair in search of counsel. But the self that gazed back at him out of the mirror was wearing only sandals and a striped woollen chlamys thrown over the left shoulder, in a style that recalled amphorae paintings from ancient Greece. Apart from the differences in clothing and hairstyle, however, the reflection conformed with Peregrine's every look and gesture. It occurred to him, within the framework of the dream, that what he was seeing might be a true, if deeply hidden, part of himself.

He moved hastily through the arch into the adjoining room. This chamber was mirrored too, and in this one, his reflection wore the short tunic and leather body armor of a Roman centurion. In the room after, he was greeted by a long-haired image of himself in a rich Byzantine dalmatic of embroidered silk. More images followed, detailed like a fantastic display in a museum of historical costume. But the face was always his own.

The strange gallery of mirrors brought him at last to the foot of a tall door. Ornately carved as the entry port of a church, it yielded smoothly when Peregrine gave a tentative tug at the latch. He felt no sense of danger, so he stepped across the threshold and paused to look around.

The chamber in which he found himself was vaulted like a Greek Orthodox chapel, its curving dome overlaid with mosaic work in marble and gold. Light spilled down from a glowing filigree lamp suspended on golden chains from the ceiling. Directly below the lamp, on an upraised dais of white marble, a curiously fashioned pedestal supported a shimmering globe the size of a royal orb.

Aware that he was still dreaming, Peregrine gazed at the orb in wonder. It had a nacreous sheen, like a great pearl. The silken beauty of it drew him like a magnet. Without pausing to consider his actions, he strode across the floor and mounted the dais, hands reverently outstretched to touch it.

The instant of contact brought a radiant flash, like a surge of heat lightning. Reeling, Peregrine flung up his arms to shield his dazzled eyes.

He took his hands away to find the chapel gone, himself suspended in an iridescent sea. Fear of falling gripped him, and he kicked out frantically in an attempt to find the floor. His violent and instinctive movement sent a wave of color surging through the opalescent matrix surrounding him. The wave folded back on itself, fragmenting in a kaleidoscopic explosion of fractured light.

Straightaway Peregrine was swallowed up in a polychrome tempest. He thrashed about in the eddying tides like a swimmer in danger of drowning, becoming more disoriented by the second. Panicking, he choked out a gasping cry for help.

A chorus of voices answered him, calling out reassurance and encouragement. They spoke in different languages, but he understood all of them. In that Pentecostal moment, he realized that they were all echoes of his own voice, all telling him the same thing: *Be still. Be still, and know that thou art lord of all.*

He stopped struggling. At once the wild fluctuations of light became less erratic. Holding himself motionless, he willed the storm to subside. By degrees, the warring colors resolved into a unified field of light, like a pearly lake—and he could walk upon it! Awed and astonished, he set off in perfect silence. . . .

A soft blue light grew up all around him, gradually overwhelming every other color. In trying to blink back focus, he discovered that his eyes were closed. When he opened them a moment later, he found himself gazing up at a painted sky full of painted stars. He was back in his room at Strathmourne.

He sat up in bed, puzzled and abstracted, as he mentally reviewed the very vivid dream he had just experienced. At the same time, a mild compulsion laid hold of him to commit the details to paper. He found pen and notebook on the table beside his bed, and he switched on the bedside lamp and began to scribble down an account of the dream's scenes and events.

By the time he had finished, it was past eight o'clock. Mindful that his host was an early riser, Peregrine rushed through his ablutions and, with his notebook tucked under his arm, hurried downstairs to the morning room where Adam habitually ate breakfast. He arrived rather breathlessly to find Adam in the act of pouring himself a steaming cup of tea, a newspaper at his elbow. The wide bow window beyond the table showed the day starting out to be a misty one.

"Good morning," Peregrine said, tendering the older

man a sheepish grin. "I hope I haven't disgraced myself by being late again for breakfast."

"Not at all," Adam laughed, putting aside his paper. "I've only just sat down myself. Join me, by all means." A discerning look produced a raised eyebrow. "Is anything amiss?"

"Not amiss, no." Peregrine slid eagerly into the chair across from Adam. "I had the most extraordinary dream, just before I woke up. Could we talk about it?"

"Certainly," Adam replied. "Did you make notes?"

Nodding, Peregrine produced his notebook and proffered it across the table. "It's all here—everything I could remember. You don't actually have to read it right now," he added, somewhat self-consciously. "You can have your breakfast first."

Adam took the notebook and hefted it in his hand, smiling.

"I think I'll do both at once," he said lightly. "I've found that such material makes far more interesting breakfast reading than the newspaper. In the meantime, by all means have something to eat. . . ."

Peregrine went through the motions of taking toast and tea while Adam read and then re-read the closely penned lines. The account ran to several pages. When at last he raised his eyes from the notebook, Peregrine abruptly pushed aside his plate, all further appetite at least temporarily fled.

"Well?" he said, a little apprehensively. "What do you make of it?"

"The textbook response from me," said Adam, "is, what do you make of it yourself?"

Peregrine grimaced. "I was afraid you'd say that." After a moment's thought, he said with some hesitation, "Based on what you said yesterday in your lecture, I suppose it's all about history—history, and the resonance that history generates. What I don't understand is, why the self-portrait gallery?"

He glanced obliquely at Adam as though inviting an explanation. Adam gave him a penetrating look from under his eyebrows and carefully set the notebook on the table between them.

"I don't think you really need my help in extracting meaning from this experience. Do you?"

Peregrine bit his lip, clearly groping for words. "No. No, I suppose I don't. But—" He shook his head impatiently, then said in a rush, "Adam, I was brought up to be a good Presbyterian. It isn't easy for me to reconcile notions of reincarnation with Christianity."

"And yet, Christianity itself embraces a multitude of different interpretations of the same basic story," Adam responded. "Otherwise, we shouldn't have all the different denominations of Christians, who all think *their* way of approaching God is best."

"Then, you think the two are compatible?" Peregrine asked doubtfully.

Adam shrugged. "That's a matter of conscience, for *you* to decide. My own feeling—and I say this as a committed Christian, and having dined with my bishop only last week—is that Christianity quite possibly embraces far greater and more universal truths than are generally accepted and taught in its various churches."

This rather pointed observation reduced Peregrine to wide-eyed silence. After a long moment, he said slowly, "This is crazy. You're a psychiatrist, yet you're telling me that you believe my delusion is no delusion at all, but the truth."

"I didn't say that," Adam replied. "But if it makes you any more comfortable, accept that the *illusion* of past resonances—past lives, if you will—is a useful metaphor for utilizing some seventh sense for which we have no adequate explanation at present. In a word, if it works, use it."

Goggle-eyed, Peregrine simply stared at him for a moment, taking it all in. Then he nodded slowly.

"I think I understand what you're saying," he murmured. "Somehow, it even makes sense—of a sort."

"*Intuitive* sense?" Adam asked, smiling.

"Maybe. But you're right about one thing: whether it's *real* real or only *seems* real, it's better than anything *I've* been able to come up with to explain what's happening to me." He fingered the notebook on the table between them, then looked up again.

"So let's assume that I *have* had several other lives before this one, just for the sake of argument. If the same is true of you," he continued in the same reflective tone, "then what I was seeing the other night, when I tried to draw you, was—resonances of *your* past?" He looked to Adam for confirmation.

"Somewhat over-simplified," Adam agreed, with a wry half-smile, "but essentially correct, as far as it goes."

Peregrine assimilated this. After a pause he asked, "Do you ever find yourself seeing shadows of *my* past lives?"

"Not spontaneously, if that's what you mean."

"Why not?"

"For one thing," Adam said, "I suspect that it's because I've developed the ability to limit my temporal perspective as well as expand it. For another, that isn't where my major talents lie."

Before Peregrine could demand a fuller explanation, Adam squared his shoulders briskly and set his cup and saucer aside.

"Are you a horseman, by any chance?"

The sudden shift of subject took Peregrine totally by surprise.

"I beg your pardon?"

"Do you ride?"

Blinking, Peregrine said, "I used to be quite keen when I was at school. Why?"

"As I think I may have mentioned," Adam said, "I've had a crew doing some badly needed clearance work up at Templemor Tower, during the past week. There's a chap coming by this afternoon—an archaeologist from Ancient Monuments. Before I give him the go-ahead to carry out a survey of the ruins, I'd like to take a good look at what's been done so far. I was planning to trek out there on horseback later this morning, and it occurred to me that you might like to come along, do some sketching. I think we can kit you out in some of my nephew's breeches and boots—he's about your size—if you think you'd be interested."

Peregrine was studying Adam with amazement tinged with suspicion. "Is this going to be another experiment?" he asked.

Adam threw back his head with a laugh. "So much for the subtle approach. Yes, it's going to be another experiment. I assume you've got a pocket sketchbook? Good, then bring it along. I'll tell you what I have in mind, once we're on our way."

John, the ex-Household Cavalry trooper who looked after Adam's horses, had Adam's favorite grey gelding already saddled by the time they found riding gear for Peregrine and got down to the stable, and was just leading out the blood bay mare that was to be Peregrine's mount. The mare nickered as she caught sight of Adam, and the grey pricked his ears and pivoted on the forehand to look too. Behind them in the stable aisle, two more heads poked out above stable doors with equine interest.

Their keeper grinned and lifted a hand in affable greeting, almost a salute, as he cross-tied the mare and began saddling.

"Morning, sir. He's all ready to go, and I'll have Poppy ready in a minute."

"Good morning, John. Thank you," Adam said. As he ran a gloved hand over the grey's satiny neck and down the near front leg, the animal whuffled softly and presented its face to be scratched.

"And good morning to you, too, Khalid," he murmured, with indulgent compliance. "Ah, you like that, don't you? Are you and Poppy ready for a little outing?"

"Oh, he'll give you a good ride today, sir," John said with a chuckle, finishing with the mare's girth and moving on to bridle her. "Not that there's a mean bone in either of them," he added, for Peregrine's benefit. "You shouldn't have any trouble, Mr. Lovat, if you've ridden much at all."

"I used to hunt, when I was still at school," Peregrine offered.

"Well, then, you'll do fine with this lady. And she'll keep pace with that great grey lump there," he said, giving

Khalid an affectionate smack on the rump as he led the mare past. "She should give you a very good ride."

After John had given him a leg up and helped him adjust his stirrups, Peregrine waited for Adam to mount and then fell in behind him as they walked the horses out of the stable yard. The mare moved out obediently in response to his legs, clearly ready to be off, if called upon to do so, but making no demands—a perfect lady, as John had maintained.

They continued walking for the first ten minutes, to let the horses warm up—and let Peregrine reaccustom himself to being in the saddle. Then, after a short trot along a drainage ditch that separated two fields, they set off across a rolling pasture at a canter. In deference to Peregrine's long hiatus from riding, Adam took them through gates rather than jumping fences and hedges, reining back to a walk as they approached the wooded slope of Templemor Hill.

It was Adam's intention to have Peregrine look at the castle ruins with an eye to locking in on some of its resonances from the past. He had set the stage in his previous day's lecture, and it had occurred to him that the artist might find it less threatening to look at a structure rather than at a person, as he began allowing his talent of seeing to reassert itself. Ahead, through the ragged lattice of wind-stripped branches, the jagged ramparts of Templemor gleamed gold-grey in the morning mist—a classic Z-plan fortalice with two headless stair turrets jutting from opposite corners of a roofless keep.

Adam stood and stretched a little in his stirrups as they approached, wondering what the man riding at his side would see when asked to look beyond the mere physical of the ruin. He was not seeking or expecting anything for himself, content merely to be present as facilitator and guide for Peregrine, as the younger man learned to harness his gifts.

Guard relaxed, then, he was startled when suddenly, in the space of an eye-blink, a fragment of his own past intruded on the present. As if by magic, a shaft of sunlight lanced through the bare branches above them and struck the castle walls, fanning in an eye-dazzling corona of golden sunfire. The alchemy of light suspended time and reason, and revealed, standing before the ruined doorway of Templemor, a tall, bearded man wearing the red, eight-pointed cross of the Knights Templar on the shoulder of his white mantle, gauntleted hands resting on the hilt of a great, two-handed broadsword planted in the earth before him.

Between one startled heartbeat and the next, the vision vanished. Adam blinked several times, hoping to recapture it, but ghosts of even older memories briefly surfaced instead, all unbidden—sitting at a table littered with scrolls in an ancient library. . . . standing at the prow of a papyrus funeral boat drifting along the west bank of the River Nile. . . .

Then Khalid stumbled on a root, and the present moment reasserted itself, and he was once more Sir Adam Sinclair of Templemor, riding toward a derelict castle in the misty brightness of a Scottish morning.

Shaken more than he hoped he showed, Adam glanced aside at the young man riding at his knee, but Peregrine seemed not to have noticed, his gaze set attentively ahead on the sun-dappled ruins. Relieved—for frightening Peregrine was the last thing he wanted to do—Adam set himself to deciphering what the vision meant.

It was not a warning of danger, as such—though the image of the armed knight might symbolize a need to be watchful, and perhaps presaged a future necessity to dispense justice on some level. In more general terms, however, such an unsolicited and unregulated intrusion of his past into his present usually signalled change—a subtle shift in the balance of powers that governed the wheeling of the universe, such as sometimes required his intervention. The warning he had received on the Inner Planes had hinted as much.

But the focus of any impending threat remained unclear; and until he understood the nature of the coming shift in balance, he could only watch and wait, until he had more information. In the meantime, his immediate concern must be for Peregrine—who, he was beginning to suspect, was being thrust into his life at this particular point in time for more reason than mere happenstance.

He glanced again at Peregrine, briefly wondering whether he was doing the right thing, where Peregrine himself was concerned. Thus far, the young artist's far-seeing had encroached only slightly upon Adam, other than in his professional capacity. The artist had come to Adam as patient to physician, wanting only to be "cured"; but Adam, quickly discerning the root of Peregrine's "problem," had more or less taken it upon himself to convert that problem to an asset—not to shut off Peregrine's special sort of seeing, but to channel it.

That was not what Peregrine had asked for. Nor was it too late to pull back and simply "cure" him, as he had requested—though a point of no return could not be too far away, if Peregrine learned as quickly as Adam was beginning to suspect he might. Right now, today, Adam still might put Peregrine and his wayward talent at arm's length, simply by retreating to the role of *only* a psychiatrist, agreeing that the far-seeing was a mental aberration, helping him learn to blot it out, as he first had wanted. And any questioning of Adam's professionalism, if Peregrine later spoke about his methods to anyone else, might be dismissed as the delusions Peregrine himself had posited from the beginning.

Reverting to mere psychiatry was not really an option in Peregrine's case, of course—though Adam always made himself examine all the likely permutations, before taking that plunge of deeper commitment on the Inner Planes. For good reason, he still might back off; but the potential reward was worth a great deal of risk: another Adept restored, ready to take his place in the Work of the Light—and possibly, a valuable ally for Adam himself. Most compelling of all was the fact that Adam Sinclair, as medical practitioner, spiritual healer, and warrior of the Light, was constitutionally incapable of turning away someone in need, whom he had the ability to help.

So. Now to see what Templemor had to offer Mr. Peregrine Lovat. Adam already had intimations that energies were stirring, or he would not have glimpsed visions of his own, merely approaching the ancient site. Casting his gaze ahead, and putting his own concerns out of mind,

Adam led the way into the narrow clearing surrounding the base of the old tower house, casually pointing out a knee-high series of foundations, just outside the castle wall, and several piles of cut stone off to their left.

"I see the lads *have* been busy," he said, reining in and dismounting. "Most of those foundations are from the old outbuildings. The piles of stone are debris they've hauled out from inside, where walls fell in and roofs collapsed. We'll leave the horses here to graze while we explore."

He forgot to worry about Peregrine while they saw to the horses, caught up in the changes just since his last visit, but a week before. The ivy was gone, for a start, and the trees formerly growing atop the first floor vaulting had been ruthlessly rooted out, along with the debris in which they had been growing. Pleased, Adam led the way toward the doorway of the castle itself.

"That was probably a family crest, there above the door," Adam said, pointing out a blurred irregularity in the stone. "I've always assumed it was the same as the phoenix you saw in the great hall, up at the house, but it could be a different Sinclair crest, or something else altogether. Unfortunately, it's so far gone that we may never know for certain."

There was no response from Peregrine. Adam glanced back over his shoulder. The artist was standing at the bottom of the steps leading up to the entry-way, his sketchbook clutched tightly in front of his chest, his expression all at once pained and rigid.

"Peregrine? What's the matter?" Adam asked sharply.

The young artist started slightly at the sound of his name, eyes screwed to mere slits behind his glasses, and looked hastily at the ground.

"I don't think I ought to have come here," he said softly.

He swayed on his feet and staggered backwards. Swiftly Adam sprang to his side and guided him to a seat on a block of stone at the edge of the clearing.

"Whyever not?" he demanded.

"It's this cursed, bloody ghost-sight of mine!" Peregrine said between gritted teeth. "If I could only blot it out—"

"No, that's the last thing you want to do," Adam

interposed with soft urgency. "Don't fight it. Don't even try to control it for now. Just relax and let the experience run its course."

"But—"

"I said relax," Adam said. His voice this time carried a sharp note of command as he laid a hand across Peregrine's furrowed forehead, steadying his head with the other hand behind. "Relax, Peregrine," he repeated, more quietly. "I want you to go back into trance for me, like you did the other night. Fighting isn't the answer. Relax. Remember your dream. Remember. . . ."

Under Adam's hands and persuasion, some of the tension eased out of the younger man's taut form. His eyes remained closed, and when he finally settled down enough to take a deep breath and let it out softly, Adam took his hands away and moved back a step.

"That's better," he said, watching his subject closely. "Just keep your eyes closed and listen to me. Don't you see? This is precisely why I brought you here today—to give you a chance to test out your various levels of vision. I thought a structure would be easier than people. Before we can explore ways of selectively controlling what you see, we need to find out what happens when you make no attempt to control it at all."

Peregrine shook his head dreamily. "I know what you're saying, but it's so—confusing. I can shut out some of the confusion, if I look straight at whatever it is, but the images in my peripheral vision—" He paused to swallow noisily. "Even with my eyes closed, I still see more than I should. It's like—like trying to see through a bunch of transparencies all stacked on top of each other."

"A good analogy," Adam agreed, "but if you'll only stop struggling, the storm of images may subside of its own accord. What did your other selves say in the dream?"

"Be still," murmured Peregrine. "Be still, and know that thou art lord of—Good God!" His eyes popped open. "Do you think I'm *causing* the turbulence?"

"There's only one way to find out," Adam said, sitting carefully on another block of stone. "Do what your other selves told you to do. *Be* still. Relax and breathe deeply.

Close your eyes again for a moment, until you find your balance. Concentrate on each breath as you take it, in . . . and out. . . ."

Peregrine obeyed. His chest rose and fell. The rigid lines of tension eased in his face. After a long moment, his fingers eased their death grip on the sketching pad.

"Good," Adam said. "Now open your eyes and draw what you see—*whatever* you see—just as you did that first night in the library. It's perfectly all right."

Peregrine cracked his lids a cautious chink. Colors—green, grey, brown—shimmered giddily before him. He took another deep, slow breath, then opened his eyes wide.

The scene in front of him flickered and flashed, oscillating between one state and another like a holographic projection. One moment he was looking at a derelict ruin, open to the sky; the next, he was seeing a manorial keep with its roofs and windows intact.

"Don't tense up," Adam's deep voice advised from somewhere off to his left. "You're seeing beyond the mere physical now, and that's good. Just let the images flow."

Peregrine managed a slight nod of acquiescence. As he continued to gaze unresistingly at the castle, even a little bit *beyond* the castle, the vision of a different Templemor began to stabilize, building up layer on layer. The twin stair turrets were capped off with square overhanging garret chambers, their crow-stepped roofs snugly overlaid with slates. The heraldic crest above the door, so badly weatherworn in the present, now showed a sharply-cut and freshly-painted device of a Maltese cross surrounded by seven stars—not the phoenix rising from the flames, as he had seen in Adam's house. The motto underneath the crest read, *Morte nunquam reget*—"Death shall have no dominion."

Peregrine blinked—slowly—but the image did not dissolve away when he opened his eyes. More confident now, and catching a little of the satisfaction that he could actually keep the thing in focus, he opened his sketchbook and began rapidly to draw. . . .

After a few minutes, Adam came to look on over the artist's shoulder. Under Peregrine's deft, busy hands, the ruin was transformed on paper into a stout tower-house, half fortress, half manor. The dormer windows sported heavy wooden shutters, and there were shot-holes in the flanking stair turrets to allow for protective fire across the main block of the building. Short parapet walks along the sides of the two overhanging garret chambers commanded a guarded view of the ground below.

For the next hour, Peregrine continued to draw, pausing only now and again to sharpen his pencil before moving into a new position, to catch a different perspective. By the time he finally handed the notebook to Adam, standing up to stretch, he had completed no fewer than a dozen comprehensive drawings.

Adam looked them over, marvelling at the wealth of detail running throughout. The restoration of the crest was particularly interesting, for it depicted a much earlier version of the Sinclair device, harking back to the time when the name had been Saint Clair, and the Templar connection had been quite unmistakable—a variation known to Adam, though not expected here, and certainly nothing that Peregrine Lovat could be expected to know. Given the accuracy of this heraldic detail, far beyond the scope of coincidence, there was little doubt in Adam's mind that Peregrine had reproduced an accurate record of the structural features of the house, inside and out.

The plan of the ground floor showed two vaulted storage chambers behind an entry hall, with the kitchen housed in the northeast tower. The great hall occupied the center of the building on the first level above the ground, with auxiliary family rooms opening off into the towers at either corner. The space on the next level up was divided into two bed-chambers, a strong room, and a solarium. The rooms on the garret level gave access to the parapet walks, where household guards would have kept watch in times of trouble. It was a plan fairly typical for castles of this era, but many of the interior details could not have been deduced merely from looking at the ruined remains, and certainly not in the short time Peregrine had spent drawing them.

"Peregrine, these are truly excellent," Adam said, looking up. "May I show them to the surveyor when he calls round this afternoon?"

The young artist had plopped down on the bottom-most step in front of the port, with his booted feet stretched out in front of him. He was looking slightly weary, but there was no longer any strain in his face. At Adam's question, he looked up and chanced a tentative smile.

"If you really think they'll be useful—certainly."

"If he's any good at his job," Adam replied, "I think 'useful' will be a gross understatement. How do you feel?"

Peregrine considered. "That's very odd," he said. "I'm tired, but you know, I feel quite relaxed—as though I'd got something bothersome out of my system."

"And your vision?"

"It's gone back to normal," said Peregrine. He added with a half-laugh, "I think your experiment worked." He sounded almost elated.

Adam gave him a knowing nod. In the last hour, they had passed the point of no return.

"I believe it did," he replied. "How soon do you think you might be ready to start looking at people again?"

Peregrine's eyes widened, but this time there was none of the fear that would have accompanied contemplation of the question, but hours before.

"Do you really think I could?" he asked.

"Why not?" Adam replied. "Was this frightening for you, once you actually got into it?"

"No."

"Well, then." Adam smiled. "People are the next step. It's the step you're going to have to take, if you really mean to see this through."

Peregrine drew a deep breath and let it out with a determined sigh.

"All right," he said. "If you think I can do it, I'll give it a try. Just tell me when and where."

Adam nodded, considering. "How about tomorrow? I've got to go into Edinburgh in the morning to offer testimony in a case before the High Court. One of the other men scheduled to be present is someone I'd like you to look at very closely. . . ."

Chapter Seven

THE following day dawned gusty and changeable. Peregrine and Adam left Strathmourne House shortly before nine, with Humphrey behind the wheel of the reliable blue Range Rover that was the workhorse of Adam's stable of motorcars. By the time they reached the Forth Road Bridge, most of the morning's rush hour traffic had subsided, leaving the roads relatively clear into the center of the city.

Humphrey let his passengers out on the front steps of Parliament House, directly across from St. Giles' Cathedral. Peregrine shifted the strap of his small artist's satchel on his shoulder and hunched down in the collar of his trenchcoat as he and Adam headed up the steps.

"You don't let a chap start out easily, do you?" he said. "I think I understand what you're hoping for, and I have to admit that the case is fascinating. But I'd still be curious to know why you want me to concentrate on sketches of the arresting officer, rather than the defendant or any of the witnesses."

Adam reached ahead to open the door into the courthouse building, holding it so that Peregrine could pass through ahead of him.

"Oh, you can sketch the others as well, if you feel up to it—though I'm not too sure I'd dwell on the defendant, at this early stage of your training. I'd rather not go into any further detail, though, because I don't want your reactions to be influenced by anything I might say. You'll understand better, I think, once you've had a chance to put your gifts to use."

"All right," said Peregrine, somewhat dubiously. "I'll do my best, in blind faith."

The case was being tried in a courtroom on the third floor. It had been in the papers for months—a gradual buildup of bizarre events involving threats of retaliation by black magic, a series of bizarre animal executions, and culminating in an attempt to burn down a house belonging to an elderly woman who kept dozens of cats. Initially, Adam had been called in to construct a psychological profile of the probable perpetrator. When the police eventually arrested the son of a prominent and wealthy businessman, Adam had been asked to perform a psychiatric evaluation on behalf of the courts—and would be presenting testimony as an expert witness in that regard today. He had reviewed his notes on the way in, familiarizing Peregrine with the essential background of the case. Now, as they stood waiting for the lift, Peregrine glanced speculatively at his mentor.

"Your suspect—he really took all of that black magic nonsense seriously, didn't he?"

"That black magic nonsense, as you so eloquently phrase it, *should* be taken seriously," Adam replied, though a faint smile softened any rebuke that might have accompanied the bald statement. "Some of what the uninformed *call* black magic can be put down to psychological aberration and delusion, I would be the first to admit. But as you yourself have cause to know, the lines between delusion, illusion, and fact can be very fine, indeed."

The stark reference to Peregrine's own situation produced the desired surprised silence, just as a soft chime announced the arrival of the lift. The doors opened, discharging a bewigged trio of barristers in their black courtroom robes. When Adam headed briskly into the empty car, Peregrine had to scramble a few steps to keep up.

"Let me see if I've got this right," Peregrine said, when the doors had closed. "Are you saying that the suspect really *was* working black magic?"

"Oh, there's little doubt he was *trying*," Adam replied.

Peregrine stared at Adam in shock.

"Did he *succeed*?" he asked.

"No." The flat denial hung in the air between them as Adam gazed somewhat distractedly *through* the lift's control panel. "This wretched young man, not content with the material advantages he already had, aspired to powers he was not entitled to. He began to practice what he fancied was a form of black magic. Unfortunately, helpless animals suffered unspeakable torture and an innocent old woman lost her home, her beloved pets, and very nearly her life. If there had been anything else to it, beyond a degree of petty and vicious immaturity, his activities might have attracted my notice sooner. As it was, he was only deluding himself in thinking that he was actually accomplishing something—which is better, I suppose, than the real thing, except that the victim still suffers, to one degree or another."

"You're implying that black magic *is* real, then," Peregrine said, obviously finding it hard to believe what he was hearing.

"Oh, it certainly can be," Adam said, fixing him with one of his bland, matter-of-fact looks. "The High Roads are many, and the Dark turnings have always been enticing to those of evil intent, who have a true affinity for spiritual power. And those who choose to travel the Dark Roads often engage in far blacker practices than animal sacrifice."

The sheer nonchalance of his tone made the actual words somehow even more ominous in their impact. Even though it was close in the lift, Peregrine shivered. Before he could press for further information, the lift grounded with a bump and the doors parted on a corridor full of people waiting to be admitted to the courtroom.

"Inspector McLeod will be sitting with me behind the Crown prosecutor," Adam murmured, as they stepped out and headed down the corridor, as casual as if they had just been discussing the previous day's racing results. "If you make for the right-hand side of the visitors' gallery, you should be able to get a reasonably good angle on his face."

The visitors' gallery extended along the back of the courtroom, with flanking extensions running halfway along the walls on either hand. Peregrine shouldered his way through a mixed group of journalists and idle spectators to secure a seat in the front row, overlooking the bench which Adam was sharing with a fit-looking grey-haired man in a tweed suit. The moustache and gold-rimmed aviator-style glasses tallied with the brief description Adam had given him. Never doubting that he had located his intended subject, Peregrine hauled his sketchbook from his satchel and embarked on his first sketch.

Other testimony occupied the better part of two hours. Adam immersed himself in the proceedings, only allowing himself a glance up at the visitors' gallery when it came time to take the stand himself. He was pleased to note that Peregrine was hard at work, his expression intensely absorbed. As Adam was sworn in, he briefly found himself wondering what McLeod would say when he learned he had been subjected to such penetrating scrutiny. After that, however, he gave his full attention to the questions of the Crown prosecuter, and then of the counsel for the defense.

Adam's testimony was finished just before the court recessed for lunch. Taken as a whole, the morning had not gone well. As he and McLeod made their way toward the back of the courtroom, moving with the flow of attorneys and witnesses and spectators, McLeod gave vent to an uncharacteristic rumble of complaint.

"Sometimes I don't know why we bother," he muttered through clenched teeth, so that only Adam could hear him. "That smirking little weasel back there is going to get off with a fine and probation, when by rights he should be locked away before he gets a chance to really hurt somebody. I'll lay you any odds you like that we get him back again within the year—and next time, it won't be just for torturing animals."

"I doubt you'll get any takers, even at those odds," Adam replied. "However, there's no point in dwelling on the limitations of the law. You're through for the day, aren't you? Why don't you join me for lunch? I have someone I'd like you to meet."

"That young man who was sketching, up in the gallery?" McLeod asked. "I thought he might be with you. Unfortunately, I'm *not* through for the day." He glanced at his watch and grimaced. "And if I don't get my skates on, it'll be my hide, too."

"What, have you been seconded for royal protection duty this afternoon?" Adam quipped, certain that McLeod was doing no such thing. "I seem to recall that a certain Royal Duke is in town."

McLeod rolled his eyes and snorted. He had little patience with what he regarded as royal baby-sitting.

"Don't you dare wish *that* on me, Adam. Let the younger chaps have the glory, so that old fogies like me can concentrate on real police work. No, this is some colonel from the S.A.S., come to teach a special workshop on using anti-terrorist tactics against inner city drug barons. I've already missed the morning session."

"Next time, then," Adam replied. "You *are* going to want to meet my young friend."

"Hmmm, then I expect I'd better make the effort. Call me later in the week, will you?"

"I'll do precisely that," Adam agreed.

The two men parted outside the courtroom. Adam found Peregrine waiting for him in front of the lift, watching McLeod disappear into the crowd. The young artist was clutching his sketchbook to his breast, his eyes bright with eagerness behind his spectacles. Sensing that Peregrine was about to thrust the drawings at him, Adam fended him off with a smile and a restraining gesture.

"No, don't show them to me now," he said. "There's an excellent French restaurant a few blocks from here. I had Humphrey book us a booth in the back, so we can have some privacy. I'd hoped the inspector could join us, but unfortunately, he has another commitment."

The restaurant was located down a stepped close off the Grassmarket. In between courses, Adam looked over the sketches Peregrine had made. He had *not* drawn the defendant.

"I could hardly bear to look at him, Adam," he said, as he handed over his sketch pad. "There was a fuzzy black line all around him, like someone had taken charcoal and smudged it. But at the same time, he looked—*slimy* is the only word that comes to mind."

"Hmmm, yes," Adam said, casting Peregrine a wry,

I-told-you-so glance as he opened the pad. "Now perhaps you understand why I suggested you not try to sketch him. Selectively is very important at this stage of the game."

But the sketches of Noel McLeod were precisely what Adam had expected. The first was a lively study of the inspector on the witness-stand, moustache bristling above a mouth set in a bulldog scowl, wire-rimmed aviator glasses lending him a slightly dashing air. Another showed him and Adam behind the Crown prosecutor's table, listening intently to testimony, both precisely as they would have appeared to everyone else in the courtroom.

The other drawings, however, were of far greater interest to Adam. In one version, McLeod's bright blue eyes stared uncompromisingly out from under a Highland bonnet with a white cockade pinned to the band. In a second, he wore the cowled visage of a medieval monk. In yet another, the police inspector of the present day had assumed the guise of a raffish sea-captain with a bushy beard. Adam smiled involuntarily.

"I always thought McLeod had a touch of the pirate Henry Martin in him," he observed out loud. "You've just confirmed that suspicion."

Peregrine looked up from stirring cream into his coffee. "You and he have more in common than first meets the eye," he said on impulse. "The inspector's another one like you, isn't he?"

Adam confirmed it with a slight smile and a nod of the head. "Though he would be slow to admit it in so many words," he said carefully, "Noel McLeod owes a great deal of his professional success and effectiveness to his hidden talents. The inspector is not alone in this respect," he added pointedly.

The startled look on Peregrine's face told him that the point had struck home.

"If you're talking about me," the artist said, "I don't see how my gift for seeing this kind of thing can be of much use to the rest of humanity."

"Keep working to perfect it," said Adam, "and you might be surprised."

So saying, he signaled the waiter to bring them the bill.

Adam's cryptic words stayed with Peregrine, cropping up when he least expected them. He pondered them repeatedly, but he was not aware of being any the wiser. Indeed, he was kept far too busy to even think very much about them, for Adam kept giving him ever more demanding exercises to develop control.

The weather had cleared after lunch, so they walked down to Princes Street Gardens, where Adam had him sketch passers-by, sometimes opening his sight to all impressions, looking for the deeper resonances, sometimes deliberately limiting himself to what he saw with his physical sight. The next day, the challenge deepened when Adam took him along on a consultation session at Jordanburn Hospital, where two of his patients had given their consent to have their portraits sketched.

This time, however, Peregrine was instructed to disregard *all* the psychic resonances he might detect—either from their former lives or from their present psychic disturbances—in order to focus on external appearances only. The task proved less difficult than he had expected. Instead of fighting to blot out the now-familiar overlay of ghost pictures, he found himself merely looking beyond them, focusing his artistic acuity by means of the deep breathing technique that Adam had taught him. In almost no time at all, the warring images seemed to dissipate before his very eyes, leaving him free to concentrate on the purely physical aspects of his subjects.

In consequence, the portraits he produced on this occasion had all the sharp clarity of feature and expression that Adam had so admired in earlier Lovat portraits. At the same time, the drawings were unclouded by the unsettling spiritual elements that had dominated his study of Lady Laura.

"Excellent!" exclaimed Adam, when he reviewed the portraits that night. "You see, you *can* shut it down, when you want to; and you don't have to let it take control of you. I believe you're well on your way to taking command of this talent of yours."

The real test of Peregrine's new-found control, however, came on Friday afternoon, when he accompanied Adam up to Kintoul to attend Lady Laura's funeral.

The service was held in the Episcopal church in the village. Though Humphrey got them there early, Adam and Peregrine arrived to find the pews filled to capacity with mourners come to pay their final respects. Fortunately, places had been reserved for them near the front of the nave, in one of the pews directly behind the family's private prayer stall. An usher escorted them down the center aisle and to the left, while the organist improvised vaguely melancholy-sounding background accompaniment.

Because Adam knelt after slipping into their assigned place, bowing his head in brief prayer, Peregrine did too, though he was not accustomed to kneeling in the church of his childhood. It was not that which made him ill at ease, however. The very air was heavy with undischarged emotion, and the church seemed all at once far too small to hold all the people present. Though it was well-heated, he suddenly felt clammy and cold.

Nervously Peregrine fingered the formal line of his starched collar, conscious of a growing tightness in his throat. When Adam finally slid back onto his seat, quietly opening the service leaflet the usher had given him, Peregrine followed his example. Sitting did not seem to help much. Trying another tack, the artist forced himself to inspect the high ceiling beams and rafters of the old church, hoping that artistic distraction might help him avoid acknowledging the reason they had come here today.

He had not expected it to work, and it did not. Inexorably his gaze was drawn toward the chancel area, just inside the communion rail. Lady Laura's coffin lay before the altar, within the protection of six tall candlesticks, looking very small under its blanket of red and white chrysanthemums. The sight unnerved him, but he would not allow himself to look away. To his infinite relief, no ghostly apparition manifested itself before his shrinking gaze.

Wondering why he should have been so afraid, Peregrine closed his eyes and took several long, deep breaths to relax, as Adam had taught him. Gradually the tightness in his throat abated. He was still searching his memory for a prayer appropriate for the moment when the organ up in the choir loft segued into a prelude by Palestrina, signaling the beginning of the service. Toward its conclusion, the clergy entered in procession: cross-bearer and candle-bearers and white-surpliced vicar.

The familiar pattern and repetition of the music had drawn and held Peregrine's attention. His emotional turmoil began to recede. The Handel introit which followed was performed by an accomplished contralto. All at once, Peregrine seemed to hear Lady Laura's voice with that of the singer, speaking comfort to him through the lilting strains of what had been one of her favorite arias:

"*Art thou troubled? Music will calm thee. . . .*"

He stopped trying to pray in words and let his spirit rest.

The theme of comfort continued with the opening hymn, this one based on a fifteenth-century poem by Bianco da Siena and set to a melody by Vaughan Williams:

"*Come down, O Love divine, Seek thou this soul of mine, And visit it with thine own ardor glowing. . . .*"

Anchored by the stability of the familiar hymn, Peregrine found himself able to join in with the rest of the congregation. Beside him, Adam's resonant bass lent added support, full of depth and latent passion. The mingled pride and reverence in the other man's upright stance reminded Peregrine of the statue of a Crusader-knight he had seen once in a chapel in Provence. The deep eyes held a faraway glow, as though they were reflecting back some measure of the brightness of his own inner vision. Abruptly Peregrine remembered that first sketch he had made of Adam—had it really been less than a week ago?

The hymn ended, and the moment passed, but to Peregrine's unmitigated relief, all the prayers and readings that followed spoke eloquently of light and transcendence.

"Behold, I show you a mystery," the vicar declared in the words of St. Paul. "We shall not all die, but we shall all be changed. . . ."

Adam had told him on the way here that the readings were Lady Laura's own choice. She had known she was going to die—had had time to prepare for it—and she had selected the words of comfort with the same care with which she had lived her life, sensitive to the end of the feelings of those she had loved and was leaving behind.

Adam had been one of the few to know she was dying. How much of his own knowledge had Adam shared with her, in those days before her passing, Peregrine wondered?

Lady Laura's eldest son came forward then, speaking briefly but emotionally of his mother's life and the causes she had loved, bidding her farewell on behalf of all the family. Then, to Peregrine's surprise, Adam Sinclair went forward, mounting the lectern and withdrawing a single piece of paper from an inside pocket.

"It was my privilege to enjoy Lady Laura's confidence and affection for many years," he said simply. "Lord Kintoul has asked that I share with you this short reading, which was one of her favorites. It comes from the final paragraph of a novel by Thomas Wolfe, entitled *You Can't Go Home Again.*"

He glanced down at the paper and slowly began to read, but it immediately became clear to Peregrine that the words needed no prompting from any written text.

Something has spoken to me in the night,
burning the tapers of the waning year;
something has spoken in the night
and told me I shall die, I know not where.
Saying:
"To lose the earth you know, for greater knowing;
to lose the life you have, for greater life;
to leave the friends you loved, for greater loving,
to find a land more kind than home, more large
than earth,
whereon the pillars of this world are founded,
toward which the conscience of the world is tending—
a wind is rising, and the rivers flow."

"We shall miss you, Laura," Adam finished quietly, in the hush of the crowded church, "but we bid you Godspeed and send you on your way with all our love and blessings."

The words had moved Peregrine profoundly, and he knew that he was not the only one to blink back tears. But as Adam made his way back to his seat, Peregrine found that his pain had gone, and with it any lingering guilt that he might have contributed to Lady Laura's death. On the contrary—and he knew this was a certainty tinged neither with pride nor with false modesty—his regular appearances to work on her portrait had given her much pleasure and comfort in those last weeks and months.

That acknowledged, he found that he could bid her an affectionate farewell from the depths of his heart, as serene now as he had been anxious earlier. He would miss her, but he knew that any lingering sadness must be for himself and not for her.

Still, as the vicar bade them kneel for the benediction, Peregrine reflected that he was glad there would be no graveside farewell. He knew it made no difference to Lady Laura, but he still shrank from the idea of anyone he loved being buried beneath the earth. Once the congregation had left, she would be laid to rest in the medieval vaults underneath the nave, to sleep with Kintouls and Kintoul wives of many another generation. She had been proud of her heritage; she would have liked that.

The prayer finished. The congregation stood. The tune of the closing hymn was by Michael Praetorius, the lyrics a translation from St. Ambrose:

> O Splendor of God's glory bright,
> O thou that bringest light from light,
> O Light of Light, light's living spring,
> O Day, all days illuminating. . . .

Freed now from all the guilt and confusion attending his vision of Lady Laura's passing, Peregrine let the words of the fourth-century bishop speak for him as well, now also free to let his newly biddable vision quest out as it would. At the same time, he again found himself hearing other voices, distinct from the general congregation. Almost without thinking, he allowed his eyes to be drawn to the singers in turn. Deeper impressions followed.

The reedy tenor coming from somewhere in front of him belonged, he discovered, to a sleek young man with a fox's clever face. Peregrine had met him once. He was a distant nephew of Lady Laura's, only present because he was hopeful of gaining something material from her will. By contrast, the gruff, tuneless baritone from one of the back rows advertised the presence of Lady Laura's elderly chauffeur, stoically accepting what he had no power to change.

Then, for Peregrine, all the other voices fell silent before a single, silver-bright soprano, soaring heavenward like the song of a lark. It was a woman's voice, but thin and pure as a young boy's, poignantly mingling piercing clarity with aching sorrow. The singer herself was somewhere off to Peregine's left and ahead, in the direction of the family stall. Eagerly he scanned the people standing there. A moment later he found her, far to the left, almost against the north wall.

She was standing in a pool of colored light cast down through the stained glass window immediately above her left shoulder. The hair that she wore swept back off her slender neck was a pale bright shade between copper and gold. Her averted profile was as delicate as that of a Botticelli madonna, traces of tears glistening beneath her lowered eyelashes.

Peregrine's heart went out to her in that instant, his perceptions quickened by compassion. Though he did not think she was any blood-relation to Lady Laura, her grief was as strong as any daughter's. Drawn by her beauty, he studied her more deeply—and was touched to discern a gracious gentleness of spirit.

Who is she? he wondered.

The recessional hymn ended on a harmonic Amen. After a moment's respectful delay, the mourners began gathering themselves to leave the church. The family made their departure by a side door, and the girl with the face of a grieving madonna made her way with them, though unaccompanied. Peregrine followed her slender figure with his eyes until she had disappeared, only coming to his senses when Adam nudged his elbow.

"Her name is Julia Barrett," Adam murmured in his ear, as he urged the younger man into the center aisle. "She's Lady Laura's god-daughter."

Peregrine half-turned, long past being surprised that Adam Sinclair should be able to read him so clearly.

"Is she?" he wondered aloud. "I can't think why we never met before."

"Her father was Sir Albert Barrett," Adam said softly. "He had holdings down south, in Buckinghamshire."

Peregrine glanced at Adam, noting the two uses of the past tense.

"Her father's dead?" he whispered.

Adam inclined his head in discreet confirmation, keeping his voice low as they made their way along with the crowd.

"A few years ago, he was involved in a financial scheme that went badly awry. When the company he had helped to found went bankrupt, he sold off his own properties in order to make good the losses to the shareholders. It was an honorable thing to do, and no word was ever spoken against him personally, but rumors hinted increasingly that his business partners might have been involved in professional improprieties. It took the heart out of him. A few months after the bankruptcy, he was found dead. The official verdict was death by natural causes, but there were some who said he had taken his own life. Needless to say, the affair put an enormous strain on his family. I think things might have gone very ill with Julia and her mother if Lady Laura hadn't stood by them."

They reached the door of the church in time for Peregrine to catch a disappointing glimpse of Julia Barrett stepping into a waiting car. He looked for her again at the reception back at Kintoul House, but without success. He was distracted from any further thoughts on the subject when the Earl of Kintoul called him courteously aside to inquire about the completion of his mother's unfinished portrait. To his own private surprise and relief, Peregrine discovered that the thought of coming back to the painting no longer filled him with shrinking alarm.

"I can resume work any time you wish, my lord," he assured the earl. "I'm doing some work for Sir Adam Sinclair at the moment, but I know he's also eager to see the portrait finished."

When the earl shortly departed to look after his other guests, Peregrine went wandering in search of Adam. He found him by one of the windows in the drawing room, engaged in absorbed conversation with a lissom, laughing-eyed blond whom Peregrine recognized as Lady Alyson MacBaird, the elder daughter of the Earl of Kilrevan. He had painted her several years before. Unwilling to interrupt what was obviously a pleasurable encounter for both parties, Peregrine was about to withdraw, when the scene before him underwent a sudden disturbing change.

A shadow seemed to pass over the brightly-lit room, like a storm cloud passing over the sun. The darkness gathered over Adam's corner of the hall, spiraling around him like smoke.

Peregrine gave a gasp and blinked his eyes hard, but the darkness remained, hovering queasily in the air like a screen of poisonous gas. Throwing discretion to the winds, Peregrine called out sharply and started forward.

"Adam!"

The older man turned his head, his expression one of question. Halfway to the middle of the room, Peregrine fetched up short as the darkness abruptly vanished before his eyes. He stumbled to a halt, feeling foolish and confused.

"What is it, Peregrine?" Adam inquired mildly.

Peregrine shifted his weight uncomfortably from one foot to the other, aware of Lady Alyson's amused blue gaze.

"I beg your pardon," he told her. "I was looking for Sir Adam, but it can wait. . . ."

Later on, however, when he and Adam were in the car driving back to Strathmourne, he related what he had seen.

"I haven't a clue what it was," he confessed. "It wasn't like any of the other things I've been seeing. A—almost an intelligent presence, perhaps some kind of elemental force—like the energy buildup before a tornado or a hurricane. It was definitely menacing. And you were at the center of it."

Adam assimilated this without speaking. When the silence lengthened, Peregrine finally asked, "Adam, are you in some kind of danger?"

Adam's mouth was thin and unsmiling. "If I am, it has yet to assume a particular shape and form."

"Have you any enemies that you know of?" Peregrine persisted.

"Yes. Who hasn't?" Adam stated shortly. Then his expression softened. "Look, I don't doubt for an instant that you've caught intimations of some form of trouble to come. But I make it a rule never to worry, until I have something specific to worry about. Sufficient unto the day," he finished drily, "is the evil thereof."

"All right," said Peregrine on a heavy note. "At least you've been warned." He added mentally, *And I'll do anything I can to help, if that will serve. . . .*

Chapter Eight

ON Saturday, the twenty-seventh, with the sinking of the sun, a cold, dank fog drifted down off the three hills of Eildon into the narrow streets of the Scottish border town of Melrose. As the night darkened, the mist grew steadily thicker, reducing street- and window-lights to ghostly smears in the gathering gloom. Before very long, the fog was so dense that it was impossible to see more than a few yards in any direction. On the east side of the town, the famous ruins of Melrose Abbey became all but invisible, drowned in a sea of cloud.

Shortly after eight o'clock, a white patrol car bearing the markings of the Lothian and Borders Police rumbled downhill along the crooked length of Abbey Street and slowed to a halt outside the entrance to the abbey's grounds. The officer at the wheel cut the engine, then rolled down his window to listen while his partner stepped out of the car to shine a torch into the mist beyond the gates. The fog diffused the beam without illuminating anything, but the stillness was reassuring. Satisfied that all was in order, the officer returned to the warmth of the car, and the pair continued on their way.

The tail lights of the patrol car vanished into the mist. As the drone of its engine receded into the distance, five dark-clad figures emerged from the shadows flanking the enclosed garden of St. Mary's School, across the street from the abbey. Silent as wraiths, they darted across the road and ducked into Cloisters Road, a single-track lane running along the north side of the abbey compound. Once inside the lane, the leader switched on a shielded electric torch and led the way to an iron gate in the churchyard wall.

The gate was locked, but one of the party made short work of it with a deftly wielded lock pick. Swiftly the little procession filed through the open gate and set out across the fog-bound lawn toward the vaulted ruin of the abbey church, skirting the eastern side of the cloister ruins and slipping through what once had been the processional door from the cloister into the church. Three of the five shouldered bundles containing an assortment of workmen's tools; a fourth carried a pair of battery-powered lanterns. The leader bore a bulky leather satchel and a narrow canvas case, the latter long and thin like a fencer's kit-bag.

Once inside the shell of the nave, the five made their way purposefully toward a small chapel set into the corner between the north transept and the presbytery, shielded from outside view by thick outer walls on two sides and the bulk of the abbey on the others. One man scurried across to the south transept to peer searchingly through a doorway in the south wall, then came back to post watch down the gravel-paved nave. Two of the others directed the dim, blue-filtered beams of the electric lanterns low against the chapel floor, while the fourth produced a whisk broom and with it swept the gravel off an oblong section of flagstone paving beneath the narrow east window. When his work was finished, the leader came forward and went down on his knees, taking off his gloves to run bare hands over the stones just exposed. A signet ring on the third finger of his right hand flashed blood-dark in the blue light.

Whatever he was looking for, he found. Getting to his feet, he gave his subordinates a nod by way of confirmation and backed off a few paces to sit on a piece of foundation stone by the chapel doorway and rummage in his satchel. One of the men came to crouch beside him, while the other two began unpacking the shovels and crowbars and pick-axes they had brought with them for excavation.

"I still think we could have done this part ahead of time, Mr. Geddes," the crouching man whispered, as the leader drew first a leaden bowl and then a length of leather thong out of the satchel.

The lead made a dull thunk as the leader set the bowl beside his boot, but he only glared at his companion before shrugging out of the left sleeve of his leather jacket and pushing up the sleeve of the black polo shirt underneath.

"You know better than to use real names," he replied, also whispering, but with an undertone that brooked no argument. "And you also know that the ritual requires that the blood be as fresh as possible. Do it! There's no time to waste."

He handed the thong to the other man and held out his left arm, at the same time shifting the leaden bowl into his lap and leaning back against the stump of a Romanesque column. His assistant offered no further comment, merely applying the leather thong as a tourniquet and then delving into his jacket pocket to produce several small items sealed in plastic packets.

From the first came a sterile wipe, pungent with alcohol. The leader straightened his arm, impassively clenching and unclenching his fist to pump up the vein as his assistant scrubbed the skin over the inner elbow, rolling the vein under his fingertips to be sure of the location in the dim light. A second packet produced a coil of clear plastic tubing, with a clamp midway along its length and a connector for attaching it to the sterile needle unit the man withdrew from the third.

"Keep your arm straight now," he murmured, swabbing over the vein a final time and then pulling off the needle's protective cap with his teeth.

His subject displayed no flicker of reaction as the needle went in. Briefly releasing the clamp in the center of the tubing allowed a dark line of blood to race into the near end, confirming accurate placement of the needle. Satisfied, the man pulled the tabs from a butterfly bandage and used it to stabilize the needle against the leader's inner arm, then ran his hand lightly down the length of the plastic tubing until he found the free end, which he set in the leaden bowl for the leader to hold in place.

"You're all set," the man whispered, loosening the tourniquet. "Shall I leave you alone for a few minutes, after I start it?"

At the leader's taut nod, his assistant thumbed the clamp, watching for a moment until blood had begun to pool in the leaden bowl, then got to his feet and backed off a few paces. The leader leaned back his head with eyes closed and began to murmur something under his breath, hugging the leaden bowl to his chest. With a slight shudder, the assistant turned away to assist his colleagues, who were uprooting the paving stones and leaning them against the chapel wall.

A few minutes later he returned. The bowl was more than half full, containing perhaps a cupful of blood. Kneeling, the man pulled a roll of adhesive tape and a pair of blunt bandage scissors from his pocket, along with a packet containing a ball of sterile cotton. He drew off a short length of tape from the roll and cut it, sticking one end lightly to the side of his thigh while he opened the packet with the cotton. The faint sound caused the leader to stir, opening eyes that, just for an instant, seemed to glow in the bluish light, almost forbidding the hand that came to close the clamp and stop the flow of his blood.

But then the moment was past, and he was handing over the leaden bowl, holding up the doubled end of the tubing so it would not drip, extending his arm for removal of the needle. When it was done, and cotton and tape in place over his wound, he eased his sleeve back down his arm and put his jacket back on while his assistant gathered the debris from their work into a plastic bag, which he stashed in the leather satchel. From that satchel he then removed an aspergillum of black horsehair, which he handed to the leader before getting to his feet, also picking up the leaden bowl of blood.

"Careful when you stand up," he warned, though he made no move to assist. "You may be a little light-headed."

The leader staggered a little on his feet as he came full upright, pausing to catch his balance on the column while he drew a few deep breaths, but then he held out his hand for the bowl.

"Give it to me," he commanded, at the same time snapping his fingers at the two men finishing up on the floor slabs. The pair immediately abandoned their activities to move to the center of the area, also joined by the man who had been assisting the leader.

The leader moved to the northern edge of the area they had cleared, dipping the tuft of black horsehair into the bowl. As he raised it, blood dripped onto the stone of the foundations there.

"*The blood of life,*" he whispered fiercely.

Turning westward then, he began pacing off a circle to include the entire chapel area, going widdershins, shaking blood lavishly to mark the outline, his voice pitched barely above a whisper as he chanted the measured verses of a ritual invocation. The men within watched avidly, bowing deeply as their leader paused at each quarter to make a sign and splash an additional measure of blood on the ground and confining stones of the walls. When the circuit was complete, the leader closed the circle with another sign. The leaden bowl was all but empty, and he wrapped it and the aspergillum in a square of fine black cloth and a plastic bag before stashing them in his satchel again.

"The temenos is sealed," he told his men. "You may now begin."

His three subordinates hefted their implements and began to dig. Earth and gravel went flying as the excavators quarried their way into the ground. Inside the guarded circle, the air rang loud with the busy tumult of picks and shovels. Outside, where the sentry kept watch along the darkened nave, it was quiet as the grave.

Two hours passed. The men continued to work uninterrupted. By the middle of the third hour, they had uncovered a deep oblong pit the size of a coffin, perhaps three feet below the level of the floor. Shortly thereafter, one of the diggers struck his shovel against something hard that rang out dully like gun metal.

"This should be it," one of the men murmured.

After that, they worked more carefully. In a quarter hour's time, their excavations had unearthed a heavy slab of fine-grained silvery granite. The leader sprinkled the face of the slab with salt that had been mixed with sulphur and muttered a word of command.

Spidery lines sprang to life, glistening in the light from

the electric lanterns. The lines flowed together to form an intricate spiral of hieroglyphics. The leader smiled thinly at his associates.

"This is indeed his resting place," he told them. "Let's raise the marking stone."

Under the combined efforts of the team, the slab came up with a hollow groan. Beneath it lay a plain stone sarcophagus. Two members of the trio heaved aside the sarcophagus lid, exposing a mummified form swathed in the cobwebby remains of a linen shroud.

The senior member of the excavation team explored the spaces on either side of the body with hands that were trembling with eagerness. He carefully shifted the corpse and groped beneath its head, back, and legs, muttering to himself when he discovered nothing there to find. The face he upturned toward his leader was black with disappointment.

"It isn't here!" he declared bitterly. "Damn it, it isn't here!"

The leader dismissed the import of this heated announcement with a laconic gesture.

"A small setback, nothing more. I came prepared against this eventuality."

He motioned his men to alight from the pit. When they were clear, he opened his satchel again and produced a handful of scarlet tapers and a stick of black chalk. The former he gave to his men to position at the four quarters of the circle he had circumscribed with blood, himself methodically chalking out an equilateral triangle at the north side of the grave slot, its apex pointing toward the body. A clay incense burner was set at the center of the triangle.

After he had completed these preparations, he returned to the satchel for the last time and drew out a carefully folded packet of black silk which, when shaken out, became a short hooded cape. This he slipped around his shoulders, drawing up the hood and carefully arranging the rest so that it fell in smooth folds, just to his elbows. Silver embroidery in the shape of a snarling beast's head glimmered to the left of the throat clasp. From an inner pocket of his leather jacket came a final piece of ceremonial regalia: a silver pendant hanging from a heavy silver chain.

The three men with him had brought similar hoods, embroidered with the same beast device, but in red. While they were putting these on, the leader lit the tapers and set the incense burning. The smoke was heavy, welling over the edges of the clay incense burner and spreading slowly over the floor, spilling down into the open coffin. As the heavily scented smoke began to obscure what lay inside, the leader unzipped the narrow canvas bag. Damascened gold and silver-work blazed cold in the light of the filtered torches as he drew out a splendid, swept-hilt rapier, fashioned in the ornate style favored by Italian armorers of the late sixteenth century.

Carefully he drew the sword from its gem-studded scabbard. Flanked by his henchmen, behind and to either side, he positioned himself behind the triangle he had drawn on the ground, with his feet all but touching the triangle's base. Extending the sword at arm's length, he traced a symbol in the air above the opened grave, then lowered the tip of the blade so that it came to rest precisely on the crowning point of the triangle. For a moment he was silent, marshalling mind, body, and spirit. Then, rousing himself, he uttered the opening cantrip of a potent and dangerous incantation.

Harsh as stone against the ear, the archaic Latin phrases built within the invisible boundaries of the warded circle. Out of realms of air and shadow, dark powers rose in answer. The three acolytes present at the graveside shuddered in mingled awe and ecstasy as their leader exerted the strength of his will to take command of the forces he was raising. His own power temporarily magnified by borrowed arcane energies, he at last reached out in spirit to wrench another soul from its orbit.

The clash of opposing wills rocked the circle, but the binding force of the ritual was strong enough to maintain it. Relentlessly, the leader of the group spoke the final words of power, summoning his victim by name. For a long moment nothing visible seemed to happen, while tensions crackled over and around the grave. Then all at once, the air above the triangle became charged with a pale, silvery mist, different from the heavy smoke still pooling in the grave.

The mist thickened, slowly gathering shape and density. Two pallid points of light flashed briefly in the midst of the suggestion of a face. Shaking his head, the hooded leader of the group moved the point of the sword to the edge of the pit, uttering another word of command.

Writhing in something like anguish, the mist descended into the grave and mingled with the smoke. Gradually both smoke and mist began to dissolve, once more revealing the mummified corpse. But this eerie miasma was not just dispersing; it was actually sinking into the corpse. And as the air grew clearer, the body itself began spasmodically to twitch.

Chapter Nine

THE heavy fog that shrouded Melrose that Saturday night extended north of the Firth of Forth as far as the River Tay. In the Fifeshire town of Dunfermline, however, the chill mists did little to dampen the spirits of the revellers who had come to attend a full-dress *ceilidh* and dinner-dance sponsored by the local churches in aid of a new counseling center. In the botanical gardens adjoining Dunfermline Abbey, a series of striped canvas marquees had been erected on the rolling lawns among the glass hot-houses. Ablaze from within like so many great Chinese lanterns, the pavilions rang merry with the sounds of mingled music, dancing, and laughter.

Adam and Peregrine were numbered among the party of guests invited by Janet and Matthew Fraser. In anticipation of a pleasurable evening of Scottish country dancing, nearly everyone had turned out in full Highland dress. Adam, never one to miss such an opportunity to display his Scottish heritage, wore the red tartan kilt of the Sinclairs with panache, a froth of lace jabot showing at the throat of a doublet that had been his father's. The sapphire brooch amid the lace had been given his great-grandmother by Queen Victoria.

He was greeting his hostess, resplendent in a gown of royal blue, with a silk sash of bright red-and-blue Fraser tartan brooched to the right shoulder and blue ribbons woven through her upswept hair. Peregrine had been temporarily waylaid by an old flame.

"Heavens, Adam! No one, seeing you, could ever

maintain that romance is dead!" Janet exclaimed, taking him by both hands to survey him by the lights on the lawn. "You look like a character out of a Robert Louis Stevenson novel!"

Adam laughed and bent his dark head to kiss her hand in gallant acknowledgement of the compliment.

"And *you* look like a heroine by Sir Walter Scott!" he told her, dropping one of her hands so he could rest his own on his heart.

> Joy to the fair! whose constant knight
> Her favour fired to feats of might!
> Unnoted shall she not remain
> Where meet the bright and noble train. . . .

"He does that very prettily, doesn't he, Matthew?" she said aside to her husband, dimpling. "It's from 'The Crusader's Return,' isn't it? But you know you really shouldn't squander your store of poetry on me. You ought to be saving it for the lady of your dreams."

The lady of your dreams. . . . Janet was at it again. The evening promised to be one of *those* affairs. As he turned his outward attention to greeting the Frasers' other guests, he briefly envied Peregrine, who had already connected with an old love and who might even bump into the lovely Julia Barrett before the night was through. Perhaps one day *he* would be so fortunate—though if he remained as uncompromising in his choice of women as he was about so many other things, that day might be long in coming.

The rollicking strains of a Scottish jig called him back to the present—and to awareness of his present companion, who was quite charming enough to command his willing courtesy. Smiling, he offered Janet his arm.

"I hear the music livening up," he said. "It's time we set a good example, and let our fine *ceilidh* band know we appreciate their efforts. If Matthew has no objections, I should esteem it a signal honor to lead you out for the next dance."

"I suppose you might as well," Sir Matthew said from

the rear of the group, peering down his handsome nose at his wife and their friend with an assumption of mock austerity. "*Some* of us came here with duties to perform," he reminded them. "By all means, enjoy yourselves. I'll join you once I've talked to the vicar, about when to present the fund-raising awards."

The rest of the party carried on into the marquee, where the couples on the floor were just finishing up a round of "Strip the Willow." The music concluded with a flourish, attended by breathless laughter and applause from the dancers. As the floor began slowly to clear, the stout, green-kilted leader of the band hefted his accordion and pulled the microphone closer.

"Thank you very much, ladies and gentlemen. Form sets now for 'Dashing White Sergeant.'"

Janet beckoned forward her brother-in-law and his wife, who were swiftly joined by Janet's sister, Lady Eloise McKendrick.

"We need one more person!" exclaimed Janet. "Adam, where's your handsome Mr. Lovat?"

Adam stood an inch or two taller than most of the other men in the room. From his advantage of height, he scanned the room and spotted a slim, upright figure in a kilt of Hunting Fraser moving toward the outer edge of the dance floor, now unaccompanied.

"Peregrine!" he called, catching the younger man's eye and waving him over. "We need another man."

As Peregrine came to join them, grinning self-consciously, Janet caught up his hand with an indulgent little laugh and urged him toward her left.

"I'm afraid we can't afford to let you stand by and observe right now," Janet said, as they squared up their line, the three of them facing the other three across the set.

Almost immediately the band struck up the introductory bars of a Black Dance reel, accompanied by ragged bows and curtsies of the dancers toward their opposite lines, as hasty final adjustments were made within the sets of six. Naturally neat-footed, Peregrine had no trouble keeping pace with Adam and Janet as the members of their set joined hands and circled first to the right, then to the left, before breaking back into their groups of three. Janet, in the middle, matched steps first with Adam, then with Peregrine, before leading the way into a figure of eight. They joined hands again then, advancing and retiring with their opposite trio, then advancing again to pass through this time, one group ducking laughingly under the upraised arms of their counterparts to meet the next set of three.

Groups joined up briefly, then broke away again to form other set combinations as they progressed round the floor. One dance tune led into another, in a spirited medley. Peregrine found himself enjoying it, laughing as he dipped his head to pass through an archway of arms—and raised it again to find himself coming face to face with Julia Barrett.

Surprise almost brought Peregrine to a standstill. This was not the grave, grieving girl he had seen at Lady Laura's funeral. Under the lively enchantment of the music, Botticelli's grieving madonna had been transformed into Flora of the *Primavera*. Rather than Highland attire, she wore a diaphanous frock patterned in traceries of flowers and vine leaves, and her rose-gold hair was flying loose except for a cascade of green silk ribbons catching back the front. Even as he faltered in his step, her gaze met his for a brief instant of electric contact.

As their respective groups merged to circle, he reached out and took her hand. Her eyes were a clear aquamarine blue, her look as guileless as a fawn's. He tightened his clasp, struggling to think of something to say to her, but before he could devise anything like a suitable remark, the conventions of the dance forced him to release her. All too soon, her two partners whisked her away, and she was lost from view among the crowds of other dancers.

They completed four more patterns before an upsurge in the melody signaled that the dance was coming to a close. When the music died, Peregrine turned hurriedly to Janet.

"Please excuse me, Lady Fraser!" he told her. "I've just seen someone I want very much to speak to."

He darted off before she could question him, slipping adroitly through the milling couples on the floor until he caught sight of a slender, girlish figure with rose-gold hair.

She was standing by the doorway, fastening the throat of a hooded green velvet evening cape she had donned over her floral gown. Peregrine quickened his pace, overtaking her just as she was at the point of stepping out into the fog.

"Hello," he said rather breathlessly. "I hope you haven't tired of the dancing so soon. The evening's hardly begun."

She turned her fawn's eyes on him, her expression faintly smiling.

"Oh, I know. My part in the festivities begins in about a quarter hour, over in the conservatory. With the air as damp as it is tonight, my harp will be badly in need of a last-minute tuning."

"Your harp!" Peregrine was intrigued. "Are you a professional musician, then?"

She laughed. "Hardly that. A dedicated amateur, at best. I don't generally perform in public at all," she continued, "but I'm a parishioner at St. Margaret's, across the road, and when the vicar asked me to take part tonight, for charity, I couldn't very well refuse."

"I suspect you're being far too modest," Peregrine said with sincere conviction. "If you play even half as well as you sing, it will be the crowning performance of the evening."

She gave him a tip-tilt look, composedly curious. "We haven't met before. Have we?"

"No, we haven't." Peregrine shook his head with a rueful grin. "I'm sorry. I ought to have introduced myself at once. I'm Peregrine Lovat."

"And I'm Julia Barrett," she returned. "If we haven't met before, wherever did you hear me sing?"

"In—in church," Peregrine murmured lamely, suddenly aware that this revelation had been thoughtless. "I—I was at Lady Laura Kintoul's funeral yesterday."

He dreaded seeing the shadow of grief return to her face, but to his relief, she merely nodded wisely.

"Ah, that explains it," she said. She smiled slightly and extended a slender hand. "I'm pleased to have met another of her friends. She was very special."

"Yes, she was," Peregrine said lamely. Her fingers felt warm and vital within the compass of his own. For a moment both of them were silent. Then he said impulsively, "Have you anyone in particular waiting on you tonight?"

Pleased comprehension lent a sparkle of mischief to Julia's blue eyes. "Well, I'm sure my uncle would like to think that he's a *particularly* favorite uncle," she said, smiling. "Come and let me introduce you to him, before it's time for me to play. . . ."

Their departure did not go unobserved.

"Really, Adam," said Janet in tones of mild reproof, "you might have warned me that your shy young friend had already set his sights on Albert Barrett's niece."

Adam accepted this censure meekly. "I'm sorry. I wasn't certain she would be here tonight."

Matthew Fraser grinned down at his wife. "Disappointed that you aren't going to be able to indulge in your passion for match-making? Never mind, there's always Adam to fall back on."

"Oh, Matthew, I am *quite* out of charity with Adam at the moment," Janet said, pretending to pout. "It would be nothing less than just, if I were next to introduce him to some garrulous old dowager with a neck like a turkey hen, and then leave him to fend for himself."

"Mercy!" exclaimed Adam. "How can I make amends?"

"You can begin," said Janet, "by fetching us all some refreshments. . . ."

The dancing and music continued. Nearly an hour later, Peregrine reappeared with Julia on his arm. Quick as ever to take command of a promising situation, Janet accosted them with the smiling suggestion that Julia and her uncle should join the Fraser party for the light buffet supper that had been laid on for the guests later in the evening. Urged on by Peregrine with a rare show of forcefulness, Julia shyly accepted the invitation. Thereafter, the two parties merged for the remainder of what Peregrine, for one, considered to be one of the most pleasurable evenings he had spent in a long time.

By two in the morning, the *ceilidh* was beginning to break up, the counseling center richer by several thousand pounds and no one able to say that he or she had not had their fill of entertainment or good food. Peregrine reluctantly escorted Julia to her uncle's car, regretful that he was not in a position to drive her home himself. He watched wistfully as the tail lights of Albert Barrett's car vanished into the fog and mist.

"She said she wouldn't mind seeing me again, Adam," he confided, as Humphrey opened the door of the Bentley for them. "She's really quite a remarkable girl!"

Lost thereafter in his own pleasant reverie, he failed to notice the wistful look of something akin to envy in Adam Sinclair's dark eyes.

Humphrey had them home within half an hour. Pleasurably weary, Peregrine bade his host a cordial goodnight and retired. He shed his evening clothes quickly and climbed into bed, fully expecting to fall asleep the instant his head touched the pillows. But though his body was glad to be at rest, his mind remained strangely active.

At first his thoughts were still dominated by Julia Barrett and the events at Dunfermline. But as the minutes ticked away, his musings unaccountably took a darker turn. In retrospect, mentally moving among the pavilions and the botanical gardens, he saw that though all was light and life and movement inside, outside the mist-shrouded grounds were haunted by shadowy figures with grasping, long-fingered hands. . . .

A wave of fog rolled over the scene, masking it behind a smothering curtain of cloud. When the cloud thinned again, Peregrine found he was no longer surveying the botanical gardens. Crooked gravestones jutted upright among the grassy mounds of a medieval churchyard, and a dim, skeletal figure was lurching unsteadily toward a gap in a high stone wall. . . .

Peregrine sat up with a start and groped for his watch. To his surprise, the time was ten minutes past six. He shook his head, realizing that he must have drifted off to sleep in the midst of his imaginings. He was about to lie down again, when he heard somewhere off in another part of the house the sudden, urgent ringing of a telephone.

By the time Humphrey knocked at the door of his apartment, Adam was already out of bed, tying on a burgundy wool dressing gown. One glance at his manservant's face told him that something important was afoot.

"I'm sorry to disturb you so early, sir," Humphrey said. He too wore a dressing gown, hastily donned over striped pyjamas. "It's Inspector McLeod, calling from Melrose."

"Melrose?" Adam was all at once aware of a pricking in his thumbs. "I'll take it in here," he said, as he moved toward the extension telephone on the table beside the bed.

Humphrey paused by the door. "Shall I wait, sir?"

"I think so." Adam lifted the receiver and spoke without preamble. "Here I am, Noel. What is it?"

The police inspector's voice came gruffly through a crackle of static on the line.

"My apologies for calling you at this unseemly hour, Adam, but we've had a rather peculiar incident down here at Melrose. I'll not go into details over the phone, but it's something that I think you'll agree requires your most particular attention."

Requires? McLeod's choice of words, along with a subtle shift in the tone of his voice, conveyed unspoken volumes.

"Indeed?" Adam said, his own inflection carefully noncommittal. "In that cause, I shall certainly come along to tender my opinion. Is there a particular place that you'd like me to meet you?"

There was a weighty pause. "Make your way to the abbey ruins," rumbled the voice from the receiver. "You'll see the police lines. If I'm not there when you arrive, one of my men will know where to find me."

McLeod clearly was taking precautions in case unauthorized ears might be listening in—which again pointed to something beyond the usual scope of police expertise.

"I'll make the abbey my starting point then," Adam said with apparent lightness. "It's—what?—a quarter past six," he went on, with a glance at a clock on the mantel. "It should take me—perhaps two hours. Fortunately, it's Sunday, so there won't be much traffic. I'll be there as quickly as I can, though."

"A man can't ask for more than that." McLeod sounded more than a little relieved. "Thank you, Adam."

"Not at all."

As McLeod rang off, Adam turned to face Humphrey, his dark eyes glinting keen as a hunting hawk's.

"I think I'd better take the Jaguar," he said. "And I'd like to be out of here in the next half hour. From the sound of things, the sooner I'm in Melrose, the better."

Humphrey nodded. "You'll want the top up, then, sir. It's á raw day outside. Shall I see to it?"

"Please do," Adam said, heading for his dressing room. "I'll want some tea and toast, too, if you can manage it quickly. But before you do any of that, I'd be very much obliged if you'd go and wake Mr. Lovat. Tell him what's afoot, and say I'd like him to come with me, if he's willing. I've a shrewd suspicion he's about to come into his own."

Chapter Ten

WELL within the half hour Adam had specified, Peregrine found himself sitting in the passenger seat of Adam's blue Jaguar. The gloved hands of the laird of Strathmourne were steady on the wheel as he piloted the powerful car south in the direction of Edinburgh. Still a little breathless from having to get ready so quickly, Peregrine eased his portable sketchbox off his lap onto the floor between his knees. Adam had instructed him to bring it, but something in the older man's manner just now made him hesitate to ask the reason why.

It was nearly seven o'clock, but the fog and overcast made it seem much earlier. The Jag's headlamps did little to illuminate the gloom, and the lights of occasional oncoming cars dazzled in the mist. The motorway was mostly deserted, as Adam had predicted, but the fog and occasional drizzle made it necessary to pay particular attention to his driving, if he hoped to make good time. Nonetheless, he found a part of himself speculating, even though Noel McLeod's telephone call had given him nothing whatever to go on besides sheer intuition. Despite all reason to the contrary, he could not help the vague, foreboding suspicion that one mystery was about to lead him and his associates into the heart of another, even more dangerous than the first.

Even with Adam's skillful driving, it was well past nine by the time they reached the outskirts of Melrose. Sunday traffic this early remained light, especially with the weather, but roadworks forced several detours, carrying them many miles out of their way. Round about Galashiels, the fog gave way to a cold, drizzling rain, verging on sleet. Adam adjusted the defoggers and increased the speed of the wipers as they approached the town of Melrose, cruising past the imposing facade of the Waverly Hotel and then reducing speed as they carried on along Waverly Road and entered the lower end of the High Street.

By-passing the police station on their right, which seemed to be a bustle of activity for a Sunday morning, they turned left into Buccleuch Street and made directly for the abbey, as McLeod had suggested. In the abbey car park, directly across the street from the main entrance to the ruins, Adam was not surprised to see a pair of white police cars, a police van, and several other unmarked vehicles, probably police as well. A barricade had been set up before the entrance itself, manned by a sturdy young constable in a yellow mackintosh with *Police* stenciled across the back. With him was a second man in plain clothes.

The Jaguar turned heads as Adam nosed it into the car park. A number of curious townsfolk were milling about outside the barricade, peering and pointing from under their dripping umbrellas, and they shifted their attention to Adam as he eased the car into a space beside one of the white police vehicles. Beyond the barricade and the black iron fence that closed off the abbey grounds, Adam could make out lines of fluorescent yellow tape strung like cobwebs among the ruins. More anonymous figures in rain-slick macks were moving around among the abbey's crumbling walls.

"Lots of activity," Peregrine observed, craning his neck. "Do you suppose there's been a murder?"

"Nothing so conventional as that, I fancy," Adam said grimly, switching off the ignition, "though perhaps something every bit as serious."

Retrieving a tweed motoring cap from behind the front seat, he eased open the door and got out of the car, hunching under its shelter and that of his taupe leather trenchcoat as he squinted against the fine, penetrating screen of mingled rain and fog. Peregrine, looking more than a little dubious, got out from his side and pulled up the collar of his duffel coat, scowling up at the sky.

"I wish I'd had the sense to bring a cap," he grunted.

Adam settled gloved hands deep in his pockets and gestured toward the car with his chin.

"There's an umbrella under the front seat," he told Peregrine. "And don't forget your sketchbook."

They locked the car, and together picked their way through the puddles to the abbey's entrance, eliciting less interest from the bystanders as they got farther from the car. The young constable came to attention as they approached the barrier, starting forward as if to warn them off, but he paused when the plainclothes man laid a restraining hand on his shoulder and muttered something in his ear.

"Come right through, Sir Adam," the man in plain clothes said with a grim smile. "I should ha' known, from that great, purrin' beast of a motorcar, but wi' yer hat pulled down like that, I almost didnae recognize ye."

"Well, Melrose is hardly my usual stomping ground," Adam said with a smile, as he and the man exchanged handshakes. "Good to see you, Hamish. Incidentally," he added, as the plainclothes man ushered them past the barrier, "this is my associate, Mr. Lovat. Peregrine, this is Detective Sergeant Hamish Kerr, one of Inspector McLeod's best men."

"Pleased to make your acquaintance," Kerr murmured, also extending a hand to Peregrine.

"So, is the inspector anywhere about?" Adam went on, casting about with an inquiring look as they moved on past the constable.

"Not here, sir. He went on up to the Angler Hotel about half an hour ago. Shall I send one of my lads to fetch him down for ye?"

Adam shook his head. "He'll want me to have a look around first, I'm sure. Can you tell me briefly what happened?"

An odd, guarded look came over the detective's face.

"It's an odd one, it is, sir. The lads have cordoned off an area inside the ruins, right up at the front. Forensic chaps were there for more'n an hour. Damnedest thing I ever saw—pardoning the language, sir."

Adam controlled a droll smile. "Why, Hamish, I do believe you're shocked—a police officer of your experience and acumen!"

"It—wasn't natural, sir," Kerr muttered. "I dinnae like it at all."

"So I gather." Adam glanced around casually, noting Peregrine's strained look of curiosity. "Well, why don't we start by letting me read over the incident report, and then Mr. Lovat and I will take a look around. You and I have worked on odd cases before, Hamish."

"Och, aye, sir, that we have."

Without further ado, the sergeant conducted them into the shelter of the entrance kiosk behind the gate. The abbey's custodian was sitting on a stool behind the counter, complaining to a constable in uniform.

"It makes honest, God-fearin' folk wonder what this world's coming to," he was saying. "*I've* never seen anything like it."

The constable merely shrugged. Sergeant Kerr reached around his subordinate and plucked a paper-laden clipboard off the counter top.

"Here's the report, Sir Adam," he said as he handed it over. He added with a grimace, "If ye ask me, somebody's been watching too many late-night horror videos. Who'd have thought we'd wind up with a grave-robbing in a quiet, law-abiding place like this?"

A grave-robbing? Conscious of a prickling at the base of his skull, Adam skimmed down the page, tilting it so that Peregrine could read over his shoulder. The account was stark in the manner of police reports everywhere. Under cover of last night's fog, some person or persons unknown had penetrated the confines of Melrose Abbey, either by climbing the fence separating the south burying ground from an access alley or by coming through a gate found open by the main road, to the north. Once inside, they had dug up a section of the floor in the northeast chapel to unearth a twelfth-century stone coffin. The coffin, according to the report, now lay broken and empty.

"The body that apparently was *in* the coffin turned up in the wine bar up at the Angler," the sergeant informed them. "It's that badly decomposed, it's no much more than a skeleton. We're all of us still trying to work out how the pranksters who dug it up could ha' gotten it out of the ground and up the road, still in one piece." He paused to shake his head. "Really makes ye wonder who'd want to do such a thing in the first place. And why."

"Indeed." Adam handed the report back, his expression inscrutable. "Thanks very much, Hamish. Now let's have a look at that grave site."

The detective sergeant led the way down through the ruins, along the nave toward the desecrated chapel by the northeast angle of the transept. As they approached the restraining lines of yellow tape strung at the crossing, Adam became aware of a subliminal chill in the air that had nothing to do with the weather.

Black Wards ahead, decaying but still potent! By all the gods that ever were, could someone really have been so foolish as to abandon a magical operation without properly dismantling it first?

Shoving his gloved hands into his coat pockets again, Adam drew a deep breath and made an invisible ritual sign of personal warding, briefly turning then to glance at Peregrine matter-of-factly, just before they reached the barrier tapes.

"Hold up just a moment, Peregrine. Do you see that frieze back there? Yes, that one, just above the side altar. I'd like you to make a sketch of it before we get involved with making any pictorial records of the grave-site itself."

He was careful to make it sound like a casual request. None the wiser, Peregrine obediently turned back and went to do as Adam had asked. With the young artist's attention safely occupied elsewhere, at least for a few moments, Adam continued with Kerr and bent his gaze on the space the police had cordoned off, letting his subtler perceptions come into play. As he had sensed from farther back, the area immediately surrounding the opened grave was overshadowed by a lingering pall of baleful psychic energy.

So. The force of what the perpetrators had left behind

was definitely on the wane, but there was still sufficient residual power in it to inflict a severe shock on anyone unshielded yet sensible to such things, as Peregrine would be. Kerr, fortunately, was either oblivious or naturally shielded. Adam wondered what McLeod's initial reaction had been.

"I'll wait here, sir," Kerr said, catching hold of the tape and lifting it so Adam could duck under. "Shall I pass Mr. Lovat, when he's finished?"

"Yes, thank you," Adam replied. At the same time, he reached deeper into his right-hand pocket and closed his gloved hand around a piece of lodestone the size and shape of a large wolf's tooth. As he advanced cautiously toward the wavering wards the graverobbers had left, he casually withdrew his hands from his pockets, keeping the lodestone palmed where Kerr would not be able to see it. He halted just short of contact to murmur an invocation that was already ancient when the great library of the Ptolemies went up in flames.

The words invested the lodestone with a spiritual potency equivalent to the drawing power of a magnet. Adam waited until he felt a lively quiver at the center of his hand, then shifted his grip. Holding the tooth-stone like a sword hilt, his first finger extended along its length, he extended it until the tip penetrated the shadowy field in front of him.

The shield imploded like a soap bubble, totally silent. He could feel the lodestone absorbing the residue of force. A moment later, all traces of malignant energy had vanished. Grimly satisfied, ignoring Kerr's puzzled glance, Adam pocketed the lodestone and moved forward again to the side of the grave-opening.

It came as no surprise to see that the pit was circumscribed by splashes of what could only be blood. The array of burnt-out tapers and the black triangle chalked at one side of the opening bore further witness to a profane act of summoning.

His patrician face grimly intent, Adam knelt down and peered into the grave itself. The up-ended slab of granite had required no little effort to raise and prop against the side of the pit. The stone coffin it had covered was roughly trapezoidal, with a circular area cut out at the head end and a great crack splitting it in two. It was like a hundred others Adam had seen over the years, many of them in this very church yard. The one thing of which Adam was certain was that its occupant had been unlike any ordinary man.

The sound of footsteps crunching on gravel interrupted his speculation, and he glanced back to see Peregrine slipping under the tapes to join him at the side of the opened grave pit.

"Here's the sketch of that frieze you asked for," the young artist began, flourishing his sketchbook. "I can't think why you wanted it—it isn't very old—but I—"

As he fell abruptly silent, Adam rose and turned in a single fluid movement. Peregrine had stopped short in his tracks. He was fumbling with his drawing pad again, hazel eyes wide and intent behind his spectacles as he scanned the desecrated chapel, seemingly transfixed. After a breathless moment, he whipped out his pencil and began to sketch rapidly.

Adam sidled around behind Peregrine and stole a swift glance over his shoulder. A scene was beginning to take shape under the artist's rapidly moving pencil: a small group of indistinct figures gathered around an open grave.

Adam realized what was happening and backed away. Leaving the younger man to work on without interruption, he ducked back under the tapes and withdrew to the nave where Sergeant Kerr was waiting for them.

"I think I've seen all I need to see here," he informed McLeod's subordinate. "As soon as Mr. Lovat is finished, we'll be on our way. You said I might find Inspector McLeod at the Angler Hotel?"

Kerr nodded. "Aye, sir. It's just a wee walk from here. I'd leave the car, if I was you. Head straight up Abbey Street till ye get to the square. The Angler's the big white place on yer right, just opposite the Mercat Cross."

Out of the corner of his eye, Adam could see that Peregrine had put his pencil away and was now folding over the cover to his sketchbook.

"Thanks very much for showing us around," he told the

sergeant. "Mr. Lovat and I can find our own way out to the street. . . ."

The Angler Hotel was easy to locate. It was a comfortable, prosperous-looking place that boasted a restaurant, dining room, and wine bar on the ground floor. A number of cars were drawn up in front of the building. Scanning the array of vehicles present, Adam recognized the big white Range Rover with police plates as the one McLeod regularly used on official business outside the city of Edinburgh. They found McLeod himself in the hotel foyer, hemmed in between a delegation from the town council and a pair of local journalists armed with notebooks.

"Aye, it was a ghoulish prank," McLeod was saying grimly, "and rest assured we'll do our best to see that there aren't any more incidents of this kind. That's why I've come down from Edinburgh to assist with the investigation."

He flashed a look in Adam's direction and drew himself up. "We're looking into the possibility that the perpetrators of last night's act of vandalism may be members of an itinerant gang of some sort. But that's all I'm prepared to say to anyone at this point. You'll get more facts if and when we have them."

He cut short any attempts to question him further with a curt wave of the hand, and stepped briskly between the two reporters to join Adam and Peregrine by the main entrance to the hotel.

"Adam, am I glad to see you!" McLeod said. "I hope no one's had the brass neck to keep you waiting."

Adam shook his head. "Not in the least. Noel, I'd like you to meet Peregrine Lovat, a young artist of considerable promise. I hope you don't mind that I've brought him along."

"I suspect that you have excellent reasons," McLeod replied, subjecting Peregrine to a shrewd look as he extended a blunt-fingered hand to deliver a firm handshake. "I remember you, Mr. Lovat. You were up in the visitor's gallery at the High Court last week, while evidence was being presented in the Sherbourne case. We were supposed to have lunch."

Peregrine looked a little surprised. "That's right, sir." He cast an oblique glance at Adam, and added neutrally, "I was there to do some portrait studies."

"Well, I hope you weren't put off by what you must have overheard in the courtroom. Not if you're here to help out in *this* case."

Before Peregrine could respond to this ominous-sounding remark, Adam interposed.

"We've already been up to the abbey," he said briskly. "Is there any place around here where we can talk in privacy?"

"There's the lounge," McLeod said, indicating the indoor entrance with a jerk of his chin. "In view of what happened there last night, it's been declared off limits to the rest of humanity until I say otherwise."

In spite of himself, Adam almost smiled. "That's sufficiently secure for me," he told McLeod. "Lead the way."

The lounge was a spacious, oblong room, with red-curtained windows and a stone fireplace at the far end. A few feet to the left of the threshold, some anonymous forensics officer had drawn the splayed outline of a human body in white chalk on the red carpet.

"That's the place where the corpse decided to lie down," McLeod said. He favored Adam with a darkling look and scowled. "I told you it was only a matter of time before something happened that was going to be difficult to explain to the press. I'm having the devil's own time convincing the locals that this whole incident wasn't really as uncanny as it looked."

Adam pulled out a wooden chair and sat down, his gesture inviting the others to do the same.

"What exactly *did* happen?" he asked.

"You're not going to like this, any more than I did." McLeod snared himself a stool at the bar and set an elbow on the counter top.

"This place is licensed to stay open till two," he explained. "Round about half past one, according to the barman, he and his customers heard a scrabbling at the door. One of the late-night patrons went over to open it. The corpse was standing up on the threshold. As soon as the door swung wide, it tottered forward a couple of steps and collapsed on the spot indicated."

His jaw tightened. "Needless to say, the witnesses in the bar were more than a wee bit upset by the incident. The barman called the hotel manager, and she called the police. Fortunately, one of my own men got wind of it pretty early in the game, and he called me at home to tell me about it. That was at about three. At that point, they still didn't know where the body had come from."

"So you came down to check it out," Adam said.

McLeod nodded. "When my man was telling me about it, all kinds of alarm bells started going off inside my head. You know the feeling. Anyway, by the time I got here, one of the local constables had arranged for the cadaver to be removed to the morgue at Borders General, while the others on night duty went on a tour of the cemeteries in the area. No one thought to look in the abbey at first, because there haven't been any burials there for years—just in the churchyard outside. As soon as it got light, though, it didn't take them long to discover the excavation left behind inside the abbey, where the body started out on its travels."

As he paused for breath, Peregrine could contain himself no longer.

"Surely you're not saying that the corpse really *did* walk here to the hotel under its own power!" he said incredulously.

McLeod glared at him from under grizzled eyebrows. "You can bet your last copper we're not! The official story is that the whole affair was engineered by a band of malicious punks, who made it out to *look* as though that's what happened." He shrugged. "That version *might* stick, if we repeat it often enough—especially since the only people in a position to gainsay us are a handful of late-night drinkers whose view of the whole situation is bound to have been at least somewhat affected by alcohol."

"An account of a walking corpse is certainly too outlandish to win widespread public acceptance," Adam agreed. "Even though at least two of us in this room know that it could very well be true."

Peregrine gasped. He opened his mouth, as though to speak, and then thought better of it.

"This business is far from finished," Adam continued soberly. "I think I'd better see the body, as soon as possible."

McLeod nodded in agreement, getting to his feet with a scraping of the legs of his bar stool.

"Right you are. We'll take my car, to make it official."

CHAPTER ELEVEN

TWENTY minutes later, a pathologist at Borders General Hospital ushered Inspector Noel McLeod and his associates into the chilly confines of the hospital mortuary. Peregrine followed close behind Adam, still clutching his sketchbook. He had not dared to look closely at his latest drawings, so disturbing had they been, and Adam had grimly bade him close the book after only a cursory glance. The smells here in the morgue made him a little queasy, especially in light of how the case was developing.

"Inspector McLeod would like to see the body that was brought in from the Angler earlier this morning," their escort told the attendant. "Sir Adam Sinclair and Mr. Lovat are his associates."

The attendant raised an eyebrow and indicated one of the smaller autopsy rooms opening off the cold room.

"He's in there, doc," the man said, switching on the lights. "I don't know what his story is, but I'd say he's been dead a long time."

The harsh overhead lights revealed a sheet-shrouded form lying on a stainless steel table. The attendant came with them into the room, starting to reach for the sheet, but McLeod tapped him on the shoulder and shook his head in dismissal.

"We'd like to view the body in private, if you don't mind. Sir Adam is a physician. It's all right."

The attendant exchanged glances with the pathologist, but neither made any objection. As soon as they were gone,

Adam approached the table and carefully drew back the concealing drape. McLeod registered no surprise, for he had seen the body in the lounge, but Adam exhaled softly through pursed lips. Peregrine took one shrinking look, then hastily averted his gaze from what lay revealed.

Mouldering shreds of a shroud and a monkish black robe hung in threadbare tatters about a form that was little more than a skeleton held together by a desiccated sheath of leathery skin. The bones protruded through the skin in places—the frame of a man near Peregrine's height but heavier, suggesting that the living individual had been sturdy and muscular in his prime. Hands like fossilized claws lay curled in stiff knots over the jutting flange of the breastbone. Empty eyesockets gaped wide and dark above a lipless death's-head grin full of yellowing teeth.

Adam studied the body for several minutes in somber concentration, unmoving, striving to read signs invisible to the naked eye. When, at last, he spoke, his voice was a low murmur of most bitter condemnation.

"It's bad enough that the perpetrators of this crime had sufficient power at their command to conjure a dead man's spirit back to the body's resting place," he said quietly. "It is infinitely worse that they were able to force that same spirit back into this wretched house of bones."

The force of his anger throbbed in the air like thunder, though his volume never went above normal conversational levels. McLeod remained impassive, but Peregrine shivered slightly, not daring to say a word.

"This is as sordid a piece of work as I've ever had the misfortune to encounter in recent years," Adam continued, in the same freezing tone. "It is the work, moreover, of dangerous neophytes. Only someone too arrogant to reckon with his own limitations would ever have attempted this rite of summoning, given the identity of the individual he was trying to bend to his will."

Peregrine finally summoned enough courage to give the mummified body a more direct look, shuddering as a wave of chill shivered down his spine, like the touch of icy fingers.

"Who—" he managed to whisper—"who *was* he, then?"

Adam did not answer. The expression on his stern face was one of shuttered introspection, as though he were privately considering alternate solutions to a difficult problem. McLeod's lip curled in a smile completely devoid of humor.

"You ought to go back to school, laddie. Melrose Abbey is traditionally the resting place of the wizard Michael Scot."

Peregrine blinked. "Michael Scot?"

This time the question penetrated Adam's reverie. "None other than Scotland's most famous magician," he informed Peregrine. "He was a man of many parts: scholar, alchemist, physician, and demonologist—not to mention sometime court astrologer to the Holy Roman Emperor Frederick II. In terms of the sheer breadth of his learning, he was arguably one of the most illustrious adepts of the twelfth century."

"The twelfth century!" Peregrine's eyes widened in disbelief. "But that's—what?—seven or eight hundred years ago! Surely there should be nothing left of him but dust by now!"

"Not necessarily." Adam's dark eyes resumed their intense study of the object of discussion. "Quite apart from the possibility that conditions of burial sometimes lead to extraordinary preservation or even mummification of bodies, you should recall that in Christian tradition—to cite a single example—it's by no means unusual for the bodies of saints and mystics to resist corruption. In fact, the phenomenon has long been accepted as a posthumous sign of an individual's spiritual potency. Scot was a wizard of incredible potency—which could explain the survival of his corporeal remains."

As Peregrine digested this bit of revelation, Adam's gaze shifted to an unfocused spot somewhere off to his right.

"One thing does disturb me profoundly, however," he went on quietly. "All my reading suggests that Michael Scot most assuredly was not a man lightly to be trifled with. Whoever summoned his spirit would have had to overcome massive resistance. I keep asking myself how the deuce they managed to do it!"

"They would've needed some kind of power focus," McLeod murmured. "Maybe a talisman of some sort—maybe even something that once belonged to Scot."

Adam nodded thoughtfully. "A power focus—aye. That would certainly account for a lot. I can't say I've ever heard that anyone has anything that Scot once owned, but—dear *Jesu*, that's it. The Hepburn Sword. That's why someone stole the Hepburn Sword."

His gaze met McLeod's.

"Oh, bloody hell," the inspector said succinctly.

After a brief, stunned silence, Peregrine whispered, "The Hepburn Sword? Isn't that the one you were reading about in the paper, just last week?"

"Yes."

"But, that was a—a sixteenth-century weapon—a swept-hilt rapier." He blinked owlishly at Adam. "You said Scot lived in the twelfth century."

"So I did," Adam replied. "However, I think you may have misconstrued what I said about the requirements for a power focus. It isn't necessary that the connection with Scot be one of previous ownership. Think about the owner of the Hepburn Sword."

"The Earl of Bothwell?" Peregrine said.

Adam nodded. "The same. In his day, Francis Hepburn—the earl of Bothwell—was notorious as a black adept. It was widely believed that he held regular intercourse with the dead. He was one of the foremost wizards of his day. Eventually, the combined forces of the Church and the Law gathered sufficient evidence against him to warrant his arrest. He only narrowly escaped to France, leaving behind everything he owned—including his sword."

He cocked his head at the artist, his keen gaze sharpening. "Peregrine, something has just occurred to me. Let's have a closer look at those sketches you made back at the abbey."

Mystified, Peregrine produced his sketchbook, shivering as Adam turned back the cover. The first sketch, finished now since Adam's initial glimpse of it in the chapel, showed a group of men in short, hooded capelets ranged about the excavated grave-slot. The leader stood at one side of the pit, where a triangle had been drawn on the ground. He wore a medallion about his neck and a ring on his right hand. With the same hand he grasped the hilt of a thin-bladed sword, its point directed toward the open grave.

Adam peered at the sword, trying for greater detail, then began leafing through the rest of the drawings—close-up studies drawn from the same scene. From among these, Adam singled out a detailed sketch of the sword itself: an elegant weapon with a swept hilt, crafted in ornate Florentine style. So far as Adam knew, Peregrine had never actually set eyes on the Hepburn Sword; yet he had drawn it to perfection. Just to be certain, Adam offered the sketch for McLeod's perusal.

"What about it, Noel? Is this the blade that went missing from the museum?"

McLeod gave a brisk nod. "That's it, right enough." He transferred his gaze to Peregrine. "You're good at your work, lad. I'm beginning to understand why Adam brought you along."

Peregrine flushed slightly under the inspector's sharp look.

"Maybe there's something else, too, then," he said, "if I was right about the sword. There was a symbol—an animal's head of some kind—inscribed on both the medallion and the ring. Try as I would, I couldn't quite make out what it was. I'm sorry."

"No need to apologize," Adam said, looking again at the sketches. "The fact that you couldn't see it clearly probably has nothing to do with you. They had very strong wards all around the working area. The sword they used was Francis Hepburn's, though, beyond all doubt. And that is sufficient to confirm our theory."

"Aye, you have to give them credit for ruthless invention, whoever they were," McLeod agreed, glowering down at the master-drawing and curling a lip. "What better way to control one dead wizard than with another dead wizard's sword?"

Adam nodded. "My thought, precisely. Almost any object used in a magical connection will pick up a charge of residual power after a while—and Francis Hepburn's sword would become a particularly potent weapon. Those who stole the sword must have tapped into that energy to bind Michael Scot to their will."

"But, *why*?" Peregrine asked, repressing a shudder. "What do you suppose they were after?"

"Well, Scot spent a lifetime collecting rare and dangerous lore from all manner of sources," Adam said. "Just offhand, I'd guess our intrepid graverobbers were probably after Scot's masterbook of spells. Many of the legends claim it was buried with him. Of course, some of the legends say he was buried at Glenluce Abbey rather than Melrose," he added, "which goes to show that one can't necessarily trust legends."

McLeod nodded ponderously. "That's true, in general. However, I'm inclined to think it *was* the spell book they were after. The question is, did they get it?"

"I don't think so," Adam said. "If it had been buried with him, there would have been no need to bring him back. They would have taken the book and been on their way. My guess is that when the book wasn't to be found in the coffin, the graverobbers used the sword to summon Scot back to his body, with the intention of forcing him to disclose the book's present whereabouts.

"I think he must have been obliged to tell them, too," he continued, his mouth tightening. "His interrogators left the graveside in a hurry—too eager to get on with the hunt to bother tying up loose ends."

"Which explains why Scot's corpse went walking," McLeod finished. He gave his head a wondering shake. "Didn't they realize that might happen?"

"I don't think they much cared," Adam said. The look in his dark eyes was steely. "That piece of criminal negligence is going to cost them, if I have anything to say about it."

"W—what are you going to do?" Peregrine whispered.

"Well, first of all, we must finish what they failed to do, and set Scot's spirit free."

McLeod made a noise under his breath that might have masked a strong expletive.

"Good God, Adam," he sputtered, "are you telling us

that Scot's spirit is still bound to *that*"—he indicated the shriveled corpse on the table, "—even as we're standing here?"

Adam shoved his hands into his trouser pockets, nodding soberly. "I didn't come prepared for anything like this, I'll confess," he admitted. "We'll just have to improvise, and hope we'll be able to undo what's been done. If we're particularly lucky, Scot may be able to tell us who summoned him, and where they might have gone from here. If not . . ."

His voice trailed off as he considered how to approach the task set for him. Peregrine's eyes were wide and frightened behind his spectacles, but Adam did not think the young artist would bolt. McLeod was his usual pillar of inscrutable support. After a moment, Adam squared his shoulders and drew himself up to his full height, a plan taking shape in his mind.

"All right," he told his two companions. "I'm going to see what kind of a rapport I can establish with Scot. Peregrine, I want you to stand by with your sketchbook. You know enough now to recognize when your deep sight is about to key in. Draw whatever strong images come to mind—in as full detail as you can manage. It may very well be vitally important."

When Peregrine had given him a nervous nod, Adam turned to McLeod. "Noel, I may need to call upon you later, but for now I'd be obliged if you would simply guard the door. This is going to be difficult enough, as it is, without risking interruptions."

The inspector nodded. "Right you are, Adam. Short of a construction crew with a bulldozer, *no one* gets into this room!"

Adam accepted this assurance with a fleeting smile, waiting until his two aides had taken up their respective positions before drawing his sapphire signet ring from his trouser pocket. He fingered it absently for a moment before slipping it onto the third finger of his right hand. Then, with the first two fingers of that hand, he traced once around the edge of the stainless steel table, moving clockwise from the head, before laying both hands flat on the shiny metal surface, as if it were an altar.

For a moment he remained thus, head erect, eyes closed, while he drew a succession of long measured breaths, sinking past surface consciousness toward levels of deeper awareness. From the island of silence at the center of his being, he raised his brief prayer of invocation:

"Star of the Sea, Wisdom most potent, be thou a light before me and behind me," he whispered. "Be thou a beacon in the darkness, a bright star to guide and protect me. . . ."

At first he could sense nothing beyond the shadowy sea-surge that was his own unconscious, ceaselessly rolling, ebb and flow, in the waiting stillness. Then, all at once, a breath of wind stirred in the darkness, moving over the face of the deep and bringing with it the invigorating kiss of inspiration. As he spoke the Word of his grade in his heart of hearts, the dawning came.

At first he could see nothing for the radiance that surrounded him. Then, as the brightness subsided, he found himself standing in spirit at the center of a bare stone chamber. Before him was a massive door, bound with iron like a dungeon port. On an iron peg to the left of the door hung a heavy, rust-encrusted key.

The atmosphere within the chamber was charged with roiling anger. Adam felt it in his nerve ends like the ionizing crackle of sheet lightning. The source of that anger lay on the other side of the dungeon door. He was seeing in symbols, but he could entertain no doubt that the identity generating that anger once had answered to the name of Michael Scot.

Adam studied the scene for a long moment, weighing up the psychic reality underlying the visual imagery. Symbolic logic dictated that he should take up the key and unlock the door in order to set Scot free. He distrusted the apparent simplicity of the solution, but could find no hidden alternatives. In the end, grimly aware that he was courting danger, he braced himself and reached for the key. It came away in his hand without resistance.

Adam mentally breathed a sigh of relief and examined the key more closely. It was solidly made and intricately whorled beneath the rust, but even under close scrutiny its precise form eluded the eye. Conscious of a warning tingle at the base of his skull, he set the key in the lock and gave it a strong turn to the right.

The mechanism yielded and the door burst wide. In the same instant, Adam's whole frame of reference exploded in flames.

Fire crackled and surged all around him. He tried to elude it and discovered that he was bound fast to a tall stake. The twin towers of a gothic cathedral loomed above him, wreathed in clouds of greasy smoke. In the courtyard below, masses of spectators were howling blasphemous abuse in the language of another age.

Searing heat lashed out at his feet and legs, charring the flesh on his bones. Within seconds his whole lower body was engulfed in a devouring conflagration. Ashes choked the tortured screams that rose in his throat as the flames rose higher. There was no escape . . . no escape. . . .

NO!

Somewhere in the midst of his agony, the voice of reason made itself heard. *This isn't Paris!* shouted the modern part of his mind. *Paris was then. This is now!*

NOW!

You're not Jauffre de Saint Clair! You're Adam! Sir Adam Sinclair—laird of Strathmourne—Baron of Templemor—Master of the Hunt!

Clinging to these phrases that were his present identity, he recited his name and titles over and over like a litany, denying the past that was past and affirming the present. The flames wavered momentarily in the face of his conviction, and he used that brief instant of respite to call up the saving powers that were the gift of Light. New strength welled up within him, like a spring of living water. The bonds that held him frayed and broke; the fire flickered out in a malevolent hiss of quenched energies. Like the phoenix of the Sinclair crest, his liberated spirit took flight out of the cinders of a previous existence. When he snapped back to normal consciousness, he was back in the confines of the morgue at Borders General Hospital.

Peregrine was staring at him, his expression acutely

concerned. As soon as he saw that Adam's eyes were open, he started forward.

"Are you all right?" he demanded.

As Adam nodded a little dazedly, McLeod's face appeared beside Peregrine's.

"What the devil happened? You cried out. I was afraid someone from the hospital staff was going to be down on us."

Adam drew a long, shuddering breath, still struggling to restore calm. "For a moment, I thought the past was about to repeat itself," he said thickly.

"You mean your own past." McLeod made it a curt statement. "What was it then, some kind of trap?"

"Not exactly." Adam frowned, remembering. "Not even so much a trap as a—an associated effect of the binding spell our arrogant friends used to restrain Scot." At McLeod's look of question, he groped for a clearer explanation.

"Let me try it another way," he ventured. "Let's say that the spell is designed to—reawaken resonances from the past. Anyone entering the field risks reliving some episode from his personal history."

"You think they were expecting interference, then?" McLeod asked.

Adam shook his head, still thoughtful. "Not on that level, certainly. I doubt they even expected knowledgeable investigation. If they had, it would have cost them far less effort simply to tidy up at the gravesite, rather than taking the time to set a deliberate trap. I'm not even certain *that* was deliberate. It may simply have been left over from what they did to compel Scot back. It's precisely this random quality to their actions that's going to make them difficult to predict and dangerous to follow. We'd better be on our guard from here on out."

Peregrine nodded, his expression one of mingled awe and uncertainty, and McLeod grunted by way of assent.

"What about Scot, then?"

"I've only broken a part of the binding," Adam replied. "There's still the physical unbinding to be done. It shouldn't be as tricky as the first, though. And if I can, I'd like to find out what he told them."

McLeod favored Adam with an appraising look, then shrugged, apparently satisfied.

"If you say so. I'll mind the door, as before."

He moved back to his post. Peregrine watched in owl-eyed silence as Adam drew a deep breath and then went through a series of ritual gestures that culminated in the tracing of a pentagram and then a circled cross in the air over the body. After that, the older man inscribed a third symbol on Scot's forehead with his thumb, then touched the thumb and fourth finger of his right hand to Scot's temples and closed his eyes with a murmured word of command too low for Peregrine to catch.

The body on the table began to shudder. The lipless mouth moved, yellow teeth chattering. The shuddering mounted to a wracking paroxysm that lasted for several seconds. Then all at once the body fell still, with only the bony fingers left twitching feebly.

Adam remained motionless for the space of several heartbeats, then opened his eyes. He took his hand away from Scot's forehead and glanced at McLeod.

"Sorry, but I'm going to need you, Noel," he said softly. "Scot's willing—eager, even—to communicate with us, but this body is too far gone. Will you be his voice?"

McLeod grimaced and gave a resigned sigh. "I was afraid it might come to this," he said, summoning Peregrine to take his place, and bending briefly to check the door lock again before crossing to join Adam. "It's a good thing the minister of my kirk isn't here to see this, or he'd have me thrown out of the General Assembly."

He made a ritual sign of recognition as he approached the table that had become their working altar, and the juxtaposition of magical gesture and pious concern elicited a faint smile on Adam's part as he answered the salute.

"Never mind the minister of the kirk," he said lightly. "What about your police superiors?"

"Aye, they'd have their knickers in a twist, too! Let's get on with it."

Moving around to the other side of the table, so that the

body lay between them, McLeod took off his glasses and slipped them into a breast pocket, then set his hands on the table's edge as Adam had done, closing his eyes. Almost at once, his respiration settled into the slow, measured rhythm Peregrine had begun to associate with the onset of a trance. Adam's face took on a relaxed, dreamlike appearance as well, though he did not close his eyes.

Silence profound settled over the room. After a long further moment, Adam reached across to lightly touch McLeod between the eyes. Then he set his hands back on the table, glancing briefly at the corpse between them.

"The door stands open to receive you," he intoned. "Enter the vessel without fear."

A heartbeat's pause. Then a shiver passed through McLeod's sturdy frame. He inhaled deeply and opened his eyes. Across the room, Peregrine stifled a gasp, for the lively intelligence reflected in the darting blue eyes was no longer that of the police inspector.

"Speak, brother," Adam's voice urged softly.

McLeod's lips parted. For an instant no sound came out. Then an unfamiliar voice spoke in tones of imperious urgency.

"What is this place?" demanded the being that had taken command of McLeod's body. "Where am I, in space and time?"

"You are at Melrose," said Adam, his own voice deep and even. "But eight centuries have passed since you were laid to rest there."

"And how long since the summoning?"

"We do not know for certain," Adam said. "At least twelve or fourteen hours, perhaps as long as eighteen."

"Eighteen hours!" Something like fear flashed behind the blue eyes. Then the piercing gaze shifted, ranging beyond Adam and Peregrine as though searching distractedly for something at a distance.

"The cord. . . . The silver cord is fraying!" muttered the voice of Michael Scot. "The heart is faltering—"

"The heart!" Adam stiffened visibly, his next words sharp with concern. "Have you, then, an identity in this present age?"

"Yes!" The presence that was Michael Scot sent a tortured shudder through its host body, growing distraction in the voice. "A child now . . . only a child. And death is perilously near!"

This declaration sent a cold chill racing up Peregrine's spine. His vision blurred. In his mind's eye, he saw the image of a young girl, barely into puberty. She was lying motionless on a hospital bed, in the icy grip of a deep coma, her face blanched white under an adolescent powdering of freckles. . . .

"Time runs short," the voice of Michael Scot murmured. "I must return at once, or abide another turning of the Wheel." The voice throbbed with sudden, desperate appeal. "By all that is holy, if thou be truly brother, I charge thee to release me! Release me, while I yet have a living body to return to!"

"And so we shall," Adam promised in swift assurance, "but first I beg you to tell us—if you know—who summoned you and why."

"Rievers from the Dark Road. . . ." Scot's tone seemed increasingly distracted. "They wanted my book, my gold—the philosophers' gold that is the secret to unlock all other secrets! They bound me, and I was powerless to hold back the knowledge of the treasure's resting place."

Scot's voice broke into a dry sob, and McLeod's blue eyes closed as a spasm of pain wracked his body.

"The book and the gold are guarded," the wizard's voice continued raggedly, "but the Rievers may yet prevail, through the power they have usurped." The eyes blazed up at Adam once again. "Swear to me that thou shalt pursue them, and I shall give thee freely what they took from me by force!"

"I swear it!" Adam said. "By my Office, as Master of the Hunt, I swear that I will do my utmost to see justice done."

This declaration won a grim nod of acceptance from Scot. Triumphant, he turned his compulsion on Peregrine. All at once the artist found himself entrapped by the burning gaze, unable to look away. Pain lanced his eyes, bringing with it a flood-tide of mental pictures, compelling him to put pencil to paper. His present surroundings forgotten, he lost himself in a feverish race to sketch down everything that passed before his inner eye.

A castle on a low cliff . . . a sweep of dark water below. A crescent of pebbled beach . . . a rock-bound cave. His pencil flying, Peregrine filled the next several pages of his sketchbook at a speed he could not control. By the time Scot at last released him, his whole hand was aching with strain. Without volition, his fingers flexed to relieve their cramping, his pencil slipping from fingers too numb to retain their grip.

The pencil struck the bare floor with a wooden clatter. Adam shot Peregrine a lightning glance, then returned to face Scot. For an instant they locked eyes. Then Adam made a sign between them in the air.

"By the authority of the Seven do I release you, brother," he declared in a deep voice that rang clear as a bell. "Go in peace, to fulfill your appointed destiny."

Air left McLeod's lungs in a rush. He breathed in again sharply and lurched against the autopsy table. The corpse before him seemed all at once to fold inward on itself. Under Peregrine's incredulous gaze, it crumbled in seconds into so much powdery grey dust.

In the same instant, McLeod lost his precarious balance and crumpled to his knees, his breath now coming swift and hard. Adam had darted around the head of the table at the first sign of distress, and had an arm under his even as he collapsed in a faint. Propping the inspector upright against his knee, he groped in his pocket for an ammonia capsule, which he snapped open with a flick of his thumb and passed under McLeod's nose.

"Steady, old friend," Adam murmured, as McLeod twitched and tried to escape the pungent aroma. Relentlessly Adam brought it under his patient's nose again. This time the inspector managed a speechless jerk of his head and opened his eyes, though they still were not quite focusing properly.

"Good man!" Adam's voice reassured, as he shifted to press two fingers to the other man's carotid pulse. "You're doing just fine. Don't try to move too quickly, though. I think he must have pulled out faster than you were expecting."

"Och, aye, he did that," McLeod muttered, sitting up cautiously with Adam's help and taking several deep, ragged breaths. "God, I hate it when they do that! My head feels like to explode."

"You'll be all right in a few minutes," Adam replied. "Do you want to try standing?"

"Aye."

With Adam's help, McLeod got his feet under him and climbed to his feet, bracing himself on the edge of the table again, apparently unperturbed that the body was now but a narrow mound of dust. Adam, when he was satisfied that the other man had his legs firmly under him again, stood back and banished the protective warding on the table with a swift sequence of gestures. Only then did he seem to remember that Peregrine was there.

"I hope all this didn't frighten you," he said. "What did you get?"

The artist was clutching his sketchbook to his chest like a life-preserver, his owl-eyed concern for McLeod only gradually fading as he realized the inspector was safe and that Adam was speaking to him. In response to Adam's look of inquiry, he blinked and hazarded a wan grin.

"Well, I got *something*, from *somewhere*," he said, looking from one to the other of them uncertainly. "Inspector, when you started staring at me, pictures came into my head, and I couldn't make them stop. And then my—hand started drawing, and I couldn't make *it* stop, either."

McLeod chuckled mirthlessly. "It wasn't *me*, laddie," he murmured.

"You're implying that it *was* Michael Scot, then," Peregrine said uneasily. "I suppose that's a relief, because—well, I certainly didn't dream this up by myself." He shifted his grip to the side edges of the sketchbook's cover, his hands shaking.

"Anyway, whatever it was, and wherever it came from, it's all here," he said, raising his chin defiantly. "Do you want to take a look?"

At this declaration of acceptance of what had occurred, Adam permitted himself a faint sigh of relief.

"Well done," he said approvingly. "You've gone far beyond the *how* and *why* and focused on the *what*. But I think we'd better wait until we've finished up at the abbey. There are still a few loose ends that we wouldn't want innocent folk tripping over, just because we didn't do our clean-up properly."

He turned to McLeod. "Are you up to moving yet?"

The inspector looked up from adjusting his tie and putting his glasses back on.

"Aye, I'm fine now, thank you. All I needed was a bit of a breather." He surveyed the dusty outline on the table and pursed his lips thoughtfully. "I suppose that was bound to happen, once the body was exposed for a time to the air—as any archaeologist will tell you."

He and Adam traded knowing glances.

"I'll be happy to certify that explanation," Adam said. "In the meantime, we'd better be getting back to the abbey."

"Right," said McLeod. "Once you and I are finished there, I'll arrange for Scot's dust to be returned to its resting place. . . ."

Chapter Twelve

BACK at the abbey, Peregrine was left to play the role of fascinated observer while Adam and McLeod systematically went back over Scot's disturbed gravesite, this time countering the residues left behind by the grave robbers with banishing signs of their own. Most of their movements were too deft and subtle for Peregrine's eye to catch, but he became gradually aware of a lightening in the atmosphere within the confines of the violated chapel. By the time the two older men had finished, all lingering traces of their adversaries' work had been effectively nullified. As Peregrine wordlessly followed Adam back to the car park, he sensed that a delicate balance had been restored.

By then it was well past one. At Adam's suggestion, the three of them convoyed to the Waverly Hotel for a much-needed meal. McLeod commandeered a small room off the main dining room for their private use; and once their order had been taken, Adam finally allowed Peregrine to bring out his sketchbook.

"Keeping in mind that waitresses will be intruding from time to time, I think it's safe enough to talk here," he said, opening the book. "Now, let's see what we've got."

Peregrine had made five sketches in all. The castle in the first drawing was a simple structure, more fort than fortress, consisting of a squat central bailey enclosed within a dry stone motte. The second presented the same castle from a higher angle, so that they could see that it occupied a high point of ground on a fist-shaped peninsula overlooking a broad expanse of dark water. The third sketch showed the same bluff from the waterside, where a crescent moon of stony beach yielded to burgeoning undergrowth below a beetling outcrop of boulders. The fourth was a more detailed view of the boulders themselves, while the fifth was an interior view of a cave hollowed out in the shape of a horseshoe. It was this fifth drawing that held Adam's gaze the longest.

"This is no ordinary cave," he said, leaving the pad open to that page and tapping the sketch with a fingernail. "Now I understand the full import of what Scot meant, when he said that his book and his gold were protected. Look there."

He pointed to a spot at the entrance of the cave in the picture, where Peregrine's pencil-strokes had come together, apparently at random, to form a curious glyph, like a quatrefoil knot of spidery lines. McLeod adjusted his aviator glasses and subjected the design to closer scrutiny. After a moment, he shook his head.

"If that's a symbol of some sort, I can't say it means anything to me," he said to Adam. "What is it, then?"

Adam's dark eyes had taken on their familiar inner luminance.

"It's a *seamrag*—the sign of the Sidhe," he said, a thin smile plucking at the corners of his mouth. "It would appear, gentlemen, that Scot's spellbook and gold are in the keeping of the 'people of the hills'— the 'unseelie coort' of the fairies."

"Fairies?" Startled, Peregrine regarded Adam with a wary eye, uncertain whether or not this was meant as a joke. He glanced aside at McLeod, but the inspector merely looked intent. Returning his gaze to Adam, the young artist said flatly, "Surely you're not serious."

"On the contrary, I'm completely serious." The light in Adam's eyes hardened to a cool gleam. "However, if you're harboring sentimental visions of pretty little flower-sprites with gauzy wings, I strongly suggest that you dismiss them once and for all. The Sidhe—to give them their ancient Gaelic name—are beings belonging to the elemental order of creation. They wield powers all out of proportion to their manifest size. All of them are capricious. Most of them are dangerous. And some have a lively appetite for human flesh and blood."

Peregrine shifted uncomfortably in his chair, no longer disposed to laugh.

"They would make formidable guardians for any valuable object," Adam continued, "all the more so because they are fiercely—in some cases, murderously—territorial. And they are not to be bought off; one might as well attempt to bribe a brushfire." He sighed.

"It *is*, however, possible to divert them, or even to fight them, provided that one has the appropriate knowledge and sufficient power. Given what our grave robbers were able to accomplish here at Melrose, their leader may well have the necessary resources at his command. Certainly, that's what Scot himself feared. And we have no choice but to proceed on that assumption."

"I'll be happy to proceed however and whenever you say the word," McLeod muttered, "provided that you can tell me *where*."

"This castle is *where*," said Adam, flipping back to the earlier drawings. "The hard part is going to be determining its location in this time period."

McLeod did not seem surprised at this declaration, but Peregrine suddenly looked crestfallen.

"Don't tell me," he said. "I locked in on past-time resonances, rather than the present."

Adam shrugged wistfully. "It isn't your fault. The images that you received were drawn from Scot's own living memories of the place—memories nearly eight hundred years old. The castle that Scot knew almost certainly has changed over the years—if it even still stands. Finding it, or even its former site, is going to present something of a challenge."

Peregrine scowled down at the sketches he had made.

"It's a pity Scot couldn't simply have given us the name of the place."

"You're assuming that it *had* a name, or that it had the same name then that it has now," Adam replied. "Locally, it may have been quite sufficient merely to call it 'the fort,' or 'the castle.' "

He paused to let this point sink in before continuing.

"At any rate, we *haven't* got a name—and we mustn't blame Scot for that. He did the best he could, given his condition at the time. If the situation had been any less critical—if he himself had been in any fit state to sustain further verbal communication—he might conceivably have been able to tell us more, in fuller detail. As it was, he was summoned and bound under torture, and was suffering acutely by the time we got to him. If we'd detained him longer, however worthy our intentions, it would have unjustly prolonged his torment and aggravated the injuries he had already sustained. I was honor-bound to release him when I did."

Peregrine lapsed into thoughtful silence. McLeod picked up the sketch pad and leafed through the drawings again.

"Looks as if we do this the hard way, then, with a magnifying glass and a fine-toothed comb," he said with a sigh. "At least we can eliminate any and all medieval sites that aren't situated near water. I wonder if there'd be any point in my checking these drawings against aerial survey photos of Scottish archaeological sites."

"If all else fails, we'll certainly try that," Adam agreed, as McLeod tossed the pad back on the table between them. "However, there may be a better way."

His two companions eyed him expectantly.

"Fortunately, we do know that Scot's spirit has been reborn in this present time, and is presently a child," Adam said. "If we can locate that child, it's possible I may be able to retrieve sufficient information from his subconscious mind to put us on the right track."

"It's a little girl," Peregrine said, before he could keep the unbidden words from popping out of his mouth.

Both men turned startled glances on him, and Peregrine shrank before their scrutiny in confusion, trying to recapture the image that had flitted in—and out of—his mind, unremembered until just that instant.

"I—before Scot had me start drawing—" he stammered, shaking his head as he tried unsuccessfully to pin down the elusive image. "I had this—this brief flash of—of—a little girl, I think. . . ."

As he looked at Adam in appeal, shaking his head in frustration at not being able to recapture it, Adam glanced beyond him, to see if anyone was coming, then reached over to lay his hand across Peregrine's forehead.

"Close your eyes and relax, Peregrine. Take a deep breath and let it out." He removed his hand as Peregrine obeyed, turning the sketch pad to a fresh page and pushing it across the table top to nudge at the slack hands resting on the table.

"Now, let your mind go back to that room at the hospital, and see the image again that Scot showed you—the image of a little girl who is Scot's present incarnation. Nod when you've got it."

Grim determination played behind the closed eyelids, but then the bronzed head nodded.

"Good." Not taking his eyes from his subject, Adam held out a hand to McLeod for a pen, and put it into Peregrine's hand. "Now, open your eyes and draw what you see. Nothing will distract you until you've finished the drawing."

Dreamily Peregrine opened his eyes, the pen already moving on the blank page before him. Hardly blinking, he bent to his task with single-minded concentration, not looking up even when a waitress brought them water and retreated. As he finished and laid the pen aside, Adam lightly touched his hand.

"Excellent. Now rejoin us, in your normal waking state."

As Peregrine breathed out with a sigh, blinking several times, Adam turned the sketch pad so he and McLeod could look at it. The inspector only shook his head as Peregrine, too, bent to see what he had drawn.

Surrounded by the stark whiteness of a hospital bed, a young girl lay with her eyes closed. She looked to be anything from ten to about fourteen or fifteen, light curls cropped short around her face, a sprinkling of freckles across her nose giving her a slightly gamine look, except for the taut pallor around the mouth, and an impression of tension in the slender body vaguely outlined beneath the sheets. To either side, a few pen strokes suggested the presence of several people keeping watch beside her bed—

whether anxious parents or medical staff was hard to determine, for the ball-point had not allowed of the fine detail Peregrine usually captured with pencil.

"This is very interesting, Peregrine," Adam said, glancing up at him. "This is what you saw, back in the morgue?"

Peregrine nodded. "I'd forgotten, until this very minute. I guess the images of the castle overwhelmed me. Is it useful?"

"Hmmm, it could be. Noel, does this mean anything to you?"

The inspector regretfully shook his head. "Afraid not. It could be any hospital, and any young girl."

"Yes, but it's a *modern* hospital, and it isn't just any young girl," Adam pointed out. "She appears to be Caucasian, perhaps twelve or so, these may be parents to either side, and—what's this at the end of the bed, Peregrine? Is it a chart?"

Startled, Peregrine bent his head to turn the sketch pad and stare. He *had* begun sketching a chart—there, just jutting above the foot of the bed. He *almost*, if he held his head just—so—could bring the chart into focus.

"Adam, put me under again," he whispered, fumbling for a pencil in his pocket.

McLeod raised an eyebrow, and Adam gave the doorway behind Peregrine a surreptitious glance, but then he cupped a restraining hand over Peregrine's wrist.

"Peregrine, what do you see?"

"I can't see it yet," Peregrine whispered. "Just put me under again, *now*! *Deep!*"

McLeod had to work at controlling a smile, for no one ordered Adam Sinclair to do anything, but Adam, after another glance behind his subject, lifted his hand to brush Peregrine's forehead again. The hazel eyes closed immediately, tension draining out of him as if the string had been cut on a puppet.

"That's fine," Adam murmured. "Settle back into trance. You can do this yourself, you know, but for now, I'll talk you through it. Relax and take a deep breath, and feel yourself go twice as deep as you were before. You see something that you didn't notice before. Something that's very important.

"Take another deep breath and go deeper. It's starting to come into focus. Keep taking yourself deeper, refining the image, and when you can see it clearly—draw it."

For several long seconds, nothing outward happened. Eyes closed, Peregrine lowered his forehead to rest on his left hand, that elbow propped on the table. For a full minute and more, by McLeod's watch, as the two older men exchanged speculative glances, all Peregrine did was breathe. Movement behind the closed eyelids suggested intense internal activity, but it was not reflected in any movement of the pencil in his hand.

Then, suddenly, the pencil twitched, the eyelids fluttered and then opened to merest slits, and the pencil hand began sketching feverishly. In far finer detail this time, the foot of the hospital bed emerged from the shaded grey pencil strokes. And at the foot of the bed, not on the chart itself but writ bold on a strip of tape across the top of the clipboard holding the chart, could be read a name: *Talbot, Gillian.*

As Peregrine wound down and the pencil stopped, Adam touched his hand again.

"Are you finished?" he asked softly.

At Peregrine's dazed nod, Adam glanced at McLeod. "All right. When you're ready, come back to full, waking consciousness. Take your time, because you've been pretty deep."

He turned the sketch pad so he and McLeod could look at it as they waited for Peregrine to come back. After a few seconds, the artist let out a very heavy sigh and opened his eyes.

"Are you sure about this?" Adam asked, looking up at him and indicating the pad.

Peregrine rubbed a hand over his face, looked at the pad, and nodded.

"As sure as I *can* be, about this stuff. If the other is real, then this is, too. It felt the same."

McLeod nodded and gave a sigh, rocking back in his chair.

"Right. Well, at least we can say that Gillian Talbot is a

good English name. Do you suppose it would be too much to hope that she lives somewhere in the U.K?"

"We can certainly give it a try," Adam replied. "I won't be up to it until I've had some sleep, but we should be able to narrow it down."

Peregrine blinked, only now realizing what was being suggested.

"You don't really mean that you're going to try to *find* her?" he asked, appalled. "Besides," he shook his head, "this doesn't make sense. How can Michael Scot be a young *girl*?"

Adam's faint smile suggested that the latter was but one more notion about which Peregrine was going to have to readjust his thinking.

"We'll discuss the psycho-sexual aspects of reincarnation on the way home," he said dryly. "Meanwhile, here comes lunch—which you, my friend, have certainly earned with this piece of work."

So saying, he closed the sketchbook and gave his attention to the meal being set before them—and to more specific discussion with McLeod of how to defuse the aspects of the case that really had no rational explanation, so far as the police and media were concerned. Peregrine, though he clearly longed to pursue his earlier line of questioning, kept his silence and merely tried to take it all in—which spoke well of his self-restraint, for times to come.

It was nearly three before Adam and Peregrine started back for Strathmourne. The Jaguar had been eating up the miles for perhaps ten minutes when the artist finally screwed up his courage, as Adam had known he would, to ask again how Michael Scot's current body could possibly be female.

"I simply don't understand," he said. "Maybe I was mistaken. I mean, Michael Scot's presence was unquestionably male. How could he be reincarnated as a woman? Isn't sexual identity a vital part of an individual's personality?"

"Speaking as a psychiatrist, of course it is," Adam said. "But when we enter the realm of the spirit, perhaps different rules have to apply. I put it to you that the human spirit, as opposed to the personality, is intrinsically neither male nor female. Rather, it possesses the potential to be either. Would you agree that the perfection of the spirit is to be regarded as an ongoing process of pursuing wholeness, with the ultimate goal of reunion with the Divine Light?"

The question took Peregrine slightly aback. "I—suppose so," he said uncertainly.

"Very well, then," Adam said. "Wholeness implies, among other things, completion—and balance. Now I ask you: How can any individual soul hope to become complete, unless life has been experienced in all its various aspects, including both kinds of sexuality according to nature?"

A glance in Peregrine's direction revealed that the concepts were finding root, but he shook his head in dismay, not yet able to frame any answer.

"Let's try another angle," Adam began again. "I can see that this is difficult for you. You have yet to realize this on conscious levels, perhaps, but there are some aspects of the Light that one may best understand as a man, other aspects that one can come to know only as a woman. To put on femininity at such times is to put on the sacramental mask necessary if one is to enter into those chambers of the sanctuary."

As he glanced again at Peregrine, the artist permitted himself a perplexed sigh.

"Let's backtrack about five steps and get down to very basic concepts," he said tentatively. "Have *you* ever reincarnated as a woman?"

"Certainly."

"Have I?"

"No doubt."

"Then why haven't I *seen* any of the female incarnations, when I've looked at you—or in my portrait-gallery dream?" Peregrine asked triumphantly.

"I suspect," Adam said archly, "that it's because you weren't yet ready to deal with your feminine side at this level. The thought simply hadn't occurred to you. I hasten to add that this is not meant as any reflection on your sexuality—I'm not saying this as a psychiatrist—but merely a statement of possibility, given your limited experience in these matters—at least in this one of *your* incarnations. You haven't been at this very long, after all. Give yourself time."

Peregrine struggled with this revelation in silence.

"If—what you say is true," he said at last, after some obviously difficult cogitation, "it rather looks as though I'm going to have to drastically revise my ideas about the nature of existence."

At Adam's slightly bemused nod of agreement, Peregrine sighed and ran a hand through his short, pale hair.

"All right. I'm not going to even pretend that I understand this; but for the moment, I'm going to take a leaf from your book and pretend that it's true. If you say so, I'll accept as a given that the wizard Michael Scot has been reincarnated as a young girl named Gillian Talbot, because that's what I myself saw. But if his spirit *has* been reborn as you say, why did it answer to us at Melrose as Scot, and not as Gillian? Which person is he?"

"He's both, of course," Adam said. "You must understand that the individual is not merely brain, or mind, or spirit, but a complex interaction of all three functions simultaneously. The brain, obviously, is physical—part of a physical body. It's the computer, if you like, that drives the physical body; but the information that it stores and processes—memory, and what is done with that memory—constitutes mind, an aspect of personality—and *that* can impinge on the purely spiritual soul. For it's through the human experience of a given personality that the soul progresses in its journey toward the Light, life by life.

"I spoke a moment ago of the soul's putting on a mask," he went on. "We might think of personality as the mask that the soul wears in any given incarnation, suitable for the time and circumstances, one mask per life. An Adept such as Michael Scot learns to retrieve those masks and change them at will, to reaccess useful aspects of earlier personalities. You can learn to do that, too. You're already learning to see other people's masks; that's part of what makes you such a fine artist. You've caught glimpses of several of *my* masks."

Peregrine nodded. Adam could tell by his expression that he was now thinking furiously.

"Some people can deal with pure spirit," Adam resumed. "We sometimes call them saints or even gods. Most people, however, need more concrete points of reference. When we're in our bodies, we're all wearing our masks; and we tend to interact more effectively with other masked beings. If a soul should be temporarily displaced from its present physical incarnation—as Scot's was—resuming an earlier incarnation to seek help is far more useful than trying to interact as a purely spiritual entity. Which is precisely what he did, and why."

"I'm going to have to think about this," Peregrine said dubiously. "But don't be surprised if it takes a little while for it all to sink in."

He fell silent after that—they were nipping around the Edinburgh Ring Road now, heading for the Forth Road Bridge—and when he began nodding off, exhausted from his accumulated exertions, Adam at last could turn his thoughts to other aspects of the day's events besides wrestling with Peregrine's logic. There were aspects to the case surrounding Michael Scot that still did not quite add up.

Aside from the appalling violation of the soul of Michael Scot, and the need to rectify its effects in young Gillian, if possible, the most important question raised by the circumstances of the case at Melrose concerned the status of those responsible, and their apparent intention to go after Scot's book of spells. Upon further reflection, Adam stood by his earlier conjecture that the thieves were neophytes. The muddled approach to their whole assault on Scot was a clear indication of their comparative inexperience.

On the other hand, he had crossed swords with the members of various black lodges often enough in the past to know that the Lodge-Masters of such fraternities were quite capable of allowing their more enterprising underlings a degree of apparent autonomy, whenever it served their own veiled purposes to do so. Was the summoning of Michael Scot no more than what it seemed: the ill-judged act of overly-ambitious apprentices? Or did it represent an opening gambit in a much more complicated chess game?

Adam was forced to admit that, on the basis of the information he possessed at the moment, he was in no position to say. And until he got some rest, he was not likely to improve on the situation. As they turned into the drive at Strathmourne, he became acutely aware of the leaden sense of fatigue he had been holding at bay for some hours now, born of the labors he had undertaken to liberate Scot and cleanse his burial site. And one glance at Peregrine, jerking back awake as Adam stopped the Jag and turned off the engine, was enough to confirm that the artist was similarly exhausted—and far less able to cope with the weariness.

"Thank you, Humphrey," Adam said, as the butler opened the door on their approach, ready to relieve them of their coats. "It's been quite a day. I'd be very much obliged if you'd bring us tea in the library—and even more obliged if you could manage to provide some sandwiches to go with it."

"I'm certain I can manage to put something together, sir," Humphrey said, with every appearance of aplomb. "And I lit a fire in the library about an hour ago. You should find it quite comfortable by now."

As he followed Adam along the corridor toward the library door, Peregrine spared Humphrey a backward glance.

"He always seems to know just what you're likely to want or need, doesn't he?" he remarked wonderingly. "I hope you're not going to tell me he reads minds. How does he do it?"

Tired though he was, Adam could not suppress a chuckle. "No mind-reading—just ease of long habit, I suppose," he said, gesturing Peregrine toward his now accustomed chair by the fireside. "If I know Humphrey, he'll be up with the tray in a trice. Why don't you have a seat and make yourself comfortable . . . ?"

Half an hour later, Peregrine found himself yawning uncontrollably over his tea.

"I'm awfully sorry," he said apologetically. "I can't think why I should be so sleepy when it's barely five o'clock. Granted, last night was a rather late one, and we were up and about early this morning, but that's still no excuse for nodding off in the middle of a sentence. And it's only been a few hours since we ate, but I was absolutely ravenous! Anyone would think I'd been out digging ditches all day!"

Adam helped himself to another buttered scone, starting to feel more human.

"A common enough misconception. Most people don't realize that psychic work can be far more exhausting than the roughest forms of manual labor."

"Psychic work?" Peregrine caught himself short in the middle of another yawn. "But I haven't been doing any work at all, psychic or otherwise."

"Ah, but you have," Adam replied. "What did you think you were doing, when you were making all those sketches?"

The question earned him an owlish look from Peregrine.

"In case you hadn't noticed," Adam went on, "today you took a rather active part in what is turning out to be a significant psychic event. The fatigue you're feeling now is a direct consequence of your participation. It's something you'll have to learn to deal with, if you think you want to become any further involved in this business than you already are."

Peregrine lifted his head. "Am I *allowed* to become further involved?" he said in surprise.

"Yes, you're allowed—and encouraged, in fact. The way things are starting to move, I can't promise I'll be able to find time to explain everything that's happening, perhaps until it's all over, but I want you to understand the nature of at least some of what you've seen today—and what you may see me do in the future."

Peregrine pursed his lips, breathing out in a low, soundless whistle as he turned his gaze to the fire, seeking a familiar anchor in the dancing flames.

"I don't know if I'm ready for this, Adam. Tell me what it is you really do—I mean, *really* do. I think I'm beginning to get a little scared."

With patience and even compassion, Adam leaned back in his chair and sighed, choosing his words carefully. In everything Peregrine had done today, he had shown himself ready to be introduced more fully to the mysteries that were

Adam's life and purpose. But what Adam chose to tell him now must be weighted very carefully, striking just the proper balance of the familiar with the mystical, lest Peregrine shrink from the destiny unfolding before him.

"As you quite possibly have gathered by now," Adam began tentatively, "I sometimes act as a physician of souls as well as of minds. In another sense, I suppose one also could say that, like Noel McLeod, I have an additional function as a keeper of the peace. I won't even *try* to define my jurisdiction for you just now, but it lies somewhere within that realm of experience that Noel and I, and others like us, call the Inner Planes. They're a—separate reality, if you will, lying outside of time and material space, but nonetheless accessible to the mind of man through the interior motion of the spirit. The Inner Planes are the wellspring of dreams, the origin of inspiration, the source of prophetic vision. The ordinary man visits the Inner Planes only by the natural accident of sleep or unconsciousness, and brings back only fractured memories of what he encountered there. The Initiate, however, may journey there at will, in full awareness of what he does; and what he brings back is knowledge."

Peregrine was listening raptly, still not looking at Adam; but all at once he had the look of a man who has just heard a distant trumpet.

"You're describing what I do when I paint," he said softly. "Not the Initiate part—the other. That's part of what my seeing is all about, isn't it? That's where my inspiration comes from. That's what you've been trying to tell me, what my portrait-gallery dream was trying to tell me. 'Be still, and know. . . .' "

Adam smiled. "It seems I should have used the language of the artist from the start. I suspect that further insight may come along when you least expect it. You aren't frightened any more, are you?"

Peregrine tensed for just an instant, a slightly anticipatory look upon his face, as if probing for a sore tooth. Then he breathed out as if a great weight had been lifted from his shoulders, turning his head finally to look Adam squarely in the eyes.

"No. I'm not."

Adam nodded. "I thought not. In that case, we'll continue this discussion in the morning. I, for one, shall be curious to see whether you dream."

Chapter Thirteen

ADAM left instructions with Humphrey for breakfast at nine. He willed himself to wake at six. Fifteen minutes later, he had showered, shaved, and dressed with the brisk self-discipline of long habit. As he made his way quietly downstairs to the library, leaving his butler and young associate to enjoy a few more hours' much-needed rest, the house was still and silent.

Peregrine had left his sketch pad on the table before the library fireplace. Adam opened it to the second sketch of Gillian Talbot as he carried it over to his desk and sat down. Rummaging in a desk drawer produced an ornately decorated jeweller's loupe of antique design, which he set on the desk atop the sketch pad. Then he spun his chair around and propelled himself with a push to the nearest bookcase.

The lowest shelf housed an assortment of maps and atlases. Adam selected a large, fold-out road map of Britain and a world atlas. He hoped he would not need the latter. Pushing himself back to the desk, he set the atlas and jeweller's loupe aside and opened the map. It covered most of the desk when he spread it out, and he pulled the sketch pad out from under it as he sat back in his chair, tapping it lightly against his hand in distracted speculation as he cast his gaze over the map. Then he drew a deep breath and shifted his gaze to the sketch of Gillian Talbot, fixing her image firmly in memory, before slipping the pad back under the map.

"All right, Gillian, my girl," he murmured, setting his right hand on the map over the bulge of the sketch pad.

"You're going to have to help me a little on this. Let's see if you're anywhere in the British Isles. . . ."

Closing his eyes, he set himself to settling into trance, focusing on the sketch pad under his hand, and the resonances echoed in the sketches Peregrine had made. He tried for the Michael Scot connection first, since his personal experience was of that identity; but that facet of the soul he sought was nowhere in evidence on the Inner Planes.

Temporarily stymied, he shifted his focus to the Gillian Talbot matrix. Here, he had less to go on from firsthand experience, for he knew Gillian only by the sketches Peregrine had made; but the Gillian identity had the advantage of being currently in incarnation, physically anchored somewhere on this planet. Her astral traces should be easier than Scot's to pick up—if he could identify them.

Patiently, eyes still closed, he began running his hand over the map of Britain, mind still and receptive, using a vast, overlapping figure-eight pattern that eventually would sweep across every square inch of the map. As he settled into the sweeping motion, he tried to put the physical appearance of the familiar map out of mind, focusing on the energies, as if they were eddies of current in some vast cauldron to be stirred with his hand. Slowly he began to detect variations within the currents, subtle shadings of temperature and pressure.

He let himself flow with them, letting his hand be a thing apart, letting it quest toward contact with the entity he sought. Slowly, gradually, the sweeps of his figure-eights decreased, at last starting to zero in on a location on the map. When the hand finally came to rest, Adam opened his eyes to see it spread squarely across the city of London.

"Really?"

He stared at the grey cross-hatching of the city in mixed relief and disbelief. To cross-check himself, for London seemed far too easy, he stood and picked up the map, closing his eyes again and turning the sheet round and round, totally at random, before laying it back on the desk.

Again he began his sweeping figure-eights across the surface, again stirring the eddies, looking for the fluctuations. When the hand had stopped a second time, it was once again resting directly over London.

"Well, well," he murmured. "That does simplify matters. Let's see if we can't narrow down the focus a bit more."

Pulling the U.K. map onto the floor of the bay behind him, Adam pushed himself back to the map shelf again. This time, he selected a large-scale map of the City of London, marked out on the national grid, and a recent edition of the London A to Z Street Atlas and Index. He put the street atlas temporarily to one side and spread the map out flat on the desktop, smoothing it with his palms and scanning it briefly. This time, a more exacting methodology was called for.

He sat back in his chair and closed his eyes, palms upturned on the chair arms in a posture of receptivity. A single deep breath relaxed and centered him. A slight shift of weight brought all the lines of his body into balanced alignment with the plane of the floor underfoot. Effortlessly maintaining that equilibrium, he drew another long, deep breath, this time releasing it with a silent petition to the Pantocrator for stability and insight.

In almost immediate response, the image of an unfinished pyramid took shape before him in his mind's eye. Holding the image, he concentrated on building it up to its apex, carefully adding each course of stones, seeing the pyramid take shape. As he set the capstone in place, the face of the pyramid was split in two, the two halves opening outward to reveal the single, All-Seeing eye at the pyramid's heart.

A tongue of flame flared within the pupil of the eye. He let the rest of the pyramid dissipate as he drew that ocular fire into his own living spirit. A corresponding point of radiant warmth sprang up at the center of his forehead, at the site of the mystical Third Eye of esoteric awareness. As it grew and glowed, he released the vision and opened his physical eyes.

For a brief instant, the room was bathed in luminous rainbows. Not only could he see objects, but also their auras, projected in every frequency of the spectrum from infrared to ultraviolet. Two items in the room stood out in white: the London map spread on the desk before him and the sketch pad holding all the images connected with the soul that Adam sought.

The rainbow effect dissipated as Adam brought his vision under the regulating influence of his will. Picking up the jeweller's loupe, he slid the sketch pad underneath the map as he had done before, then put the loupe to his eye, training it on the upper left region of the map where the area had been marked into squares on a grid. Then, with deliberate care, he began scanning the grid, inch by inch, from left to right and back again.

Names flashed past him, borough by borough: Edmonton, Walthamstow, High Gate. More boroughs—Hampstead, Islington, Hackney—and still no sign of what he was seeking. He shifted his attention down to the next row on the grid and scanned past Stepney, Westminster, and Kensington without getting any response. Then his eye lighted on the area of Hammersmith.

A point of blue light flared beneath the crystal lens of the jeweller's loupe. Adam paused, adjusted his eyepiece, and looked more closely. A fleeting expression of satisfaction crossed his face as he caught the pulse of blue again.

"So, she's in Hammersmith, is she?" he murmured softly, sitting back in his chair and lowering his glass. "Let's see if we can draw the net closer. . . ."

He reached for the A to Z street guide, consulted the index, and turned to the pages showing the street plan of the Hammersmith district, south and west of Hyde Park and Kensington. Weighting the book open with a gold letter-opener, he set his loupe in place again and repeated the scanning process. His survey of the left-hand page brought no response, but when he shifted his activity to the right-hand page, he got a telltale flicker of blue to the south of Hammersmith Tube Station. Closer inspection enabled him to pin-point the location more precisely: Charing Cross Hospital.

Frowning, Adam lowered the loupe and sat back in his chair, pulling the sketch pad out from under the map. He did not doubt that Gillian was there. And as a physician, gaining access to his prospective patient should be relatively easy. He knew several of the senior consultants on staff at Charing Cross, if assistance was needed.

But he had hoped not to find Gillian Talbot in hospital at all. The fact that she was still there gave him a prickle of uneasiness. The reunion of spirit and body *should* have signaled a return to normal good health.

It was possible, of course, that the girl's attending physician was merely retaining her for observation, out of professional caution. Healthy children normally did not lapse into spontaneous coma, for no good medical reason. But it was equally possible that the period of soul-separation had been the cause of extensive damage. And if that was the case, Adam reflected grimly—quite aside from the possibility of damage to Gillian herself—his chances for reestablishing contact with the submerged personality of Michael Scot might well be reduced from slim to nought.

But, first things first. Before he went haring off to London, he needed to confirm that Gillian Talbot was, indeed, at Charing Cross Hospital. He trusted his methodology, but whenever possible, it was also wise to double-check one's findings by more conventional means. Pulling out a London medical directory, he skimmed down the *Hospitals* section until he found the entry for Charing Cross. While he dialled the number and waited for it to be picked up, he formulated his plan.

"Charing Cross Hospital."

"Good morning," Adam replied, deliberately omitting to identify himself. "I'm trying to locate a patient by the name of Gillian Talbot. She would have been admitted sometime yesterday morning. Could you tell me whether you have someone by that name?"

"What was the name again, sir?"

"Gillian Talbot."

"Hold for a moment, please, and I'll check."

The line clicked, then reconnected to a recording of what sounded like the chimes of Big Ben played on a child's xylophone. Grimacing, Adam glanced at the receiver in disbelief. Midway through the third repetition, the operator's voice broke back in.

"We do show a patient listed by that name, sir. It's a

child, though. She was admitted to Pediatrics at about half past ten yesterday."

"That's the one I'm looking for," Adam said. "Who's the attending physician, please?"

"That would be Dr. Ogilvy," came the prompt reply. "Shall I put you through to Pediatrics?"

Adam had started automatically jotting down the doctor's name, but his pen paused at the question. He did *not* want to speak to the unknown Dr. Ogilvy just yet; not until he had invented some plausible explanation for his interest in Gillian Talbot.

"That won't be necessary just now," he said, thinking fast. "I know your people are terribly busy, this early in the morning. What times does Dr. Ogilvy usually finish rounds?"

He could hear the crackle of pages being turned.

"She usually signs out by about one," came the reply. "I expect her within the hour. Shall I take a number, and ask her to ring you?"

"No, I'll catch her later. I'm not certain where I'll be. Thank you very much."

Before the operator could ask any more questions, he hung up, carefully reviewing his conversation as he sat back in his chair. He had avoided leaving his name. Nor, on analysis, did he think he had aroused any undue curiosity. Anyone could inquire about a patient's presence in hospital, and the name of the attending physician. And by skillful direction of the questioning, Adam also had learned that Gillian was in Pediatrics, and that her attending physician was a woman doctor who had not yet arrived to begin rounds.

Now, if he hoped to gain any more information before actually going down to London, he had best make his follow-up inquiry fairly quickly.

He checked his directory again, hoping for a separate Pediatrics listing, then shook his head and dialled the general number again. His luck held. The voice that answered this time was slightly different from the first one.

"Pediatrics, please," he said.

"One moment," came the brusque reply.

Adam drew idle circles around Ogilvy's name while he waited for the call to be transferred, focusing again as a voice announced, "Pediatrics, Matron O'Farrell."

"Good morning, matron, this is Dr. MacAdam," Adam said, using a name he had used before when wishing to retain his anonymity. "You have a patient on your ward, a young girl named Gillian Talbot. Dr. Ogilvy admitted her yesterday morning. Can you tell me how she's doing today?"

His tone was authoritative but not demanding, as if he had every right to be asking what he was asking. That, plus the cachet of the medical title, apparently diverted any reluctance Matron O'Farrell might have had about releasing information.

"Ah, the Talbot girl. Yes, doctor. She regained consciousness yesterday afternoon, as you probably know, but she's remained totally out of touch with her surroundings. The house psychiatrist on Pediatrics is to look in on her sometime today, and Dr. Ogilvy has scheduled more tests for this morning."

"I see," Adam said. "Ah, what tests have been ordered, please?" he added, almost as an afterthought.

"Just a moment, doctor." The sound of rustling paper intruded briefly. "Yes. She's ordered more blood work and a CAT scan. Is there some problem with that?"

"No, not at all. Thanks very much for your help, matron."

"You're very welcome, doctor. Shall I have Dr. Ogilvy call you? She should be here within the hour."

"Thank you, no," Adam said again. "I won't be reachable by telephone for the next few hours. Perhaps I'll check back later in the day."

When he had cradled the receiver, Adam sat back thoughtfully in his chair.

So. The two telephone calls had gained him a great deal of useful information, but only so far as it pertained to getting him in to see Gillian Talbot. Unfortunately, he was not likely to learn anything else of use until and unless he could examine the girl—and hopefully, reestablish communication with that part of the soul that once had been

Michael Scot. Whether or not he could accomplish that would depend, at least partially, on luck. If the damage had been great, re-integrating the soul's present personality might be a long and tedious process.

There was another aspect of a trip to London that might not depend so much on luck, however. As Adam folded away his maps and stashed the jeweller's loupe in its drawer again, it occurred to him that if his own line of investigation proved in vain, perhaps Peregrine's burgeoning talents might provide an alternative avenue of approach. Of more immediate urgency than repairing the damage that might have been done by Scot's tormentors was the thwarting of their intentions concerning Scot's book of spells and his gold.

To do that, Adam and his colleagues needed to know where the perpetrators were headed—and *that* information might well yield to more conventional methods of investigation, especially if augmented by Peregrine's increasing ability to see on many levels. The artist already was as deeply involved in this affair as either McLeod or himself—not least because Michael Scot had singled him out as the recipient of information he hoped would enable his rescuers to bring his summoners to justice. And, Adam reminded himself, however inexperienced Peregrine might be in his present life, his soul was still that of a trained occultist.

Once an Initiate, always an Initiate, he thought, and put his lingering doubts behind him.

He stood up and stretched, then glanced at his watch. He and Peregrine were about to have another busy day. Though it was just approaching eight o'clock, he knew Humphrey would be up by now—probably in the kitchen already, dealing with breakfast. He picked up the in-house telephone and rang there first. Humphrey answered on the second ring.

"Mr. Lovat and I need to go down to London today," he informed Humphrey, settling briskly down to business after exchanging good mornings. "I'd be obliged if you'd ring the airport as soon as the reservation desk is open and book seats on one of the midday flights. Route us into Heathrow, if you can, and notify me as soon as you have the details."

"Certainly, sir." Humphrey's voice was imperturbable as ever. "Will you be staying overnight?"

"I think so," Adam said. "You'd better pack a bag for me, just in case. And book us rooms at the Caledonian Club, if you can get us in. If not, one of my other clubs will do."

"Very good, sir. Shall I arrange for a car and driver?"

"No, we'll make do with taxis this time, I think."

Peregrine entered the breakfast room just before nine o'clock, wearing grey flannels and his navy blazer, for Humphrey had already alerted him regarding the impending flight to London. He found his mentor already seated at the table, dressed for the city in a navy three-piece suit, riffling through his morning's mail. He had a stack of books at his elbow.

"Good morning," Adam said, with one of his wry smiles. "I hope you're feeling fit for active duty."

"Never better," Peregrine said. He seated himself opposite Adam and pretended casual interest in unfurling his napkin. "Humphrey tells me he's booked us seats on the noon flight to Heathrow. He also said I ought to bring along at least one change of clothes."

"That's correct," Adam said. "I've been able to locate the precise whereabouts of Gillian Talbot."

"*Have* you?" Astonishment and relief mixed in Peregrine's expressive eyes. "Where is she, then?"

"She's a patient at Charing Cross Hospital, in Hammersmith," Adam replied. "I rang there just a few minutes ago. There seems little doubt that she is, indeed, the child we're looking for."

"That's amazing!" Peregrine declared, his expression then changing to one of concern. "But—why is she still in hospital? I thought you said she'd be all right, once Scot got back."

"I had hoped she *would* be," Adam replied. "Unfortunately, the news in that regard is mixed. As you rightly surmised, she was in a coma for a time. She was brought in as an emergency case yesterday morning. She regained consciousness yesterday afternoon—you can guess at about what time—but she appears to be completely out of touch with her surroundings. I know the name of her doctor now, and what tests have been ordered—not that they'll tell anyone much. It's my plan to go to the hospital and try to see her, try to get a few minutes alone with her without arousing unwanted curiosity."

"You don't want me there, then," Peregrine said. "I don't know anything about hospitals. I've never even been a patient."

"No, I've got a separate commission for you in another part of London," Adam agreed. "How's your Latin?"

Peregrine gave him a quizzical look. "Rusty, I'm afraid. It's been a few years."

"You may be surprised at how quickly it comes back. Here."

Adam passed Peregrine the topmost book from his stack: a handsome volume bound in brown Moroccan leather, with creamy pages the quality and texture of good watercolor paper. The gilt lettering on the spine read: *Miscellany of the Maitland Club—Vol. IV, Pt. I.* Opening to the title page revealed that the *Miscellany* was a collection of "original papers and other documents illustrative of the history and literature of Scotland."

"Look at the second entry," Adam directed, "beginning on page twenty-one."

"*Brevis Descriptio Regni Scotie,*" Peregrine read aloud. "A Brief Description of the Kingdoms of Scotland." He looked to Adam in question.

"The *Brevis Descriptio* is a thirteenth-century account of Scotland as seen through the eyes of an itinerant Englishman," Adam explained. "In the absence of any contemporary maps, it's the earliest surviving document of recorded locations in Scotland. The original manuscript is in the British Museum. I want you to go and take a look at it."

"All right," Peregrine said. "But what exactly am I supposed to be looking for in the original, that isn't in here?"

"Psychic correspondences—if any," said Adam, "between the *Brevis Descriptio* and your own drawings from Melrose. If that castle Scot showed you was still in existence at the time the *Descriptio* was made, you may be able to pick up sympathetic resonances between your sketches and the manuscript that will give us a clue to the castle's general location."

At Peregrine's growing expression of dismay—and self-doubt—Adam paused and smiled.

"You needn't worry," he said. "I would not send you on this errand, if I did not think you were capable of the task. The process is not unlike setting up an electrical conductor between two points. Here is the method I recommend that you use. . . ."

Peregrine listened intently as Adam proceeded to explain, incredulity gradually changing to eager agreement.

"I think I *can* do that," he said, when the older man had finished. "Not only do you make it sound easy, but somehow the idea doesn't daunt me at all—though if you'd told me, even a week ago, that we'd be having this conversation, I'd have said at least one of us was daft."

Adam smiled. "Life is an ongoing learning process—and the learning stretches from life to life as well."

"I think I almost believe you," Peregrine replied. "There's one practical aspect of this that still worries me a little, though. I understand what I'm to do, once I get my hands on the appropriate manuscripts. But getting the museum staff to let me see the manuscripts in the first place may pose a bit of a problem. I don't have any academic credentials for this kind of research."

"No," Adam agreed, "but fortunately I do. I've prepared a letter of introduction for you—stuck there in the back of the book—addressed to an acquaintance of mine in the Department of Medieval Antiquities. He's a specialist in medieval geography and cartography, and will give you all the assistance you may require."

The noon flight from Edinburgh touched down at Heathrow Airport only a few minutes later than its scheduled arrival time, amid an autumn haze of thin fog backed by pallid sunshine. En route, Adam pointed out an article in that morning's edition of *The Scotsman: Bizarre Grave Desecration at Melrose Abbey.* His own copy of the article had already made its way into his files. After reading it,

Peregrine could only exchange an amazed look with his mentor. The article did not even hint at supernatural goings-on. Noel McLeod had done his job well.

With only carry-on baggage to contend with, the two made their way out of the main terminal at Heathrow with reasonable efficiency, though engaging a taxi proved more difficult than usual. The drive to the Caledonian Club also took far longer than Adam had hoped, though the doorman at the Caledonian recognized Adam at once, and took charge of their luggage with cordial efficiency, necessitating scarcely any delay at all.

The Caledonian Club lay just off Belgrave Square, in Halkin Street, near Hyde Park Corner. It was Adam's favorite London club, of the several to which he belonged, and it was also quite centrally located for what both he and Peregrine had to do. Had time not been of the essence, he would have had their taxi double back and drop him at Charing Cross Hospital before taking Peregrine on to the British Museum—or hailed another taxi. But the doorman told him that taxis seemed to be in short supply today, and they already knew that traffic was moving very slowly.

Fortunately, Adam's destination was reasonably convenient to the London Underground—which would be far faster than fighting surface traffic. Accordingly, he had the taxi deposit him by one of the entrances at Hyde Park Corner, passing a folded wad of currency to Peregrine to cover the fare and instructing the driver to continue on to the British Museum. The artist had his Melrose sketches locked away in the briefcase clutched across his knees, along with his letter of introduction, and he gave Adam a "thumbs up" sign just before the taxi pulled away.

Adam had forgotten how busy the London Underground could be, even outside rush hour. Fortunately, the correct train was waiting at the platform as he stepped off the escalator. Six quick stops later he was alighting at Hammersmith Station, following the signs that directed him along the pedestrian tunnels to surface on Fulham Palace Road, just under the Hammersmith Flyover. He paused briefly to get his bearings, then struck off along Fulham Palace Road, the collar of his trenchcoat turned up against a wind that suddenly had grown chill. Five minutes later, he was mounting the steps to the main entrance of Charing Cross Hospital.

He shed his trenchcoat as he entered the hospital lobby. Without it, outside and on the Underground, his three-piece suit would have set him a little apart from most of the men around him; here, he blended right in. Drawing anonymity from the "uniform," he made his way purposefully to the hospital directory, confirming that Pediatrics was up in the west wing, where he remembered. A casual inquiry at the reception desk revealed that, as hoped, Dr. Helen Ogilvy was not in.

"I'm very sorry, doctor," the receptionist told him. "You must have just missed her. If it's urgent, you could probably reach her at the children's hospital in Great Ormond Street, in about half an hour."

Reassured that he probably would not have to deal with Gillian Talbot's physician, Adam thanked the receptionist and made his way to the escalators on the other side of the lobby. Visiting hours had just begun, so he was able to blend in easily with the many other non-staff people moving about. He alighted on the first floor amid half a dozen people, obviously concerned parents, heading toward Pediatrics and followed along with them toward the nurses' station. Scanning the status boards behind the desk, he found the name *TALBOT,G.* printed with two others in a space indicating a four-bed ward at the end of the corridor. Without stopping at the nurses' station, he headed in that direction, hopeful of making his first contact without interference.

The door was open. It was not difficult to decide which bed was Gillian's. The two closest to the door were occupied by younger children, one with a plastered leg in traction and one sporting an arm in a cast and supported by a sling, each engaged in contented chatter with a doting parent. The third bed was empty. The child in the fourth one, next to the windows, had to be Gillian.

She was sitting bolt upright in her bed—a slender, angelically fair creature with short blond curls, an engaging spray of freckles, and a rosebud mouth—with wide blue eyes staring fixedly at the wall just to the right of the door. The round, childlike face was utterly devoid of expression, and the small-boned hands lay curled aimlessly in her lap, occasionally plucking at the edge of the blanket.

Adam watched her for a full minute from the far side of the corridor, assessing her condition with growing concern, noting the hands and skirted lap of someone sitting close beside the bed on the right, though he could not see the rest of the person. When he finally decided to enter, a comely blond woman in her late thirties started up from a chair at the bedside. So marked was the resemblance to the girl in the bed, Adam had no doubt they were mother and daughter.

"Good afternoon, I'm Dr. Sinclair," Adam said, smiling. He left his coat draped across the foot of the bed as he came to take her hand. "You must be Gillian's mother."

The woman's eyes met Adam's, wide and frightened, but when Adam retained her hand, she made no move to withdraw, already engaged by his direct gaze.

"Yes, I'm—Iris Talbot, doctor," she admitted, with confusion and apprehension mixed. "Did—Dr. Ogilvy ask you to look in on Gillian?"

"Not exactly," Adam said truthfully. "But I heard about Gillian's case, and thought I might be able to help." He neglected to mention just how he had heard. "I'm a specialist in psychiatric medicine. I've dealt with similar cases in the past."

"Then, it's *isn't* hopeless!" Iris Talbot whispered. "There is *some* hope—"

"There is *always* hope, Mrs. Talbot," Adam reassured her. "I must urge you not to expect miracles—these things sometimes take time—but rest assured that I shall do everything within my power to bring Gillian back to her previous, happy state."

"Oh, if only you *could* help," Mrs. Talbot murmured, both adulation and desperation edging her voice. "Gillian is our only child, and the doctors—"

She was on the verge of tears, exhibiting every sign of nervous anxiety—for which Adam could hardly blame her. But she also was primed to listen to anything he might say, eager for any shred of reassurance that things were not as bad as they seemed.

To find out whether that was true or not, Adam needed a few uninterrupted minutes with Gillian—which meant diverting her mother's attention for a little while. He had already done the groundwork, by the confident projection of his medical authority. With a little care, he should be able to guide the situation in precisely the direction necessary.

"Why don't you sit down and tell me a little more about it, Mrs. Talbot?" he urged. She made no resistance as he gently guided her back to her chair, sitting as he released her hand. "In fact," he continued, as he moved to pull the drapes around the bed cubicle to afford at least a little visual privacy, "before you tell me that, perhaps I should first assure you that I find no fault whatever in Dr. Ogilvy's handling of your daughter's case so far. On the contrary, she has done everything I would have done, had you been referred to me in the first place. In psychiatric cases, however, there are sometimes limits to what conventional medicine can accomplish. I hope to overcome those limitations."

As he returned from the curtains to stand beside her, he casually slipped his pocket watch from his vest pocket and let it dangle from about six inches of antique gold chain, spinning and gently swinging to and fro so that the gold caught the afternoon sunlight in small, rhythmic flashes. Mrs. Talbot's troubled gaze was drawn to it immediately, as Adam had intended it should be.

"Tell me what happened, Mrs. Talbot," he urged softly. "When did you first notice that something was wrong with Gillian?"

"Yesterday morning," Mrs. Talbot said, watching the watch turn and spin. "Her father and I tried to wake her for school, and she—wouldn't wake up."

"So you called the doctor, didn't you?" Adam murmured, "and she was brought here to emergency."

Mrs. Talbot nodded, her blue eyes a little unfocused, her voice going a little flat and sing-song as she continued.

"They said she was in a coma. They couldn't wake her

either. They ran some tests. And then, sometime early in the afternoon, she woke up—but she wasn't herself. . . ."

"In what way was she not herself?" Adam questioned, lifting the dangling watch a little, so that she had to look up.

"She just lay there and—and stared at the ceiling. It was as if she couldn't hear us. We couldn't get through to her. Dr. Ogilvy said it was au—autistic behavior."

"I think I understand," Adam murmured, gently laying his free hand on her shoulder and continuing to let the pocket watch catch the light. "You're very, very tired, aren't you?"

As she nodded dreamily, swaying a little under his hand, he went on.

"So tired—and who can blame you? I can see you've been too distressed to sleep. Why don't you take a little nap right now? It will do no harm if you close your eyes for just a few minutes' rest. I'll call you if your daughter should need you. It's all right to rest for a while. . . ."

As he continued speaking softly, her eyelids drooped heavier and heavier. Within only a few minutes, under his skilled guidance, she had settled into a passive state of hypnotic relaxation, her eyes safely closed.

Adam noted the time before pocketing his watch again and spared a swift glance at the curtains around them, cocking his head for the background sounds. Nothing seemed to have changed, but he might have only a very short time to accomplish what was needed. If nothing else, visiting hours would not go on forever—and who knew when a curious nurse might notice the closed curtains and come to investigate?

Turning his back on the mother, and also interposing himself so that her view of her daughter would be blocked, should she come out of trance before he was finished, Adam took one of Gillian Talbot's slack hands in his own. He laid his other hand on her forehead, easing her back until her head was resting on the pillow.

She made no resistance, even when he brushed his fingertips down over her eyelids, holding them there until the eyes stayed closed. Because time was short and he had no idea when someone might walk in on them, he used a shorthand method for casting a protective circle of warding around himself and his patient—a rapid sketching of the circle with a circular, clockwise motion of one up-raised forefinger, accompanied by the appropriate interior petitions of dedication and empowering. That accomplished, he set up a scenario for visual misdirection, should anyone come in, pressing his fingertips to Gillian's wrist as if counting her pulse rate, head bowed over the pocket watch in his hand once more, eyes closing as he began his real work.

A single deep breath took him deep into an altered state of consciousness. Carefully, like a man testing his way across a rickety bridge, he moved in spirit out of himself and into the borderlands of Gillian's inner being. He had expected the changeover to be profound, with so little time to make the passage, but entering her world was like stepping from a lighted room into a wilderness.

The interior landscape was like a scene from an earthquake: all cracked earth and heaps of rubble. Off in the distance, Adam glimpsed broken outlines of structures that might have been buildings, now fallen into ruin. Even as he steeled himself to set out across this wasteland, a subterranean rumbling broke out in the deeper regions below. A moment later, fresh upheaval rocked the ground.

The surrounding landscape began to break up. Whole patches of earth crumbled and fell away, leaving only chaos behind. He quit the unstable ground to hover above it, scanning all about him in growing dismay. The degree of psychic disruption was appalling. In all his years of function on the Inner Planes, he had rarely encountered such a complete breakdown of personality.

All around him spun floating clusters of psychic debris—thoughts, memories, fragments of personality. It was as though a cyclone had swept through a room full of jigsaw puzzles, scrambling up the pieces and scattering them far and wide in indiscriminate confusion.

All the diverse elements that had gone into the making of Gillian Talbot were out there somewhere, along with those elements belonging to Michael Scot—and doubtless others besides. In time, one might sort out the pieces, put the puzzles back together, rebuild the masks. But only in time. For now, Adam was forced to concede that bringing Michael Scot back in any meaningful way, at least in the immediate future, was out of the question—which meant that any hope of timely assistance regarding the Melrose incident lay with Peregrine. And repairing the damage to Gillian Talbot was another question entirely.

He was just starting to withdraw into his own body again when the sound of the curtains being briskly swept back catapulted him precipitously back to normal waking consciousness. He schooled himself to make no outward sign of alarm, composing himself in that space of two or three seconds before he calmly turned to look at the nurse standing between the parted curtains. Her expression was one of incensed disapproval.

"Here, now, what do you think you're doing?" she demanded, looking from Adam to the startled Mrs. Talbot and back again.

Affecting no concern whatsoever, Adam pocketed his watch and produced several business cards from inside his coat.

"You needn't alarm yourself," he said, handing her one of the elegantly engraved cards. "Mrs. Talbot asked me to examine her daughter. I've agreed to transfer Gillian to a clinic nearer my usual practice, if her condition does not improve within a few weeks." He jotted a number on the second card with a gold fountain pen and handed it to Mrs. Talbot.

"I've noted a second number where I can be reached at any hour, Mrs. Talbot," he went on, closing her hand around the card and holding it for just a moment, to underline the post-hypnotic suggestions he was placing. "Please do call me again, if I can be of any assistance at all."

As Mrs. Talbot nodded agreement, still looking a little dazed, the nurse read the card Adam had given her, eyes widening at the professional credentials listed.

"'Sir Adam Sinclair, Fellow of the Royal'—I *am* sorry, Sir Adam," she said, looking up at him apologetically. "Dr.

Ogilvy didn't mention that you'd be seeing Gillian. When I saw the curtains drawn—"

"I'm sorry, I should have checked at the desk," he said, bending over Mrs. Talbot to take her hand in farewell. "Don't get up, Mrs. Talbot. I'm expected elsewhere, so I really must go now, but I'll have a look at Gillian's chart before I leave. I did mean what I said before, however. If her condition does not improve, don't hesitate to call me."

"Yes—I will," Mrs. Talbot agreed.

"Brave lady," Adam whispered, patting her hand a final time before releasing it.

He retrieved his coat from the end of the bed, gesturing for the nurse to accompany him as he said, "I'll see that chart now."

Then he was leading her out of the room toward the nurses' station. He managed to take back his card as well, when she laid it down to fetch Gillian's chart.

But the chart told him little he did not already know or expect. All the blood work was normal, the neurological tests were normal, the CAT scan was normal. Everything was normal—except that it was not normal for healthy twelve-year-old girls to end up in the condition Gillian Talbot was in. Adam resolved then and there to apprehend those responsible—and to bring them to his own sort of justice, if the Fates did not supply a justice of their own.

Chapter Fourteen

MEANWHILE, Peregrine had parted company with Adam in a state of suppressed excitement. As the taxi crawled up Park Lane and then right, into Oxford Street, he drummed impatient fingers on the armrest of his seat and scowled abstractedly out the window at the people crowding the pavements on either side. The air was acrid in his nostrils, heavy with exhaust fumes. He was relieved when at last they reached the quieter streets flanking the museum.

Not that the museum itself was quiet. Peregrine stepped out of the taxi into a bustling exchange of visitors coming and going. Just inside the museum entrance he was overtaken and engulfed by a uniformed troop of schoolchildren, and had to wait while their teacher consulted the curator at the information desk concerning how to get to the exhibition of Greek sculpture. As the group moved noisily away, Peregrine reflected that if the reading rooms in the Manuscript Section were half as busy as the rest of the museum, he was going to have a hard time carrying out his intended mission without attracting undue attention.

He half-expected his own credentials to be questioned when he presented Adam's letter and asked to be directed. But the uniformed woman behind the desk merely nodded politely and reached for the telephone at her elbow. After only a brief exchange with someone on the other end of the line, she turned back to Peregrine with a brisk smile and informed him that Mr. Rowley would be along very shortly to meet him.

In person, Peter Rowley proved to be short and broad,

with a spiky fringe of black hair wreathing a bald crown. Rowley's black eyes were disconcertingly shrewd behind their old-fashioned bifocal lenses. But after reading over Adam's letter of introduction, he extended a hand with every appearance of cordiality.

"You not the first person who's come to examine the *Brevis Descriptio*," he stated genially. "But if Sir Adam has seen fit to take you on as his assistant, I expect you'll make better use of it than some might. Let's go down to my office."

Rowley's office was located deep in the bowels of the museum's underground vaults.

"This place is a veritable warren," he commented, as they threaded their way along several connecting corridors. "Still, if you want to get anything really useful done in the way of research, you've got to get as far away from the general public as possible. Here we are."

He opened a door with his name on it and ushered Peregrine into a small, cramped anteroom lined with file cabinets and overflowing bookshelves. From an island at one side of this academic clutter, a grey-haired secretary looked up inquiringly from the console of a very up-to-date word processor.

"Mrs. Trayle, this is Mr. Lovat," Rowley informed her. "He's here to do some work on folio 239 of Cotton MS Nero D.II. Would you fetch it for us, please? That, and some tea."

He led Peregrine on through an inner door giving access to a slightly larger but no more tidy office beyond.

"I expect you'd rather look over the manuscript someplace where you can count on a bit of privacy," Rowley observed matter-of-factly. "I've got a lecture to give over the road at the university in half an hour's time, so you might as well make use of these humble premises while I'm gone."

His gaze connected squarely with Peregrine's. In that instant, Peregrine caught a flickering succession of companion images overlaying the cartographer's rubicund face. Adam, quite clearly, had had more than one good reason for sending him to Rowley.

"That's uncommonly kind of you, sir," he found himself saying, without any lingering trace of doubt. "I'm not terribly familiar with the museum, and I was wondering where I might find a quiet corner to work."

The secretary intruded briefly to deliver the requested manuscript, returning a moment later with a laden tray. Rowley stayed long enough to drink a cup of tea, giving Peregrine a few brief instructions on how to handle historical documents, before suddenly glancing at his watch and starting to shovel a sheaf of lecture notes into an untidy folder.

"Good gracious, where *does* the time go? I'm due across the street in five minutes. I shouldn't be much more than an hour," he continued, pulling on coat and hat as he paused by the door. "If there's anything more that you require in the meantime, Mrs. Trayle will attend to it."

Left alone, Peregrine opened his briefcase and took out the sketches he had made at Melrose. He laid them carefully to the left of the manuscript containing the *Brevis Descriptio*, then sat back in his chair, mentally rehearsing the instructions Adam had given him. His heart was racing with repressed excitement. He felt, he realized, almost like a criminal poised to execute some illicit operation.

For God's sake, you idiot! he told himself in exasperation. *You're trying to retrieve information, not rob a bank!*

He took a firmer grip on himself and concentrated on bringing his breathing under control. As his respiration slowed, his heartbeat returned to normal. Continuing to breathe in disciplined measure, as Adam had taught him, his present situation lost its strangeness. All at once he felt calm and clear-headed, as sure of his ground as one treading a familiar path.

The feeling of certainty brought with it an attendant sense of self-mastery. He became conscious of being in control of all his faculties, as he could not recall ever having been before. Without stopping to think, he laid his left hand on the stack of drawings, palm down. With the other, he smoothed flat the folio page in front of him and began to study it in detail.

Using his right forefinger as a pointer, he traced over the

whole manuscript once from beginning to end. At first the medieval script looked strange and crabbed, a chaotic collection of minims, smudges, and run-on lines. But by the time he returned to the start of the entry, he discovered he could, in fact, disentangle word from word quite easily. His concentration narrowing, he began slowly to read.

An hour earlier, he might have been surprised that the thirteenth-century Latin should be so readily decipherable to his untrained eye. Now he hardly gave the matter a second thought, translating without conscious effort the lines spread out before him. The author of the *Brevis Descriptio* treated each Scottish province by name, beginning with the border areas of Teviot and Lothian. Peregrine passed over them without sensing any response, and continued reading:

Postea est terra de Fif in qua est burgus Sancti Andree et castrum de Locres. . . . Next there is the land of Fife in which there is the city of St. Andrews and the castle of Locres—Leuchars, by modern spelling. . . .

Subsequent entries dealt with the province of Angus and the Grampian Mountains, known to the writer as "Le Mounth."

Oblivious to the passage of time, Peregrine read on past mention of the east-coast cities of Aberdeen and Elgin until he came to another natural break in the text. The next sentence conformed grammatically to the ones preceding it: *Et postea est terra de Ros. . . .* But as Peregrine came to the word "Ross," he felt a sudden tingling in the palm of his left hand where it rested over the drawings Michael Scot had prompted him to make.

He returned his index finger to the place-name and held it there, stationary. The tingling in his opposite hand became stronger, ceasing altogether when he briefly lifted his hand from the stack of drawings and resuming when he made contact once more.

That's it! he thought triumphantly. *Scot's castle must be somewhere in the ancient kingdom of Ross!*

He knit his brows, casting his mind back over what he remembered of the medieval period of Scottish history. The kingdom of Ross, he recalled, had taken in a wide area between Loch Ness to the south and the mountains of

Sunderland to the north—still a great deal of ground to cover.

Peregrine sighed and shook his head.

If only I had a map to go along with this piece of text! he thought.

No such map existed, of course, but the notion suggested another tangent of speculation.

"How early are the earliest maps of Scotland that *do* survive?" he wondered out loud.

"If you're prepared to consider Great Britain as a whole," said Rowley's voice from the doorway, "the *very* earliest ones in our collection date from the thirteenth century. They're cartographical drawings, actually—not really maps in the usual sense."

Peregrine looked up with a start.

"I'm sorry—I thought you heard me come in just now," the cartographer added. He gestured toward the *Brevis Descriptio*. "Did you find what you were looking for?"

"Yes, I think so," Peregrine said. "At least in part. But I've still got a lot of unanswered questions." He paused to adjust his spectacles. "Would it be possible for me to take a look at those maps you just mentioned?"

Rowley shrugged. "I don't see why not. But I must warn you, they're wildly inaccurate when it comes to Scotland. The man who drew them, Matthew Paris, was an Englishman, a monk of St. Albans. His practical knowledge of Scottish geography seems to have been limited to the region south of the River Tay."

"I'd still like to see them, if I may," Peregrine said. "What else have you got, that's more accurate?"

"Let me see . . ." Rowley pursed his lips and searched the air slightly above Peregrine's head. "The earliest would be Lansdowne 204, an untitled map by one John Hardyng, dated roughly 1457. It's not much more of a map than the Paris ones—in the nature of an illustrated diagram, actually—but it's got about fifty place names on it. After that, there's a parcel of sixteenth-century maps by various people. Are you interested in printed maps, or only in original manuscript drawings?"

"I wouldn't mind having a look at whatever there is

dating from before sixteen hundred," Peregrine said. "Provided that you can spare the time."

"I'll make time," Rowley said cheerfully. "I could do with a diversion." He lifted a bushy eyebrow. "How do you want to do this? In chronological order?"

"Unless you can think of a better way," Peregrine replied.

"So be it, then." Rowley poked his head back out into the front room. "Mrs. Trayle, can you spare a moment? I need you to pull a few more items for me. . . ."

For the better part of the next two hours, the two men pored over a whole series of early maps, concentrating on those that showed the area of the ancient kingdom of Ross. At first Peregrine was shy of demonstrating his eccentric method of investigation in front of Rowley. At the same time, however, he could see no way of avoiding it. After his first assay, he fully expected Rowley to question him quizzically about what he was doing. Instead, the museum's cartography expert treated the situation with an offhand manner suggesting that this sort of thing was nothing new to him.

Rowley's matter-of-fact attitude put Peregrine at his ease and made his self-appointed task that much easier. At the same time, the work itself proved singularly unproductive. Some of the maps Peregrine looked at were portularies—maritime charts showing only coastal regions. The rest proved to be insufficiently detailed in other respects. By the time the clock in the outer office struck six, Peregrine was forced to accept that, much as it galled him to admit defeat, there was nothing more to be gained from continuing.

He swallowed the lukewarm dregs of his third cup of tea and sat back with a heavy sigh. Rowley, watching him, gave a sympathetic nod.

"I know just how you feel," he said philosophically. "In my experience, most research is ten percent discovery and the rest a waste of valuable time." He cocked his head in inquiry. "Do you want to carry on?"

Peregrine flexed tired shoulders and shook his head. "Thanks for the offer, but no. If I haven't turned up anything by now, I doubt I ever will—not from these sources, at any rate." He gave the other man a rueful grin. "I suppose I'd better be on my way, and let you be on yours. Thanks for your help, all the same."

"Don't mention it," Rowley said robustly. "Just tender my regards to Sir Adam." He waited until Peregrine had finished putting his drawings back into his briefcase, then offered his hand. "Don't hesitate to call on me again if I can be of any further assistance."

As they shook hands, a telephone jangled loudly in the outer office, interrupting any protracted response on Peregrine's part, and a moment later, Rowley's secretary ducked her head around the door-frame.

"It's for you, Mr. Rowley: Dr. Middleton."

"Ah!" Rowley moved toward the telephone on his desk.

"Go ahead and take your call, sir," Peregrine said, raising a hand in farewell. "I'll hand these maps back to your secretary and find my own way out. And thanks again."

Rowley gave him a nod and a wave before picking up the receiver. Snatches of his end of the conversation filtered through into the adjoining room as Peregrine lingered long enough to allow Mrs. Trayle to take the requisite inventory of the documents involved.

"Hullo, William! So, how was the Highlands and Islands Conference? Oh? Oh, really? I'm sorry to hear that. Still, Raeburn was bound to be there, wasn't he? After all, he's got business interests in Inverness, as well as academic ones. . . ."

Peregrine realized he was listening in, and gave himself a mental shake, mildly surprised at himself.

Whatever they're talking about, it's hardly any concern of yours, he told himself as he made for the door. It puzzled him that fragments of that conversation continued to echo in his mind long after he had left the museum.

He had forgotten about the incident completely, however, by the time he had hailed a taxi and made the short trip back to the Caledonian Club. He entered the main hall to find Adam already there, sitting in a club chair in the angle of the staircase and thoughtfully sipping at a whiskey. The older man looked up immediately at Peregrine's entrance, raising his glass in invitation to join him.

"Hullo," Peregrine said, flopping his briefcase on the settee next to Adam and pausing to shed his trenchcoat. "I hope I haven't kept you waiting."

"Not at all," Adam replied. "I've only been back a little while myself. How did you make out at the Museum?"

Peregrine sat down beside Adam and gestured to catch a waiter's attention, pointing to Adam's glass in signal for another of the same.

"I'm afraid my luck was variable," he said. "In going over the *Brevis Descriptio*, I was able to narrow down our area to the kingdom of Ross. But that was the best I was able to do with the materials available." He sighed and grimaced. "Most of the maps Rowley showed me were prints rather than drawings. Maybe I'd have done better if I'd had access to the manuscript originals. . . ."

"Don't be too quick to underrate your achievements," Adam said. "Ross narrows the field considerably. You've provided us with a clue that may prove vital—not the least, because it's the only clue we have at the moment." Seeing Peregrine's startled expression, he went on to explain.

"I saw the Talbot girl. She *is* the individual we're looking for. Unfortunately, the information we need is, for the moment, completely inaccessible."

"Why? What's happened?"

"The summoning and binding at Melrose had far more destructive consequences than I supposed," Adam said bluntly. "There's been a complete breakdown of personality. At all levels."

"Did she not come out of her coma after all, then?" Peregrine asked.

Adam allowed himself a weary smile and shook his head, bowing his forehead briefly to press against the cool side of his glass.

"I wish it was that simple, Peregrine," he murmured. "Clinically, the girl is conscious; but she's in an almost catatonic state. She displays classic autistic responses—or non-responses. No, the personality has been fragmented, at all levels. I know. I was there."

Peregrine's brow furrowed in confusion—and concern for Adam's apparent exhaustion—but before he could pursue either question, a waiter delivered his drink. He gave a distracted nod of thanks as the man discreetly withdrew, sipping automatically and then with more focused attention before raising the glass slightly in approval.

"This is very good," he remarked, rolling the flavor on his palate. "Single malt?"

Adam nodded. "The MacAllan. You were about to comment?"

Peregrine swallowed and nodded, gesturing slightly with his glass.

"You said her personality was fragmented—but isn't Michael Scot a separate personality?"

"Yes, but remember that I likened the personalities of successive incarnations to masks," Adam replied, keeping his voice down as their conversation got more specific. "The *spirit* is the essence of what is ongoing, immortal—what wears the mask in a given incarnation. But pure spirit, unless it is *extremely* evolved, cannot interact with incarnate humans except through the agency of a mask—either a past one or a current one.

"I would venture to say that *all* of the masks once accessible to the spirit now occupying the body called Gillian Talbot have been fragmented—including the Michael Scot mask. Until that one, at least, can be reassembled, we'll get no further access to information that would have been accessible to the Michael Scot incarnation."

Peregrine's eyes had grown round behind his spectacles. "Is there anything you can do to repair the damage?"

"Not in the short term," Adam said. "I've offered to take Gillian under my care as a private patient. If her parents decide to avail themselves of my services, there are some grounds for hope. Otherwise . . ."

He shrugged and took another deep pull from his drink, and Peregrine's eyes gradually went cold and grim behind his spectacles.

"The people responsible for this," he said after a moment. "They're the ones who dug up the abbey, aren't they? The ones I sketched."

At Adam's grave nod, the artist leaned a little closer.

"Well, then, let's *find* them, Adam," he whispered. "They can't be allowed to get away with something as—as bloody awful as this!"

"My thought, precisely," Adam agreed.

"So, what do we do next, then?" Peregrine demanded.

"For tonight," Adam said, "we have a proper dinner and early to bed. And in the morning, I propose that we pay a visit to the Scottish Geographical Society—which, illogical as it might sound, has its headquarters here in London."

Peregrine furrowed his brow. "Will they have materials Rowley didn't have at the British Museum?"

"They'll have different *kinds* of materials," Adam replied. "And from those, we shall learn everything we can about fortified sites in the ancient kingdom of Ross."

Chapter Fifteen

LESS than twenty-four hours later, on the Isle of Skye, in a castle that had been the seat of the Chiefs of Clan MacLeod for more than seven hundred years, a present-day MacLeod regaled yet another group of visitors with tales of the clan's past glories. Finlay MacLeod was not the Chief, but he was proud to be one of the Chief's principal retainers—what would have been called a henchman, in the old days.

Henchmen no longer were expected to bear arms for their Chief in any literal sense, except for ceremonial occasions, but in fact, Finlay *had* borne arms at his Chief's command—during the Second War. He carried pieces of German shrapnel in his knee to this day, and walked with a stick when the weather was bad.

Now Finlay and his wife lived in honorable retirement, as live-in caretakers for the castle, and extra household staff when the Chief was in residence. During the tourist season, they also filled in as castle guides, especially toward the end of the season, when the extra staff hired on for the summer had gone home and the visitors began to thin out, as the harsh weather of late autumn and winter approached. Today Margaret was manning the ticket desk in the main entry hall, while Finlay circulated in the castle drawing room. The Chief was in America, attending one of the large highland gatherings, and was expected back the following week.

Finlay gravitated back toward his customary post near the white-painted window bays as another shoal of visitors began to drift through the room, flicking an imaginary speck of dust from an imposing Bösendorfer grand piano. The last lot had been a busload of Japanese, with expensive cameras and only a smattering of English. The current batch appeared to be the more usual mix of western Europeans, mostly Scots and Brits and a fair number of Americans.

Finlay enjoyed his job. He enjoyed people, and he particularly enjoyed trying to guess the origins of the castle's visitors, especially if he could identify them before an accent gave them away. Over the years, for example, he had found that he could almost always spot Americans by their clothes: the older ones in new London Fog raincoats and tartan or Burbury scarves, and the younger ones uniformly sporting running shoes, backpacks, and puffy down jackets.

Finlay liked the Americans, even though some of them were a bit brash and loud by local standards, because often they came looking for their MacLeod roots—which was one reason that all the castle staff wore some item of MacLeod tartan when on duty. Margaret and the other two women working this afternoon favored sashes in the bright yellow-and-black tartan affectionately called "loud MacLeod," worn baldric-fashion and brooched to the shoulder with cairngorms or agates set in Scottish silver.

Finlay preferred tartan trews in the predominantly green sett known as MacLeod of MacLeod. He noticed that several of the visitors in the current batch wore ties or scarves in that tartan. As one looked expectantly in his direction, Finlay cleared his throat genially and clasped his hands behind his back, preparatory to beginning his customary spiel.

"Good afternoon, ladies and gentlemen. On behalf of our Chief, I bid ye welcome again to Dunvegan Castle. This is the drawing room, which is one of the oldest parts of the castle. Its Georgian decor may not suggest great age, but just through that door and around the corner, on t'other side o' that wall," he gestured to his left, "ye can look down into the old bottle-neck dungeon—hardly a Georgian feature. I will nae waste yer time by dwellin' on things that ye can read about for yerself in the guidebook, but I *would* like to point out perhaps the greatest treasure of the Clan MacLeod, which is kept in this very room: *am Bratach Sìth*, the Fairy Flag."

As he indicated the wall between the two seaward windows at his back, all eyes turned toward the antique frame hanging there—an impressive gilded thing measuring perhaps three feet wide by four feet high, hung against a background of peachy-salmon.

The flag itself was a tattered web of translucent gossamer the color of parchment, with patches of brown and scarlet where the fragile fabric had been mended in centuries past. To preserve it from further deterioration, it had been mounted behind glass on a stabilizing mat of natural-colored linen. Figured brocade draperies of a burnt orange on ivory were drawn to either side of its frame, with a pleated sconce of the same material hiding the curtain mechanism above. Finlay's staunch Presbyterian sensibilities would have been affronted at even the hint that he condoned religious frippery, but it did not seem at all odd to him that the flag's setting should resemble nothing so much as a High Kirk religious shrine.

"There are several versions of how the MacLeods got the Fairy Flag," Finlay said, his voice dropping into the awed silence as his audience moved in for a closer look. "Some historians believe that it was the war-banner of Harald Hardrada, lost during his defeat at Stamford Bridge and brought to Skye by his descendants. Others believe that it was a Saracen banner captured during the crusades and brought back from the Holy Land."

Several people in the front row nodded approvingly, for what remained of the fabric behind the glass did resemble oriental work.

"MacLeods hold, however, that the Flag came from no earthly source," Finlay went on, "but was the gift of a fairy lady to a beloved MacLeod Chief, with the promise that future Chiefs might unfurl it three times when the clan was in need, and the fairy folk would come to their aid. Tradition says that the Flag has been unfurled twice already, an' that the fairies did come, so ye can imagine how carefully each new Chief considers whether he should be the one to unfurl the flag for the third an' final time."

"That's ridiculous," a male voice murmured from the rear of the group, to which a female voice responded, "Shut up, George. I wanna hear about how the fairies gave them the Flag."

Finlay smiled indulgently. After more than a quarter century of dealing with the public, he was well used to coping with scoffers.

"As with most old stories, we have several versions of how the fairies happened to give us the Flag," he went on blithely. "The one I like best tells of a MacLeod Chief who fell in love with a beautiful fairy lady, an' she with him. Though both families opposed the match, eventually it was allowed—but with the stipulation that the fairy lady might remain with her human lord for only a year or until the birth of an heir, whichever came first.

"Well, the Chief an' his fairy bride were deliriously happy, an' just before the year was out, she bore him a son. But then she must return to her people, across the Fairy Bridge ye can see just north o' the castle here.

"But during the festivities to celebrate the birth of the Chief's heir, his nurse left him sleeping in his cradle in the tower, back where ye've been, next t' what is now the dining room. As will happen, th' wee bairn kicked off his blankets and began tae fret. His nurse didnae hear his cries, but the mother did. Drawn by her love for her bairn, she came back across the Fairy Bridge tae comfort him, an' wrapped him in her shawl against the cold. She fled when the nurse returned, but there was no mistakin' where the shawl had come from.. An' *that* is where the Clan MacLeod got the Fairy Flag—or so the legend goes."

His droll delivery elicited the expected chuckle, and several of the Americans crowded in for a closer look, including a middle-aged couple with a prepubescent boy in tow.

"Excuse me, sir," the boy said tentatively, "but you don't *really* think the Flag came from the fairies, do you?"

Finlay leaned down and gave the lad his grave appraisal. "What, do ye no' believe in fairies, laddie?" he asked.

As the boy shrugged noncommittally, Finlay nodded.

"I see. Well, I wouldnae presume t' tell a man what he ought to believe, but I can tell ye this," he confided. "The Fairy Flag stands for th' luck o' the MacLeods, wherever it came from. During the Second War, many young MacLeod flyers carried a photograph of the Fairy Flag as a good luck charm. An' do ye know what? Every single one o' them came back."

The boy was goggle-eyed, and even his parents looked impressed.

"Is that really true?" the boy's father asked.

Finlay smiled and slowly took out his wallet, thumbing through the contents of one inside pocket until he could extract a yellowed and dog-eared photograph of the Flag in its frame.

"Mine brought *me* back safely," he murmured, showing it to them. "That's one reason I feel privileged to guard the Flag itself." He gestured at it over his shoulder as he slid the photo back into his wallet for safekeeping. "Ye can *believe* what ye will, regardin' how the Flag came to be in MacLeod hands; but I *know* that it was given tae my ancestors by th' Fairies."

The remark served as a conversation-stopper, as it always did; and after looking more closely at the Flag behind its glass, the three wandered on out of the room with the other visitors. A few more drifted through, but the numbers were dwindling as closing time approached. Looking at his watch, Finlay knew that Margaret would have admitted the last of the day's ticketholders a quarter hour ago.

The clock on the mantelpiece chimed five. Finlay heard the last lot coming along the corridor from the dining room and met them at the door, ushering them through the drawing room with courtesy, but not encouraging them to linger, either. They moved on to look at the dungeon, and then at the other MacLeod treasures in the two display rooms beyond, eventually heading downstairs to the Clan Center and gift shop.

Noises filtered up from the front hall downstairs—a genial hum of voices that eventually was silenced by the hollow closing of the front door. Assured that the last of the day's visitors had departed, Finlay made a leisurely circuit of the drawing room, noting everything in its familiar place, easing around the piano to close the window in the left-hand bay. Some fifty years before, following a serious fire in the castle, a metal fire-escape ladder had been run up the side of the building from the gun court below, whence great cannons once had guarded Dunvegan Castle from attack by sea. Safety regulations required that access must be kept available during the day, when visitors were coming and going, but the window was always locked during the night, lest a burglar climb up from below and break in. Of course, one would have to breach the castle's outer walls first. . . .

Nonetheless, checking all the windows had become second nature to Finlay MacLeod after decades at the castle, so he gave the matter hardly a second thought as he secured the window latch and drew the drapes in the bay.

The Fairy Flag was another matter entirely, and never, *never* received perfunctory, unthinking service. Coming around to face the Flag squarely, old Finlay drew himself smartly to attention and raised his right hand in a brisk, formal salute. He held for a moment, remembering the yellowed photo in his wallet, before slowly lowering his hand.

Then, just before he drew the brocade drapes that covered the Flag at night and protected it from the light when the castle was not open, he kissed the fingertips of his right hand and touched them fondly to the lower right-hand corner of the frame. The gilt was a little worn there, from years of Finlay's devotion, and he smiled as he eased the drapes into place. He gave the room a last, fond glance as he headed for the door, turning off the lights before making his way downstairs to the foyer.

Margaret was still in her seat behind the ticket desk, counting up the proceeds from the afternoon. She greeted his arrival with a cheerful wink and held up a finger while she continued counting, warning him not to interrupt. Finlay acknowledged with a companionable nod and moved toward the nearest bench. Before he could sit down, there was a sudden, peremptory knock at the door.

"Hello, is anyone in there?" called a muffled female voice from outside. "Please, could you open up a minute?"

The voice sounded distressed. Finlay's wife shot him a look over the top of her spectacles.

"Sounds like someone's forgotten something," she said, with a slight frown. "Better see what she's wantin'."

"Aye." Finlay strode over and unbolted the door.

The forlorn figure waiting on the doorstep was a young woman he vaguely recalled seeing in the castle during the last hour or so, drab and anonymous in a brownish suit of nondescript tweed. In fact he would not have remembered her at all, except that she had spoken English without a trace of regional accent. He had decided at the time that she must be Canadian, or perhaps American—maybe a nurse or a secretary.

Probably a secretary, he decided now, as he eyed her anxious expression and the hands twisting nervously at the strap of a plain leather shoulder bag. On closer inspection, he judged her to be thirtyish, with dark brown hair cut in a neat bob and a clear-skinned oval face that was neither plain nor pretty, framed by dark-rimmed glasses. The pale eyes behind the lenses were worried-looking.

"Oh, thank goodness someone's still here," she said. "I'm awfully sorry to bother you, but I seem to have misplaced my car keys. I had them when I came in, because I remember putting them in my bag when I paid my admission, but I can't find them now—and I certainly can't go very far without them. I can only imagine that they must have fallen out in the gift shop—or maybe in the drawing room. I did open my bag when I was there, to take out my guide book. Do you think we could go and look?"

All the while she was speaking, she had been pressing forward. Before Finlay knew it, she was across the threshold and in the entry hall. This discovery was slightly disconcerting, but a Scottish gentleman could hardly ignore the pleas of a lady in distress.

"Och, aye, we'll go up and take a wee look 'round," he said indulgently, with a sidelong glance at his wife. "I didnae see any keys in the drawing room, but mayhap Mrs.

MacCrimmon has found 'em downstairs. If they're anywhere about, we'll find 'em, never fear."

"Oh, thank you so much!" their visitor exclaimed. "I really am sorry to disturb you this way, after closing time and all. I don't know how I could have been so silly! I'm not usually this scatterbrained."

"Och, dinnae worry, dearie," Margaret said comfortably. "I must've done the same myself half a dozen times or more. On ye go now, Fin, and see what's tae be done. I'll wait for ye down here, tae lock up."

Finlay led the way back up the wide stone stairs, flipping on lights as he went. At the top he paused to unhook the guard-rope that had been placed there to direct the flow of tourist traffic left, toward the dining room rather than right, toward the drawing room. As soon as the rope was down, the brown-haired woman slipped past him and threw open the drawing room door. Taken slightly aback, Finlay sprang after her.

"Here—gi' us a moment," he admonished, and reached for the light switch just inside the doorjamb.

The room sprang to life again. Without waiting for Finlay, the brown-haired woman darted over to the left-hand window bay, plopping her bag on the piano and feeling across its surface.

"I remember resting my bag here while I went after my guide book," she said over her shoulder to Finlay. "They aren't here, though. Maybe they fell on the floor."

Together they made a search around and under the piano on hands and knees, though without success. The brown-haired woman sat back on her heels with a sigh of mingled apology and exasperation.

"Well, they don't seem to be *here*," she said. "Maybe I *did* leave them in the gift shop—though I could have sworn I only took out my change purse down there."

Finlay repressed an avuncular impulse to cluck his tongue at such carelessness. "Mrs. MacCrimmon'll no' hae gone home yet," he said. "I'll take ye down and let ye have a word with her."

"You're very kind." The brown-haired woman beamed at him gratefully and made a move to get up, giving a small shriek as her hand inadvertently snagged the strap of her shoulder bag and pulled it off the piano, spilling its contents onto the polished wooden floor. Cosmetics and toiletry items scattered, and loose change bounced in all directions.

"Oh, no!" she cried. "How could I be so clumsy?"

Finlay wondered the same thing, but a gentleman did not say that to a lady in distress. Murmuring reassurances, he left his companion to gather up the more personal items while he chased after errant coins and pens that had gone farther afield. With his back turned, he did not see her take a swift sidestep to the window and trip the latch that unlocked it. By the time he rejoined her, she had gone back to returning her scattered belongings to her purse.

"Thank you so much," she murmured, as she got to her feet. "I really don't know what's come over me. I broke a mirror, too." She showed him the shattered glass in a cheap pink plastic compact. "They say that's seven years of bad luck."

"Och, dinnae worry about that, miss," Finlay reassured her. "Here at Dunvegan, ye have the luck o' the MacLeods to cancel out any bad luck. We'll go down now an' see if Mrs. MacCrimmon has yer keys."

They left the room as they had found it, in darkness. Unaware that anything suspicious had occurred, Finlay ushered his companion down the stairs and into the gift shop, where a birdlike little woman with silvered black hair was making notes in a well-worn ledger.

"Hullo, Mrs. MacCrimmon," he said genially. "Ye've no' found a set of keys lyin' about, have ye? This young lady's lost hers, an' she thinks she may ha' dropped 'em in h—"

His good-humored explanation faltered as he realized that Mae MacCrimmon's face had suddenly gone white and stiff. She was staring not at him but past him, at the young woman with the brown hair. Nonplussed, Finlay turned his head to see what she was staring at—and found himself gazing down at a very lethal looking automatic pistol levelled at his midsection.

Shock rendered Finlay momentarily speechless. The pistol had been fitted with a silencer—which meant that this woman was no amateur. A part of him noted that he had taken similar weapons off Gestapo officers at the end of the war. It probably was a fairly small caliber, but the muzzle looked like it would fire cannonballs, seen from the business end. His heart gave a queer fluttering lurch, reminding him why his doctor had been cautioning him for months to retire.

With a curt motion of the barrel of the gun, the young woman with the brown hair beckoned Mrs. MacCrimmon to join them. Wide-eyed as a rabbit, the older woman did not move, apparently paralyzed with fright.

"Come on!" their captor snapped. "I haven't got all night."

She pointed the weapon at Mrs. MacCrimmon, finger tense on the trigger. Hastily, Finlay reached out for Mrs. MacCrimmon's arm and drew her from behind the counter, glaring at their captor with all the dignity he could muster.

"All right," he said sourly. "We can see ye've got a gun. If ye want tae go ahead and empty the till, neither of us will try tae stop ye."

The young woman with the brown hair smiled thinly. "Some other time, perhaps. Right now, I'd like you both to put your hands on your heads and move slowly towards the door."

Mrs. MacCrimmon's face went a shade paler, and Finlay was afraid she might faint.

"Wh-where are you taking us?" she stammered.

"Upstairs to the drawing room," said their captor. "If you do as you're told, you won't be harmed. Now *move*, while I'm still in the mood to be polite."

Not daring to disobey, Finlay mutely hurried Mrs. MacCrimmon up the steps, conscious all the while of the gun aimed at the small of his back. If she fired, the bullet would likely go right through him and hit Mrs. MacCrimmon as well.

A chilly stream of air came rushing down the stairwell to greet them as they ascended. When they reached the top and made the turn back toward the drawing room, Finlay was surprised to see the drawing room door standing open, and the lights on. He was even more surprised, when they entered the room, to see the fire-escape window gaping wide, with curtains billowing wildly in the cold sea wind.

"Over there, by the piano," their captor ordered.

Finlay obeyed, herding Mrs. MacCrimmon with one hand and keeping his other hand raised. Glancing aside at the window, he saw smears of mud on the broad sill where a second intruder evidently had gained entry by way of the fire-escape. In the same moment, they all heard a scuffle of movement below, and footsteps started up the stairs from the direction of the front hall. A voice that Finlay recognized as his wife's said indignantly, "It's well for ye that the Chief himself's no' at home just now. Otherwise, ye wouldnae be havin' things all yer own way!"

Ah, feisty Margaret. She was first through the door into the drawing room, but Finlay's hope that the intruders might have missed out on Mrs. McBain, the library docent, died stillborn when she stumbled across the threshold a step behind his wife, looking terrified. The second member of the intruder's party was a man in a ski mask, dressed in the sort of tight-fitting black clothes that Finlay had seen worn by spies and cat burglars in the movies. However theatrical his appearance might be, there was nothing fanciful about the silenced pistol he, too, was carrying. His close-set black eyes ranged briefly over Finlay and Mrs. MacCrimmon before meeting the gaze of his counterpart.

"Any trouble?" he inquired.

The brown-haired woman shook her head, her expression disparaging. "No. They came along like lambs."

The man in black nodded, apparently satisfied, and turned to the prisoners to gesture with his gun.

"Now then, all of you: Over there."

To Finlay's consternation, the intruders herded the four of them into the adjoining guardroom. From here, a heavy trapdoor gave access to the castle's fourteenth-century dungeon: a steep-sided pit nearly fifteen feet deep, cut right into the castle rock. The man in black caught Finlay by the shoulder and gave him a shove in the direction of the closed trapdoor.

"Pull it up," he commanded.

Mae MacCrimmon made a small noise between a gasp

and a sob. "Oh, not down there, *please*!" she whimpered. "There might be rats, and—"

The man in black turned to face her squarely, raising the silenced muzzle of his pistol to point directly at her forehead.

"Perhaps you'd prefer the alternative?" he suggested.

Mrs. MacCrimmon wilted into shivering silence, cowering with the shaking Mrs. McBain in the circle of Margaret's arms as the man returned his attention to Finlay.

"How about you?"

The old caretaker needed no further encouragement. Being dropped into the pit wasn't going to be pleasant, but it was better than a bullet. Within seconds, he had the trap door open and was glancing up expectantly.

"Go ahead. Put 'em in."

Dutifully Finlay lowered the women into the chilly darkness of the pit—Margaret first, so she could help the other two land, for it still was a nasty drop, once he lowered them to arm's length. It also got her farther away from the man's gun. The women shrieked and cried out, but he wished they would save their breath; there was no one to hear them.

"All right, old man. Now it's your turn," the man said, when the women were down, gesturing with his gun.

Glowering like a thundercloud, and wishing he was twenty years younger, Finlay stiffly eased his way to a sitting position at the edge of the dungeon mouth, feet dangling over the edge, then turned to support himself on his hands and forearms and start lowering himself. Shoulders protesting, he had let himself down to hang by the length of his arms when the man in black gave his clutching fingers an impatient nudge with a boot.

Finlay lost his grip and plummeted into the midst of the shrieking women. He landed crookedly, and bit back a curse as his ankle turned under him. In the darkness of the dungeon Margaret MacLeod groped for her husband's hand. The intensity of his grip told her he was in pain.

"A curse on ye, whoever ye are!" she shouted up at their captor, a dark silhouette against the lighted opening above their heads. "By the luck of the MacLeods, I hope and pray ye may get what ye deserve for this night's work!"

The intruder's response was a sneering laugh and then the hollow boom of the trapdoor being closed over the opening again, shutting out the light. . . .

As soon as her male accomplice had herded his prisoners into the next room, the brown-haired woman set her weapon aside on the piano long enough to close the window and draw the curtains back into place again, to keep up appearances from the outside. That done, she slipped her weapon back into a zippered compartment in her bag and carefully drew out a small red snap-pouch of Chinese silk.

Inside was a heavy silver medallion slung from a silver chain. She slipped the chain over her head and turned toward the wall between the two seaward windows, where the Fairy Flag hung behind its sconced curtains. When she moved, the pendant caught the light, revealing a device like the snarling head of some predatory beast.

She opened the curtains and caught a brief, slightly distorted glimpse of herself mirrored in the glass that covered the Fairy Flag. She did not like this job. One of the stories the old man had told her tour group this afternoon was that anyone besides a MacLeod who touched the Flag would go up in a puff of smoke. That obviously did not refer to the frame or the glass, because she had touched both when the caretaker wasn't looking, but she mistrusted these ancient legends. You could never tell when there might be a grain of truth to them, and she *had* broken her mirror. . . .

But that was just as ridiculous as imagining that the medallion would afford her any protection, if the stories *were* true—though she wore it, because they had told her to. Still, when she reached out with both hands and grasped the ornamented sides of the frame, she smiled as nothing untoward happened.

She shifted it back and forth to test its weight, then took a firmer grip on the moulding and lifted the frame down off the wall. The frame was large, but it was not particularly heavy. Its size simply made it awkward to carry.

Resting it briefly against the wall, she closed the draperies again, so its absence would not be noticed immediately. Then, carrying her prize gingerly in front of her, she moved off toward the door that led to the stairs, making her way cautiously down to the front hall to wait for her accomplice.

She knew he was on his way down when the lights began to go out in the stairwell. When he had joined her, he let them both out through the front door, locking it with keys he had taken from the ticket-taker's desk. It was nearly dark outside, so no one could see them cross over the castle bridge and climb down the embankment toward the single-lane drive normally used by the Chief and his family and staff.

She had left the car in the shadows under the trees, a dark coupe almost invisible in the gathering gloom. The man in black unlocked the car and got in on the driver's side while his female associate carefully loaded the Fairy Flag into the back seat, covering it with a tartan lap rug. As she took the passenger seat in the front, the driver started the engine, driving without lights as they moved slowly up the lane in the direction of the main road.

A short drive brought them along the water's edge to a little rock-bound inlet. At a wooden dock jutting out into the shallows, a small cabin cruiser floated quietly at her moorings.

The driver of the car flashed his headlamps. Aboard the cruiser, someone beamed an answering signal from one of the cabin ports. A moment later, two dark figures emerged onto the deck into the open air.

The two thieves climbed out of the car, the woman again handling the Fairy Flag in its frame. With her accomplice following, she carried it out along the dock to where her employers from the cabin cruiser were waiting to receive it. When she arrived, the shorter member of the pair bent down to examine the frame and its contents by the glow of a pencil flashlight. As he did so, the light glanced rosily off the fine carnelian signet ring he wore on his right hand.

"Very good, indeed," he commented, raising his eyes to meet hers. "Excellent, in fact."

The woman raised an eyebrow in sardonic acknowledgement.

"Thank you. As jobs go, it's more dignified than mud-wrestling. And it pays better. Excuse me while I get rid of this."

Hooking her fingers in the hair at the front of her face, she gave a backwards tug. Short blond hair gleamed pale in the fading light as the brown wig came away in her hand, and she shook her head lightly as she ran her free hand through the hair to riffle it. The man with the carnelian ring watched her from under hooded lids.

"I assume you'll want your pay, so you can be off," he said, motioning to his colleague to take the frame as he reached into the breast of his jacket for a fat brown envelope. "I think you'll find everything in order."

His colleague wore a medallion like the one still around the woman's neck. She eyed it as she reached for the envelope in the other's hand, not noticing that her erstwhile accomplice was moving in closer from behind, drawing his silenced pistol from behind his leg.

In the same instant that her hand touched the envelope, the man in black pressed the muzzle of the silencer just behind her left ear and pulled the trigger. The quiet cough of the shot was inaudible even on the shore, much less in the castle or on the road above. And the second and third shots he fired into her heart, once she was down on the dock, were no louder.

Her employer did not spare her a second look, only turning to follow his underling below decks with the Flag. The man in black knelt briefly to remove the silver medallion from around the woman's neck, then pushed her body over the edge of the dock with no more concern than he would have given a sack of rubbish or a dead cat.

Then, as the boat's engines rumbled to life, the man in black cast off the line securing it to the dock and leaped lightly aboard. Ten minutes later, boat, passengers, and stolen treasure had disappeared into the twilight, leaving only a faintly phosphorescent wake that faded steadily with the lowering dusk.

Chapter Sixteen

MEANWHILE, as planned, Adam and Peregrine had spent their second day in London at the Docklands headquarters of the Scottish Geographical Society. Upon their arrival, Adam introduced himself to the receptionist as Dr. Sinclair, at the same time presenting Peregrine as his research assistant. He did not mention that his title was that of a medical doctor rather than an academic one. A seemingly offhand reference to the talk he had given the previous week at Gleneagles helped to reinforce the impression that he was a historian gathering material for a series of scholarly lectures.

"Oh, dear," said the woman behind the desk, though she clearly was favorably impressed with Adam's manner and appearance. "I'm afraid we don't seem to have you written into our appointment book, Dr. Sinclair, but maybe something can be arranged—since you're only here for the day. Why don't you and Mr. Lovat have a seat, and I'll phone upstairs to ask if someone might be free."

"That's very kind of you," Adam said warmly. "Of course we'll wait. And thank you very much."

It took some doing, but in the end they were able to secure the services of one of the senior archivists, a stocky, middle-aged Glaswegian by the name of Ronald McKay. Under his guidance, Adam and Peregrine spent the morning reading through microfilmed articles on archaeological fieldworks in Ross-shire. After lunch they examined the Society's accumulated wealth of pictorial data—survey photos and reconstruction blueprints—in comparison with the sketches Peregrine himself had made. By the end of the day, after exhausting every available file on the subject, they had managed to compile a list of four Ross-shire castles worthy of further investigation: Foulis, Strome, Eilean Donan, and Urquhart.

"Whew! I hope we don't have to do *that* again, any time soon!" Peregrine exclaimed, as they climbed into a taxi to return to the Caledonian Club. "One hour more, and I would have had a headache the size of Blenheim Palace!"

Adam smiled distractedly, mentally reviewing the four names on the list. All four were located on sites overlooking water, and all four had been in existence at the time Michael Scot had lived, but beyond that, they had not managed to narrow the field any further.

"Well, we might have done worse," he said with a sigh, "but I must confess, I had hoped we might do significantly better."

Peregrine grimaced. "I know what you mean. Any one of the sites on our short list could turn out to be the castle we're looking for—or none of them, for that matter. I may be totally off base."

"Do you think you are?" Adam asked.

"No. But unless you know of any other documentary sources we haven't yet considered, I can't think of any way to narrow down the list to one."

Adam shook his head. "I'm afraid you're quite right. We've done everything that paperwork could accomplish. Our only recourse from here is to visit these places in person."

Peregrine looked slightly daunted. "You mean, go there?"

"Yes."

"But—won't that take rather a lot of time?"

"A day or two," Adam admitted. "But if we don't begin, we shan't find out, shall we?"

"I suppose not," Peregrine said. "Will we be flying back to Scotland tonight, then?"

A line appeared between Adam's dark brows, and he leaned back against the vinyl-upholstered seat of the taxi, looking suddenly weary.

"No, we'll catch an early shuttle in the morning," he said. "We've done enough—more than enough—for one day. Nothing hampers the mind like fatigue. I want us well rested before we set out for the Highlands."

Back at Adam's club, they ate dinner early, while the dining room was still largely empty. Once the meal was over, Peregrine found himself more than ready to retire to his room. His neck was stiff from the unaccustomed hours he had spent hunched over the microfilm reader, and his eyes were burning from the effort of doing too much close work in poor lighting. A hot shower helped to alleviate the worst of his aches and pains, and he fell asleep almost as soon as his head touched the pillow.

Dreams came and went, most of them quite unmemorable. But sometime in the dead of night, he woke suddenly to what he thought at first was the angry braying of a trumpet. He started up in bed and listened intently, but his straining ears could pick up nothing but the omnipresent rumble of traffic moving through the midnight streets of the capital.

I must be imagining things, he thought with a shrug, and lay back down.

But echoes of the strange, angry alarm continued to reverberate at the back of his mind, like a memory of the warhorns of Elfland wildly blowing. Eventually he fell asleep again, with the half-formed intention of relating the incident to Adam the next day; but in the cold light of morning, the whole thing seemed too trivial to be worth mentioning.

Keep on like this, and before long, you'll be running around claiming the sky is falling, he told himself with a grimace, as he finished knotting his tie and ran a comb through his hair. *Adam's already got enough to worry about, without you inventing new distractions.*

With this admonition in mind, he put the matter aside and went downstairs, appearing promptly at seven, as agreed the night before. He decided that Adam must have spent a restless night as well, because his mentor was uncharacteristically silent and even a little testy over breakfast. His usual perusal of the morning paper seemed more intent than usual, as if he were looking for something specific; but he offered no explanation, and Peregrine did not press the issue.

Still on schedule, so far as Peregrine could tell, they were walking out the front door of the Caledonian Club well before eight, their few bags in hand. But no sooner had they emerged onto Halkin Street, intending to have the doorman hail them a taxi to the airport, then Adam eyed the already heavy traffic of morning rush hour and instead began herding Peregrine in the direction of Hyde Park Corner.

"I'll swear the traffic gets worse, every time I come to London," he said sourly, consulting his watch. "I hadn't reckoned on it being this heavy, this early. We'll have to take the Tube. It will be standing room only, at this hour, but I'm afraid it's the only way we're going to make our flight."

The Tube *was* standing room only. Flowing with the expected crush of morning commuters, in an atmosphere increasingly redolent of stale clothing and warring perfumes, they boarded the first available westbound train and spent the next forty-five minutes clinging precariously to handholds along the ceiling, bags braced between their feet. Only past Acton did the crowd begin to thin out, and even then, they had to stand for several more stops.

They arrived at Heathrow with a scant twenty minutes to spare before the 9:30 shuttle. Fortunately, Adam had booked seats the night before, and they had only carry-on luggage, so securing their tickets and checking in was a relatively rapid procedure. After signing off on the credit card slip, Adam sent Peregrine off to buy a Glasgow newspaper while he telephoned Strathmourne. There would be copies of *The Scotsman* aboard the shuttle, so he would check that during the flight up.

"After looking at where we've got to go, I've changed my mind about taking the Jag," he told Humphrey, after verifying that they would, indeed, be arriving on the flight Adam had designated in the previous night's call. "I think you'd better pick us up in the Range Rover. And please pack us each a change of clothes suitable for stomping around uncertain terrain in uncertain weather. If my suspicions are correct, and time *is* running short, we can't afford even slight delays in getting under way."

"I understand, sir," Humphrey replied. "I'll make all the necessary arrangements."

The loudspeakers were announcing the final call for their flight. All he and Peregrine had to do now was make the plane. They were not the last ones aboard, but delays at security screening had him fidgeting for a few minutes. As he and Peregrine buckled up and the plane started to taxi out to the runway, Adam at last allowed himself to relax a little—which only gave him time to feed his growing apprehension.

Something new was brewing, almost certainly some new facet of what they had left behind in Scotland. He searched for it in the copy of the Glasgow paper Peregrine had brought him and in *The Scotsman*, but nothing spoke to him.

Were the obstacles they were encountering a part of some emerging pattern of opposition on the Inner Planes, or were they random? He told himself that most of the obstacles could be chalked up to coincidence; but another part of him worried that it was all part of some sinister design being carried out by an enemy he had yet to meet face to face. Until he knew more, all he could do was trust to the innate survival instincts of his higher self, and hope that their adversaries would soon show themselves—and hopefully, make a mistake.

Their flight was routine, though the air turbulence increased the farther north they flew. The skies over southern Scotland were patched with racing scuds of dirty grey, and their aircraft descended through gusty showers. They touched down at Edinburgh on a wet runway and taxied to the terminal amid windblown outbursts of rain.

By the time the jetway was run alongside and they were permitted to begin deplaning, Adam had decided to ring Noel McLeod as soon as they got inside the terminal building. With single-minded impatience, he led Peregrine toward the arrival gate, raising a hailing hand as he spotted Humphrey, waiting just beyond the barrier.

But his valet was not alone. Adam stiffened as he

recognized the moustached figure in the trenchcoat, all the slowly-building apprehension of the past twelve hours or so finally crystallizing.

"What is it?" Peregrine asked.

"There with Humphrey—it's Noel McLeod," Adam replied. "And unless I'm very much mistaken, his presence confirms the trouble I couldn't find in the papers this morning. Come on!"

Leaving Peregrine to make his own way, Adam lengthened his stride and darted forward, weaving his way through the intervening throngs with an evasive skill a professional soccer-player might have envied. Humphrey and McLeod converged to meet him. The inspector's craggy face was looking uncommonly grim, and his mouth was tight.

"Why do I get the distinct impression you're about to give me news I don't want to hear?" Adam said to McLeod, at the same time handing off his carry-on to Humphrey. "I was going to call you as soon as I could get to a telephone. Peregrine, get in here, so he doesn't have to tell it twice."

Peregrine hurried to join them, looking slightly ruffled and mystified. McLeod greeted the artist with a curt nod and ushered them all aside, Humphrey taking up a station with the bags a few paces away, to deflect passers-by.

"This comes totally out of left field," McLeod said, "but suddenly everything starts to make sense. Not quite two hours ago, I received a phone call from my clan chief. He's in New York right now. He'd just had words with his staff up at Dunvegan Castle. It seems that the Fairy Flag has been stolen."

Neither of his listeners needed any explanation of what the Flag was. The Fairy Flag of the MacLeods was one of Scotland's most famous artifacts, and the legends surrounding it were common knowledge to anyone with even a modicum of interest in Scottish folklore. More knowledgeable than most, Adam experienced a sick, sinking feeling in the pit of his stomach.

"When did this happen?" he asked.

"Late yesterday afternoon, some time between five and six o'clock, as near as anyone can make out," McLeod replied. "We're a bit short on details yet, but it seems the thief was a woman posing as a tourist. She had a male accomplice, but he wore a ski mask, so we have no description of him. Both of them were certainly armed."

"Was anyone harmed?" Adam asked.

"No, thank God. At least nothing serious. A twisted ankle, some bumps and bruises. There were four members of the castle staff on duty, and the thieves put them down the castle dungeon for the night. It's one of those bottle dungeons—a nasty drop, but they were safe enough, once they were down.

"They'd probably be there still, except that a busload of English pensioners showed up for a prearranged tour, before regular opening hours, and got concerned when they saw cars in the staff car park but couldn't rouse anyone inside. The local police are investigating, checking out every car in a fifty-mile radius, but you know as well as I that the perpetrators could be anywhere by now. They've had all night to make their getaway."

Peregrine had been looking more and more incredulous as McLeod's story went on, and by now could not contain his indignation.

"This is incredible. How did they get in? It's a *castle*, for God's sake! That's hardly the usual target for breaking and entering."

McLeod favored the younger man with a sour smile. "The woman apparently played the damsel in distress—came back to the castle, minutes after closing time, claiming to have lost her car keys somewhere on the premises. The caretaker, being the trusting sort, let her in—and *she* managed to let in her accomplice. The rest you can gather for yourselves. The staff were all old-age pensioners themselves. What kind of fight could they put up against armed and determined robbers?"

During the course of this recital, most of the other newly arrived passengers had dispersed, leaving the three of them standing alone at the side of the concourse. Humphrey waited patiently beside their luggage, affecting not to overhear their conversation. McLeod glanced briefly up and down the concourse before going on.

"Anyway, the MacLeod himself has appointed me to act on his behalf," he said, his blue eyes bright and sharp. "He's *most* concerned that the perpetrators be tracked down and the Flag recovered, before they get a chance to misuse it or even destroy it. I phoned Strathmourne as soon as he'd rung off, and when Humphrey told me he was just leaving to collect you, I thought it would save time if I passed on this latest development in person. I'm acting in a private capacity, of course, but I've arranged for a chartered plane to fly me up to Skye in about an hour. There's seating room to spare, if you think you might be able to come along. I've a feeling that this may all tie into the fun and games last Sunday at Melrose."

"We'll come, of course," Adam said, "though I'm wishing I'd known in time to have Humphrey bring along a few useful accoutrements."

At the mention of his name, Humphrey cleared his throat and moved a step closer.

"Begging your pardon, Sir Adam, but I believe I may have anticipated this eventuality. After speaking with the inspector earlier this morning, I took the liberty of bringing along some additional items besides what you specifically requested. You know the ones I mean, sir—in that medical bag that you often take on house calls."

A brief but pleased smile flitted across Adam's otherwise stern demeanor.

"Humphrey, somehow you always manage to make me look far better than I would on my own accord." He turned to the waiting McLeod. "And Noel—it appears we're better prepared than I thought."

"Is that the royal 'we,' or will Mr. Lovat be coming as well?" McLeod inquired blandly.

"Well, of course I'm coming!" Peregrine said indignantly.

"Not so fast, son," McLeod warned. "It could be dangerous—probably a damned sight more dangerous than you imagine."

"Oh, bother *that*!" Peregrine declared. "Do you think I can't handle myself in a pinch, or that I want to miss out on all the excitement? I've put in my time with the books and musty documents, Adam. Please let me come."

McLeod looked askance at Adam. "You know how hairy it's apt to get, if this means what I think it does. Do you really think he's ready for this?"

"Actually, I think we may well need him," Adam replied, to Peregrine's unmitigated relief.

"Right then. If you want him along, that's good enough for me. Humphrey, are those all the bags?"

"Yes, Inspector."

"Then I suggest you take them over to the lounge at Hangar B," McLeod went on, "if that's all right with you, Adam. They're gassing up our plane and doing the pre-flight checks. We've just about got time for a quick sandwich and cup of coffee before we head over—God knows when we'll have time to eat again. Meanwhile, Humphrey can bring in your changes of clothes. Our pilot tells me the weather's blowing up something fierce, over by Skye."

A few minutes and a short phone call later, to alert Airport Security that Humphrey would be arriving, the three of them were tucked into a booth at the back of the airport cafe, continuing their discussion of the theft at Dunvegan over stale sandwiches and tepid coffee. Adam was frowning as he chewed, his dark eyes fiercely thoughtful.

"I detect an ugly pattern emerging here," he murmured. "The theft of Francis Hepburn's sword, the violation of Michael Scot's grave—and of Scot himself—and now this. It all has to be the work of the same people. And whoever they are, it's plain they're quite determined to get what they want."

"But, what do they want with the Fairy Flag?" Peregrine asked, looking from Adam to McLeod and back again. "Presumably they aren't MacLeods. No MacLeod would do what they've done. So what earthly use would they have for the Fairy Flag, unless—" A look of sudden enlightenment came over his face.

"Of course! It isn't an earthly use at all. It has to do with fairies. And Scot's book and his gold are hidden in a fairy cave!"

"Precisely," Adam agreed. "And just offhand, I would guess that our thieves believe the Flag has power to protect them from the cave's guardians, just as they intend to use the Hepburn Sword for that purpose." He glanced at McLeod. "You're the expert here, Noel. *Have* they the right of it? *Will* the Flag keep the Sidhe at bay?"

McLeod scowled down at the coffee stains left in his styrofoam cup. "That's going to depend on how they handle it," he said slowly. "One of our very ancient traditions states that if anyone *not* a MacLeod were to lay hands on the Flag, he'd go up with a bang, in a puff of smoke. It would appear that the thieves left the Flag in its frame when they took it, so *that* legend hasn't been tested yet. But whether or not they can use it for their own purposes, without actually touching it, is an open question. Maybe they intend to leave it as it is, and use it literally as a shield."

"What if they were to try unfurling it?" Adam asked.

McLeod shook his head. "It wouldn't muster up the fairy host to give victory to the summoners, if that's what you're thinking. Only a Chief of the MacLeods can do that, and only on behalf of the clan."

At Peregrine's look of question, Adam pushed aside his empty cup.

"When the Fairy Flag first came into the possession of Clan MacLeod," he explained, "the Chief at the time was told that the Flag would guarantee victory in battle to whomever should unfurl it. However, this favor would be limited to three occasions. Since then, the MacLeods have twice unfurled the Flag to save the clan from defeat and destruction—once at the battle of Glendale in 1490, and a second time at the battle of Trumpan Brig in—1530, was it, Noel?"

"Aye. What worries me, on a purely personal level, is that the Flag may be destroyed—whatever else may happen. If they *are* intending to use it as a shield, and its frame gets broken open in the process, that could be tragedy enough, the thing's that ancient and fragile."

"Unfortunately, I think they probably *will* use it as a shield," Adam said. "Even in its frame, if they know what they're doing, they may be able to harness its power in another way. It's a fairy talisman, after all—use fairy power to control fairies. I suspect that's what they're banking on."

Peregrine's expression had been growing steadily more indignant throughout this recital.

"That's appalling!" he exclaimed. "Where is this all going to end?"

"At the castle where Scot hid his book and gold," said McLeod, "and where those who seek that treasure will also use Francis Hepburn's sword to ward off the treasure's rightful guardians. God, if we only knew which castle it was!"

"Well, we're closer than we were, thanks to Peregrine's work in London," Adam said. "We think we've narrowed down the choices to four castles in Scot's old haunts. Perhaps the final clue we need is waiting for us at Dunvegan." He consulted his watch. "Which reminds me that we'd better be on our way, if you think the plane is ready. Unless I miss my guess, matters may very well come to a head *tonight*."

"Why tonight?" Peregrine asked.

McLeod pulled a mirthless smile as he rose and began gathering up their luncheon debris.

"In case you may have forgotten, tonight's the last night in October, Hallowe'en, the night before All Hallows. We Christians call it All Souls' Night. Others might prefer to call it Samhain."

"Samhain . . ." Peregrine repeated. McLeod had pronounced it in the Highland manner, *Sow-an*, and the younger man savored the name uncertainly on his tongue.

"Samhain, the Witches' Sabbat," Adam said. "Perhaps the single most perilous night in the year. The night when the doors that separate the physical world from the worlds of the spirit are thrown wide, and all objects and entities of power are at the height of their influence."

His dark gaze strayed beyond the confines of their immediate surroundings. "Yes, it would be an appropriate time to hazard a confrontation with the People of the Hills. The Fairy Folk themselves will be powerful enough, but the occult influences of the sword and the Fairy Flag also will be at their most potent, from the rising of the moon tonight. . . ."

As planned, they made a brief detour to the Hangar B lounge, so that Adam and Peregrine could don the more serviceable outdoor clothing Humphrey had brought: tweed trousers, stout walking shoes, and a tough, thorn-proof hacking jacket over a good Arran sweater for Adam; and cords, a turtleneck sweater, and a quilted shooting vest for Peregrine. Outer wear had been provided as well: Peregrine's navy duffel coat and the green waxed jacket that Adam wore riding when it was wet. As Peregrine was lacing up a stout pair of hiking boots, he glanced up just in time to glimpse Adam slipping something long and narrow and shiny black into the inside breast pocket of his hacking jacket.

"Necessities of the hunt," Adam remarked, seeing Peregrine's interest, though he made no move to show Peregrine what it was or to offer any further explanation.

Pretending he had not really seen, Peregrine hastily averted his gaze and finished with his boots, wondering if this might be one of the items from the mysterious black medical bag Humphrey had mentioned. Now that he thought to look for it, he noticed it sitting at Adam's feet, closed, but with the latch unsnapped. Whatever it might contain, Adam's manner suggested that it was something to be kept private, at least for the present.

They left their extra luggage with Humphrey, taking only a shaving kit apiece, Peregrine's sketchbox, and Adam's black bag before going outside to join McLeod. He was pacing the tarmac beside a trim Cessna six-seater whose starboard engine was already warming up. Their gear fit easily with his in the plane's small tail hold, and he gestured impatiently for them to board.

As Adam settled into the seat behind the pilot, Peregrine stuffed their coats into one of the rear seats and buckled in beside him. McLeod closed the cabin door and came forward to take the copilot's seat as the port engine roared to life. The craft's twin propellers spun whirring ghost-circles in the air as they moved out along the taxi strip and headed toward an active runway. Within a matter of minutes, they were in the air and on their way.

The flight took nearly two hours. In the smaller plane, the turbulence Adam and Peregrine had experienced on the approach to Edinburgh was more pronounced, and increased as the Cessna winged its way north-northwest amid buffeting crosswinds. Very quickly, the green, rolling hills around the Firth of Forth gave way to the higher, darker slopes of Strathclyde. The rugged highland landscape beneath them showed plum-brown and grey-green through the tears in the clouds.

North they flew along Loch Linnhe, heading westward between Loch Eil and Loch Arkaig, and then picking up Loch Hourn as it led up toward the Sound of Sleat. Beyond loomed the Isle of Skye, its stony headlands overshadowed by a lilac pall of mingled cloud and rain. They curved right to parallel the sound, then followed the curving coastline around to the seaward side. Looking down, Peregrine caught sight of the island ferry ploughing its way unevenly across the channel through a choppy expanse of white-capped waves. Very shortly, the Cessna banked sharply left again and started to descend.

"Airstrip ahead, gents," the pilot called back over his shoulder. "Check your seat belts and brace yourselves. It's going to be a bit bumpy coming down."

The island's airfield turned out to be little more than a windswept expanse of grey-black tarmac overlooking the white-capped water. No other planes were on the ground, and the place looked utterly deserted. Their pilot taxied the plane in front of a small hangar with white plastic siding, just inside the barbed wire perimeter fence, and cut the engines. They could feel the wind buffeting the plane as he made his way to the rear and opened the door, jumping down to offer a steadying hand as his passengers also began to disembark.

"Not much of a place, is it?" the pilot remarked, pitching his voice loud into the spanking breeze. "There *is* a control tower, over in that portable building, but they don't man it except on special occasions—mostly in the summer. Here, I'll get your gear."

Opening the hatch to the Cessna's small cargo bay, he began handing out what little personal baggage his passengers had brought with them. Peregrine shrugged on his duffel coat and buttoned it, turning up the collar against the gusting wind. As he picked up his shaving kit and portable sketchbox, he noticed that both Adam and McLeod had bundled woolen scarves around their necks, and he dug into his own pockets for a pair of fingerless woolen gloves.

The pilot closed the cargo hatch and clamped his cap more firmly to his head, his freckled face puckering with concern as he peered up at the thickening clouds.

"I hope you're planning either a very short visit or quite a long one," he said, "because I'm going to have to get out of here pretty sharpish. The Highland weather service started handing out storm warnings on the way here. It's gonna get a whole lot worse before it gets better."

He pointed across the airstrip to where a bright orange windsock was flapping wildly against its moorings. "You can see for yourselves how the wind's freshening. If I hang around, I'm likely to find myself grounded."

"Go ahead, then, while you still can," McLeod said. "You've done your bit, getting us this far. We'll make our own arrangements from here."

"If you say so," the pilot said with an amiable grin. "I'm off, then. Cheerio. . . ."

He climbed back aboard the Cessna and closed the door, waiting until the three had moved a few yards away before starting up the engines. As the little aircraft trundled down the runway and again became airborne, side-slipping as gusts buffeted it, the men left on the landing strip turned their backs to the wind and drew closer together. Blowing on his exposed fingertips, Peregrine cast a dismal eye over their surroundings.

"I hate to say this," he announced, "but I don't see any sign of a telephone."

"There isn't one," McLeod said matter-of-factly. "That's why I brought my own."

He unzipped one of the side pouches on his overnight bag and extracted a cellular phone unit. He was about to switch it on when a grey Volvo estate car came rumbling into view along the unpaved track that connected the airfield with the main road.

"Perhaps you won't have to bother with that," Adam said. "It would appear that someone's sent a welcoming party."

The Volvo was moving fast, its wheels throwing up sprays of wet gravel as it negotiated the ruts. As McLeod straightened to watch, it rattled noisily across the cattle grid that lay just outside the open gate, shooting on through the gap and coming to an abrupt halt but a few yards from where the three of them were standing. A fair-haired young man in a cloth cap rolled down the window and gave McLeod a wave.

"Hullo, Inspector!" he called. "Would ye be needin' a lift, now?"

McLeod's craggy face creased in the first smile Peregrine had seen all day.

"Sandy!" he exclaimed. "How did you know when to come? I was just about to put in a call to the castle, and here you are!"

"Och, we saw the plane comin' in, so I thought I'd better get down here. My da had word direct from the Chief tae say ye'd be handling this case for us, so we figured it had tae be you. We dinnae get that many planes, this time o' year." He threw open the door and stepped out onto the turf, unfolding to well over six feet. "The Chief said ye were tae have all the assistance we could give ye. Dad took that tae mean *not* leaving ye tae cool your heels at the airstrip any longer than anyone could help. Can I help ye with yer bags?"

McLeod chuckled with genuine good humor as he turned to Adam and Peregrine.

"You see how helpfulness and good sense run in the MacLeods," he said. "I want you both to meet Alexander MacLeod. His father is head caretaker at the castle. Sandy, I'd like you to meet Sir Adam Sinclair of Strathmourne and his associate, Mr. Lovat. They're going to be giving us a hand with the investigation."

Sandy gave a tug at the brim of his cap. "I'm sore pleased

tae meet both of ye, gentlemen. An' if ye can help the inspector get the Flag back for us, ye may be sure of the friendship of the MacLeods forever—for the luck of the clan stands or falls by it."

CHAPTER SEVENTEEN

RELIEVED to get out of the wind, Adam and Peregrine slid into the rear seat of the Volvo, stowing their scant luggage behind the seat and leaving McLeod to sit up front. With an admonition to hang on, Sandy swung the car around in a tight U-turn and headed back up the lane toward the main road. Within minutes they were roaring along the A850 toward Dunvegan Castle.

The road was narrow and winding, and fortunately empty. Sandy drove at top speed, making scant allowance for dips and bends, cutting the inside of curves. As they bore left at Sligachen, changing to another "A" road, Peregrine braced himself and briefly closed his eyes, taking but little comfort in the assumption that Sandy MacLeod must know this stretch of road like the back of his hand. White-knuckled and silent, he soon abandoned all thought of admiring the scenery as they raced through the hills under a lowering pall of cloud.

They ran into a squall just north of the village of Bracadale. The driving downpour eased a few minutes later, but the wind persisted, whistling shrilly through the wet heather on the high ground. By the time they reached the fork in the road leading up to Dunvegan, the broken cloud banks had begun to close ranks, and the turbulent air carried the bitter tang of ozone, like a threat of impending lightning.

"I don't like the feel of this," McLeod muttered over his shoulder to Adam and Peregrine. "There's something uncanny about the way the wind keeps changing."

"Changing?" Adam was instantly alert.

"Aye," said McLeod. "Hadn't you noticed? It's chasing itself around in circles, widdershins. Whatever else it is, it isn't natural."

He spoke with authority. It reminded Peregrine that McLeod had spent at least one previous lifetime battling the elements at sea. Adam peered out the window for a moment at the racing scenery, and presumably the errant wind, then shook his head.

"I wish I could reassure you that it's nothing to worry about," he said, "but unfortunately, I can't. If it's what I suspect, this may be even harder than we thought. But there's nothing to be done about it just now."

On that enigmatic note, he fell silent—which only made Peregrine worry more, for he had not a clue what the other two were talking about. The wind just looked like wind, to him. He glanced at Sandy, hoping the younger man might offer some additional comment, but Sandy seemed intent on his driving—for which Peregrine was grateful, for the driving conditions were atrocious. Still, his silence did nothing to reassure Peregrine about the enigmatic wind.

Their route to the castle took them steadily northwest, eventually skirting briefly along the eastern shore of Loch Dunvegan. About a mile short of their destination, within sight of the weathered timbers of Dunvegan Pier, Sandy suddenly emitted a grunt of surprise and began applying the brakes.

As the Volvo lurched to a halt, its three other passengers saw that a police barrier had been set up across the road. A broad figure in a fluorescent macintosh stepped out from behind the barrier and strode forward to meet them, sergeant's stripes bold on both sleeves. Sandy cranked down his window as the wearer came around toward the driver's side.

"What's goin' on, Davie?" he asked. "Have ye no' had enough trouble for one day?"

"Aye, ye'd think so," the sergeant replied. "As if it wasnae bad enough ye had the robbery up at the castle, Tam Dewar's just pulled a body out o' the water, out past the seal colony. Happened about an hour ago. He an' his brother were checkin' their lobster pots."

Beyond the barrier, two police cars and an ambulance van were pulled up on the left-hand shoulder of the road. The wind-driven stretch of exposed beach below was dotted with moving figures, anonymous in glistening macs and rain-hoods, and there was more activity on the pier.

McLeod threw a sneaking glance over his shoulder at Adam before asking, "Was the victim somebody local?"

The Island policeman eyed him in unconcealed surprise. "An' who might ye be, sir?"

"Now, Davie, there's nae need tae gawk like a mackerel," Sandy said tartly, before McLeod could answer. "This is Detective Inspector Noel McLeod. The Chief's called him up from Edinburgh, tae look into last night's theft. Show him yer ID, Inspector."

"I'm not here in any official capacity, understand," McLeod said, as he produced his police credential. "Just as a favor, from a clansman to his clan and Chief. I'm sure your people are quite capable of handling the police side of things."

The sergeant's troubled face cleared slightly at the statement of confidence, and as he verified the ID.

"Weel, now. That's all right, then, isn't it? If the Chief called ye in. . . . Tae answer yer question, the dead woman wasnae anyone from around here. We didnae find any identification on the body, but all her clothes had foreign labels. We think she may hae been Dutch—or possibly Scandinavian. We'll know more, maybe, when we get the fingerprint report back from Fort William."

"How did she die?" asked Adam. "Did she drown?"

The sergeant turned to gaze at Adam as though seeing him for the first time.

"This is Sir Adam Sinclair," McLeod said crisply. "He's a physician. He and his associate, Mr. Lovat, are here to lend me a hand."

"As ye say, sir." The police sergeant accepted McLeod's explanation with a nod, before returning his attention to Adam. "No, she didnae drown. She was shot in the side o' the head, at pointblank range, and she took two more bullets tae the heart."

At Adam's noncommital, "Ah," McLeod scowled even more darkly.

"Are you saying it was an execution, Sergeant?"

The sergeant shrugged. "Weel, I wouldnae go so far as that," he said. "Granted, we dinnae get much o' this sort o' thing around here, but—weel, it did look tae me like the killer made a professional job of it. Ye might care tae have a wee look at the body for yerselves, before the medics ship it off tae the hospital morgue in Portree. The bullet that killed her made a bit of a mess o' her face, but otherwise, she fits the general description o' the woman who took part in yer robbery."

"I think we *will* have a look at that body," McLeod said, already opening his car door.

Sandy stayed behind with the Volvo. Adam and McLeod set off down the beach in the company of the police sergeant, shoulders hunched against the buffeting of the off-shore gale. Peregrine lagged behind long enough to retrieve his sketchbox from the back of the car, then followed after. A random gust sent a shiver up the back of his neck, but he told himself it was just the cold and hugged his sketchbox closer to his chest.

He caught up with his companions halfway along the length of the pier. The body was lying stretched out on a heavy sheet of tarpaulin a few feet short of the pier's end. The men from the ambulance were getting ready to transfer it to a black plastic body-bag.

"Hold up a minute, Geordie," the sergeant called. "We've got a couple o' experts here tae take a look at what we've found."

The men stood back to make room for the newcomers. While McLeod looked on, Adam crouched down to examine the body. Peregrine hung back, white-knuckled.

The woman appeared to have been in her early thirties, with blond hair clipped so short it was almost crewcut. An overnight immersion in seawater had washed away most of the blood, but the cause of death was unmistakable. The bullet had entered just behind the left ear, exiting below the right eye. From the sergeant's description, Adam had expected major facial disfigurement, but in fact the damage was fairly minimal—not that the face elicited any twinge of recognition.

Sighing, Adam turned his attention to a superficial inspection of her body. The chest wounds were self-evident; and other than a few lacerations on the legs—apparently made after death, since there was no bruising—he could find no other visible marks, no signs of a struggle. The hands were neat and well-manicured, the fingers slender and tapering, blackened at the tips from taking a set of fingerprints.

"Good hands for a thief," McLeod grunted at his elbow. "I'll wager a month's salary she's got a police record someplace—even if it isn't here in Scotland."

"A professional, done to death by a professional," Adam said quietly. "And you think she *was* involved in stealing the Flag?"

McLeod nodded. "I feel it in my bones, Adam. I don't know why she was killed, but she's our lady thief, mark my words."

Adam looked around for Peregrine. The young artist was clinging to one of the pilings closer to shore, fair hair feathered wild by the wind. He was gazing out at the tossing waves with a wooden expression on his thin face. It was clear that he was not finding it easy to come to terms with the physical evidence of premeditated murder.

Adam got to his feet and went over to him. At his approach, Peregrine turned and gave him a hollow look.

"I thought it couldn't be worse than Melrose," he said bleakly, "but somehow, it is."

A white-crested wave crashed into the pier, sending seawater splashing high into the air. Both men shrank from the flying spray, and Adam steadied Peregrine with one strong hand.

"I think I know what you're feeling," he said, his voice carrying clear and low through the surge of wind and water. "Sudden and violent death is always disturbing. That's what makes it something to be resisted with equal intensity." Continuing to watch Peregrine closely, he added, "Noel and

I don't always enjoy the work we do, Peregrine. But it still has to be done."

The younger man lowered his head. "I'm sorry. I didn't mean to be difficult. Did you want me to make some sketches?"

Adam tilted his face to the stormy sky. "*Can* you, in these conditions?"

"I'll manage," Peregrine said, squaring his shoulders.

Moving closer to the corpse, he shielded his sketchbox with his body and took out a drawing pad and pencil. Seeing what he was about to do, McLeod moved over to help Adam screen him from the force of the wind. Peregrine's face was stiff and pale at first, as he stared down at his subject, his initial pencil strokes tentative and halting.

Then all at once he seemed to relax. His gaze focused and sharpened, and his sketching became swift and decisive. Intrigued, Adam and McLeod watched over his shoulder as a finely detailed image took shape.

The portrait was that of the murdered woman—not as she was now, but as she must have appeared shortly prior to her death. The face and clothing were unchanged, but the hair now was longer and dark, cut in a fashionable bob. She wore glasses, too—missing now, after her buffeting in the sea.

More significant still, to Adam's way of thinking, was the fact that Peregrine had drawn a large medallion hung on a chain around his subject's neck. As if in response to what was in Adam's mind, the artist indicated the pendant with a touch of one forefinger.

"There's another one of those medallions, like the one I drew at Melrose," he murmured dreamily. "I'd swear it carried the same device—only I still can't make out what it is."

Adam laid a quieting hand on his forearm. At his touch, Peregrine recollected himself, closing his sketchbook self-consciously and then making a nonchalant show of putting it away. Thoughtful, Adam turned back to the Island policeman, who had been watching all with undisguised curiosity.

"Mr. Lovat is a forensic artist," he explained, stretching

the truth only a little, to defuse any further speculation. "Tell me, was this woman wearing any jewellery when her body was recovered?"

The sergeant shook his head, apparently satisfied with the explanation.

"Jewellery? No, sir. Not a ring, not a brooch, not even so much as a wristwatch. I know the men who found her," he added, "and I'll vouch for their honesty. Tam's an elder o' the Kirk."

"That's fine," Adam said. "I wasn't questioning—just wondering."

As he and McLeod traded glances, the inspector drew him a few steps farther away, leaning in so that his mouth was close to Adam's ear.

"I guess that confirms what we already suspected: that the folk who engineered this job are the same ones who summoned Michael Scot at Melrose and who stole Francis Hepburn's sword."

Adam nodded. "I agree. And it occurs to me that this murder has some of the same earmarks of another unsolved murder that I've remarked upon before. I wonder if your mystery drug-dealer, over in Glasgow, could actually have been hired to steal the sword, and then was killed for his efforts, with it made to *look* like a bad drug deal. I'd guess this woman was also an outsider—a small-time professional, hired on for this particular job and then killed to safeguard the identity of her employers."

Peregrine huddled in closer to follow what they were saying.

"But—if she wasn't a member of the gang," hc ventured, "why give her a medallion?"

"Not a gang," Adam corrected. "More in the nature of a magical lodge, I'm beginning to suspect—a lodge of black magicians, by the evidence so far. And to answer your question, they would have given it to her for protection."

"Protection from the Flag," Peregrine asked, "because she wasn't a MacLeod?"

"Quite likely," Adam agreed. "The Fairy Flag is a powerfully charged artifact. Even insulated behind glass, which *probably* would make it safe to handle, it still represents a potentially dangerous source of elemental energy.

"So the woman's employers took what measures they could to make sure she would survive long enough to perform her function. They let her wear one of their medallions. The fact that you can't see its design clearly, Peregrine, tends to confirm that it, too, was a powerfully charged talisman of some sort, perhaps representing a symbol peculiar to this particular black lodge."

McLeod sighed heavily. "I was afraid it might come to this. Do you think she was shot as soon as she handed over the Flag?"

Adam thought a moment, then nodded. "I do. And my guess is that the shooting probably took place somewhere along the shore here, since I doubt the killers would have bothered to transport the body any great distance. That suggests they may have intended to take the Flag away by boat, rather than by car."

"Which means that the Flag really could be anywhere by now," McLeod said, glowering out at the sea beyond the dock. "If they didn't take it in a car, that throws an entirely different light on our investigation."

"Not necessarily," Adam said. "If we're right about their motives, then they're going after Scot's book and gold tonight. Those are hidden somewhere right here in the Highlands, probably in or near one of the four locations Peregrine and I have identified. I suggest we go on up to the castle and see where the Flag was stolen from, and see if we can pick up a lead on where it went from there."

A respectable drizzle had started up again while they talked, and they took leave of their helpful police sergeant with a hurried word of thanks before beating a prudent retreat to the Volvo. Sandy was pacing the ground at the side of the road, anxiously awaiting their return. McLeod was the first to reach him.

"We were right to stop here first," he told the younger MacLeod. "It seems someone shot your lady robber. I think we'd better go on to the castle now."

Sandy needed no extra encouragement. After creeping around the police barrier, he accelerated sharply up the hill, skilfully negotiating the tight turn between the piers at the gate and heading along the tree-lined lane used by the castle's residents and staff. Very shortly, they were pulling up outside the main entrance, just to the landward side of the bridge that led up to the main door. A sign just to the right of the door read, "Castle closed today."

The police had already departed, having done all they could for the time being. As Adam and his companions followed Sandy MacLeod into the vestibule, they were greeted by a grizzled man on crutches and a plump, grey-haired woman with eyes bright as a sparrow's behind twinkling spectacles.

"So, *there* ye are, Noel McLeod!" the latter called, coming to embrace him with a swift hug, damp trenchcoat and all.

"Margaret. Finlay," McLeod replied. He and the man shook hands as his companions gave their damp outer wear into Sandy's willing hands.

"They were on duty last night, when the bastards stole the Flag," Sandy said, when he had finished introductions. "Da got his ankle bunged up, when they threw him in the dungeon. They'll gi' ye a first-hand account of what happened."

"Nah, there's no' much more tae be said, than what Sandy's probably already told ye," Finlay muttered, his lantern-jawed face furrowed with remorse. "When the lady came knockin' on the door, 'twas I that had the bad sense tae let her in." He paused and gave his head a rueful shake. "I wish now I'd turned a deaf ear tae all her talk o' lost keys!"

"Hush, Fin! It was no fault of yours," his wife admonished, giving him a pat on the arm.

"Be that as it may," said Finlay, "I'd rather ha' lost my right arm than tae have failed in my duty tae the Chief—an' the Flag."

McLeod pulled a sour grimace and stripped off his sodden trenchcoat.

"If you'd had the ill fortune to meet up with the mastermind behind the theft," he said, "you might have lost more than that, Finlay. Your persuasive lady thief was shot dead not long after she left here—apparently by a superior who had no further use for her. They've just brought her body ashore at the pier."

Finlay and his wife exchanged wide-eyed glances.

"It was that black-masked man that did it!" Margaret stated. "Och, he was a mean 'un! I didnae like his voice!"

"Och, never mind *that*," Finlay said. "What about the Fairy Flag?"

"We believe it's in the hands of whomever hired her to do the job in the first place," Adam said. "Hopefully, we can still recover it, but there's no time to be lost. Which way to the drawing room?"

Chapter Eighteen

BECAUSE Finlay was on crutches, it fell to Margaret to lead them upstairs, muttering that she did not know what good *that* would do, since the Flag was no longer there. Adam had slipped on his signet ring during the drive from the airstrip, and now, as they climbed the broad main stair, he caressed the ring's band with his thumb, beginning to trigger the higher level of consciousness he would need as he searched for clues at the scene of the crime.

Extrasensory input assailed him as he and his companions entered the drawing room, at once drawing Adam's gaze to the wall between the two seaward windows. Damask curtains had been drawn back from a blank oblong where the salmon-colored paint showed a shade darker than the surrounding wall. From that entire quarter of the room, Adam could detect residual traces of super-elemental power.

"The Flag was there?" Adam asked, gesturing in that direction.

Margaret looked a little surprised. "Aye."

"I thought as much."

The concentration of residual power increased as Adam came within an armspan of the wall, palpable as the warmth that lingers over a firepit after the embers themselves have died. Willing himself to center and open, Adam stared for a moment at the empty space where the Fairy Flag had hung, then briefly closed his eyes.

Blurred colors resonated before him, stabilizing into the ghost image of a tattered swathe of brownish silk, mounted flat within a golden frame. Fixing that image fast in his mind for what he proposed to do next, he opened his eyes and redirected his attention to Margaret, who was hovering uncertainly by the doorway.

"Mrs. MacLeod," he said, "do you suppose you might find me a photograph of the Fairy Flag?"

"Aye, we hae postcards doon in the shop," she replied. "Shall I bring ye one o' those?"

"That will be perfect," Adam said. "Would you know if the shop also has ordnance survey maps of the area? This whole western region, if possible, perhaps as far north as Inverness."

Margaret looked more doubtful at this request.

"Aye, sir, we do carry those normally—if we havenae sold out. It's the end o' the tourist season, ye know."

"I'm sure you'll do your best," Adam said. "Could you check on those for me now, please? I'll need a bit of string, too—or heavy thread would be even better."

"Aye, sir, whatever ye say."

"Thank you. Mr. Lovat, why don't you go with Mrs. MacLeod and bring those things back, so she won't need to climb the stairs again? She looks tired. I'm sure she must be exhausted, after the strain of the last twenty-four hours."

Adam's observation had the force of compulsion. Margaret blinked and gave in to a wide yawn, as if his words had granted permission at last to succumb to her fatigue. Peregrine looked a little startled, but a brief eye contact with Adam was sufficient to forestall any questioning on his part. Putting on one of his most ingratiating smiles, he offered his arm to the older woman with a gallant flourish.

"Please lean on me, if you're feeling tired, Mrs. MacLeod," he said. "And after we've collected those things Sir Adam wants, you can put your feet up and have a nice cup of tea."

"Aye, a wee nap wouldnae go amiss," Margaret agreed, yielding him her hand and looking a little dazed. "We'll gae doon the back way."

He ushered her out of the room without a backward glance, passing the dungeon room and heading for the back stairwell. When they had disappeared from sight, McLeod subjected Adam to an inquiring stare.

"Did you do that?"

"Did I do what?"

"Never mind. It's got rid of our good lady for the time being, which is obviously what you wanted. Now, what are you thinking to do?"

Adam smiled thinly. "Nothing you haven't seen before—though I think it might have alarmed our good hostess, had she stayed, and I'm going to have to make some adjustments to avoid startling Peregrine. Our basic problem is that conventional evidence can only tell us what has already happened. If we're to have any chance at all of getting the Flag back before it's too late, we're going to have to look at things from another angle. . . ."

Five minutes later, the sound of footsteps on the stairs heralded Peregrine's return. He came through the doorway brandishing a sheaf of maps in one hand and several spools of thread in the other.

"Mrs. MacLeod wasn't sure what you wanted to do with the thread, nor was I, so she gave me three different kinds. One's carpet thread, I think, and she said this green one, folded up in a skein, was for embroidery. And since I wasn't entirely sure what you meant by *this area*, I've brought maps of Skye and the next two sheets over and up. They'll form a continuous map, if you put them together, including all four of the castle sites we isolated. And here's the photo of the Flag."

"You're becoming a credit to your training," Adam said with a fleeting smile, as he ran his eyes over what Peregrine had brought and started unfolding maps. "Yes, these should do nicely. Let's open them out on the piano, here—that's right. Skye and Glen Cannich on the lid, and the Torridon one on the piano bench. Be sure we get them properly aligned, Noel, so north is really north. You can leave the photo and threads right there.

"Is this what you want?" McLeod asked.

"Yes, it's perfect. Now, if you gentlemen would do me the favor of minding the doors, we'll see what we can discover."

"Just keep a sharp lookout by the other door," McLeod said, at Peregrine's look of question, himself heading for the entrance from the main stair. "We don't need to *close* the doors; we simply don't want to be interrupted. This way, you can watch what Adam's doing, too. I think you'll find it interesting."

Interesting was not the word Adam would have chosen to describe what he was about to do, but he hoped it at least would not be frightening.

"I'm going to start by performing a brief warding ritual," he said, mainly for Peregrine, "because I don't know how powerful our opposition might be, or what nasty surprises they might have left behind. A warding is simply a form of psychic protection. It will take a minute or two, so bear with me."

Putting Peregrine out of mind then, he moved to the center of the room and faced east, opposite to where the flag had hung, and bowed his head for a moment to collect himself, the fingertips of his folded hands pressed lightly to his lips. Then, with his left hand resting on his breast, he raised his gaze and his right hand far above his head.

Gently the first two fingers curved as if plucking something from the air and drawing it downward to touch his forehead. In his mind, the words were in Hebrew—*Ateh, Malkuth*, *Ve Geburah*, *Ve Gedulah*, *Le Olahm*—but he said them aloud in English for Peregrine's benefit.

"Unto Thee, O God . . ."

The words brought a deeper silence to the room, intensifying as his hand moved downward to touch his solar plexus and he said:

"The Kingdom . . ."

Then it moved back up and to the right as his fingertips brushed first his right shoulder, then his left—

"The Power . . . and the Glory . . ."

As the hand came back to fold with the other again, he completed the formula—"Unto all the Ages."

And as his head bowed once more, he whispered the final, "Amen."

For a few breathless seconds he could feel the silence and the centering, but he could also feel Peregrine's eyes upon him—incredulous, a little awed, but not frightened. Ordinarily, he next would have traced pentagrams in all four directions, charging each with a different Name and aspect of Deity, but he decided Peregrine was not ready for that yet; nor was such formality really necessary. A mere sealing of his aura would suffice for now.

The prayer he chose as vehicle for the procedure was an old monkish formula, not terribly long-lasting, but potent while in force. It should serve for whatever protection he needed for the next little while. Spreading his arms in a cross, he threw back his head and turned his face heavenward, speaking softly but with unshakeable conviction.

"By the power of the Christ of God within me," he said, "Whom I serve with all my heart and with all my soul and with all my strength." He began turning slowly to his right, visualizing a circle being defined by the span of his outflung arms. "I encompass myself about with the Divine Circle of His protection, across which no mortal error dares to set its foot."

When he had turned full around, completing the circle, he sealed the rite as he had begun it, again tracing the Qabalistic Cross over his body with his right hand. The sapphire set in his signet ring seemed to leave a trail of luminescent blue that only faded from vision when he took a step into it and absorbed it. He knew McLeod had been aware of it; and by Peregrine's expression, the artist had seen it, too.

"Well, then, that's done," he said, giving Peregrine a nonchalant glance as he headed for the piano. "Now, let's see what useful things we can learn."

Returning to the piano, and facing where the Fairy Flag had hung, he moved the photo of the Flag in front of him, then took up the spool of carpet thread and unreeled about an eighteen-inch length, which he snapped off between his two hands. Doubling the thread and making a knot at one end, he removed his signet ring and fed the knot through, running it through the loop at the other end and pulling it snug. Then he held the knot between the thumb and forefinger of his right hand and let his elbow rest on the piano top, allowing the ring to dangle over the photo like a pendulum.

Now he must establish appropriate responses to make the pendulum a tool. He had used this technique often before, with excellent results. Drawing a deep breath and slowly exhaling, he willed himself to center and relax, focusing his attention on the picture of the Flag. Concentrating on the reality the photo represented, he framed the first question in his mind—one that could only be answered *yes*.

Is this a true likeness of the Fairy Flag?

He held the question in his mind and waited. Gradually, through no conscious effort on his part, the pendulum began to swing up and down, along the length of the photo.

Very well. A *yes* answer would be signified by an up and down motion.

Nodding, he stilled the pendulum with his free hand and framed the second question, which would establish a *no* response.

Is the Fairy Flag still in this room?

This time, after a few seconds, the ring began to swing from side to side.

Stilling it again, Adam concentrated on the third sort of query he might need to make.

Will we be able to retrieve the Fairy Flag before irreparable damage is done or the Flag is destroyed?

It was a question no one could answer just yet, so Adam was not at all surprised to see the ring start to circle slowly clockwise, signifying, *I don't know* or *I don't want to answer*.

"Very well," Adam said softly, glancing briefly at McLeod and Peregrine. "I've established the responses for *yes*, *no*, and *I don't know*. Now it's time to ask some questions to which we *don't* know the answers."

Drawing another deep, centering breath, he concentrated on the ring again.

"*Is the Fairy Flag still on the island?*" he asked.

With little delay, the pendulum swung back and forth, signifying no.

"No. *Did the woman who was shot take the Fairy Flag from this room?*

At the pendulum's *yes* response, Adam nodded.

"Yes. *Did she take it on a boat?*"

When the pendulum signaled *no*, he frowned and glanced over at McLeod, who was watching and listening with great interest.

"It says no. *Did she take it in a car?*—yes."

"But she didn't take it very far," McLeod said. "She *couldn't* have done. I would've sworn she'd taken it to a boat, and that's where they shot her."

"I thought so, too," Adam replied, "but it said she didn't—ah! *Did she get on the boat?*—no.

"*So she took it* to *a boat—in a car*? Yes."

He smiled a little as he glanced up at McLeod again. "Now I think we're getting somewhere. We have to remember how literal this technique requires one to be. That makes sense, though. She put the Flag into a car to run it down to the dock, turned it over to someone on a boat but didn't go aboard, and then was shot for her pains.

"So now we need to ask, *Was the Fairy Flag taken away in a boat?*

"Yes, the pendulum says.

"*Is it still on a boat?*

"Yes, again."

"Then, maybe it *isn't* all that far away," McLeod said. "With the seas running the way they've been, how far could a small boat go?"

"Let's not make any hasty assumptions," Adam warned. "*Has the Fairy Flag been on a boat all this time?*—no."

"*No*?" McLeod cried. "Was it landed somewhere and put in a car again?"

Adam held up his free hand for silence and stared at the pendulum again.

"One question at a time, please. *Was the Fairy Flag taken off the first boat and put*—wait, I'll rephrase that. *Was the Fairy Flag taken off the first boat?*—yes.

"*Was the Fairy Flag placed in a land vehicle of some kind?*—yes.

"*And it is now on another boat?*—yes."

Throughout this exchange, Peregrine had been watching and listening with growing amazement.

"Adam, do you really *believe* the information you're getting this way?"

Adam allowed him a tiny smile. "It's been proven correct before. Do you have any better suggestions?"

"Well, no, but—"

"Just listen, then. Noel?"

"Yes?"

"We haven't a clue who's behind all of this," Adam said, "and we could play Twenty Questions all night, without getting any closer. Therefore, I'm going to propose switching my inquiries to a more specific focus on the Flag's whereabouts."

"I understand," McLeod replied, and glanced pointedly at Peregrine. "No further interruptions, please, Mr. Lovat. He's going to need all his concentration."

As Peregrine nodded solemnly, Adam moved the photo of the Fairy Flag off the map, leaving his left hand resting lightly upon it, and then positioned the dangling ring over the spot marking Dunvegan Castle on the map of the Isle of Skye, his right elbow propped on the piano.

"All right, my pretty," he murmured under his breath, addressing the photo of the Flag. "Where are you *now*? I know where you've been, and I know you've been wrenched from your rightful place by violent humans, for their own purposes, but you're going to have to help me, if I'm to help you. Use me and the pendulum, to show me where you are. I know we can make the connection, if we try."

For a moment he was perfectly still, eyes shuttered and slightly unfocused, marshalling his concentration for the task at hand. Mentally invoking the astral image of the Fairy Flag, he breathed gently on the ring to set it spinning, at the same time inviting the resonances vested in the Flag to communicate its present whereabouts.

At first there was no response. His breathing light and controlled, Adam closed his eyes and threw wide the doors of his own spirit, petitioning the living wisdom of the Light both to amplify the magnetic influences of the Flag and to enhance his own receptivity. A tingling energy stirred at the center of his being, rising and uncoiling—the serpent power, coursing up his spine and all along his extremities.

A complementary pulse went resonating up the thread, with the ring for its conductor. The two currents met and merged at his fingertips in a burst of confluent powers. Contact brought with it an unexpected awareness of something more: a great and growing anger, manifested in the storm that was descending upon the Isle of Skye. The source of that anger was a swirling conflagration of elemental presences which Adam recognized immediately for what they were: the Fairy Hosts of earth, sky, and sea.

The tide of their anger washed blindly over him and rolled on, circling now in the room itself, coalescing in a maelstrom of coruscating fire and shadow. He saw it in his mind, suddenly swirling in the space between the piano and the wall where the Fairy Flag had hung, and when he opened his eyes he saw it with his sight as well—and a glance at his companions confirmed that they saw it, too.

A skeletal face began to focus in the maelstrom as he looked back in surprise, shifting and mutating, terrible in its beauty. He could only guess its particular identity—perhaps the elemental essence of the fairy that had ensouled the Fairy Flag—but its type was that of the *ban-sidhe*, snake-like locks writhing around its head, greenish fire glowing in the empty eye sockets, clawed talons flexing and flashing, poised to reach out and rend.

"Hold your anger, Child of Nature!" Adam said evenly, his voice reverberating on psychic levels as well as audible ones. "I am not your enemy. I am a friend who would help you right the wrong that has been done here."

Humans are but false friends to the Sidhe! the being replied, in a voice that wailed like ripping silk and sent mortal terror surging involuntarily down his spine. *Tell me why I should not slay you where you stand! How dare you summon me, when your kind have violated my sacred trust?*

Trembling despite his control, Adam made himself bridle his fear, forcing himself to look into the hell-fire pits that were the being's eyes.

"Do you think you are alone in your outrage?" he challenged. "Those who have offended you have offended me as well—I, a Councillor of the Seven, who am charged by my Superiors to safeguard the Light and all the forces of Nature who serve It, both human and fairykind. By summoning from beyond the grave the wizard Michael Scot, a man once beloved of your kind, these rogue practitioners of the arts magical have transgressed immortal Law. They have shattered the personality of Scot's present vehicle—an innocent girl, who may never regain what was taken from her. Undeserving, these offenders seek Scot's treasure, which your kind guard. It is they who should be subject to your just wrath—not I, who would stop them, if I can."

The maelstrom roiled and flickered, fresh anger warring with the fragile thread of logic Adam had just presented. Adam was aware of McLeod and Peregrine staring, transfixed with horror, but the unfettered power immanent in the center of the room would not let any of them move. As the being towered above him, threatening to engulf him, Adam threw back his head and looked up at it unflinchingly, vesting all his hopes in one final plea for mercy.

"I am not the one you want," he said. "The ones you want are the ones who stole *am Bratach Sìth*—who carry it even now, intending to steal Scot's book of spells and your fairy gold! Show me where that is, and I shall do my best to stop them. Nor shall I or mine do any harm to what rightfully belongs to Faerie. Furthermore, if I can, I swear that I shall restore *am Bratach Sìth* to its rightful place."

He could feel the being's encroaching power prickling at the edges of his soul, threatening oblivion. He swayed on his feet, unable to help himself, but he not would let himself look away from what threatened to overwhelm him. Brazenly he lifted the photo and the dangling ring on its thread.

"*Show me!*" he commanded.

At his words, the being let out an unholy shriek and came for him, talons raking the piano top and sending maps and thread spools flying.

"*Show me!*" Adam commanded again, flinching involuntarily, but never shrinking from the challenge.

Then a sound reverberated in his mind like a thunderclap and shook him into unconsciousness. He must have been out for only a few seconds, but he came to on the floor beside the piano, with his head raised on one of McLeod's arms and Peregrine kneeling stricken beside him. The photo of the Fairy Flag was still in his left hand, but the ring on its thread was nowhere to be seen.

"Thank God, yer alive!" McLeod whispered, reverting to a broader Highland accent in his agitation. "Good Lord, man, ye goaded her! Whatever possessed ye?"

A little dazed still, Adam struggled to a sitting position. "It's all right, Noel. I think I knew what I was doing. And Peregrine, don't look like you've seen a ghost. It was only a banshee."

"A banshee?" Peregrine breathed. "But—"

"I think, in specific, it may have been the spirit of the Fairy Flag," Adam continued, trying to get his feet under him. "Help me up, you two. Since I'm alive, I think it must have worked. I want to know where my ring has gone."

"Your *ring*?" McLeod yelped. "Don't ye know ye've just been that close to oblivion, man? Take it easy, or you'll pass out again. Where's one o' those ammonia capsules, when ye need one?" he added, patting down several of Adam's pockets. "You doctors never come prepared!"

Making wordless, placating gestures, Adam struggled to his feet anyway, hauling himself up with both hands on the edge of the piano and casting his gaze over the aftermath of a banshee's rage. The map that had been on the piano stool was on the floor with the spools of thread, and shreds of technicolor paper scraps all around the piano told the fate of one of the maps that had been on top. The piano itself was deeply scored with six long parallel scratches, but they ended next to the map remaining. And on that map, a gold-set sapphire winked in the light.

"Oh, *there's* your bloody ring," McLeod said, starting to reach for it. "An' lookit what's happened to the piano!"

But Adam stayed his hand. For the ring, its thread extending straight as an arrow back to Dunvegan Castle, had landed partway down Loch Ness, the bright gold of the band encircling the words, *Urquhart Castle*.

CHAPTER NINETEEN

STUNNED, the three of them crowded around the piano to stare at the words encircled by the ring on the map.

"Urquhart Castle!" McLeod murmured.

"Does that mean what I think it means?" Peregrine asked, apparently a believer at last.

Eyeing the gouges on the piano top, Adam prodded at the ring with a tentative forefinger, then picked it up and took off the thread.

"It means," he said, slipping the ring back on his finger, "that Urquhart Castle is the hiding place of Michael Scot's treasure—and that the Fairy Flag is being taken there to help hold the treasure's rightful guardians at bay."

"Urquhart," Peregrine repeated, looking distractedly off into the distance. "So we were on the right track all along." He shook his head wonderingly. "It makes perfect sense, of course. When I remember what I drew, and compare those sketches to the photos we looked at, it's plain to see how the castle evolved, over the centuries. In fact, the references did say there were caves in the area—some of them underwater."

"Aye, and the Loch Ness monster is also guarding the treasure, if it's even there!" McLeod muttered under his breath. "Adam, are you *sure* it's Urquhart, where we're meant to go?"

Adam had begun scanning the map around Loch Ness more closely, and now he looked up at McLeod just a little impatiently.

"Noel, I've just put my life and maybe my very soul on

the line—not to mention my word as an Adept—to induce a *ban-sidhe* to tell where a fairy treasure's hidden. And helping the Sidhe protect that treasure isn't all that's at stake."

"I know that," McLeod replied.

"No, I'm not certain you do," Adam said. "You're worried about the Fairy Flag of the MacLeods, as well you should be. But making unlawful use of the Flag is only the beginning. If the thieves are successful, they'll get their hands on Michael Scot's book of spells—a fearful enough prospect, in its own right—but they'll also get the fairy gold. Do you hear that wind outside?"

"Of course."

"Well, you were right when you said there was something uncanny about it," Adam went on. "This *isn't* just another seasonal storm. It's being generated through the agency of the Sidhe—and it's going to get worse until they're appeased, one way or another."

"What exactly are you saying?" McLeod said stonily.

Adam's long mouth tightened before he spoke. "The fairies gave the Flag to the MacLeods as a rare token of their favor. Its theft represents an offense against the whole realm of Faerie. The Sidhe have never taken such offenses lightly. And stealing their gold will merely add insult to injury. Already, their anger has unleashed elemental forces that, unchecked, could devastate the Highlands."

His last word was cut short by a sudden skirl of wind that set the seaward windows rattling violently. Peregrine flinched and looked around apprehensively, instinctively moving a little closer to the other two men.

"I think I'd better tell you about the odd dream I had last night," he said uneasily. "I was going to mention it over breakfast, but it seemed so trivial in the light of day."

"Go on," Adam urged.

"Well, I thought I heard horns blowing in the distance—like trumpets sounding a call to battle. In view of what's happened, I think it must have been some kind of warning—only I didn't know enough then to recognize it as such."

Adam's face had grown increasingly troubled as Peregrine made this revelation, and now he sighed heavily and leaned both hands on the piano, glancing down.

"I wish you *had* told me," he murmured. "Not that it would have made any difference in what we have to do."

"Why? What did it mean?" Peregrine asked.

"Well, it wasn't exactly a warning," Adam said slowly. "More like a call to arms—maybe even the summoning of the Faerie Rade—the Wild Hunt. If that goes unchecked, I hate to even contemplate the possible consequences."

McLeod looked stricken, and could hardly raise his eyes to meet Adam's.

"Adam, I'm sorry. I didn't know."

"Nor did I. None of us did. But it makes our task just that much more urgent."

Shaking his head, Adam drew a deep breath and seemed to take a grip on himself.

"All right, gentlemen. We now need to formulate a plan of action. We know that the fairy gold and Scot's book are at Urquhart Castle. Presumably, the thieves know that too, and are on their way there now, with the Flag, intending to do—whatever it is they're going to do—as soon as it's properly dark and the forces of Samhain are at their peak." Adam scanned the map between Dunvegan and Urquhart, running a finger along the red lines of the roads they would have to take, rather than going as the crow flies.

"From the pendulum, we also know that the Flag is on a boat," he continued, glancing up at McLeod. "That means they must be coming either up or down Loch Ness. But Urquhart is their destination, whichever way they're coming. How fast do you think we can get there?"

McLeod drew closer to the map, adjusting his glasses and using his thumb and first finger as calipers to estimate the distances.

"Well, it's near fifty miles to the ferry, and you've seen that road."

"Yes—"

"I'm not as familiar with the one from there to Urquhart," McLeod went on, "but it looks like, oh, seventy or eighty more, allowing for the twists and turns." He shook his head and grimaced. "I'd say—close to three hours, allowing for the weather and the ferry crossing. And that presumes that the ferry is running—which, in this kind of weather, is not at all certain."

Adam glanced at his watch and then began folding up the map. "We'll worry about that when we get to the ferry crossing," he said. "Meanwhile, we'd better get going, because it's past five already. That means we can't expect to make Urquhart much before eight."

"Is that a problem?" Peregrine asked.

"I hope it won't be," Adam replied. "The critical time factor has to do with the beginning of Samhain. If *I* were running their operation, I'd want to delay beginning until well after sunset—and after moonrise as well—when the powers of the sword and the Fairy Flag will be at their peak. But sunset is going to seem to come early tonight, because of the storm. If they get too greedy, they might try to start sooner—so it's essential we get there as quickly as we can. Noel, can you get us a car?"

McLeod nodded. "I'll commandeer the Volvo. After all, the MacLeod did authorize us to take whatever we need. And before we leave, I want to ring my counterpart in Inverness and see about some mundane reinforcements. Magic is all very well and good, but the Opposition have already used firearms at least once, and I doubt they'll hesitate to do so again. I'll have a police boat sent down the Loch."

He took a last look at the ruined piano top and sighed.

"I can cope with possibly ruining the Chief's car. That goes with the job. I just wonder how I'm going to explain about the piano."

With that disgruntled observation, he turned and made for the door leading to the main stairs, Adam and Peregrine falling in behind him. They had taken only a few steps when all the lights in Dunvegan Castle suddenly flickered and then went out.

"Damn, that's all we need!" McLeod muttered, groping for the wall as the others stumbled to a halt behind him. The darkness was not absolute, as their eyes adjusted, for the windows still showed a flat, lighter grey, but it was too dark to see very well.

"What do you think's happened?" Peregrine whispered.

"Storm's probably taken out a power line, or blown a transformer," Adam murmured. "Have they got an emergency generator, Noel?"

"Aye. It should kick in any minute."

Standing shoulder to shoulder in the murky darkness, they could feel the stone floor vibrating under their feet as, outside, the mounting storm waves beat about the rock on which the castle was founded. But after a few seconds, as predicted, the lights came back on, to the accompaniment of a mechanical hum from somewhere deep in the bowels of the building.

"At least *something's* working," McLeod muttered. "It may not last, though. Keep close behind me, and mind the steps on the way down."

Together they made their way down the wide main stairs, keeping to the railings on either side, lest the lights fail again. Before they reached the bottom, the lights resumed their flickering. Sandy MacLeod met them in the entry hall, a lighted oil lamp in one brawny hand and a look of concern on his face.

"I was just on my way tae fetch ye down tae the parlor," he told them. "Something's no' right wi' the generator. Da's gone down tae the basement tae see what he can do."

"Never mind the generator," McLeod said. "Are the phones working?"

Sandy goggled at him. "I couldnae say. I dinnae think anyone's thought tae try 'em."

"In that case, let me do the honors," said McLeod. "Is there one here, in the lobby?"

Sandy turned and pointed. "Aye, over there—under the desk."

Scowling, the inspector strode over and whisked the telephone out onto the desktop. He lifted the receiver to his ear, sighed, and pumped the call button several times, pausing intermittently to listen. After several attempts, he shook his head.

"No joy here. The line's dead as a bloody doornail."

"What about that cellular phone you brought with you?" Adam asked.

"It's still in the back of the Volvo, in my bag," said McLeod.

"I'll go get it for ye," Sandy volunteered. "It's the blue bag wi' the pockets?"

"Aye."

Rain gusted into the entry hall as Sandy dashed outside, wind wailing up the staircase and raising chills not altogether born of the cold. The lights continued to waver on and off. In a few minutes, a rather damper and more windblown Sandy returned, McLeod's bag clutched close to his chest. He watched with undisguised fascination as McLeod unzipped one of the side pockets and took out the cellular phone.

"I don't know whether this is going to work," he warned his companions. "These things are none too reliable at the best of times. Still, nothing ventured . . ."

Moving closer to the doorway, where there was apt to be less interference from the stone, he activated the phone. After listening for a dial tone, he punched in the number of the Inverness constabulary. The line rang through for two short rings, then cut out in a sudden, fierce burst of static.

McLeod disconnected and tried again. Seconds after he finished dialling, the same angry crackle burst from the receiver, popping and snapping like an amplified electrical short. McLeod killed the noise with a stroke of his thumb and rolled his eyes in bleak exasperation.

"Distance could be a factor," Adam said. "Why don't you try Fort Augustus? It's about the same distance from Urquhart, but it's forty miles closer to us, as the crow flies. Do you know the number?"

"No, but I've got it here somewhere," McLeod said, already thumbing through a small notebook he had produced from an inside pocket. "Here it is."

He punched in the number, juggling notebook and phone and grimacing the while, his face brightening as the number began to ring.

"A-ha! It's ringing, at least. I can't say this is a much better line," he said over his shoulder to his companions, "but so far—hullo? Is that the constabulary? Very good. This is Inspector Noel McLeod, Edinburgh branch . . .

hullo, are you still there? I want the officer in charge, please. . . ."

In the course of the next few minutes, McLeod struggled through outbursts of static to outline as much of the situation as he dared. Eventually his conversation was cut short when the line abruptly went dead. McLeod uttered a single well-chosen epithet as he switched the phone off and turned back to his friends.

"Well, that's that," he stated peevishly. "If we're lucky, the lad I just spoke to got enough of what I was saying to send up the units I requested. But I wouldn't count on it—especially with this storm moving in."

"So it's up to us?" Adam asked.

"I'm afraid so." McLeod sighed wearily. "It's typical. Whenever you want something done right, you generally end up doing it yourself."

As he knelt to stash the phone back in his bag, Sandy could contain his curiosity no longer.

"Ye're no' really goin' tae Urquhart, are ye?"

"Aye."

"But, why would anyone want tae tak' the Fairy Flag *there*?"

McLeod rose and clapped Sandy on the shoulder. "If I'm right, I'll explain later," he said. "And about the piano upstairs. Meanwhile, we're going to need a vehicle. How's the Volvo for petrol?"

"Och, she'll get ye there, easy, but I dinnae know how ye propose gettin' off the island. The ferry'll no be runnin'."

"We'll worry about that when we get to the ferry," McLeod replied. "Are the keys in it?"

Sandy looked dubious. "Aye, they are. But if ye *are* determined tae go out in this, at least come intae the mud room an' tak' some proper rain gear. Ye cannae go wi' just what ye wore before; ye'll get fair soakit."

To this concession, at least, McLeod was forced to agree. He had not really allowed himself to think about what they might have to do, once they *reached* Urquhart, so concerned was he about simply getting there; and the prospect of doing it wet and freezing was daunting, indeed.

"Sandy's right, Noel," Adam spoke up, before McLeod

could answer. "We can't work at peak efficiency if we're cold and wet."

"This way, then," Sandy said. "The mud room's here, underneath the stair. We've a good assortment, between what belongs tae the staff and what visiting members of the family hae left behind. Take whatever ye need, an' I'll gae tell Dad what's afoot. . . ."

He vanished down the back stairs, leaving them to sort through the contents of the mud room. Among the several dozen pairs of rubber Wellington boots lined up along two walls, they easily found three pairs to fit; and loose-fitting rain slickers layered over their own clothes seemed the best choice for protection from the wet. McLeod exchanged his trenchcoat and suit jacket for a thick sweater and a waxed jacket like Adam's. They had scarcely finished kitting themselves out when Sandy returned, accompanied by his mother. Margaret MacLeod was carrying a small wicker picnic hamper, which she presented to McLeod.

"Trust a man tae go chasing off after those rascals wi' no thought for yer tea till it's too late," she told him, with a matronly cluck of her tongue. "Here's sommat tae take with ye in the car. It's no' very fancy—just sandwiches an' scones—but it should keep ye going till ye can find time for supper."

McLeod accepted the hamper with a grateful nod of the head and passed it off to Peregrine without comment, before clumping back into the entry hall to pick up his blue bag. Sandy and Margaret followed to see them off. At the door, as the three of them donned caps and scarves and zipped up slickers, preparing to brave the elements, McLeod glanced aside at Adam.

"Shall I drive, or would you rather?" he asked.

Adam shook his head. "You're the professional. Why don't you let me navigate, and be an extra set of eyes, if the going gets really bad? The visibility out there is going to be worse than bad, once it really gets dark."

"Aye, there's no arguing that," McLeod agreed. "All right, let's go!"

The wind wailed as Sandy opened the front door of the

castle and held it, gusting rain into the entry and sending Margaret scurrying for cover.

"I dinnae suppose ye'd want another pair o' hands?" the young man offered, as Peregrine and then McLeod bolted for the car.

A brief smile touched Adam's lips. "Not this time, I think—though the offer is appreciated. What you *can* do, if you would, is to stand by, if the Chief should call, and tell him where we've gone. If we do succeed in recovering the Fairy Flag, he should be on hand to receive it."

"Aye, sir, I'll do that."

With that, Adam clapped him on the shoulder and dashed into the rain, taking his place up front beside McLeod.

"Everybody buckle up and hold tight," the inspector warned, giving the ignition key a turn. "It's going to be a rough ride."

The trees lining the avenue were thrashing crazily back and forth, and bare branches lashed at the sides of the car as it eased back up the narrow avenue. The flickering lights of Dunvegan Castle receded into the gathering gloom behind them, disappearing well before they reached the main road.

Turning right, the big car picked up speed along the road toward Dunvegan village. No lights showed in any of the houses and shops along the High Street, and the rain-swept pavement was empty. A truck had stalled out in the junction leading off to the north, but McLeod barely slackened speed as he whipped the Volvo around and carried on, past the outlying buildings and on toward the rugged country beyond.

The road wound back and forth between rain-drenched ridges of high ground. The wind that blew down off the heights carried an eerie whistling note, like the keening of inhuman voices. McLeod drove with single-minded concentration, taking each successive bend in the road with calculated precision. In the back seat, Peregrine clung white-knuckled to the nearest armrest and the back of Adam's seat, hardly daring even to think about the miles still to go before they reached the ferry, somewhere beyond the airstrip.

They sped through Struan and Bracadale and carried on

toward Drynoch. Rain whipped across their path in driving squall-sheets, leaving the tarmac slick as an oil-spill. McLeod held the Volvo ruthlessly to the roadbed at speeds well in excess of what Peregrine considered to be safe. Sitting motionless in the seat next to McLeod, Adam fingered the sapphire on his hand but said nothing.

Forty minutes after setting out from Dunvegan, they rolled into Kyleakin to find ongoing traffic at a standstill, with cars being turned back at a barrier ahead. As McLeod crept up to the barrier, a slicker-clad policeman armed with an acetylene lamp trotted up to the side of the car.

"Sorry, sir, but the ferry isnae running, on account of the storm," he informed them, when McLeod rolled down the window. "I'm afraid ye'll have tae turn around."

Scowling, McLeod reached inside his coat and produced his police ID.

"I'm afraid I can't do that, laddie," he said. "I'm on official business, and we've got to get over to the mainland as quickly as possible."

The policeman's face fell. "Well, now, that *is* a problem, sir. But it's the ferry captain's decision. Ye cannae blame him for no' wanting to venture out o' port in such a storm. He made his last run half an hour ago, an' I dinnae think he's going anyplace."

"Well, maybe I can persuade him to change his mind." McLeod's blue eyes were glinting behind his spectacles. "Where can I find this ferry captain?"

A look of incredulity crossed the policeman's face, but he was better trained than to argue with a superior about a matter that really did not concern him.

"Please yourself, sir. I think he may still be aboard. If he isnae there, ye'll probably find him and his mate holed up in their office. It's at the end of this row of cottages."

"Thank you," McLeod said, with tart satisfaction. "Now, if you'll shift that barrier out of the way, we'll be on about our business."

Once clear of the barrier, they made a swift descent along the sloping street that led down to the water. Off to their right, a covey of small boats jerked and tossed at their anchors behind the stone breakwater protecting Kyleakin's small harbor. The ferry itself was close-moored to the pilings at the end of the pier, its superstructure dimly visible in the blustery storm-gloom and the harsh yellow illumination of sodium lamps. A wide concrete ramp sloped gently down to the water beside the pier, and McLeod eyed the waves rolling up on it as he halted the car at the top.

"It doesn't look so bad, once you get out a bit—mostly swells," he observed. "The tricky bit will be getting the car across the ramps—timing ourselves, so we don't end up in the drink."

"*After* you've persuaded the ferry captain to go out at all," Adam said. "How bad *is* it, Noel?"

McLeod managed a wry smile. "I've sailed in worse. Now let's see if *he* has. Mr. Lovat, why don't you stay with the car?"

He did not wait for Peregrine to reply. Turning up his collar, he opened the car door and got out quickly, as did Adam, heading purposefully down the pier. Lights showed aboard the ferry, in the little purser's office on the car deck, and McLeod and Adam darted across the heaving gangplank and headed there. The door to the office had a round glass porthole, and through it they could see a stocky, balding figure in a shapeless grey pullover and battered captain's cap, drinking coffee. A younger man was with him, tall and lean, with a shaggy thatch of ginger hair.

McLeod gave a perfunctory knock at the door, but he did not wait to see if the men inside had heard. ID in hand, he opened the door and entered, Adam at his back. The two men looked up in surprise.

"Here, what's this?" the younger man began.

"Detective Chief Inspector Noel McLeod," he announced, holding up his ID and addressing the older man. "Sorry to disturb you, but are you the skipper of this vessel?"

"Aye. Archie MacDonald's the name," the captain said. He indicated the young man behind him with a jerk of his thumb and added grudgingly, "This here's my mate, Charlie Baird. Wha's amiss?"

McLeod didn't mince words. "We need you to ferry us back to the mainland."

"What, *now*?" MacDonald was incredulous.

"Yes, now."

"Ye must be daft!" MacDonald stated flatly. "In case ye havenae looked outside lately, it's blowin' up a right gale out there. If the wind doesnae drive us all the way tae Loch Duich, the waves'll toss us about like a rugby ball. Take it from me, ye wouldnae enjoy the ride."

"We're not looking to take a pleasure cruise," McLeod retorted. "This is police business, not an outing for the Boys' Brigade!" Seeing that the two were still looking mulish, he added testily, "If I have to, I'll commandeer this vessel. I have the authority."

"Do ye now?" MacDonald said, bordering on belligerent. "And who's going tae pilot her, if I might ask?"

"I'll pilot her myself, if need be," McLeod snapped. "I've held a master's rating, in my day, and I could do it as well as yourself—"

"If we don't get across," Adam interjected with quiet emphasis, "many other lives besides ours could be at stake. If this wasn't an emergency, we wouldn't be asking you and your associate to take this risk. But it is, and we must."

His tone, like his bearing, conveyed a subtle force of authority. The captain gazed across at him with grudging respect.

"An emergency, eh?" he said, somewhat mollified. "What kind of an emergency?"

"I'm afraid we're not at liberty to tell you that just now," Adam said, in the same well-modulated tone. "You'll simply have to accept my word for it that people besides ourselves are in danger. I assure you," he went on, "we are telling you as much of the truth as we can, under the circumstances. Will you do as the inspector asks?"

Adam's mellow voice carried the ring of incontrovertible sincerity. The ferry captain gnawed thoughtfully at his lower lip, clearly wondering what Adam's status might be, but after a moment longer, he cast a look over his shoulder at his mate.

"Well? What about it, Charlie?"

The mate shrugged. His eyes, too, were on Adam. "I'm game, if you are, skipper."

The ferry captain accepted this verdict with a bob of his head. Drawing himself up, he returned his attention to Adam.

"All right, we'll gi' it a try," he said heavily. "But I'll do the piloting myself," he added, with a sidelong glance at McLeod. "The old tub may no' be much, but I'm fond o' her. If anybody's going tae scuttle her, it'd better be me."

He pulled a well-worn yellow slicker off a hook and shrugged into it, his mate following suit.

"Ye can ride out the crossing in here, if ye like. Just dinnae be sick on my clean deck."

"Perhaps we didn't make ourselves entirely clear," Adam said smoothly. "We have a third passenger waiting—and a car."

"A car." MacDonald paused in the act of doing up his slicker, exchanging an incredulous glance with his mate. "Ye think ye can get a car aboard, in weather like this?"

McLeod's reply was stark and succinct.

"Yes."

MacDonald eyed the inspector long and hard, then slowly nodded.

"Weel, ye just might get her on, this side. But gettin' her off, at t'other side, may be another matter. She'll end up in the drink."

"We'll take that chance," McLeod replied.

With a snort of disbelief, the captain shrugged and threw up his hands.

"All right, since ye seem determined. But I'll no' accept liability."

"That's understood," Adam said.

"Get back tae yer car, then, an' wait till ye hear me sound the horn before ye come down the ramp. Charlie an' I'll do our best tae hold her steady."

Outside, McLeod and Adam trotted back along the pier toward the waiting car. As soon as they were back inside, Peregrine sat forward eagerly.

"Is he taking us, then?" he asked.

"Aye—and hopefully, the car too, if I can manage it."

"*Can* you?" Adam asked.

McLeod nodded, eyes straight ahead on the surging waves and fingers clenched tight on the steering wheel.

"Aye. But leave the doors unlocked, and be ready to hit the release on your seat belts. If I *do* put this beast in the water, I'd rather just worry about explaining it to the Chief. I don't want to feel guilty that I've drowned the two of you as well."

Peregrine shut up at that, as the peril of their next few minutes became clearer. Time seemed to stand still, drawn out longer still by the shrill keening of the wind, the crash of the surf on the concrete ramp. After a moment, McLeod restarted the engine and turned on the wipers, letting the engine idle to keep it warm. Through the rain-spattered windscreen, they could make out the blurred amber dots of the ferry's maritime running-lights, moving slowly from behind the end of the pier.

McLeod switched on the headlights as the ship edged closer, illuminating heavy turbulence churned up by the ferry's stern engines as her master fought to line her up with the concrete ramp. She eased in very close, her horn hooting as her forward loading ramp started coming down. As soon as it was past the horizontal, its edges awash, McLeod popped the car into gear, holding it with one foot on the brake until just the right moment.

"Here we go," he muttered—and set the Volvo in motion down the concrete incline.

His timing was impeccable, as was the ferry captain's. Just as a giant swell receded, bringing the ferry's steel ramp into grating contact with the concrete, the big car bumped jerkily over the meeting point and carried on, up onto the car deck. In perfect coordination, the steel ramp rose behind them in a backwash of brine. The incoming swells lifted the ferry up and away from the ramp and out into the channel, heading north and east toward Kyle of Lochalsh.

As soon as the Volvo was stationary, McLeod engaged the emergency brake and killed the engine. No one said anything for several seconds.

"How—how long does this crossing normally take?" Peregrine finally asked, when he could breathe easily again.

"Normally?" McLeod let out a snort and gave a wry

smile. "About five or ten minutes. Tonight—your guess is as good as mine."

In the silence that descended, punctuated by the whine of the wind and the crash of the waves outside, Adam sighed and glanced at his watch.

"It's after six," he said quietly. Then, "What's it going to be like at the other end?"

"Worse," McLeod replied. "The pier's more exposed, and I seem to recall that the ramp is steeper. If it really looks bad, we may have to go ashore on foot and find other transport."

"I'd rather not do that, though," he went on, scowling. "I think I can construe all of this as legitimate police business, after the fact, but commandeering a vehicle could be dicey. Besides, you never know what you'll get. This old bus isn't the high-performance vehicle I'd prefer for a run like we need to make, but at least I've gotten to know her on the way here. She'll get us to Urquhart in good time—if we can get her off the ferry."

This pronouncement produced an even deeper silence than the one before. The ferry ploughed through the waves like a pregnant sea cow, engines laboring at full throttle. Rain and spume beat against the car windows as the deck pitched and rolled, the salt smearing under the wiper blades. The opposite shore was only dimly visible as an opaque black mass, a shade darker than the lowering sky. The water on all sides showed sharp white peaks like gnashing teeth.

Minutes crawled by. The mainland shore loomed closer. The ferry's forward floodlights cut pale, watery swathes through the tossing spindrift, revealing a sudden, blurred glimpse of the pierheads of Kyle of Lochalsh.

The ferry wallowed like a mired pig as the captain brought her in under the lee of the land, trying to align her with the floodlit loading ramp. Some of the waves were breaking nearly to the top of the ramp. A warning hoot from the ferry's Klaxon drew their attention away from the shoreline.

"That's our cue," Adam said thinly. "Time to get ready to disembark—if we can."

The wind was keening like a banshee. McLeod started

the Volvo's engine and crept the car closer to the raised ramp that closed off that end of the car deck as MacDonald brought the ferry in close under half speed. Battered by incoming waves, the vessel fishtailed clumsily into the water gap between the pierheads. Rumbling rustily, the exit ramp began to fold downward.

There was a jolt like a minor earthquake as the ferry's flat keel struck the submerged concrete of the sloping ramp. Smoke billowed up from the ferry's exhaust funnels as her diesel engines labored to bring her back into alignment. The end of the ferry ramp moved to within several feet of the concrete, then surged away again on a heavy swell.

"He's going to have to do better than *that*," McLeod muttered.

Adam only nodded, suddenly gone very quiet.

Three more times the ferry approached the concrete landing ramp, only once lined up squarely and coming closer than about two feet. As the captain lined up for yet another approach, McLeod was shaking his head.

"I was afraid of this," he said. "He isn't getting in close enough."

"Can *we* even get off the ship?" Peregrine asked. "I don't know about the two of you, but I don't think *I* could jump across that gap."

"Maybe not," Adam said thoughtfully. "But I wonder if Noel could jump the *car* across."

As he glanced sidelong at McLeod, the police inspector stared at him.

"*Jump* the car?"

Adam nodded. "Didn't you ever jump a car off a ramp, when they put you through that anti-terrorist driving course?"

"As a matter of fact, I did—several times. But this is—"

Calculating, he looked out at the wave-swept ramp, at the water separating it from the end of the ferry ramp, at the distance between the end of the ramp and the car—then out the Volvo's back window.

"It might just work," he said thoughtfully. "If I were to back up to the other ramp, it would probably give me enough of a run forward. Traction might be a problem, though, on these steel decks."

"I saw some sand in those fire buckets, up by the stair to the pilot's bridge," Adam said. "We could spread that under the wheels."

McLeod turned to look him full in the face. In the back seat, Peregrine was practically holding his breath, hardly able to believe they were actually discussing it seriously.

"You really want me to try it, don't you?" McLeod said. "Adam, I wasn't joking before, about putting the car in the drink. And that wasn't even with jumping involved. What'll I tell the Chief, if I screw up?"

"You'll tell him you screwed up," Adam said, "but at least you'll have tried. And meanwhile, as you pointed out before, we can always commandeer another car. But we're wasting time right now."

"Right now," Peregrine pointed out, as the engines changed their pitch and the ship lurched, "the question may be academic. I think the captain has given up."

His elders turned their attention forward once more. As Peregrine had noted, the ferry was falling away from the loading ramp, turning to head for the pier, and the front ramp was going back up.

"You'd better come with me," McLeod said to Adam, putting the car in Park and setting the handbrake. "I may need your particular persuasive ability. Mr. Lovat, I'll ask you to stay with the car again."

Hunching down against the driving rain, McLeod and Adam made a mad dash across the car deck and up the outside stair to the pilot's bridge, where the figures of MacDonald and his mate were silhouetted by the cabin lights.

CHAPTER TWENTY

"YE want tae do *what*?" MacDonald gasped, staring at the two intruders on his bridge as if they had just announced their intention to walk on water. Behind him, hands frozen on the ship's throttles, the mate also was staring.

"I know it's taking a bit of a risk," McLeod conceded, "but I told you, lives are at stake. The worst that can happen is that I'll grossly underestimate and end up in ten or fifteen feet of water."

"Aye, an' what if ye cannae get oot? I dinnae want anybody drowning on account o' me!"

"Captain, we don't expect to drown," Adam said reasonably. "In fact, we don't even expect to get very wet, if you do your proper part."

"My proper part? I've *done* as good as I *can*, man! In this sea, I dinnae think anybody could hae got her in closer."

"We hadn't decided to try the jump, when you did it before," McLeod said. "Just repeat that performance—bring her in that close—*just three attempts*—and I'll either go or give it up."

MacDonald looked him up and down appraisingly, cast a similar glance over Adam, then returned his gaze to McLeod.

"Ye swear ye'll gie it up, after three tries?" he said.

"After three tries," McLeod agreed.

"And if we even get to *attempt* the jump," Adam added, reaching into an inside pocket, "I'll send each of you a £100 bonus. Here's my card. I assure you, I'm good for it."

MacDonald took the card and eyed it tentatively.

"*Sir Adam Sinclair, Bart.*," he read. "*Fellow of the Royal College of*—ye're a doctor?"

"I am."

"A psychiatrist, it says here?"

Adam nodded.

"An' he's no' crazy?" MacDonald asked, gesturing toward McLeod.

"No, only a little desperate. And while you're dithering, lives are still at risk. Now, do you want the bonus or not?"

At MacDonald's glance at his mate, the other man only shrugged and nodded. Tight-lipped, MacDonald turned back to McLeod.

"Three tries, then—an' I sure hope ye know what ye're doin'. Flash yer headlamps when ye're ready for me tae bring her in."

As they clattered down the outside stair again, hunched down against the rain, McLeod glanced back over his shoulder at Adam.

"Thanks, Adam. I could've just ordered them to try it again, but your offer certainly sweetened the deal. If we don't make it now, it won't be because our chaps didn't give it their best shot."

"Nothing like a little extra incentive," Adam replied.

They retrieved the buckets of sand on their way back to the car, Peregrine joining Adam to help spread it while McLeod backed the car to the very rear of the car deck, back bumper nearly touching the raised rear ramp.

"Same drill as before," McLeod told them, as they piled back into the car. "Be prepared to bail out, though, if I botch it."

"You aren't going to botch it," Adam said confidently, as they watched the front ramp starting down again. "It's merely a matter of timing."

McLeod said nothing. After flashing the headlights in signal, he set his left foot hard on the brake and shifted into Low. With his right foot he revved the engine, eyes fixed on the end of the ramp and the shrinking expanse of water between it and the wave-washed target of the landing ramp, as the ferry slowly moved into position for an approach.

The first attempt was no good. A swell caught the ferry and slewed it sideways just at the critical moment, so that a corner of the steel ramp struck the concrete instead of making square contact. The impact echoed through the ship's steel, and the engines roared as they fought to bring her steady. The retreating swell carried the ferry out the same way, wallowing and pitching on the angry waves, so that it took several minutes to line up for the next approach.

Peregrine braced himself against the back of the seat behind Adam and peered anxiously ahead. Just visible in the rain and the glare of the lights up on the pier, they could see several slickered figures moving along the top of the concrete ramp.

"I hope those chaps have enough sense to get out of the way," Peregrine murmured.

"*If* we go," McLeod retorted.

"We'll go," Adam replied confidently.

Ponderously the ferry began her second approach. She started out a little too far to the left, but a gust of wind brought her directly in line, heading right for the concrete ramp.

"Hang on, this may be it," McLeod warned, as the distance closed.

Time seemed to slow almost to a standstill. Slowly the gap narrowed from ten feet to eight feet to six, and still was closing. If everything stayed steady—

With a hoarsely whispered, "Now!" McLeod released the brake and punched the accelerator. The big car shot forward, fish-tailing a little on the slick deck, even with the sand under the tires, but moving fast—hitting the end of the ramp as it came within about a yard of the concrete. The car went briefly airborne, then made contact with the front end, in a shriek of metal bumper scraping concrete, and a gigantic splash as the rear end hit about six inches of water, fortunately receding with the swell that also was carrying the ferry away again.

"Hang on!" McLeod shouted. "We're not home yet!"

Fighting the wheel to keep the car straight—and from sliding back down the ramp and into the sea—he bore down on the accelerator. Spume spun off the rear wheels as the

Volvo fought for traction—the exhausts were underwater, blowing smoke furiously—but after a heart-stopping moment of foundering, the tires gripped the concrete and the car shot up the ramp with a roar, seawater streaming from its undercarriage.

Slickered figures scattered, an array of blue-flashing emergency vehicles becoming visible as the Volvo crested the top of the slope. McLeod had a wolfish grin on his face as he jammed on the brakes and brought the car sharply to a standstill, and he gestured back toward the ferry in his rear-view mirror as he glanced at Adam.

"Grab that big torch and send him *V for Victory*, Adam!" he said triumphantly, paying no heed to the several figures now converging on the car from the direction of the flashing blue lights.

As Adam cheerfully complied, flashing three short flashes and a long one out his window in the direction of the ferry, his salute was answered almost immediately by the ferry's Klaxon—three short hoots and a long one that reverberated all the way to the diaphragm.

All three of them were laughing as Adam repeated the signal and was answered again. The broad-shouldered figure in fireman's gear who came splashing toward them, his torch aimed at the driver's window, was not laughing.

"Just what d'ye think ye're doin', mister?" he sputtered, leaning down angrily to peer into McLeod's window. "I dinnae like yer humor! Another few inches tae th' right, an' ye would've had me for a hood ornament!"

Still chuckling, McLeod rolled down his window and showed the man his ID.

"Sorry. We aren't laughing at you. It's sheer, quaking relief at having made it off that bloody ferry! Didn't mean to give you such a scare. We've got a rather urgent police matter on our hands."

"Weel, then, that's different," the man said, his anger deflating into grudging respect. "An' I haftae say, I havenae seen driving like that 'cept in the films. I didnae even think the boat was running."

"It wasn't," McLeod said, "but we persuaded the captain

it was his civic duty to get us across. What's the road condition between here and Fort Augustus?"

The man snorted, garrulous good nature returning, in the face of their common dilemma.

"Now, that I couldnae tell ye. We've enough tae worry about, right here. This storm is really queer-like. I've never seen anything like it. Nae warnin' frae the weather service—an' it's rippin' roofs off buildings, an' knockin' doon power lines— We lost the phones hours ago."

Behind him, the disarray gave mute testimony to his words. Off to their left, the wind had lifted the roof off a small concession kiosk, hurling one twisted roof panel through the front window of a nearby shop. Broken glass and sodden newspapers littered the surrounding pavement, and men were trying to board up the windows of a nearby cottage whose windows also had fallen victim to the storm. The pungent smell of gas proclaimed a ruptured main somewhere. Rescue workers in fluorescent armbands were laboring to clear away the debris that lay between them and the source of the problem.

McLeod nodded sympathetically. "I don't envy you your job. Have you got a radio?"

The fireman paused to wipe the rain off his face before answering.

"Aye, but I cannae promise that ye'll get through. There's weird electrical stuff goin' on, with the thunder an' lightning an' all. But ye're welcome tae try."

"I'd appreciate that," said McLeod. "If we can raise Fort Augustus, maybe somebody there can put me in touch with the police."

"We'll do our best," said the fireman. "Best move yer car first, though. There's a petrol station over there." He pointed off behind him. "It's closed, but ye can pull up under the overhang tae give yerselves a bit of shelter. I'll meet ye over by the truck. . . ."

While McLeod was away, Peregrine remembered the hamper they had been given by Margaret MacLeod, and dragged it up onto the backseat beside him.

"How about a sandwich, while we're waiting, Adam?"

he asked, starting to rummage in it. "We may not get a chance to eat, later on."

Adam, studying their map with the aid of a small penlight, merely shook his head.

"Nothing for me, thanks. This kind of work is best undertaken on an empty stomach."

"It is?" Peregrine put down the sandwich he had been about to unwrap and looked at Adam quizzically. "Why is that?"

Adam turned his head partway toward Peregrine and smiled. "Do you want a medical explanation or an esoteric one?"

"Oh. You mean, there's more than one?" Peregrine asked.

Adam chuckled good-naturedly and half-turned in his seat to rest his arm along the back.

"The reasons are akin, actually. Physiologically speaking, the digestive process draws blood away from the brain—which means that mental functions are going to be less than optimum after eating. That's why one often feels like taking a nap after a good meal."

Peregrine nodded. "That makes sense. And the esoteric explanation?"

"Taking in food is a grounding process—which is why it's recommended that one have something to eat and drink after meditation or any other psychic procedure. Remember how I fed you, that first night you showed up on my doorstep?"

"Yes."

"But if one is about to work on the higher planes, it follows that one would *not* want to be grounded," Adam went on. "One wants the brain to function at peak efficiency. So one fasts—or at least goes light on food. We could have something to drink, if it's nonalcoholic."

Peregrine produced a thermos flask from the hamper and opened it, sniffing at the mouth.

"Tea," he announced, as the aroma filled the car and confirmed his opinion. "Is that all right?"

"That's fine," Adam replied.

They sipped at steaming cups of it while they waited for

McLeod to return. It was sweet and strong, and warmed cold fingers as well as insides, as they cupped their hands around it. After a few minutes, Adam set his on the dash and twisted around to glance at Peregrine.

"Hand me that phone out of Noel's bag, would you? I doubt I'll be able to get through, but we just might be able to enlist some additional backup for what's waiting at Urquhart."

Wide-eyed, Peregrine passed the phone forward, watching as Adam lowered his window slightly, extended the phone's antenna through the opening, and punched in a series of numbers. He could hear the static, even in the backseat, and had begun to lose interest by the time Adam tried the fourth or fifth call.

"A-ha," Adam murmured. "This one's ringing. And what do you want to bet I'll get the answering machine?"

His expression, as the line picked up, confirmed the prediction. Thus Peregrine was startled to hear Adam leaving a most cryptic message.

"This is Adam, at—six thirty-seven PM on the thirty-first," he said, glancing at his watch. "In an hour or so, Noel and I are going to be hunting rather nasty game. If you get this message in time, I want you to go to the club and join us. Alert the others, if you can; I'm calling from a cellular phone, and can't raise anyone else. This is most important. That is all."

As he turned off the phone and shoved the antenna back into the receiver, Peregrine gaped at him.

"How many others of you *are* there?" he breathed.

Adam's smile, as he cranked his window back up, was enigmatic.

"Enough to give the Opposition pause, when need be," he said.

McLeod's return precluded further questions. As the inspector got back into the car, pausing to shake the worst of the rain from his slicker, Peregrine poured him a cup of tea. McLeod gulped the first few swallows gratefully, setting it aside then, while he polished his rain-spattered glasses with a dry handkerchief.

"I tried to raise the others, while you were gone," Adam

informed him, passing the phone back to Peregrine. "No luck, except for Lindsay's machine. I left a message, but I doubt it will be picked up in time to do any good."

"Sounds like it's up to us, then," McLeod replied, retrieving his tea. "Actually, I'm amazed you got through at all. The radio certainly wasn't much use. The storm's blanked out everything east of Loch Cluanie."

"And the road?" asked Adam.

McLeod gulped down the rest of his tea and shook his head. "Nobody has a clue. We'll just have to take our chances."

On that dismal note, he handed his empty cup back to Peregrine and started the car, hooking up his seatbelt and switching on windscreen wipers and headlights again and letting the engine warm for a few seconds, for the rain had gone much colder, even in the short time he had been gone. Peregrine eyed the sandwiches wistfully as he put the thermos flask and cups away, but all thought of food quickly fled at McLeod set the big car in motion. A heavy gust hit them broadside as they emerged from the shelter of the garage, strong enough to rock the Volvo on its tires and make Peregrine grab for an armrest and the back of Adam's seat.

"Damned good thing we're not driving a Mini," McLeod muttered, and took a firmer grip on the steering wheel.

Creeping among the emergency vehicles still ranged around the pier area, they slowly made their way out of the village and started heading east. The storm whirled round them, howling like a wolf. Off to their right, the waters of Loch Alsh threatened to burst the boundaries of the shore. The wind hurled scuds of sea froth across their path as they battled their way down the coast toward the village of Dornie.

The causeway just before Dornie was all but under water. Foam flew like shrapnel as white-capped breakers crashed against the raised levee that carried the road. At the end of the causeway, they could not even see the grey hulk of Eilean Donan, which should have been looming only a few hundred yards off to the right.

"Another hour, and we'd have found ourselves cut off,"

McLeod remarked grimly. "I wonder how much worse this is going to get."

The weather notwithstanding, they made good time along the five-mile stretch beside Loch Duich, even though the darkness was now complete. Skirting the end of the loch, however, the rain got worse. Glen Shiel opened before them, a black wind-tunnel running east and west through the mountains of Kintail, and the rain grew even heavier, pelting onto the windscreen almost faster than the wipers could strike it away. The headlights pierced the storm no more than a car-length or two ahead. McLeod's jaw was clenched tight as he manhandled the Volvo around a series of zigzag curves, slowing more with each change of direction.

"It's no use—I can hardly see past the bonnet," he told Adam, as they crept along a straight stretch at no more than fifteen or twenty miles an hour. "If we're to carry on, I'm going to need some assistance."

Adam nodded wordlessly, clipping his penlight onto the edge of the map to free his hands. The road ahead was barely visible through the sheeting downpour.

Squaring himself in the seat, feet braced wide against the Volvo's firewall, Adam cupped his left hand over the sapphire on his right, bowing his head and drawing a deep breath as he closed his eyes. As he exhaled, centering to his intent, he murmured a silent invocation to the Author of Lights:

Domine noster,
Lumen semper ardens,
Ubi sunt tenebrae,
Fiat lux!

He could feel the Light suffuse him in answer to his prayer, radiating from the stone that was its focus and spreading all along his nerve-paths until his every fiber tingled with its presence. The warmth spread inward, touching heart and mind, and upward, to fill his mind and surround him.

That moment of inner illumination brought with it the

power to see the outer world by the light of his own internal vision, not so much changing what he saw, but enhancing his ability to sort out the information coming to him by other senses besides the mere visual. Lifting his head to look at the road ahead, he now found himself better able to interpret the grey subtleties of pavement and curve, to filter out the blustering chaos of wind and rain.

It was no objective difference that he could quantify with instruments or even by describing with words, but it was nonetheless real. Where before the road had been obscured by the darkness and driving rain, now his vision extended as it might have done, had the rain not been there; and potential hazards, hidden only moments before, were now at least vaguely visible.

McLeod had slowed to a snail's pace while Adam prepared, keeping his eyes straight ahead and intent on the road, trying to maintain what headway he could. Now, as Adam raised his head, McLeod glanced at him briefly.

"Ready?" Adam asked.

"Aye."

Smoothly Adam reached across and set his right hand on the steering wheel just below McLeod's left, making sure their hands touched. McLeod drew a long, deep breath, shrugging the tension out of his shoulders, then gave his attention back fully to the road, hands steady on the wheel, craggy face composed. Peregrine looked on in owl-eyed silence, wondering what his two companions could possibly be up to.

"We're clear ahead," Adam murmured, "and you've got a comfortable margin of space on either hand. Fortunately, we're most unlikely to meet oncoming traffic. Guide on the center line and start accelerating. I'll tell you when to ease off."

With Adam's hand on the wheel with McLeod's, the Volvo began picking up speed. The needle on the speedometer edged up from twenty to thirty, then to thirty-five.

"That's fine . . . that's good enough for now," Adam continued, in the same low, level voice. "Take her ten degrees to the left . . . now back to twelve o'clock . . . now fifteen degrees right . . . now steady on. . . ."

Under Adam's direction, McLeod brought the Volvo's speed gradually up to fifty. They held to that speed for the next twenty minutes, while Adam continued to read the road ahead for bumps, curves, and obstacles. Like a pilot flying blind on instrumentation, McLeod accepted Adam's instructions with confident assurance, his hands responding to the minuscule promptings of Adam's. Watching from the backseat, Peregrine began to suspect that this was not the first time his two companions had worked together to pull off such an extraordinary feat of teamwork.

They left Glen Shiel and began to skirt Loch Cluanie. The banks of the loch were full to overflowing, and the road was flooded in places. Twice they were forced off the tarmac to creep along higher ground on the left-hand shoulders. Each time, Adam was able to guide them safely back onto the highway, with only a few precious minutes lost.

When the loch was safely behind them, Adam passed the map back to Peregrine, never taking his eyes from the road.

"Check the map, Peregrine," he said softly. "We should have a junction coming up, and I don't want to miss it in the dark."

Briefly Peregrine used the penlight to confirm their route.

"You want the left-hand fork," he said, looking up. "It should be marked A887 or Inverness—if the signs are still up."

Even as his eyes strained to penetrate the rain and darkness, Peregrine caught a sudden, blurred glimpse of a road-sign as they flashed past it in the storm.

"Any time now," Peregrine warned. "Actually, it's more of a bearing left than an actual turn."

"We're coming up on it," Adam told McLeod. "Slow down and get ready to bear left with I give the word. Easy . . . *now*—and straighten out. Well done, both of you."

Those words of praise gave Peregrine welcome comfort after simply rattling along as a passenger for so many miles, beginning to wonder why they had even brought him along. He consulted the map again, but there was only one more turn to be made, just as they actually got to Loch Ness and headed north. Still, he kept track of the few tiny villages through which they passed; it gave him reassurance that he was a part, however small, of what was going on.

Thunder rumbled low on the horizon ahead and to the left, and lightning lit the sky increasingly as they continued north and east, along the swollen torrent of the River Moriston. Road work along the route necessitated several slight detours onto unpaved stretches, slowing their progress, and a few miles past the village of Dundreggan, they came around a sharp bend in the road to find their way blocked by a flock of wet, bedraggled sheep.

McLeod braked even as Adam's mouth was opening in warning, bringing them to a halt mere inches from the nearest animals.

"Bloody stupid beasts!" McLeod muttered. "If we'd hit one, our trip might well have ended right here. Let's see if I can shift them."

He tapped the horn without result, then eased the Volvo forward. Rain-sodden and bewildered by the headlights, the sheep edged nervously aside from the car's long bonnet. One wall-eyed ewe stood rooted to the spot, only shying away when the bumper nudged her shoulder. The rest blundered toward the verges, finally leaving the car a narrow space to pass through.

With the sheep safely behind them, McLeod gradually picked up speed again. Very soon they passed the wind-twisted remains of a signpost. The route sign itself was lying facedown at the side of the road several yards away.

"This must be Invermoriston," Peregrine said, peering between the front seats as they slowed through the village. "We should have a junction with the A82, any time now. You'll want to bear le—"

"Flares ahead!" Adam suddenly said. "Look out!"

Hissing under his breath, McLeod braked to a crawl, slowly approaching a man in oilskins who was putting out more flares. Behind him, an articulated lorry lay on its side, the trailer and cab still connected. A car was stopped beside it, emergency flashers adding a yellow glare to the red of the flares.

"I hope no one's hurt," Adam murmured, as they crept closer. "As a physician, I'm bound to offer aid."

As they crept even with the man laying the flares, Adam took his hand off the wheel and McLeod cranked down his window.

"Anyone hurt?" McLeod called.

The man grimaced, holding a newly-lit flare out and away from his body.

"Only my pride," he said. "And it didn't do me rig any good. I was trying to make it down to Fort Augustus, but the winds got so bad, I thought I'd better stop. Should've stayed on the main road. A gust caught me, coming around this curve, and blew me right over."

McLeod nodded sympathetically. "I doubt you'll get a recovery vehicle out tonight," he said. "What's the road like, heading north?"

The man shook his head. "I wouldn't advise trying it. The road's clear, but the wind is really bad, and visibility is minimal. There was some thunder and lightning, too, a bit farther north. And the loch's really choppy."

"I'll watch myself," McLeod said, raising a hand in thanks. "Good luck to you."

"Aye, and to you."

As they crept on around the overturned lorry, making the transition onto the main road, Adam put his hand back on the wheel beneath McLeod's. The inspector glanced at him, then returned his attention straight ahead as he crept their speed up once more.

"How are you holding up?"

Adam's face was showing signs of strain, but he smiled slightly, not taking his eyes from the road.

"It can't be much more than fifteen miles from here to Point Urquhart. I'll manage."

The car shuddered as if struck by a giant's hand as they came onto the edge of Loch Ness, heading north in the direction of Inverness. The wind, funneled by the long, narrow confines of the loch, could sweep for more than twenty miles without resistance, to batter the edges of the loch with the full fury of the storm.

More heavily traveled than the route through Glen Shiel,

the highway here was dotted with stranded vehicles of all shapes and sizes, their drivers forced to the shoulder by the blinding fury of the tempest. Some had not been totally in control when they did so, and rested with one or more wheels in a ditch or with a front fender crumpled against a stone wall.

With Adam still guiding him, McLeod threaded the Volvo swiftly in and out along a ten-mile obstacle course of stalled cars and minor road accidents. Off to their right, the black water of Loch Ness raged along the shore below, gnashing at the rocks like a live thing possessed.

But the focus of the fury lay ahead of them. As they drew nearer to Glen Urquhart, even Peregrine became aware of a ghostly, blue-white glow flickering in and out of phase on the fringes of his vision. It was different from the lightning that also lit the sky periodically—a lambent luminance sensed more with inner perceptions than with physical sight.

He could see that it worried Adam and McLeod, too. The inspector kept glancing off at it, even though Adam seemed still to be focused on the road ahead. Far ahead, at the level of the loch, streamers almost like the aurora borealis thrust ghostly fingers upward to unite with the powers of earth and sky. Thus entwined, they formed a centrifugal whirl of elemental energies, brooding ever more threatening above the highland hills.

The significance of the manifest shape was not lost on Adam, even though his focus seemed directed elsewhere. He knew it for what it was, and what it meant: The denizens of the realm of Faerie were raising up a cone of power in their righteous wrath, investing it with all the unbridled fury of the elements. Unless the fairy anger could be appeased, its force would fall indiscriminately on everyone and everything caught within range of its influence. And the only way to appease the offended fairies was to compel their offenders to answer the harsh, uncompromising balance of High Justice.

Adam glanced ahead at the sky again. In the same instant, as they came into a turn, something large and dark broke out of the darkness on the left and bolted across the road in front of the car.

McLeod uttered a startled exclamation and veered sharply to the left. He missed whatever it was, but the Volvo went into a skid and left the road, bouncing over the remains of a low freestone wall and coming to a rest with a sudden, thick-sounding splash, partway down a sloping embankment. One headlight went dark, but the remaining one showed a water-filled ditch just beyond their front wheels.

For a heartbeat or two, the only sound was the pelting of the rain on the car's roof and bonnet and the low purr of the engine. Then McLeod drew a deep breath and eased his grip on the steering wheel.

"Everybody all right?" he asked.

At Adam's steady, "Yes," Peregrine leaned shakily forward from the backseat, his face pale and inquiring.

"What happened?" he asked.

"We almost hit something," said McLeod.

Peregrine glanced at Adam. "Did you see what it was?"

"Not clearly," Adam said. "From the general outline, it might perhaps have been a deer."

Certainly, the image resonating in the back of his mind was that of a horned shape in flight. Beyond that, however, he was not prepared to speculate out loud. McLeod shot him a curious side glance, but probed the matter no further.

"Well, whatever it was, it's gone now," the inspector said. "And so, I fear, is our transportation."

He shifted the Volvo into reverse and slowly pressed down on the accelerator, but the rear wheels only spun. The big car remained anchored to the spot.

Scowling, McLeod killed the engine and got out of the car, gingerly working his way down the slippery slope to inspect damage to the front end. He came back along the left side, steadying his balance on the fender. As he came even with Adam's door, Adam rolled down his window and handed him the big electric torch. McLeod was longer at the back of the car, and did not look happy when he rejoined them.

"Well, we aren't going anywhere without a tow truck,"

he announced. "Even if I haven't torn out the underside by going over that bit of wall, we're mired up to the axle in front, and the rear wheels are dug in. Sorry, Adam."

"No matter," Adam murmured. "No one else could have done any better. I should have given you warning. At least no one's hurt. We'll simply have to go the rest of the way on foot. Let's have a look at that map, Peregrine."

Peregrine handed the map forward, and Adam consulted it briefly under the dash light, then glanced back out McLeod's side and out the rear window at the light show still visible ahead and behind the embankment of the road.

"I don't see how we could be much more than about a mile from Urquhart Castle," he said, his brow furrowed in calculation. "That's no great distance to cover on foot, even in this storm. In fact, going the rest of the way on foot might even be an advantage—give us more of an element of surprise. It's beastly weather for it—but it's no better for our comrades at Urquhart."

The brief flash of his grin in the dim light was almost predatory, and McLeod answered it with a grim chuckle.

"Aye, that's true enough," the inspector said. "Mr. Lovat, if you'll be so good as to pass my bag up here, we'll arm ourselves for the hunt, as it were. Adam, do you need yours as well?"

"No, I have what I need," Adam replied, as Peregrine wordlessly passed McLeod's bag forward and looked at him in question. "I believe I do have an extra torch, however. You might fetch that, Peregrine."

Peregrine did as he was bidden, lifting the black doctor's bag onto his lap and gingerly opening it. He was peering into its shadowed depths, trying to spot the torch, when Adam leaned back over the seat and shone the big torch into it, at the same time extracting the second torch and handing it to Peregrine. During that brief moment of illumination, Peregrine caught just a glimpse of small boxes and vials and plastic-sealed disposable syringes—the usual paraphernalia one might expect in a doctor's bag—but also several oddly-shaped items wrapped in what looked like white silk. He looked up in question as Adam snapped off the torch.

"Tools of my various trades," Adam said, by way of

explanation. "But I won't need any of the rest of that tonight. You can put it back behind the seat."

Wide-eyed, Peregrine obeyed. He was curious, but Adam's instruction precluded further discussion. Besides, McLeod had just pulled a very serviceable-looking automatic from his bag. Upholstering it, the inspector shoved an ammunition clip into the butt, then pulled back the slide to chamber a round, letting it snap back with a deadly-sounding click.

"Browning Hi-Power," McLeod said, thumbing on the safety and sticking it determinedly into the front of his waistband. "It's a 9mm automatic—fires the standard NATO round. Gives me fourteen shots before I have to reload."

As he pulled two more clips from the bag and stuck one in each coat pocket, Peregrine gaped in dismay.

"Do you really think you're going to need that?" he asked.

"I hope I won't," McLeod replied. "But I want to be ready, if I do. We know that they've killed at least once. You saw the body on the dock."

Feeling a little queasy, Peregrine nodded. Until that very moment, even through the ordeal of the ferry crossing, it had not truly occurred to him just how dangerous this might be. The banshee had threatened a peril of its own, of course, but somehow that did not represent the same kind of danger as bullets.

"Take heart," Adam said. "If I'm right in my speculations, our gun-toting thieves are going to have a lot more on their minds than worrying about us."

With that assurance, he flung open his car door to the storm, McLeod doing likewise. As the two climbed out, Peregrine unhooked his seat belt and followed.

Chapter Twenty-one

THE temperature had dropped even more since leaving the ferry at Kyle of Lochalsh. They stayed reasonably dry at first, in the gear they had borrowed from Dunvegan, but the full force of the wind hit them when they climbed up the slippery embankment and emerged on the road, chilling to the bone, and the wind-driven rain stung exposed hands and faces like icy needles.

Shivering, Peregrine hunched deeper into his collar and pulled a fold of his borrowed scarf closer around his neck and lower face to keep out the rain, wishing he had thought to borrow proper gloves. His fingerless ones were not much good; besides they were soaked through already.

Adam was not even wearing gloves, though Peregrine knew he had some, for he had heard Humphrey mention putting a pair in the pockets of the green waxed jacket, back at the airport. He was carrying his electric torch in one bare hand, with the other thrust into a coat pocket; and whenever the exposed hand got too cold, he would shift the torch to the other hand and shove the frozen one into a pocket to thaw. McLeod, likewise, was gloveless—though at least his torch was one of the long, metal-cased police ones, long enough to clamp under one arm while he burrowed both hands into his pockets—a bit awkward, but it would keep his hands supple enough to handle his pistol, if need be.

This perception led Peregrine to wonder what Adam was going to do for a weapon, when they eventually reached Urquhart Castle. He had a feeling that the narrow, hand-length black object he had seen Adam slip into his jacket, back at the airport, might be a weapon of some sort; but he was virtually certain it was not a gun. Whatever it was, Peregrine doubted whether it would be effective defense against fairies; Adam certainly had not produced it when threatened by the banshee. And Adam's torch, no bigger than his hand, was hardly a weapon—though McLeod's might qualify.

Not that the torches were much use in *this* rain. As they trudged single-file along the right-hand shoulder of the road, Adam leading and McLeod bringing up the rear, Peregrine decided that one of the worst things about being out in the weather, besides getting cold and wet, was that one's glasses got streaky and fogged. McLeod would be contending with the same annoyance, though Peregrine was pretty sure the inspector only needed his for reading. Peregrine briefly considered simply pocketing his spectacles, for the rain was so heavy that he could only see a few feet past Adam anyway; but he put his head down instead, deciding it was better to see things through a blur of rain, if there eventually *was* anything to see, than to remove the glasses and be sure of seeing nothing. Not that he was eager to see anything like the banshee again. . . .

The rain continued to pelt down steadily. Like automatons, the three of them trudged along for nearly a quarter of an hour, the eerie light-show ever before them and to their right, thunder rumbling almost continuously above the wail of the wind. They met no traffic. As they got colder and wetter, they began to encounter pockets of hail that battered down across their shoulders like a rain of hard gravel.

"Adam, is it my imagination," McLeod called hoarsely from the rear, "or is this getting worse?"

"Well, it wasn't *hailing* before," Adam replied.

Before Peregrine could comment, a louder rumble punctuated the general thunder and lightning, even reverberating through the soles of their boots. At the same time, greenish light flared down at the level of the loch, ahead and to their right, giving a fleeting glimpse of black water and also, to their astonishment, the ragged silhouette of a ruined medieval castle. Ahead, but twenty yards or so, the castle's modern-day car park opened off the road into a flat, paved plateau overlooking the ruin.

"Look! That must be it!" Peregrine cried, pointing ahead with a cry of excitement. He started forward impulsively, but McLeod caught him by the sleeve.

"Easy, laddie," the inspector warned, quickly switching off his torch. "That'll be Urquhart, right enough, but you can see for yourself there's something bloody peculiar going on down there. It'd be poor tactics to go rushing in before we've had a chance to take our bearings."

Beside him, Adam likewise had turned off his torch, and distractedly drew the other two men closer—for his attention was still on the lights below.

"Noel's right," he murmured. "Let's see if we can get a better look from the car park. And no more torches, if we can possibly manage without," he added, pocketing his. "With the lightning flashes, and what's going on down there, I think we can see well enough, if we keep to the edge of the road. But there's no sense announcing our arrival before we're ready to act."

Bending their heads to the wind, the three managed the few remaining yards to the near end of the car park without incident. A railing brought them up short along the downhill side, and they lined up along it, crouching to peer down. The eerie green light continued to flicker in cold flashes along the cliffs fronting the loch, apparently coming from behind the south end of the castle.

"Well, whatever it is, it certainly isn't lightning," Adam said.

"Aye," McLeod agreed. "Apart from the sound, if I didn't know better, I'd say there was artillery fire going on down there."

"Unfortunately," Adam replied, "it may well be akin to that. When we start down, we'd better be prepared for a fight."

Even as he spoke, a deep, sonorous boom shivered the air, echoing up from the water's edge like the aftershocks of an explosion. All of them ducked instinctively as green sparks fountained upward behind the shoreline bluffs and hung there, whizzing and darting like a swarm of incandescent bees. The glow was enough to illuminate the trail down to the castle quite clearly.

"I believe we may be just in time," Adam murmured. "Unless I miss my guess, someone has just opened up Scot's Fairy Cave! Let's have a closer look."

The fence at the edge of the car park was a two-rail affair of tubular steel, with bars as thick as a man's wrist. Ducking his head between the two, Adam swung up a booted leg and wormed his way through, aware that McLeod and Peregrine were following as he started down the footpath toward the castle. Avoiding a potentially noisy flight of wooden steps, they skidded down the embankment to one side, clinging to the railing to slow their descent, then clambered unceremoniously over the barrier at the kiosk where tickets were usually sold.

They kept their heads down as they trotted down a long, gradual slope almost to the level of the castle walls, guided by the railings that ran along either side. At the bottom, the path made a sharp left down a slippery flight of timber and concrete steps and then continued along a wooden catwalk that led toward the bridge spanning the castle fosse, but Adam led them to the right instead, down another short flight of steps, heading for a small outbuilding set just outside the south rampart.

They paused in its shadows to peer ahead, for beyond that, a muddy path led downward among storm-tattered trees toward a narrow crescent beach. Beyond the beach, the black waters of the loch frothed with the storm. Between lightning flashes, the whole area pulsed with a fey, greenish light that shimmered and snapped like static electricity.

"Listen," McLeod whispered, as the wind brought them the faint, mechanical thrum of a diesel engine. "D'ye hear that?"

Silently the three slipped along the side of the building and crouched again at the end, peering ahead for a glimpse of the source of the sound. From their new vantage point, they could just make out the bulk of a powerful speedboat drawn up close to the crescent-shaped beach. A man in black oilskins and cap was at the helm, holding the craft steady, with its prow nudging the rough shingle, a stone's throw below the mouth of a horseshoe cave.

Adam tugged at Peregrine's sleeve to get him down as the three of them cautiously dashed across the path and took cover farther to the right, behind some bushes, where they could get a better angle on the cave. The entrance was raw as a wound. The huge stones flanking the opening and scattered across the beach looked as though they had been newly quarried. Inside the cave, the air was dense with flecks of bright green light, whirling and flying like sparks from a blacksmith's forge.

"The records say nothing about a cave here," Peregrine whispered. "Do you really think they just now opened it?"

"Almost certainly," Adam replied.

The man in the boat was watching the entrance expectantly.

"The rest must be inside," McLeod muttered, warily scanning around them, in case all were *not*. "Care to estimate how many that might be?"

Adam peered at the boat and the cave, calculating. "I'd guess maybe five or six more, if they all came in the boat—which is likely, since there were no cars in the car park. Given that men like these don't like to share the loot, that also suggests keeping numbers to a minimum. If it *is* five or six more, do you think we can handle them?"

McLeod snorted softly. "Do we have a choice?"

"No," Adam said, "but we do have the element of surprise."

"For now, aye, but keep your heads down," McLeod cautioned.

He shoved his torch into his left-hand pocket and padded off down the slope, Adam and then Peregrine following. At the point where the path hooked right, he ducked to the left into a thick stand of wet elderberry bushes. A crouching, ten-yard scramble through the underbrush brought him to the base of a large, saddle-topped boulder, half the size of a small car. Beyond, the ground fell away brokenly toward the beach and the mouth of the newly-opened cave.

The wind had died down under the cliff, leaving the air cold and still, and the rain had petered out to a chill, saturating mist. The sudden, localized lull was ominous, like the zone of calm at the eye of a hurricane. As Adam flattened himself against the boulder beside McLeod, he wondered how long the calm would last.

A showery rustle in the shrubbery heralded Peregrine's arrival. The young artist threw himself down next to Adam, his eyes wide with excitement.

"Have you seen anything yet?" he breathed, rearing up cautiously on one elbow to get a better look at the play of lights inside the mouth of the cave.

Adam tugged him downward with a hiss of warning.

"Careful!" he breathed.

"But, what are all those flecks of light?" Peregrine whispered. "They're flying about almost as if they were alive."

"They *are* alive," Adam murmured, "or hadn't you guessed? Those are the denizens of the cave."

"*Fairies*?" Peregrine caught his breath and stared.

"That's right," McLeod muttered, from Adam's other side. "And they'd just as soon eat you alive as look at you. I'm serious, boy—don't look at me like that!"

As Peregrine gasped at his two companions, speechless, Adam slipped the sapphire ring from his finger and held it out to the artist.

"Here. Take this and put it on," he said. "Whatever happens from here on out, you're going to need some protection. If we should come under attack from the Faerie Host—which is likely, before this is all over—the virtues vested in the stone should keep them at bay—at least for a little while."

"But, aren't you going to need this yourself?" Peregrine asked, gloved hand closing automatically on the ring.

"No, I have other weapons."

Partially unzipping the front of his slicker, Adam reached his right hand deep inside. It came out clasping a small, black-sheathed dagger.

Or, no, not just a dagger, Peregrine amended. It was a *skean dubh*—the Highland blade customarily worn with a kilt, stuck in the top of the hose.

But even in the erratic light, Peregrine could see that this was no ordinary *skean dubh*. The sheath alone was a work of art, half the overall length of about seven inches and mounted with exquisite silver interlace at throat and tip. He could not see the details of the carving on the hilt, because of Adam's hand, but the pommel was set with a clear blue stone nearly the size of a pigeon's egg. When Adam unsheathed the weapon, slipping the sheath back into his pocket, the polished blade shone like quicksilver under the lowering sky, a pale blue light flickering about its edges like reflected moonlight—or like the reflection of powerful intent.

At the same time, McLeod had pulled the Browning automatic from his waistband, thumbing the safety off with a faint but audible click as he raised it, ready, beside his head. However, it was not the sight of the gun that made Peregrine blink; he had done that already, back in the car. It was the sudden flash of blue fire off the back of McLeod's gun-hand. A closer look revealed that McLeod was now wearing a sapphire ring almost identical to Adam's.

Both men had in their eyes the intent, preoccupied look of hunters on the trail of dangerous prey. Gazing at his companions in owlish silence, Peregrine suddenly became keenly aware that he was seeing them in a wholly new light. During the past few weeks and even hours, he realized that he had come to accept, almost casually, that Adam and McLeod had powers and abilities he could not begin to understand. Now that they were preparing to close in on their quarry, Peregrine realized he hadn't a clue what they might do.

He had no idea, for that matter, what he was going to do himself. It was not a comfortable reflection. Glancing down involuntarily at Adam's ring in his hand, he hastily pulled off his gloves and slipped the ring hastily onto the third finger of his right hand, as he had seen Adam wear it. The fit was loose, but its presence somehow made him feel less vulnerable. As he returned his attention to the distant cave, he squared his shoulders and closed his fist tightly, so the ring would not slide off, hoping he would not prove to be more of a hindrance than a help.

Even as this thought crossed his mind, a sudden, high-pitched screeching broke out below. The angry dance of emerald lights quickened to a feverish tarantella, and a sullen glow flared deep inside the tunnel, spreading unevenly toward the mouth of the cave. A moment later, a cluster of black-clad figures became barely visible at the cavern's horseshoe-shaped entrance.

The man in front was tall and slight, moving with arrogant grace, both arms raised above his head. The three men following behind him looked bulky by comparison. Two of them were staggering under the weight of a smallish metal-bound chest that seemed inordinately heavy for its size. The man who brought up the rear was carrying a large oblong picture frame elevated like a shield between himself and the motes of light that whirled menacingly above him.

"The Fairy Flag?" Adam murmured to McLeod.

"Aye, and the chap at the front must be controlling it. Look! He's got a sword. You can't see it except when he turns just right."

Peregrine craned his neck for a better look, so much that Adam had to tug at his sleeve.

"I think it's the Hepburn Sword!" he whispered eagerly. "If only I could get a closer look—but I'm nearly certain it is!"

"No doubt it is," Adam replied. "But if you don't keep down, you're liable to get a much closer look at it than you'd care to."

As the party emerged fully from the mouth of the cave, under the milling cloud of the Faerie Host, more details became apparent. All of the men were wearing hooded black macs, but the leader also was masked across the eyes like an executioner, with a silver chain of office about his neck that Peregrine was willing to bet held a medallion he had tried several times to draw. He was holding the sword horizontal above his head, one beringed hand gripping the basket hilt, the other clasping the naked blade a few inches from the point.

A baleful greenish light played about the damascened blade, but the source was not the sword itself, but the frail fabric of the Fairy Flag, held aloft in its frame by the party's rear guard. The sword seemed to draw light out of the Flag like a spindle gathering floss, subtle as spider-silk, weaving a ghostly canopy above the procession. Green fairy-motes swooped down on the four from all sides, only to sheer off and retreat as though repelled by an invisible wall of force.

"Is the Fairy Flag doing that?" Peregrine whispered.

"Aye, that and the Hepburn Sword," Adam replied. "The sword is an implement of summoning and control. The leader is using it to call forth and direct the Flag's protective influence, against the very creatures who gave the Flag its power."

"But, how can he *do* that?" Peregrine wanted to know.

McLeod glared down at the procession's leader in mingled revulsion and disbelief.

"Not by any honest means, that's for certain," he muttered. "But it's bound to be costing him dear." He glanced at Adam. "How long do you think he'll be able to sustain the power-link?"

"Probably long enough to allow his party to reach the boat with their plunder," Adam said. "Unless, of course, we provide a suitable diversion. Noel, do you think you could work your way around to the far side of the cave without being seen too soon?"

McLeod cast a shrewd eye over the ground above the cave-mouth. "I'll do my best," he agreed, and began edging away through the undergrowth to the left.

"What about me?" Peregrine whispered eagerly.

Adam flashed him a swift, commanding look. "You stay here and keep watch—and try to avoid being eaten."

Before the artist could react, Adam was gone, slipping lightly down the hillside and over the rocks. At the lower end of the rough incline, he stopped with one foot braced against a knee-high boulder and leveled the point of his *skean dubh* at the cluster of men struggling across the flat toward the boat, drawing himself up to his full height. Power welled up within his grasp, tingling at the center of his palm, but he held that power in check as he drew breath to call out.

"That's far enough, gentlemen. Halt where you are!"

The little cavalcade started around at the sound of his voice, someone muttering an imprecation as they spotted him. The leader whirled to face him, silencing his followers with a sharp command, but he did not lower his arms. His left hand opened and then closed on the end of the blade, as if he longed to turn the sword against his challenger; but Adam knew he dared not, lest he lose control of the Fairy Flag.

"Who the devil are you?" the man demanded, the voice hard and cool against the continued drone of the fairy voices. "And just what do you think you're doing here?"

"You may address me as Master of the Hunt," Adam replied, keeping an eye on the boatman as well. "As for my purpose—I am here to see justice done."

This announcement elicited a murmur of uncertainty among the leader's subordinates, but the leader himself only curled a sneering lip.

"Justice, indeed? And what are our alleged crimes?"

"They include, not least, the injuries done to one once known as Michael Scot of Melrose, for the purpose of gaining unlawful possession of his property," Adam said sternly, pointing at the chest. "I believe you have it there.

"In addition, there is the matter of the Fairy Flag of the MacLeods, which you have wrongfully appropriated and grievously profaned. The sword in your hand is also stolen, I believe. If you are wise, you will relinquish the artifacts you have stolen and submit yourselves to the temporal authorities, while there still is time to make reparation for your grosser crimes against the laws of the Inner Planes."

The air above the four was seething with bright fairy-shapes, the mounting buzz of their anger like the buildup of an electronic overload. Watching helplessly from behind his concealing boulder, Peregrine cast an anxious glance in the direction McLeod had gone. The inspector's head and shoulders showed briefly above the boulders overshadowing the cave's entrance, and then a ripple in the bushes beyond marked his progress toward a sizeable outcropping of stone on the opposite side of the archway.

Down on the shore, the masked man was staring at Adam in bristling defiance.

"I think you overestimate your own importance, 'Master of the Hunt,' or whatever your true name might be. My colleagues and I do not recognize your authority. Nor do we accept your right to judge our actions."

"You mistake me," Adam replied. "Your own actions have already condemned you. I am here to demand your surrender—and to compell it, if necessary."

By now, McLeod had had time to reach his chosen lair among the rocks to the right of the cave-mouth. From his concealed vantage point, he saw the hooded leader of the opposition make a covert sign to the pilot of the speedboat. The man nodded almost imperceptibly and reached below the craft's steering console. As he straightened, McLeod glimpsed the sleek, deadly silhouette of an Uzi in his hands.

"Adam, look out! The boatman's got a gun!" he shouted.

Chapter Twenty-two

ADAM had already seen the boatman move, and threw himself flat as a chuttering spray of bullets cut the air where he had been standing a heartbeat before. In the same instant, the gunman swung around on McLeod's position. Rock chips flew and shrubbery disintegrated under a withering volley, but McLeod was already pressed flat against the inside face of the outcrop, bracing himself to return fire.

Another salvo brought down a clump of sapling trees to his left. The gunman paused briefly to let the debris settle, and in that scant interval McLeod reared up from cover, steadied his wrist, and squeezed off three quick rounds.

The first shot ricocheted off the speedboat's hull; the second and third shattered the windscreen. The gunman flinched aside, then fired off another burst, but McLeod was already down. Lead thudded harmlessly into the seamed cliff-face above his bent head, but then, before he could dive out of the way, the weakened section of the wall collapsed, partially burying him under a stunning battery of loose earth.

Adam started up in alarm, all but certain McLeod was shot, but the gunman fired off another burst in his direction, forcing him to hug the ground again. Meanwhile, the rock slide that had knocked down McLeod rumbled on down the hill. Catapulting stones hit the shingle and rebounded. The flag-bearer at the rear of the party recoiled before the shower of flying gravel, and as he gave a yelp and sprang backwards, he collided with his nearest companion.

The impact jarred his grip on the sides of the Flag's

protective frame, and it twisted in his hands. As it did, one corner struck the ground sharply and the frame burst apart with a dissonant tinkle of shattering glass.

Instantly the protective canopy above the party collapsed. The leader gasped. Shrilling triumphantly, the hovering Faerie Host swooped in for the kill.

The men carrying the chest dropped it, screaming and beating the air around them as the fairies tore at them with needle teeth and claws, like tiny, ravening piranhas made of light. The Fairy Flag lay on the ground, tangled in a debris of glass and ruined frame. Crazed by fear, his exposed face and hands already running with blood, the flag-bearer made a panic-stricken dive to retrieve the only source of protection he could think of. But as his profane hands touched the sacred relic, there was a sudden, sulphurous bang and a greasy surge of black smoke.

As the smoke thinned, no trace of the flag-bearer could be seen. Stunned by what he had just witnessed, Adam cautiously lifted his head again just in time to see the fairy vanguard descend on the next man. As the man sank screaming under a seething blanket of tiny, glowing forms, his horrified leader clutched hard at the shoulder of the remaining porter and gestured toward the boat, still brandishing the Hepburn Sword above his head with one hand.

"Help me get the chest aboard!" he ordered shrilly. "They can't follow us over water!"

The man's face and hands were a mass of bloody gouges, but somehow he managed a comprehending nod. The fairies seemed still intent on tearing their other adversary to bits, and the leader's sword kept the occasional scout at bay. Between them, the two managed to manhandle the chest over the remaining yards of rocky beach. The boatman, no longer under fire from McLeod and unable to see Adam, threw aside his machine gun and slewed the boat around sideways, reaching over the side to help.

"Get the chest on board!" the leader shouted. "I'll keep them off!"

Leaving his subordinates to wrestle the chest over the side, he turned to beat back the advancing Faerie Host with fierce, slashing sweeps of the Hepburn Sword. Scores, perhaps hundreds, of glowing shapes snapped and buzzed about his head like a swarm of enraged wasps, but every time the sword connected with one, sparks crackled at the point of impact and a tiny light went out, in a curl of wispy smoke. A look of triumph was beginning to light the leader's face when suddenly he spied an upright figure moving from behind the fairy cloud, heading directly for him.

Adam was holding his *skean dubh* elevated before him like a holy relic, the pommel uppermost rather than the blade. The blue stone set in the hilt gave off a soft, shimmering glow like the clear light of summer twilight. The fairies shied away from him as he passed among them to halt only a few paces from the masked man.

"Two of your companions already have perished needlessly," Adam said sternly. "Leave the chest and put yourselves under my protection, before you pay for your obstinacy with your lives."

The masked man hackled like a jackal.

"You go to hell!" he shouted. "I've paid for this chest, and the cost wasn't cheap! I'll be damned if I'll let you have it for nothing!"

With a sudden savage backlash, he whipped out at Adam with the blade of the Hepburn Sword. Instinctively, Adam raised his *skean dubh* to parry the blow. Peregrine, who had been creeping nearer while the leader was distracted, let out a horrified cry of protest as the two blades clashed in a flash and a crackle of blue-white fire. In that instant, all the intimations of mortal danger he had seen hanging over Adam in the days gone by came surging back to memory.

Without thought for what he might be able to do once he got there, Peregrine broke from cover and dashed across the dozen yards still separating him from Adam and his foe—and the fairies—praying that Adam's ring would give him some protection from the latter. Blood-hungry motes of light closed around him in a screeching throng, but he flailed at them with his bare hands and continued, half-blind, toward the place where he had last seen Adam. Abruptly, two dark shapes loomed before him, one on one knee on the ground, bathed in a pale blue light and reared back on one supporting hand, the other poised above him with steel death in his hand, already starting his downward blow.

The Hepburn Sword flashed green as it descended. Not thinking of the possible consequences, Peregrine grabbed for it with both hands. His left briefly blocked the other's wrist jarringly at the basket hilt, slowing it, but not with enough force to keep his right hand from impacting solidly with the blade, right across the palm and back edge of his hand. Searing pain flung him backwards against Adam, rolling him into a tight ball as he clutched his right hand to his chest, fire searing down his fingers and shooting up his forearm. All he could think, in that infinite instant of first agony, was that he might never paint again.

But before he could even draw breath to scream, a heavy boot took him bruisingly in the ribs, with enough force to tumble him farther across the rough shingle. Somehow he managed to protect his head, and not to lose his glasses, but what he saw as he twisted round gave him no comfort as his adversary turned to attack Adam again.

Shouting wordlessly, his lips drawn back in an almost feline snarl, the swordsman lifted his blade to slash. But as the blade descended, Adam was already lifting his *skean dubh*—not with the hilt uppermost this time, but with the point directed toward the air between them, to rapidly sketch an arcane symbol.

Blue fire left a visible trace as the *skean dubh* flashed. It was nowhere near the intended path of the descending blade, but suddenly the sword was diverting to meet it, like steel drawn to a magnet. White-eyed with disbelief, the swordsman tried to correct, but Adam merely made a sharp, wrenching movement with the *skean dubh*.

His adversary gave a hoarse cry as the basket-hilt twisted in his grasp. Unable to hold onto it, he flung the weapon from him in defiant anger and turned to make a desperate running leap for the side of the waiting speedboat.

He never reached it. Alert for just such an opening, the Faerie Host swooped down again with greedy shrills of elation, blood spattering from their midst as they snapped and snarled and tore like piranhas in a feeding frenzy, keening their triumph. Adam flung himself protectively across Peregrine, at the same time closing his free hand around the hilt of the Hepburn Sword.

The two remaining men on the boat did not linger to see any more. They had their chest aboard. Terrified, the man at the helm gunned the engines and swung his craft around in a flurry of white water. Peregrine managed a dazed glimpse of the vessel pulling away from the shore, but he bit back a sob as fire shot up his right arm again from his wounded hand.

Half a dozen yards away, the fairy cloud was lifting from a fading crimson smear on the rocks, their keening almost deafening as they realized their foes were escaping. A few tried to pursue the boat across the water, but they could not maintain altitude and fell into the waves, perishing in high-pitched screams and puffs of steam.

Peregrine stifled a little sob, dazedly cradling his hand against his chest, not daring to open it for fear of what he might see. He was still wearing Adam's ring, but dark blood was welling between his fingers, dripping onto the wet shingle of the beach.

"Where's Noel?" Adam demanded, dragging Peregrine to his feet and looking around worriedly. "Do you see Noel anywhere?"

"No, I—"

"Here, take this and stand back to back with me!" Adam said, handing him the *skean dubh*. "They'll be coming after *us* next. Use the blade to cover yourself."

Even as he spoke, the shining emerald cloud yammered at the shoreline and then converged upon them, borne on a piercing skirl of high-pitched fairy voices. Numbly Peregrine raised the *skean dubh* as he had seen Adam do, though every fiber of his being shrieked that it was hopeless. . . .

Meanwhile, up on the high ground to the right of the cave-mouth, McLeod stirred groggily to find himself half-buried under earth and rubble. Somehow, his pistol was still in his hand, but he had managed to lose his glasses.

He turned his attention down to the beach. He could see no sign of the black-clad shore party, but a greenish swarm of lightmotes was whirling angrily just at the shore—and just beyond their reach, the speedboat was laboring desperately, trying to make headway against the dark chop of the loch. He could make out two black-clad figures in it.

Scrambling to one knee and locking into a combat stance, McLeod took careful aim and squeezed off half a dozen rounds at the men in the boat, even though he knew they were probably out of range. They were—but before he could even begrudge them their escape, his attention was arrested by new movement by the fairy column, now spiraling up from the water's edge—and swooping down on two familiar figures standing back to back at the shore.

With a hoarse croak of dismay, McLeod launched himself down the slope, skidding on his butt and barely getting his feet under him as he hit the bottom. He was already in motion as he staggered to his feet and started toward them—and nearly tripped over the smashed frame of the Fairy Flag.

Intention sprang into his mind even as his body already was moving in response. Jamming his pistol back into his waistband, he bent over the Flag, in its shattered glass. No doubt assailed him, for he was a MacLeod—and he had not seen the flag-bearer perish for his presumption.

But Adam had—and realized what McLeod was about to do.

"Noel, don't touch it!" he shouted, trying to ward off the menacing fairies and watch McLeod at the same time. "The legend is true! The flag-bearer went up in a puff of smoke!"

"Then he wasn't a MacLeod!" came the inspector's defiant reply, hardly even faltering.

Reverently he gathered the Fairy Flag out of the ruins of its frame, lifting it triumphantly in MacLeod hands—and did not die! MacLeod blood singing to the music of ancient battle tunes, he draped the Flag around his shoulders like a mantle and then bounded toward his beleaguered companions, shouting the ancient MacLeod motto at the top of his lungs: "*Hold fast!*"

Heedless of the milling fairies, he plunged into their midst to thrust himself between the astonished Adam and Peregrine. A strong, blunt-fingered hand clasped each firmly by the shoulder as he raised his voice fearlessly above the din.

"Avaunt ye, children of Earth, Air, and Fire! In the name of the MacLeod of MacLeod, Chief of all the Clan MacLeod, I, Noel Gordon McLeod, take these men under the protection of the Fairy Flag of Dunvegan! Harm them not, lest the ancient covenant be broken between MacLeods and the Faerie Folk!"

At once the ear-piercing skirl of inhuman voices subsided to a sullen buzz and the cloud lifted slightly, though the fairies continued to swarm angrily above their heads.

"*Lower your blades*," McLeod muttered, in an emphatic aside to his two companions. "I've got to convince them that *we* are not the enemy. You've seen what steel can do to them."

Without hesitation, Adam lowered the Hepburn Sword, Peregrine more reluctantly letting the *skean dubh* sink to point at the ground. As the hum of the fairy voices wavered, McLeod raised his face toward them again.

"Ye have, indeed, been grievously wronged, O People of Peace," McLeod began again, "but do not vent your just anger on those who would be your allies. It is not *we* who have despoiled your treasure! Out *there* lie your enemies!—" he gestured briefly with the hand on Adam's shoulder—"not here beneath the Fairy Flag!"

For several breathless heartbeats, all three of them waited—Adam and Peregrine with blades still poised, McLeod standing defiantly between them, his arms spreading the protection of the Fairy Flag across their shoulders. But then, to their infinite relief, the tornado whirl of the Faerie Host slowly began to unwind, the column lifting gradually above their heads.

However, the host did not disperse. Instead, the dancing motes of light spread along the water's edge like a diaphanous ribbon of emerald separating earth and sky, keening softly. The surface of the loch had gone flat, and an eerie silence fell, pregnant with expectancy.

"They're waiting for something," McLeod muttered in Adam's ear. "What in the *world* could they be waiting for?"

Above the loch, pale lightning was flickering erratically

among low-lying clouds. By its light, out on the loch, they could still make out the shape of the fleeing speedboat, laboring southwards. The low rumble of its diesels was clearly audible above the rising whistle of the wind, and off to the left new lights were approaching—not the expected police backup from Fort Augustus, if it came from that direction, but two smaller craft, no doubt attracted by the pyrotechnic show of the last little while. Their searchlights lanced across the gloom, first one and then the other eventually spearing the escaping craft in their beams—though their quarry had the advantage of speed, and was starting to draw away toward the south.

But then an odd thing happened. All at once, an eye-searing bolt of greenish lightning struck the water directly in front of the fleeing speedboat, accompanied by a simultaneous crack of thunder. For just an instant, the dark waters of the loch lit up in an eerie, fluorescent green all around the boat.

Abruptly the speedboat lost power, all systems knocked out by the near lightning strike. Off to the left, still several hundred yards away, the other two boats had also lost their engines, and the focus of their searchlights became more erratic as the occupants bent their attention to balky mechanical devices.

But there was nothing mechanical about what was happening in the vicinity of the first boat. As it drifted to a stop on the tossing swells, dead in the water, its two stunned passengers began shouting and frantically trying to restart the engines—for not far astern, between them and the shore, the dark waters were beginning to boil. Illuminated only sporadically by the now random bobbing of the searchlights, and more dimly by the luminescent waves, a dark, triangular head smoothly broke the surface, rearing upward on a long, powerful neck to turn two eye-points of fire in sentient scan of the surrounding darkness.

"Bloody, bloody hell!" McLeod breathed, almost reverently. "Does everyone else see what I see?"

Neither Adam nor Peregrine answered, but the Faerie Host greeted the creature's appearance with shrieks of malevolent glee. For a moment the creature hung there in the verdant gloom, almost as if listening to the sound of voices only it could hear. Then the great head dipped as if in acquiescence, and the basilisk gaze turned purposefully toward the stalled speedboat.

Majestically the great neck crested, the motion rippling along dark, serpentine coils that seemed to have no end. Then, with a languid sweep of its mighty tail, it began moving in on its chosen prey, bearing down with ever-increasing speed.

"Oh, my God!" Peregrine whispered. "They're sending it after the boat!"

The speedboat rocked and bobbed as its two occupants frantically renewed their efforts to start the engines. The searchlights still swept the area randomly, but the occupants of the other boats did not seem to realize what was happening. In a *vee* of luminescent emerald wake, the creature drove toward its target. One man snatched up the Uzi and started firing wildly, but the great head merely submerged and the *vee* kept coming.

It never rammed the boat, though. In the end, it was the great, dark coils of the creature's body that surged upward, under, and around the vessel, swamping the helpless craft and sucking it under. The man with the Uzi disappeared without a trace, but faint screams carried thinly over the water as the other man surfaced and tried to swim away, thrashing in blind terror—until white water burst around him and he, too, disappeared from sight.

As those ashore watched in fascination mixed with awe, the great head broached once more, a weakly struggling human form pinned in its jaws. But then man, monster, and the shattered remains of the boat disappeared in a whirlpool of foam as the creature bent its neck and sounded, carrying its struggling prey into the bottomless depths of Loch Ness.

As the churning waters subsided, utter silence settled on the leaden surface of the loch, finally broken by the diesels coughing back to life aboard the other two vessels, searchlights tentatively beginning to quarter the dark waters for survivors who did not appear.

The fairies, meanwhile, seemed appeased at last. Rising in joyful chorus, the dancing green motes of the Faerie Host careened in mad circles above the heads of the three men left standing alone on the shore—though for one breathless instant, Peregrine feared they might be gathering to renew their assault.

But then, instead of attacking, the fairy vanguard suddenly wheeled about and streaked back toward the mouth of the cave. The rest of the host followed. They poured into the tunnel in a rushing torrent, carrying rock and soil after them in the gale-wind of their passing. As the last of the host swept into the cave, the cave mouth closed up behind them with a crack like a clap of thunder. In the brittle silence that followed, the sky overhead began to clear, a bright galleon of a moon emerging from behind scudding clouds.

McLeod sat down heavily on the nearest boulder, looking more than a little drained, then slowly and carefully began lifting the tatters of the Fairy Flag from around his shoulders. Peregrine had sunk to his knees in trembling after-reaction, clutching his wounded hand and the *skean dubh* to his chest. Adam, with a wordless glance at the sword in his hand, turned toward the fairy cave, now visible only as a raw depression in the face of the cliff.

For a moment he stared at it, giving silent tribute to the powers that had spared them. Then he lifted the blade in grave salute, ending by thrusting the point into the pebbled beach at his feet. As he released it, the basket hilt swayed slowly back and forth like a heavy pendulum. Beyond, the dark waters of Loch Ness had settled under a moonlit sky, giving lie to the violence only minutes past. The two small boats continued to search the waters fruitlessly, and off in the south, new lights were approaching.

"I think we're about to have more company," Adam said, bending wearily to take the *skean dubh* from Peregrine's unresisting hand. "Your police backup, perhaps?"

McLeod craned his neck to look southward, then slumped back on his rock as the sound of very large engines drifted across the loch and searchlights criss-crossed the water ahead.

"*Now* they get here!" he muttered, easing out of his slicker and using it to wrap around the loosely-folded Fairy

Flag. "Not that it would have made any difference, if they'd gotten here sooner. In fact, it's probably best they didn't."

Adam took the *skean dubh*'s sheath out of his pocket and slipped it back on the blade, then tucked the whole back inside his coat, still looking out at the approaching lights. Seen by the moonlight and the reflection of her own searchlights, the newcomer was a stout forty-foot cruiser with a canopied upper deck.

"She looks like a pleasure boat," Peregrine observed, trying not to think about his throbbing hand.

"Aye, she is." McLeod rose to have a better look, then turned back to them, shaking his head. "She's called the *Queen of Alba*. During the tourist season, she operates as a tour boat out of Fort Augustus. But she gets seconded for Coast Guard duty every now and again, if a police vessel's needed in the area. Christ!" He slumped back down on his rock and shook his head. "How am I going to write the report on this? If I write what I really saw, they'll haul me off to the department shrink—no offense, Adam."

"None taken," Adam said with a distracted smile, taking out his pocket torch and crouching down to reach for Peregrine's wounded hand. "How about holding this light for me? I'd like to see what the damage is to Peregrine's hand, before we get inundated with people asking difficult questions."

Peregrine's heart was still pounding in after-reaction to what they all had seen, but now a new fear gripped at his heart as McLeod took the torch and Adam carefully began uncurling the bloody fingers.

"Adam, I'm an artist," he whispered shakily, squinting against the glare of the light in McLeod's hands. "I can't feel anything in my fingers."

"Good, then it won't hurt as much as I straighten them out. Yes, indeed. . . ."

"Adam, I'm going to pass out," Peregrine managed to gasp.

"No, don't do that." Adam peered at the hand and nodded. "Come over here closer to the water and let me rinse off some of the blood," he said, helping the younger man move. "You're fine. Just take a good, deep breath.

You're not going to faint. This isn't going to hurt nearly as much as you think. The water's cold. Good man!"

He sluiced the hand in the icy water and took a closer look, pressing around a shallow gash across the heel of the hand and part of the palm, then carefully worked his ring off the third finger, also slightly lacerated, and passed the ring to McLeod.

"Well, the ring's going to have to be redone," he said lightly, probing at the bones in the area around the wound, "but whatever else it may have done for you, I do believe it's saved you two fingers. Have a look at what the band stopped."

A little dazedly, Peregrine glanced at the ring McLeod proffered on the palm of his free hand. The heavy band had a deep gouge in the gold, angled where the blade of the Hepburn Sword had struck.

"You're lucky nothing's broken," Adam said, rinsing the hand again and then wrapping it with a handkerchief that McLeod offered. "You'll need a few stitches, but I don't think you'll even have much of a scar. Now, if only the rest was going to be as easy to explain. . . ."

On the loch beyond, the whoop of a police siren announced the approach of the *Queen of Alba*, one of her searchlights lancing through the darkness to spotlight the three crouching on the beach.

"Ahoy there!" came an authoritative voice, amplified by a loud-hailer. "This is the police. Who are you?"

Chapter Twenty-three

THE discovery that McLeod was a senior police officer, well out of his own jurisdiction, produced more confusion than clarification at first—though the sergeant aboard the *Queen of Alba* soon realized that it was McLeod whose garbled call had summoned them. After ordering the two remaining boats to stand by, the *Queen of Alba* touched in at the tour dock north of the castle, long enough to disgorge several officers, then joined the boats still searching the waters offshore for any survivors of what already was being described as a freak accident. During the next hour, reinforcements began arriving from Inverness: half a dozen police cars, a forensic van, and an ambulance.

McLeod's statement that he had been pursuing the thieves who stole the Fairy Flag seemed to come as no great surprise to his police colleagues. They had heard about the theft through normal police channels, and did not seem to think it at all odd that a MacLeod had managed to trail the thieves to Urquhart with it, following a "hunch."

The conjecture that McLeod himself presented was that an unidentified group of ne'er-do-wells had stolen the Fairy Flag of the MacLeods for reasons yet to be determined. He did not attempt to explain the murdered woman back at Dunvegan.

As for the pyrotechnic display reported by the occupants of the small boats—though interestingly, to McLeod's way of thinking, they offered no speculation regarding what had actually sunk the speedboat—McLeod pleaded uncertainty, due to being stunned by a fall of earth during an exchange of gunfire—a claim substantiated by the police surgeon who examined him and the recovery of expended shell casings in the area where he said he had fallen. Based on the scant evidence emerging in the pre-dawn hours, the theory was evolving that the gang who had stolen the Fairy Flag, desperate enough to murder and attempt murder—for reasons of their own—had somehow gotten themselves killed in pursuit of some likewise unknown objective.

"Sounds like a little more than a Hallowe'en prank gone wrong, if you ask me," one officer was heard to remark.

Satisfactory answers to the questions of "how" and "why" continued to elude them, however. And there was a limit to how much information Adam was prepared to offer in the interest of making matters clearer.

"I believe that Inspector McLeod was called in privately, by the Chief of the MacLeods, after the Fairy Flag was stolen," Adam told the sergeant taking his statement, as they stood in the shelter of the forensic van. "The inspector knew of my concern for the preservation of Scottish national treasures, through a long-term personal friendship, so he invited me along."

"And this Mr.—ah—Lovat?" the sergeant asked, referring to his notes.

Behind them, Peregrine was sitting on the back bumper of the ambulance, having his hand looked at. Before the first officers came ashore from the *Queen of Alba*, the three of them had agreed on the basics of the story they would tell.

"Oh, Mr. Lovat is an artist," Adam replied glibly. "He's been doing some sketches for an article I'm writing, on the lesser-known treasures of Scotland. We'd been going over some of them when Inspector McLeod rang. So naturally, he asked to come along."

"Hmmm, right," the sergeant murmured, scribbling busily in his notebook. "And you say he cut his hand on some glass?"

"That's correct. In their rush to get aboard the boat and escape, the thieves dropped the Fairy Flag, shattering the glass and utterly destroying the frame. Naturally, we were concerned that this priceless artifact would be damaged by the rain, so we tried to rescue it. Unfortunately, Mr. Lovat's zeal was not matched by his dexterity. In helping to extricate the Flag and get it out of the weather, he cut himself rather badly."

"Yes, I see," the sergeant said patiently, convinced—as intended—that Adam's involvement, if a trifle eccentric, was certainly innocent. After all, he *was* a respected member of the medical profession.

"Now, you mentioned the getaway boat, Sir Adam," the sergeant continued. "I believe Inspector McLeod said he thought it must have hit something in the water. Can you verify that?"

"Well, I should imagine it *must* have hit something—a submerged log, perhaps, or something like that."

The sergeant glanced up at him, pen poised. "*Did* it, sir?"

Adam arched one eyebrow and allowed a faintly mocking smile to touch his lips. "Come, now, my good man. I'm a psychiatrist. You surely don't expect me to tell you that I saw the Loch Ness Monster sink it?"

The sergeant grinned, shaking his head as he ducked it to write in his notebook again.

"You'd be amazed at the stories I hear, sir. I've been working out of Inverness for nearly twenty years, and I drive along this loch almost every day. Sometimes I think the place *attracts* loonies!"

"Hmmm, some places *do*," Adam agreed.

"So. You think the boat hit a submerged log?" the sergeant said, still writing.

"I honestly can't say—though it must have been *something* of that sort. Actually, I was a bit preoccupied with Mr. Lovat's hand. It's rather a nasty cut, you know, and he's an artist."

"Yes, well, thank you, Sir Adam," the sergeant replied, closing the cover of his notebook with a sigh. "We may want to ask you some further questions, later on, but for now, I think the ambulance blokes have got some hot coffee. You look like you could use some."

The real investigation could not start until first light, of course, though the *Queen of Alba* and the other boats continued their sweep of the loch, looking for anything they could find of the wrecked speedboat and its occupants, and police secured the area around the south end of the castle. With the dawn, they could begin combing the beach, searching for any minute clue as to what might have happened.

By noon, the sum total of evidence was minimal and grisly: McLeod's expended shells, shattered pieces of wood and fiberglass, shreds of torn clothing, fragments of lacerated flesh, and splashes of dried blood. It was the new depression of raw earth below the castle-walls that eventually gave rise to a theory of sorts: that there had been some kind of an explosion, perhaps involving a live hand grenade.

"I suppose the cave area *does* look a bit like a shell crater," Peregrine remarked dubiously to Adam. "But now they're thinking in terms of a *terrorist plot*? What's to terrorize, at an ancient monument? It isn't as if Urquhart is even a symbol of Scottish nationalism, or something like that."

They were drinking coffee in the back of one of the police cars from Inverness, having just returned from having Peregrine's hand sutured. The attending surgeon had done a masterful job, surpassing even Adam's exacting standards; but the local anaesthetic had worn off more than an hour ago, and the hand gave a twinge as Peregrine remembered, too late, not to try using it to open the window a crack. In the car park beyond, a police van and several more police vehicles were drawn up at odd angles, and yellow police tapes were stretched across both entrances to the car park, with a constable assigned to keep the public out.

Watching the constable pace back and forth before the farther entrance, Adam took a sip from his styrofoam cup and glanced speculatively at Peregrine.

"I'll grant you that a grenade sounds a bit far-fetched—to *us*. But it's the tale—however improbable—that best fits the facts as the police know them. People have learned to cope with the notion of terrorism, however distasteful that might be. How do you think the general public would react to the truth?"

Peregrine fingered the bandage on his right hand and grimaced, suddenly aware that even the truth of how he had gotten his injury would only raise questions that none of them were prepared to answer.

"I suppose I take your point," he said, after a moment. "Still, they might have done better than to give out that the speedboat cracked up on a floating log."

"Ah, but such things *do* occasionally happen," Adam said. "Back in the fifties, a chap named Campbell hit a log while trying to establish a new speed record, in a boat called the *Bluebell*. At least everyone *said* it was a log. Eyewitnesses to another racing accident described a sudden turbulence in the water ahead of the boat, just before it capsized and exploded." He gave Peregrine a sardonic grin.

"For that matter, during the Second War, a high-speed Royal Navy launch is said to have hit precisely what we all know we saw last night. In trying to explain the damage to the bow, I believe the captain described what he hit as 'soft and squelchy.' Hardly a log—but boats *do* hit logs sometimes. At least often enough to lend credence to *this* incident."

As Peregrine considered these incidents, Adam allowed his gaze to stray across the castle car park once more. Down by the south entrance, the grey Volvo from Dunvegan was parked on the tarmac. A crash recovery truck had towed it out of the ditch an hour earlier. Apart from a liberal coating of mud and festoons of weeds trailing from the underside—and the broken headlamp McLeod had noted at the time—it seemed little the worse for the mishap.

Beyond the car, McLeod was deeply engaged in conversation with a tall, distinguished-looking man in a well-cut tan trenchcoat. A police car had brought him in half an hour before. Following Adam's attentive gaze, Peregrine noticed for the first time that McLeod's companion was wearing a Balmoral bonnet with three eagle feathers brooched on the band—the designation for a full Highland Chief.

"Adam," he murmured, "is that who I think that is?"

Adam nodded, a faint smile playing about the corners of his long mouth. As they continued to watch, McLeod carefully took a flat, plastic-wrapped bundle from the breast of his borrowed waxed jacket coat and tendered it to the Chief. To mere vision, it appeared to be only a folded lump of beige fabric, flecked with bits of vermilion, but to Peregrine's inner sight, even in the sunshine, it seemed to shimmer still with the pale, greenish glow of fairy magic.

The tall man received it with the same sort of reverence they had observed in the inspector, what seemed like a lifetime ago, as he lifted it from its shattered frame. Then, after shaking McLeod's hand warmly, he stood aside to let the driver's door be opened for him, slipping behind the wheel and carefully depositing his treasure on the seat beside him as McLeod firmly closed the door.

McLeod stood back as the man in the highland bonnet started up the engine and eased the big car out of the car park, past the police barricade, raising a hand in farewell as it made the turn onto the main road and headed south, on the return route to Dunvegan. He joined them a moment later, slipping into the front passenger seat with a sigh of mingled weariness and satisfaction.

"Wasn't that evidence we just saw you give away?" Adam said, smiling, as the inspector poured himself a cup of coffee from the flask in the front seat.

McLeod snorted and took a sip of his coffee, making a face at the taste.

"Faugh! How can you two drink this stuff? What evidence? It was recovered property, apt to sustain further damage if it wasn't put into responsible hands. I've signed for it. Besides, we couldn't have the entire West Highland Constabulary going up in smoke—other than MacLeods, of course."

"*Would* they have?" Peregrine asked. "I mean, did that man *really* go up in a puff of smoke when he touched the Fairy Flag?"

McLeod laid his arm languidly along the back of the seat and gave Peregrine a droll glance across his shoulder.

"You're asking *me*? *You're* the one who saw it, my friend. *I* was having a nap under some rocks and earth. Of course, the official version is that the chap met with a nasty mishap involving a grenade."

He started to take another sip of his coffee, then thought

better of it and cracked his door open to dump the contents of the cup outside.

"Oh, and by the way, Mr. Lovat," he added, glancing back over his shoulder at Peregrine as he closed the door again, "you didn't do too badly last night. Just remember to follow orders next time."

"*Next* time?"

As Peregrine's eyes widened behind his spectacles, Adam gave a contented chuckle.

"Noel is having a little fun with you, Peregrine," he said easily. "He means you've passed your entrance exam."

"Beg pardon?"

"You may recall that I told you, several days ago, that I had several functions besides being a psychiatrist. Noel and I are part of a small group of—shall we say, specialists?—whose responsibility it is to deal with affairs of this kind: criminal cases involving elements of what the uninitiated would call the supernatural. I suppose one might call us a kind of—ah—occult police force."

Peregrine had gone very still and quiet, and he could not seem to take his eyes from Adam's.

"You—you aren't joking, are you?" he whispered.

"I think you know the answer to that," Adam said, still smiling. "It's our job to see to it that mischief of the kind you saw last night isn't allowed to run its course. And because a little knowledge is a dangerous—not to say, terrifying—thing, it's also our job to see to it that the circumstances surrounding these cases are suitably camouflaged, for the peace of mind of the rest of the population."

"Take this particular case," put in McLeod. "As far as the man in the street is concerned, the events of last night were merely a series of accidents—bizarre accidents, maybe, but still explainable according to material logic. Even though we may be stretching credibility a long way, human beings generally believe what they expect to see—and that lets us supply and support the appropriate cloakery."

He glanced back at Adam, who gave Peregrine a confirming nod.

"All this is by way of an invitation," Adam said. "Your

manifest talent for *seeing* marks you out as one of us in spirit. We would like you to become one of us in common purpose—a part of the team. If you think you might be willing."

Peregrine could feel the blood pounding in his temples. He stared at Adam for a long moment, trying to fathom the full extent of what the older man was asking, but only new questions came to mind—not answers.

"I—*think* I understand what you're saying," he began carefully, "but I– *Yes*!" he blurted, throwing caution to the winds. "I *am* willing. I want to be a part of it! I haven't the first notion what to do, but—"

"Fortunately, it isn't so much a question of *doing* anything," Adam interjected smoothly, "as it is as a matter of *becoming* something more than you are at present. You have enormous potential, as I believe you've convinced even yourself in this past week or so. I would be both pleased and honored to help you fulfill that potential and put it to constructive use. But the decision must—"

"Hold on a minute, Adam," McLeod murmured, raising a warning hand. "There's a constable headed this way, looking purposeful."

As the man drew nearer, McLeod rolled down his window expectantly.

"Are you looking for me?" he called.

"Aye, sir. Supervisor wants you, over by the van."

"I'll be back as soon as I can," McLeod murmured, as he got out and went with the officer.

Left alone with Peregrine, Adam considered for a moment before picking up the thread of their conversation.

"As I was about to say, the decision must be yours," he said. "The offer we've just made you was not made lightly, and I shouldn't want you to make any binding answer without due consideration. You remarked that you didn't know what to do, and I replied that it isn't a matter of *doing* but, rather, *being*. However, there *is* something you can do to help the process along, if you're serious."

"Yes?"

"It's quite within your ability, I assure you," Adam replied, smiling at Peregrine's look of anxious inquiry. "I should imagine they'll be done with us in the next hour or so. We should be able to get a flight out of Inverness—or a train, at least. And with any luck, we'll be back at Strathmourne by bedtime. In the morning, after you've rested, I would suggest that you do a portrait of yourself. I think that may give you all the further guidance you need, in deciding where to go from here."

"A self-portrait . . . ," Peregrine murmured.

"That's right. Think about the sketches you've done of me, and of Noel, and then ask yourself whether you're ready to draw the inner Peregrine Lovat. Think about it."

Adam could almost hear the tumult of thoughts racing through the younger man's mind. And when Peregrine slowly nodded, breathing out with a long, soft sigh, Adam smiled and got out of the car, satisfied that he had given his new colleague something more to think about than the horrors of the previous night.

Strolling over to the railing, he gazed down idly at the police still moving on the slope below. Beyond, Loch Ness stretched bright as a blackened mirror under the noonday sun, hiding—

"Adam, could you step over to the van for a moment?" McLeod said, startling him out of his reverie. He had an odd expression on his face. "Something's just come to light that I think you ought to see."

The police van was parked at the entrance to the car park. The back of the van was open. Just inside, Adam caught a glimpse of the Hepburn Sword, bagged in plastic and with an evidence tag looped through the basket hilt, lying on the floor. Waving off the constable standing guard beside the van, McLeod reached past the sword and plucked a clear plastic evidence envelope out of one of the collection bins. He handed the envelope to Adam.

"See what you make of that," he said gruffly.

The envelope contained a bloody fragment of a human finger. Caught between the knucklebones was a carnelian signet ring. Pressing the plastic closer against the stone, Adam could see that the device on the ring was that of a feline visage with tufted ears and cheeks, its jaws agape in a defiant snarl. He stared at the ring for a long moment, then handed the envelope back to McLeod.

"The Sign of the Lynx," he murmured evenly.

McLeod gave a heavy sigh and tossed the bag back into the proper bin, sinking wearily onto the bumper of the van to rub at his forehead between the eyes.

"I thought it was," he said, "though I couldn't be certain, without my glasses. It's been a long time since I last saw a signet like that—and I must say, I was hoping I never would again. Does this mean that the Lodge of the Lynx is becoming active again?"

"I'm afraid," said Adam, "that it can mean nothing else."

For a moment he stood silent, lost in thought. The finding of the ring lent sudden weight to Peregrine's premonitions and his own sense of dark events set in motion. Now he knew what the young artist had been trying to draw, on unseeable rings and medallions. Adam had dealt with the Lords of the Lynx in times gone by. That the Lodge was mustering again promised trouble to come.

For the moment, however, the situation was under control. He and Noel were forewarned, with a new recruit to train up for the Hunt—and in all likelihood, the Opposition would not know who had thwarted their intentions.

Not that inquiries would not be made, once they learned what had happened to their confederates. But Adam would make his own inquiries—tonight, when he returned to Strathmourne, as soon as he had rested. The Inner Chiefs must be informed—and must ratify the recruitment of Peregrine Lovat.

So. The Hunt was being called again. But when the time came for further confrontations, as it surely must, he and his would be ready. In the finest of Templar tradition, they would not shy away from battle, however adverse the odds might be. And there were others willing to do their parts—if he could finally get past telephone answering machines!

Adam shook his head, smiling at the idiocy of it all, and glanced at McLeod.

"We'll have to alert the others," he said quietly, closing his hand in his pocket around the symbol of his own Lodge.

"We'll need feelers put out all around. If the Lodge of the Lynx *has* gone active again, there're none of us immune to attack, once they find out we're on to them."

McLeod snorted and got to his feet, squaring his shoulders as he turned his face to the freshening wind.

"You're not *worried*, I hope."

"Worried? Not really. Challenged, perhaps?" Adam smiled. "As I recall, one Sherlock Holmes had the right phrase."

Grinning slyly, McLeod glanced at Adam and nodded.

"Aye," he said. "The stakes may be a bit different, but the object's still the same. The hunt is up. And as Holmes would say, 'The game's afoot!' "

Epilogue

TWO days later, when the incident at Urquhart had hit most of the newspapers, a woman sitting at a desk in a Glasgow office tower scanned over the day's newspapers while she sipped her morning coffee. The Urquhart article caught her eye as soon as she turned to the second page, and she read it through twice before picking up one of the three telephones on her desk.

"Get me Mr. Raeburn," she said.